A NOVEL BY FARHANA UDDIN

SECRET SOCIETY OF KINGS, WITCHES AND SPIRITS

Written and edited by Farhana Uddin
https://linktr.ee/farhanabooks

Human-generated content. All the words and ideas within this novel were created solely from the author's own writing skills and wild imagination. There was no use of any AI-generators in the making of this novel.

ISBN: 979-8-9892524-2-8

For all my witches.
We love the darkness
because we're always looking
for the brightest stars.

Contents

Chapter 1: Collect Calls from Heaven

"It's a blessing."

"It's a curse."

"It's a blessing."

"It's a curse."

The phone kept ringing.

"It's a blessing, I tell you," said the young child.

"It's a curse, damn you," said his fraternal twin brother.

"Don't curse at me, Jason-John," the boy said warningly. "And it's a blessing!"

"Don't tell me what to do, John-Marlowe," his brother, the elder by three life-altering minutes, refuted. "And it's a curse!"

The phone kept ringing.

"Curses are nothing but blessings in disguise, everyone knows that!" insisted John-Marlowe Quartermaine.

"Blessings are destined to become c—"

"Children, please desist at once," admonished Lana. "I'm about to answer the phone, and riveting as your debates are, I'd rather not converse in the midst of one."

"Sorry, Godmother," the brothers muttered in unison, the edges of their mouths dropping to pouts.

"Why don't you boys take a nice *long* stroll outside in your Godfather's hedge garden?" suggested Lana hastily. She gestured toward one of the Knights at the door, beckoning him over. Once the man drew near, she whispered, "Take them outside, but keep them out of the sun."

The phone kept ringing.

"Yes, let's go to the maze garden." Jason-John's eyes ignited, practically matching the colour of his auburn hair. "If we get lost in there, then the King will have to fly around to find us... Again!"

The phone kept ringing.

"And then he can fly us back to the castle, just like last time, Jase!" quipped John-Marlowe, throwing his tiny hands in the air in excitement.

They both raised their voices to hear themselves over the phone, which, incidentally, kept on ringing.

"Yeah! I bet knowing we're in trouble will wake him from this curse!" shouted Jason-John, responding with equal levels of delight by jumping up and down.

"It could certainly work. He never misses an opportunity to play hero," said John-Marlowe.

"Nor has he ever passed up a chance to lecture us," said Jason-John.

"That's true," nodded John-Marlowe. "Saving people and scolding them are two of his favourite things!" They'd seen it happen numerous times: their Godfather-King rescuing someone from a dire situation only to berate them for it afterwards.

"Let's go, Marshmallow!"

The boys sprinted for the bedroom exit, only to come to a rapid halt by the double doors. As if remembering something – or rather, remembering themselves – they wheeled around to face Lana and gave deep bows. Deference was a big part of the protocol.

Lana was their Godmother, but she was their Queen first, and their eldest brother, Nick-Ray, had drilled the importance of maintaining royal decorum in the presence of the Golden Royal Family.

"There's a reason they call that castle 'The Gilded Cage.'" Nick-Ray Quartermaine, their eldest brother and current guardian, had sat them both down and prepared them for their sojourn in the Gold King's primary residence. "Don't be fooled by its opulent appearance. It's like living inside a nest of eagles... or, griffins, I should say... Wait, do griffins have nests? They're half-eagles, half-lions and lions have dens, not nests, I suppose they could have both dens and nests ... I digress... Brothers, the point is... What was my point? ... Give me a moment, it'll come back to me... The point is that you must mind your manners," Nick-Ray had said warningly before leaving them in

Lana's care. "Remember, we're the King and Queen's godsons, but we're not their sons."

"Why not?" John-Marlowe had asked. "Mama and Papa are both gone. Why can't the King and Queen be our new parents?"

"It doesn't work that way," Nick-Ray said, softening his tone. He loved his brothers, but he hated the significant age gap between them. He was an adult, well into his Fifth Century of life, and they were still children. It was one thing to be orphaned as an adult, but it was an entirely different ordeal to lose your parents before surpassing your first decade of life.

"But—"

Nick-Ray cut his brother off with a stern sigh, "We're not family to them, and we must never forget our place with them. Understood?"

The memory slipped through their eight-year-old minds as they looked solemnly at their Godmother-Queen.

"May we please be excused, Godmot— Your Majesty?" said John-Marlowe.

Lana tried to smile indulgently, but the phone was persisting. "Of course, my darlings."

With a small crew of Knights at their heels, the boys shot out of her bedroom and into her personal drawing room, out another set of double doors and into Lucien's personal drawing room, before dashing out yet another set of double doors and hastening down a long corridor.

Lana flicked her dainty wrist, rings of golden light appearing at her fist. By the trigger of her hand, nearly all the doors in the adjacent rooms slammed shut at her silent command. She kept the bedroom doors leading to her private room wide open.

Slowly, she walked into her den. Though, to an observer, it would have looked like she was gliding into the room, the long silk white train of her dress chasing after her. That was how the world saw Gold Queen Lana Valenta – a beautiful, youthful-looking woman who glided across life, instead of walking and tripping through it like everyone else.

She came to a stop once she reached the phone by the small white oak table.

Aesthetically, it was a plain, beige princess phone. It didn't have a caller-ID. It didn't even have more than three push buttons. There was nothing flashy about the phone. It was, quite honestly, a mildly hideous item in an exceptionally beautiful room furnished with gold silk wall panels and classical furniture.

Logically, Lana knew this phone wasn't in the room for its aesthetic appeal. Only certain types of calls came from this phone. It was an emergency phone. There were quite a few planted around the Cage. Those types of phones were meant to be secure lines for King Lucien to receive breaking news and distress calls from their allies – both in- and off-planet. On rare occasions, there had been a few who had somehow managed to break past the security layer to send Lucien an assassination threat or two. Lana remembered overhearing one a few years ago:

"Oh, care to kill me, do you?" Lucien had unleashed a laugh so polite it was rude. "It's a sin to kill a Chosen King, you know?"

"I'm aware," the ominous-sounding caller on the other end had said.

"Don't suppose you have any experience with it?"

"I do, as a matter of fact."

"What about the Grey King? Ever tried to kill him?" Lucien had asked, genuinely curious.

"I have."

Lucien tossed his head back and laughed snootily. "My dear boy, if you couldn't even scotch out that clumsy oaf, then you certainly wouldn't be able to get within seven feet of my impenetrable aura – not without prostrating yourself, I suspect."

It sounded like arrogance, but there was an element of truth to it. Lana had seen it before: people – both admirers and haters – literally dropping to their knees in submission before the Gold King like he was a messiah.

"Have a blessed day," Lucien had said brightly before hanging up.

The phone was ringing. It was still ringing. It had been ringing for the better part of ten minutes with no end in sight – or rather, no end in sound.

Answering the phone would have been the easiest and most obvious solution. Only… Lana had never used a phone in her entire life.

She was a Queen, and Queens didn't answer phones.

If she ever needed to relay or receive messages, there were staff members around to carry out all her communications. None of those staff members were around now. She had dismissed them all. She knew she could easily summon a servant. There were plenty of hidden buttons in every room to call upon staff and security. But given the *current* circumstances, Lana didn't want anyone near her bedroom – more specifically, she didn't want anyone near *the body* currently laying comatose in her marital bed.

It was now eleven minutes in, and the phone was still ringing. Lana had the feeling the phone would ring on for all the hours of eternity if she didn't pick it up right then. Strangely, instinctively, she knew this call was meant for her.

"I told the boys I would answer the phone," she said to herself, "So I shall answer it."

She picked up the receiver. It was ridiculously clean and yet she held it away from her like it was a dirty wipe. Reluctantly bringing it to her ear, she muttered, "Hello?"

"Lana?" came Lucien's booming voice from the other end. "Hello! Lana? Is that you?"

Shoulders sagging in relief, Lana sighed. "Lucien! Thank goodness. Yes, it's me."

"For security purposes, my dear, I must confirm, this is *my Lana* I'm talking to, isn't it? My queen for nine centuries, my wife for over a millennium? Full cosmic address: Gold Kingdom. Planet Earth. Solar System. Orion Arm. Milky Way. Local Group. Virgo Supercluster. Laniakea Supercluster. Univers— "

"Lucien, it's me!" she bursted out irritably. "And if you're going to do a security check. You should be asking me what our address is, instead of giving it away."

"Lana? Hello?"

"I'm here."

"Is that really you?"

"It's me."

"Are you sure?"

"Yes, I'm bloody well sure! There's no other Lana in the universe, multiverse, or anyverse, stupid enough to marry the likes of you!"

"What was that?... I didn't quite catch that last bit. The line's a touch scratchy… Lana, are you there?"

"I'm *here* alright," Lana gritted out as she glided back to her bedroom in haste. Thankfully, the antiquated-looking phone was cordless. "I'm right here next to your body," she said sternly while gazing down at Lucien's corporeal form. His features were youthful, beautiful and unmoving. Lana couldn't decide whether he looked as though he were peacefully asleep or had just died peacefully in his sleep. "Your seemingly comatose body, which brings forth the question: Where the bloody hell are you?"

"Really, Lana, you shouldn't let your tongue loose with that sort of language! Need I remind you, you're meant to represent the zenith of Golden womanhood," he admonished, before acknowledging, "But I suppose it's a fair question. Pity I can't provide a straightforward answer."

"I assure you my womanhood is as Golden as ever," Lana bit out. "Now explain what's happening. You've been asleep for the past 22 hours!"

"Did you try waking my body?"

"Of course I did, you fool!" Lana shouted into the receiver. "I talked to it. I yelled at it. I poked it. I shook it. I slapped it. I threatened severe bodily harm on it."

That last example was a bit of a stretch. She said *severe bodily harm*, but what she really meant was that she had threatened to shave his head. Lucien would never take a death-threat seriously, but he was vain enough not to take any risks when it came to his hair or any other aesthetic aspect that made up his perfect physical features.

"Lana! It's a grave sin to vandalize the physical vessel of a Chosen King, and you know it."

"Lucien, are you purposely being obtuse about the severity of this situation? That I'm looking at your body while talking to you on the phone?" She released a long exhale. "For a second, I thought I had woken up beside a corpse."

"Am I—"

"Relax. You're still breathing."

"No, it's not that. I was going to inquire about the state of my body… How does it look?"

Lana desperately wanted to reach down and tear all his hair out right then. "Are you seriously worried about your precious good looks right now?"

"I may be several digits and dimensions removed from my realm, Lana, but I'm still the Gold King, the First Chosen King and Emperor of the Golden Empire across our galactic postal code," he stated proudly, and Lana could picture him on the other end of the line, lifting his pretentious nose in the air as he said all this. "I have a reputation for upholding the highest standards and maintaining perfection in all areas of life, including appearance. And I'm relying on you to keep my person polished and unsullied until I return."

"Return from WHERE? Where the hell are you?!!"

"Ahhh." An uneasy little laugh came from the other end. "We've circled back to this question, have we?"

"Lucien," she hissed forebodingly.

"You see, my dear, I can't say with absolute certainty where I am," admitted Lucien. "My first assumption was that I was lucid dreaming."

"People don't stay asleep for hours on end because of a lucid dream. And they can't make phone calls to the physical world from a dream either."

"That's where my line of reasoning fled to as well," said Lucien, and for the first time in centuries, he sounded uncertain. "Which leads me to believe I may not be dreaming at all… in fact, I predict I may be in Heaven, or at the very least, one of the circles of Heaven. The higher circles, naturally."

After a beat too long, Lana said, "People can make phone calls from Heaven, can they?"

"Apparently so, otherwise, we wouldn't be able to converse like this." Lucien didn't know how to explain it to her. He was sure he had been dreaming at some point until he walked into a forest that was entirely tinted in shades of purple. Hanging right above all the violet-coloured trees was a massive full moon with three large fishes – one black, one white, and one silver – swimming clockwise around the rim, circling each other in an eternal dance. He didn't know how long he walked through the ostensibly endless forest until he came across another living being... Upon reflection, perhaps, it wasn't appropriate to call it living or a being.

"Sweetheart, all I can tell you is that I came across an...entity, let's call it, with unconventional features." Unconventional was putting it politely. The entity had six red wings and four different faces, two of which appeared to be rather zoomorphic. Lucien didn't know if he should express it out loud, but he was pretty sure said entity was a Cherubim, an Angel of the Lord. "Anyhow, I explained my unique predicament, and he—it—manifested a telephone booth for me."

"A telephone booth?" said Lana dryly. "If this *entity* could do that, why couldn't it send you back home? Or wake you up? Or, I don't know, give you clear and precise directions back to the land of the living?"

"Believe me, those options were all high among my requests. I certainly would have preferred a map and a compass to this antiquated-looking device – there's not even a single button nor dial on it. As it is, this phone was all it provided me before swanning off," Lucien said with a huff.

"If there aren't any buttons, then how did you get it to work?"

"I told it to call you... or, rather, I asked it to '*call Lana.*' Next thing I know, I'm going through every Lana in every registry in every reality in existence. I had to get through 73,208 other Lanas throughout time and space until I got to you and not all of them were sympathetic to my exceptional circumstances," he said, thinking back to the 52,300-ish Lanas who had cursed him out before hanging up on him. Many of those Lanas didn't appear to be from his world at all. A few of them told him they hailed from some strange, unknown land called Canada. It all sounded very primitive to Lucien. "I hope you can at least appreciate all the effort I made there."

"You're calling from a phone booth that signals all throughout time and space?" Lana bit her lip and nodded. "Of course, you are. Because this could only ever happen to you!"

"Keep your voice down, Lana!" he said in a fierce whisper. "I hope there's no one in the room with you. I shan't have rumours spreading that the Gold King loiters about in phone booths, celestial or otherwise."

"Put your vanity on the shelf for two minutes, will you?" Lana sighed. "First things first, how did this happen to you? When you went to bed the other night, you seemed perfectly fine."

"I was perfectly fine," agreed Lucien. "Still am."

"Then what happened? Do you think someone's behind all this?"

"It's always a possibility. Unfortunately, my enemies are endless. A fussy bunch of wannabes who wish to be me. Then again, I suppose I would too if I were them. I've got it all and they only wish they had mere a fraction of what I have," he said haughtily. "It's all jealousy and misdirected energy, I tell you. So much valuable time wasted in hatred, when they could have put all that vigor into gazing upon my person with admiration the way my subjects do."

Lana rolled her eyes. "Lucien, tell me you have a plan. Tell me you know how to get back here. And fast."

Lana knew Lucien. She had been married to him for more centuries than she cared to admit, and she knew practically everything about him. He wasn't a man who had many tells. There were less than a handful of things that gave him away and Lana knew all of them. All he had to do now was say *yes*. If he said yes, then there was nothing to worry about. A *yes*-answer meant Lucien knew exactly what he was doing and everything would resolve itself. But if he said *of course*, then Lana knew they were in danger. An *of course*-response from Lucien meant he didn't have a plan, and everything was on the verge of free falling into a boiling pot.

Holding her breath, she tightened her grip on the receiver and stared down at her husband's body, waiting to hear his answer.

"Of course I do, my dear!" Lucien released his most pompous-sounding laugh to date.

Lana released her breath and shut her eyes briefly in misery.

"You know me, even my plans have plans," he said, the remnants of his fake laughter now fading away. "You needn't concern yourself. Surely, our sons can hold down the fort until my speedy return. I suspect I'll be back within the hour. If anyone asks, tell them I'm taking the day to attend to my gardens or having my sideburns properly restructured."

"And if you're not back within the hour? What then, hmm?" Lana prodded. "Let's be honest. What are we going to do if a pseudo-day off stretches out into a sabbatical?"

Lucien went quiet on the other end. No boisterous laughter. No pretentious prattling. It made Lana feel even more apprehensive.

"Very well," he said, after a stretch of silence. "Let's give it seven days. I shan't be any longer than seven days," he stated with such conviction that Lana almost believed him.

"Mind you," he added, "Clocks appear to be nonexistent where I am." When he thought about it, it made sense. Time was a man-made concept that didn't exist outside the Physical Realm. Lucien had declared he could return anywhere from an hour to seven days, but in all honesty, he wouldn't have known 22 hours had passed if Lana hadn't told him. It felt like only seven minutes had ticked away. At the same time, it had also felt like seven centuries had flown by. The entire ordeal was almost akin to waking up one morning without any memory of falling asleep the night prior.

Time was like an imaginary concept here in Heaven, just like eating or drinking. It was then that Lucien realized he wasn't the least bit hungry or thirsty. He didn't yearn for the necessities that the mortal body craved. The only yearning he had now was to return home to his family.

"With that in mind, you may have to remind me about our timeframe the next time we converse," he said, "And if anyone inquires after me—

"You're the King. They're *all* going to inquire after you!"

"—Stick with the sabbatical story. Tell them I'm on a spiritual sabbatical, out in the desert."

"Absolute monarchs don't take sabbaticals, spiritual or otherwise." Lana thought about the Senate and the Counsel, both of which operated under Lucien's control. "They're always at the ready, 24-7-365."

"My Divine energy is still present, is it not? It must be. I can still access it, even away from my body."

"It is." Lana wouldn't have been able to telekinetically move objects if Lucien's Golden energy had disappeared. She gazed down at her hand. Within seconds, her palm lines began to glow, looking like gleaming scars of gold across smooth skin. "Yes, it's still here. We would've all had full-blown panic attacks if it didn't."

"That's a blessing, at the very least," said Lucien. "No one will question anything provided the Golden energy remains steady and active."

"Wait, your powers still work in—wherever you are now?"

"Of course it does," said Lucien. "It's limitless power from *Divine* energy. It works everywhere."

"Then why haven't you used your *limitless* powers to come home?"

"I tried," said Lucien softly. "It didn't work." Ever the idealist, he quickly corrected himself. "That is, I mean to say, it hasn't worked *yet*."

"What about your Totem?" inquired Lana. "Has it said anything to you?"

Totems were entities of Divine light and energy that appeared to the mortal eye in specific colours and shapes. In their world, Totems were the ones that chose a new King for a new nation or the next King in an already established realm. Once a Totem's light synergized with its chosen mortal vessel, that person then became the proprietor of that Divine energy, giving them the ability to wield that power however they pleased.

When Lucien had first met his Totem, so many centuries ago, it had appeared to him as pure golden light shaped like a griffin. Lucien had allegedly been the first of the First Chosen Kings. The others – like the Red King, Blue King, Green King, Grey King – emerged soon after.

"Well?" pushed Lana. "What did it say?"

Like most people, Lana didn't know much about Totems. That was because a Totem could only be seen and heard by its Chosen King. They were invisible to everyone else, like a well-kept secret among Kings only.

Everything everyone knew about Totems was based on the word of Kings. Lucien had told her bits of information, over the centuries, about his Golden Griffin-Totem. But Lana heavily suspected her husband was revealing the bare minimum seeing as he only gave away three details:

- it was shaped like a Griffin (which he'd already told the general public),
- it was an Angel of the Lord and
- it spoke to him regularly, offering advice whenever it deemed necessary.

"It hasn't said anything," Lucien confessed with a sigh. He had tried calling upon his Totem for guidance and received nothing in return. "Been as silent as unanswered prayer."

Lucien's heavy exhale on the other end of the line was most revealing. At that moment, she realized her husband's cavalier attitude, up till now, had been nothing but a glossy shield to put her at ease while simultaneously covering up his own unease. Lucien must have tried everything he could think of, everything she could think of, everything anyone could think of to get back home.

"But have a little faith, in your Husband-King," said Lucien encouragingly, willing optimism back into his voice. Because when it came down to it, Lucien was an eternal optimist. From his experience, prayers never remained unanswered for very long. They manifested miraculously in the most unexpected ways and during the most unexpected times.

"As long as my Golden energy remains intact, I assure you my homecoming is imminent," he insisted. "If I can fly my way home across our physical realm, then who's to say I can't do the same from the celestial realm?"

Lana cracked a small smile. Lucien always had unwavering faith in his own abilities. There were many people, like her husband, who insisted there was no limit to what a King could manifest with their Divine energy. But it was obvious to everyone else that certain Kings were predisposed to certain manifestations. Lucien's Golden energy, for example, gave him significant flight capabilities and allowed him to easily conjure up thunder, electricity and protective shields. To top it off, his powers made him a gold-making machine, literally. In many ways, Lucien had it a lot better and far easier than his contemporaries, like the current Red King, who – much like his predecessors –couldn't seem to stop incinerating his own land.

"Lana? Are you still there?"

"I'm here." Lana said into the receiver as she reached down to stroke his dark hair. Her hand slid down to the side of his handsome face. She wondered if he could feel her touch across time and space. A tiny part of her was glad he wasn't here to see her looking at him so lovingly. It would've enabled his overinflated ego, no doubt.

She lifted her palm up, inspecting the glints of gold emanating from it. Lucien had given her full access to his Golden energy. Kings could do that. They could share a fraction or the full breadth of their powers with others. Lucien's Knights – the Volucris, as they were called – had restricted access to the Golden energy and were able to use it solely for security and defense purposes. His immediate family, which included Lana and their sons, were given unlimited access to said energy.

It was called a King's Gift. Those who were granted such a privilege – regardless of whether their privilege was regulated or limitless – were among the Gifted. But Lana certainly didn't feel gifted, not when it came to the Golden Gift, at least. Lucien could create electric storms. He could make thunderbolts out of thin air, send them into neighboring realms and get those flashes of lightning to report back to him. Lana, by contrast, could open and shut doors with a semi-dramatic flair.

"I've given you limitless power, Lana! Use it!" Lucien used to constantly tell her.

Yes, he kept telling her to use it, but he never showed her how to use it. How was she to force the Golden energy to do her bidding? Gold was a demanding energy to say the least. It demanded perfection, strength and an unshakeable resolve. Like Lucien, the Golden energy demanded all of you and never settled for the slightest bit less.

"Lana??? You've stopped listening to me, haven't you? I can feel it."

"I'm here." Lana turned away from the bed with a sigh and strode back into the den. "I was just thinking."

"About what?"

"Are you sure no one did this to you?" They had gone up against and defeated the craziest of foes in the physical realm. But they had never encountered anything like this before.

"As I said, it's a possibility," conceded Lucien. "But I can't think of anyone capable enough to lead me down this peculiar garden path."

Arrogance, once again. And yet there was still a lot of truth to it. Lucien was considered the most powerful King in the world. Loved amongst his subjects and feared amongst his fellow Kings.

"Never you mind," said Lana. "As of now, you need to place all your focus into… waking up. Do whatever you must to get back to us. Michael, Gabriel and I will take charge in the interim. And, if anyone was behind this … well, we'll sort it all out upon your return."

"Ah yes, alert our boys," agreed Lucien. "But no one else must know. No matter what happens, you mustn't let anyone else near my body."

Lana frowned. There were already a small handful of staff members and Knights who knew that Lucien was still seemingly asleep. It had been unavoidable since there was always someone around to attend to the King. But Lana wasn't worried about them. They were hired help, and they were bound by nondisclosure agreements sealed with Lucien's energy, which meant they'd literally choke to death before they could dish out a single word about the private affairs of the Golden Royal Family. Their godsons, however, were a different situation. Luckily, she knew a way to ensure their silence as well. But it was a problem that would have to be resolved a little later.

"Your body will remain as untouchable as ever, Lucien, rest assured," she said. "I'm assuming the telephone will be your preferred method of communication until you awaken?"

"It's my *only* method of communication, thus far," scoffed Lucien. "But yes, provided it doesn't disappear on me, I'll call you back if I have to… Hopefully, I won't have to."

"I'll leave you to it then," nodded Lana. "See you in seven days or less."

"Yes, I shall return in time for our anniversary!"

A beat of silence.

"You forgot again, didn't you?"

Lana hated how smug he sounded. "I did not," she said.

"You did," bellowed Lucien with the return of his rudely polite laughter. "Can't say I'm surprised. You haven't remembered an anniversary in the last five centuries. Not very romantic of you, is it, my dear?"

Lana gritted her teeth. She wasn't great with dates and numbers, and Lucien always loved to lord it over, both privately and publicly, especially since it made him look like the doting husband while depicting her as the ungracious wife.

"I'm hanging up now," she said petulantly.

"While we're on the topic of anniversaries and romance, I feel the need to remind you that my absence, brief as it may be, does not give you permission to bat your long lashes and wander your silver eyes toward anyone who bothers to look your way," he said condescendingly. "You and I are still considered a pair in perpetuity, bonded by the laws of God, and it is a severe sin to break such a bond. That said, I fully understand you're a woman with needs, and this is likely a great physical inconvenience to you. You must know it was never my intention to leave you lusting and thirsting over me. Therefore, you have my permission to seek comfort from my soporous body as you please. Even in a state akin to sleep, I'm sure all my necessary parts still function—"

Lana promptly hung up the phone, slamming it back down onto its face plate. Letting out an annoyed puff of air, she looked up. Her eyes caught her own reflection on a large ornate mirror – one that had tiny growling griffins carved into its golden frame – attached to the wall. She didn't look a day over the age of 24, even though she was now into her Second Millennia of life. Such were the perks of being a *valensman*. Minutes equated to centuries, and decades equated to millennia. From a physiological perspective, time was exceptionally kind to humans who were classified as valensmen. From a situational perspective, however, time was indiscriminately cruel.

Seven days. They had seven days or less to sort everything out.

She turned her head over her shoulder to glare back at the man in her bed. She hadn't had a peaceful night's sleep since she married him. Even if he left her widowed, she was sure he would expect her to stay up all night, pining away for him until her final breath.

Shaking her head, she willed herself to focus. She needed to talk to her children. There wasn't a moment to waste, so out she went – through a set of double doors into Lucien's den, out another set of double doors, down one long corridor after another, sweeping past portraits and tapestries, exiting the east wing, going down three flights of stairs, turn left, then right, only to continue down another massive stretch of a hallway lined with large windows. It would take a while until she reached her destination: the north wing dining area where her children were having their breakfast.

As she trudged on, flanked by two Volucris guards, she wondered how she was going to explain everything to her sons. Out of everything they had endured as the Golden Family – assassination attempts from psychopaths, invasion attempts from rivals, kidnapping attempts from convicts – this had to be the worst and weirdest thing to have ever happened to them.

Chapter 2: By the Silver Sea

"This is the best thing that's ever happened to us! Oh, what a coup!" exclaimed Gabriel, as he paced back and forth across the sandy bluffs on his family's rocky tidal island.

Far behind Prince Gabriel stood the Gilded Cage in all its majestic glory. Officially, the castle was called the Chrysos Citadel, but everyone – except Lucien – called it the Cage.

The golden sun shot out of the dark grey clouds to shine against the stained-glass windows of the castle. Even from afar, they could make out the griffin gargoyles perched atop the crenelations.

Ahead of Gabriel came the soft roar of waves from the Silver Sea. It was actually a lake, but because it took up a walloping 145,000 square miles, it seemed fair to mark it down on a map as a sea. And, as for labelling it *Silver*, that had been Lucien's choice, long ago when he first established the island as his primary residence. Lana hadn't the slightest clue as to why he had decided to call it that. It was obvious to anyone with healthy eyesight that the water was bluer than a robin's egg.

"As if it wasn't enough for Father to be Divinely Chosen to rule the world, well the better part of it at least. Now, his soul has been granted permission to explore the celestial realms that govern our cosmos!" Gabriel went on. "From what I've heard, people usually need to undergo death to have that little white permission slip signed. And somehow, he's managed to acquire it while still drawing breath. How lucky is our Father-King, Mike?"

"Luckier than he deserves," said Prince Michael stonily. His face was expressionless – as it often was – but his eyes kept sweeping back and forth like a pendulum, as if to follow his brother's pacing from his seated position.

They had forgone breakfast upon hearing of Lucien's dilemma. After the Princes had checked in on their Father-King, the Valentas had decided to abscond to the bluffs to discuss the matter. Their staff had set up a cozy round table and several chairs over the sand and left them with a light lunch course of native lobster, caramelized carrots, topped with a vibrant pomegranate purée, which was offset with a smooth buttermilk purée. The entire meal was paired with a bottle of Lana's liquid dynamite, her homemade gooseberry wine.

The four of them were alone now. Or, as alone as one could be in a royal residence. There were still Volucris Knights guarding them from a distance. And a few feet away, their special guests, the Quartermaine twins, were running loose and having a swordfight with their parasols, which Lana had given them for the purpose of keeping out of the sun.

It wasn't that Lana was against sunlight. She simply thought the sun was overrated and overadored, especially considering how it would wipe out their planet in a few billion years' time. That, of course, was a problem for future generations. Her problem with the sun was that it could boost chemicals in the brain and provide people with more energy, which sounded appealing on paper, but wasn't so pleasing when it was applied to two hyperactive, hyper-spirited, hyper-extroverted young boys in her care. Lana loved her godsons, her little tornado twins, but the last thing they needed was more energy.

From her perch, Lana shot a quick glance toward her godsons before directing her attention back to her children. She was seated at the table with her son, Michael, and her baby daughter, Alexandra – Lexie, as they all called her – who was now snoozing away peacefully in her bassinet. Her other son, Gabriel, however, was far too excited to sit down for a meal. Hence, the incessant pacing.

The Gold Queen's silver eyes darted back and forth between her sons in confusion. This wasn't the reaction she had expected. "I'm sorry, am I hearing all this correctly?" she said. "You're both happy that your Father is seemingly in a coma and likely trapped in another dimension for an indefinite amount of time?"

She turned to Gabriel, who gave her a cheery smile.

She peered down at Lexie, who wasn't going to lose any sleep over it.

She glanced sidelong at Michael, who merely said, "I'm not unhappy about it."

Lana doubted Michael even knew the difference between happiness and misery anymore. She hadn't seen him crack a smile since the 12th century.

Michael Valenta was the eldest son, the First Golden Prince. Gabriel Valenta, younger by a century, was the Second Golden Prince. Both men were in their Ninth and Eighth Centuries of Life, respectively. Neither man looked a day over 18, ostensibly.

By valensmen standards, the Valenta brothers weren't that far apart in age, but they were as different as night and day. Gabriel had inherited Lana's thin and lanky frame, and Lucien's pointy, aquiline nose and dark eyes. Whereas Michael had a muscular physique complete with broad shoulders and strong biceps. Michael was practically the spitting image of his handsome Father-King and nearly just as tall to boot. The only physical trait Michael had inherited from Lana was his eye colour, which was a distinctive shade of silver.

The differences didn't end there. The brothers were not only displayed differently, they functioned differently as well. Gabriel was Lucien's Chief Science Advisor. Over the centuries, he had presented many inventions for the benefit of his Father's Kingdom, including spacecrafts and computers. He had also helped his Father-King design nuclear weapons, which were melded with Lucien's Divine energy. Meanwhile, Michael was Lucien's Golden General and Chief Military Strategist. He had spent much of his time conquering lands and expanding the Golden Empire in the name of his Father-King.

Despite their differences, it was obvious to everyone that the two men were forever bonded by blood, mutual respect, and unconditional love.

As for her daughter, Lexie… She had Lucien's dark eyes and Lana's delicate beauty. She was still far too pure, far too much of a novelty. She hadn't even surpassed her first decade yet, let alone her First Century. But being Lucien's daughter, Lana suspected it wouldn't be long before Lexie started to attract global attention and wreak havoc on a universal scale.

"Oh Mother, I doubt he's *trapped* there," said Gabriel, bringing Lana's attention back to him.

There was a chill in the air, but thanks to his incessant pacing, Gabriel was starting to work up a sweat. Along with his wool tailcoat, Gabriel had removed his collar and tie, leaving him attired in his light cotton twill trousers and shiny silver-velvet patterned vest. Michael wore a near-identical ensemble, only it was coloured entirely in black.

"Divinely energetic entities exist to serve God. They don't roam about entrapping people," Gabriel told his Mother-Queen. "And as for his corporeal property, I've given him a thorough health inspection."

Upon learning about Lucien's *coma*, Gabriel had sprung to action and went about converting his parents' bedroom into a makeshift intensive care unit, complete with IV-drips and heart- and brain-wave monitors.

"He appears perfectly healthy. There's no trace of hypoglycemia, hemorrhage, or any infections and diseases," said Gabriel. "The only anomaly I could find was that his heart rate was far lower than what's considered natural. But upon reflection, I've concluded that's hardly an anomaly, considering that he's likely in the Delta state… besides Father has plenty of experience decelerating his heart rate purposely, what with all those Full-Body Shields he's had to create during wartimes."

At Lana's perplexed expression, he explained, "You remember what an FBS is, don't you? It's when Father outlines his entire body with Golden energy, creating an impenetrable forcefield. No bullet, sword, or laser can puncture it. The only drawback is that it's so impenetrable that not even oxygen can get through. That's why Father had to learn those deep breath-holding techniques from—"

"Yes, I already know all about his Full-Body Shields," said Lana. "What do you mean by *Delta* state?"

"Oh. Delta's a type of brainwave that's commonly found whenever someone falls into a deep sleep." Gabriel had thought it was obvious to everyone, but he didn't mind explaining. "You see, our minds produce different kinds of brainwaves, called Gamma, Beta, Alpha, Theta, and Delta. Each of these operate at a different frequency. Some go very quickly, while others are rather slow. Alpha waves are slower than Beta and Gamma waves, but faster than Theta and Delta waves. Theta waves are slower than Alpha, but faster than Delta, and—" Gabriel faltered mid-sentence. He could see Lana's eyes glazing over in a way that suggested she was only half-listening. In an effort to recapture her attention, he said, "Mother, you needn't be concerned with any of this."

"Oh, needn't I?" said Lana wryly.

"This is a remarkable breakthrough for us," said Gabriel, ignoring Lana's sardonic tone. "Father and I have always wanted to discover what exists in the celestial realms. And I shall be the one to chronicle his first-hand experience and publish it throughout our galactic postal code."

Gabriel was the most modest of the Valenta clan, to be sure, but there were a few occasions where even his ego exceeded Lucien's. This was one of them. "It'll certainly put Durante di-Alighiero-degli-Alighieri in his place, I can tell you that," he added snidely.

"Dante? Oh, darling, please tell me you're not still hung up about that?" Lana shook her head. "It's been centuries, literally."

Centuries were mere minutes to a valensman, especially one like Gabriel who held a mild grudge. "The man gets hammered on exotic mushrooms from the Green Kingdom, writes a few fluff poems about Heaven, Hell and Purgatory, and gets praised across the literary spectrum." Gabriel grabbed hold of a chair, his fingers clenching tightly around its top rail. "I found it completely appalling. I still can't believe Father knighted him for that! The things he wrote were blasphemy!"

"Your Father has a fondness for egregious poetry, both reading and writing it," sighed Lana, who had been obligated to make appearances at Lucien's public poetry readings. Worse yet, were the times she had to listen to his "*fireside chats*" where he recited his biblical poetry over the booming speakers within the castle.

"Even so, I was most disappointed in your behaviour during that whole ordeal, Gabe. There was no reason for you to go into a jealous fit just because your Father threw a little fanfare his way," she said. "Nor did you have to order the Pope to excommunicate that poor boy."

"That's what the Pope is here for, Mother, to serve God and the King in equal measure … and by extension us, as the King's blood." Gabriel nodded firmly. "And need I remind you Dante's in his Sixth Century of Life, hardly a boy."

"Need I remind you that for our kind, any age under a millennium is comparable to a fetus," Lana shot back, smiling a little when Lexie snorted like a baby swine in her sleep.

"It matters not." Gabriel waved a dismissive hand in the air. "What matters is what's happening now. This will be a true triumph for me—for us, that is. A true scientific breakthrough. Once Father awakens, I can—"

"Gabriel, I hate to cut your wings off, but chronicling your Father's partial account of where he *thinks* he is, and what he *thinks* he's seeing right now, does not equate to scientific backing, and you know it." Looking between Gabriel and Michael, she continued, "I must say, I'm surprised to see you boys taking this in your stride. Are you truly fine with all this? No concerns?"

"There's no cause for concern," said Gabriel. "I shall ensure Father's body remains functioning and intact." Indicating to Michael, he said, "And should any pressing matters relating to national security arise, Mike is more than capable and experienced."

"I see," said Lana primly. "And what should I do while you boys are overseeing everything? Lie down on a fainting couch and wave a hanky in the air in utter despair?"

"Mother, please, we would never trivialize your role as Queen," said Gabriel, finally taking a seat. "You have an essential role to play in all this. You must keep an ear out for any more messages from Father. And if he calls again, please summon either myself or Michael immediately. Granted, under normal circumstances, I wouldn't advise you to operate a telephone. It's most inappropriate for a woman of your caliber to be picking up unsolicited phone calls. I shudder to think what would happen if word got out."

"It would be a scandal, to be sure." Lana rolled her eyes.

"I wouldn't jest about such a thing, Mother. It is the 19th century, after all, and sadly, there's been a heinous spread of spam messages, scam calls, and sketchy characters with too much time on their hands, making obscene noises and breathing heavily on the other end," ranted Gabriel. "I find it completely appalling. My team and I have advanced technology by three centuries, give or take. If it weren't for us, everyone would still be sending hand-written messages through a courier or riding a horse at 10 miles per hour instead of using an automobile. Can you imagine living so barbarically like that in the Year of Our Lord 1828? And instead of receiving gratitude for everything we've invented, what do we get in return? People have taken advantage of our innovations by utilizing them for sinister purposes—"

Lana held back another massive eyeroll as her second son carried on. Gabriel always loved to go on at length about technological innovations, and yet all the great scientists of the world were completely inept when it came to other significant matters. *Such as the state of women's apparels*, Lana thought with a wince as she remembered all the whalebone corsets she had to painfully endure during formal events. At least here, in the privacy of her own home, she could dress more comfortably in less constrictive corsets and ditch the crinolines all together. On occasion, she was even seen traipsing around the castle in *trousers*.

"There is one item of concern," Michael said stiffly, cutting through Gabriel's verbal tirade. "Two, technically." He jutted his chin forward. They all turned left, looking out into the short distance where two tiny red-haired boys in identical maroon frockcoats were playing about in the sand.

"Ah, yes the Quartermaine boys," acknowledged Gabriel. "They should not have been informed of the situation at hand, Mother. They're not family."

"They weren't informed. They went into my bedroom looking for me and came across Lucien in his sleeping-beauty pose," said Lana.

Gabriel sighed as though he'd underwent a minor inconvenience, like coming across a traffic jam or misplacing a sock. "In the future, these sort of incidents shan't happen. Father's working on installing Golden Shields behind every door in the Cage. Only people with authorized access, such as ourselves, will be able to traipse through them."

"And as for being family," Lana continued. "They're as good as, as far as I'm concerned. Their mother was one of my dearest friends. I promised her on her deathbed, I'd look after her three boys."

"Where's the third?" asked Michael, inquiring after Nicholas-Ray Quartermaine, who in recent years had been bestowed by Lucien with the duchy of Firefinch.

From one eldest sibling to another, Michael did have an ounce of empathy for the oldest Quartermaine brother, even though he'd never display it. He knew what a rigorous responsibility it was to parent one's own sibling. Michael, himself, had to be both a brother and a father to Gabriel, especially during their formative years when Lucien was frequently absent and away, expanding his empire. Nevertheless, Michael saw it as an unavoidable obligation, and he would not allow Nick-Ray to shirk such a responsibility or delegate it to Lana.

"Nick-Ray is out-of-Kingdom at the moment, away on a personal matter, concerning a cousin of his over in the Red Kingdom," explained Lana.

"Send them there then," ordered Michael. It was the best course of action, in his opinion, to send the boys away. Their household staff and sentry were permanently and contractually bound to privacy. Those kids, however, were not. They knew too much.

"I shan't send them away, and certainly not to the Red Kingdom of all places!" said Lana fiercely.

"They aren't your responsibility," Michael reminded her. "They have a guardian."

"Did you not hear me when I said I swore an oath on their mother's *deathbed*?" Lana bit out. "And, officially, I am their godmother – that makes them my responsibility. Besides, there's only so much a young valensman like Nick-Ray can do on his own. I dread to think how those boys will turn out in the absence of a consistent feminine influence in their lives."

"And that female influence must come from you?" said Michael.

"Why not? No one thrives at motherhood better than yours truly, am I right? Look at how beautifully my two boys turned out." With a smile, she lifted a hand to stroke Michael's hair back.

Gabriel flushed a little at the compliment. Michael looked like he hadn't received a compliment at all.

"Uncle Gabriel! Uncle Michael!" John-Marlowe cried enthusiastically as he and his brother ran over to the Golden Family.

Gabriel flinched in irritation at the honorific. It seemed inappropriate for these children, who were not blood-relatives, to refer to him as an *uncle*, but Lana had insisted. "*Unless you want them to call you brother, instead?*" was the threat she had beamed at him. Gabriel had vehemently protested. He was more than happy to dote on his sweet baby sister. But he had no interest in acquiring a bratty little brother, let alone two.

"Yes, what is it?" Gabriel asked them.

"Can you use the Golden Gift to make a sandcastle for us?" asked Jason-John. "His Majesty made one for us the last time we were here. It was so big it nearly reached the sky."

"It almost touched the sun," amended John-Marlowe.

"The sky," said Jason-John forcefully.

"The sun!" insisted John-Marlowe.

"The sky!"

"The sun!"

"The sky!"

"The sun!"

"Yes, of course, we'll make one for you," Gabriel cut in. He wished he could use the Golden Gift to transport these boys far, far away with a snap of his fingers. Glancing over at Michael, he asked with a twinge of embarrassment, "Well, Mike?"

Lana smiled sympathetically at Gabriel. She might have been inadequate with the Golden Gift, but Gabriel was completely useless when it came to it.

Michael had some proficiency with the Gift, but even his skills were inconsistent at best. Most of Michael's success as a military leader came from his natural physical prowess, quick instincts, and cunning.

All three of them had the King's Gift, but when it came down to it, none of them were considered Masters for none of them had conquered the art of bending the King's energy to their will whenever they pleased.

From the bassinet, Lexie unleashed another loud snort. Lana beamed down at her. *Maybe you'll have better luck with it*, she thought fondly. *It'll certainly make your Father happy if you turned out to be a Golden Master.*

"Go on, Michael," she patted her eldest son's shoulder.

Michael fixed his gaze on a spot in the sand, several feet away. It took a few minutes, but eventually the sand began to bulge as though a head were emerging from beneath the surface. It continued to grow for a few more moments, before coming to an abrupt stop.

"There," said Michael.

The Quartermaine twins visibly drooped, their shoulders deflating in disappointment, at the sight of the provisional castle. If one could even call it that.

When King Lucien had made them a sandcastle, it had been tall and towering, a glittery sandy replica of the Gilded Cage, outlined in a sheen of translucent gold. It was so robust and magnificent that not even the tide had been able to wash it away. Prince

Michael, by contrast, had given them a small igloo tinted in a hue that looked more mustardy than gold. The waves could – and no doubt, would – wolf it all down in one gulp.

"Problem?" asked Michael, his cold eyes daring them to make a remark that was anything short of gratitude.

"Uh, no sir, not at all," said Jason-John apprehensively as he nudged his brother to concur.

"It's—it's, errr, it's marvelous, Uncle Michael," agreed John-Marlowe.

"Thank you, Your Royal Highness," they said in unison, both bowing deeply before running off, far away from Michael and his intimidating aura.

"I hate to say this," Gabriel reluctantly acknowledged when the boys were no longer within hearing distance, "But it may be best to keep them quarantined here for the time being, ensure that nothing slips. Mind you, it's unlikely anyone would believe those kids, especially considering their blood ties to the Red Kingdom and Lord knows where else." Slouching into his seat a little, he said, "Nevertheless, we mustn't take any risks and let anything leak out. As it is, the public are prone to leaping to assumptions and we all know stupidity can easily spread like a kingdom-wide epidemic without a cure. Last thing we need is for people to falsely assume that the Golden Empire is under peril."

"Who's to say it's not?" said Michael.

Gabriel's posture shot up immediately. "What?"

"Gabe, I know you're eager to hear about your Father's celestial expedition," Lana started softly, "But we need to consider the possibility that maybe he wasn't being blessed with a holy permission slip. Maybe someone has cursed him into a deep, unshakeable sleep and confined him in another dimension."

"Nonsense," said Gabriel with a sniff. "Out of all the tellurian Kings, Father undoubtedly has the most powerful Divine energy. Why, I daresay his energy is like a second sun. He's got enough electrical fluid in him to light up the world... or blow it to smithereens, if he so wishes. There's no one powerful enough to imprison him anywhere."

Gabriel had a fair point. Lucien certainly appeared to be overpowered at times. It made many people, Lana included, wonder why he didn't simply conquer the entire planet for himself. That was his original plan when he was first chosen to lead, way back in the year 1027 AD. She sometimes wondered why he hadn't followed through with it.

"Aside from that," Gabriel carried on, "We're living in a time of relative peace, Mother. We have treaties and alliances with most other Kingdoms, and they wouldn't dare break it."

"Most. Not all," said Lana curtly.

Michael remained silent, only nodding once in agreement with Lana's sentiment. He wasn't as optimistic as Gabriel. He had grown up being a Warrior-Prince, and he knew from experience that peace was nothing but a delusion. There wasn't any open fire among the tellurian Kingdoms right now, but Michael knew a greater, colder war still lingered. There were spies everywhere.

"Do you suspect the Greys were behind all this?" asked Gabriel, and before Lana could answer, he abruptly turned to his brother. "What do you think, Mike?"

Michael paused for a beat to gaze out at the sea. With his stare locked on the tide, he said, "I think we should all focus our energies where they're needed – do whatever we need to do." His eyes returned to his brother as he commanded, "Gabe, you need to find a way to resurrect Father's body and make haste."

Michael wasn't concerned for his Father-King's well-being, but he did care about the rest of his immediate family. They needed Lucien back to ensure their Kingdom and their family's place as monarchs remained intact. Bloodlines didn't determine succession in their world, not anymore, not since the year 1027. Totems selected the Kings, and the Golden Totem would be the one to choose the next King if Lucien didn't return. It wasn't likely that it would choose Michael. Thus far, in their history, a Totem had never chosen a Prince or Princess to inherit their parent's throne.

At Gabriel's nod, Michael continued, "I'll connect with our counter-intelligence – keep an eye out for any unusual energies lurking about."

Michael suspected there were spies splattered around them, some possibly even hiding in plain sight. The biggest menace was the Grey Kingdom. Outwardly, the Greys didn't appear to pose a threat. Situated northwest of Golden soil, the Greys were a small realm with a failing economy and poor infrastructure. The only card the Grey King had up his sleeve was that his Divine energy was practically undetectable. Most Divine energies were *loud*, to say the least. Their presence was easily felt, and very quickly picked up with energy detectors. The Grey energy, however, was the exception. It was difficult to trace, and nearly impossible to spot unless you had access to it. For this reason, Michael knew better than to underestimate them.

As his silver eyes darted over to Lana, he said, "And Mother—"

"Yes, I shall be lying about, waving a white hanky in the air," she said bitterly.

"Right." Gabriel nodded. "Good plan, Brother."

A tiny wail suddenly came between them, drawing all their attention.

"Oh, sssshhh," Lana cooed down at Lexie. "We've woken her."

"I'll take her for a quick stroll." Gabriel shot up and strode around the table to carefully gather his sister up in his arms. "She loves it when I walk with her." Giving her a sunny smile, he said, "I suspect I'm her favourite out of our bunch."

He made to leave, only to turn back to his Mother-Queen once more. "Mother, I know this must be quite the tribulation for you, what with Father leaving you here by your lonesome. But you needn't fear in the absence of your Husband-King. Michael and I shall always be here to protect you."

Gabriel was always like this with Lana, treating her less like a formidable Queen and more like a delicate, powerless swan. He always said the same thing whenever Lucien went away for one reason or another. *We're here for you. We'll protect you. We'll care for you.*

It had sounded cute coming from Gabriel when he was eight years old. It sounded condescending now that he was in his Eighth Century of life.

"You have no idea what a comfort that is to your Mother's heart," she said sardonically.

Failing to pick up on her sarcasm, Gabriel smiled and leaned down to kiss her cheek. "May God bless you, Mother." After giving her a nod of deference, he trailed off with his sister clutched softly and securely to his chest.

Lana looked over her shoulder. She made sure he was several feet away before she rolled her eyes again. When she turned around, she noticed an abandoned item on the table.

"Oh, Gabe left his journal." Without hesitation, she picked up the black lambskin leather notepad and opened it.

"That's private," said Michael bluntly.

"I am your Mother," Lana reminded him severely as though he could ever forget. "Nothing concerning you boys is private. Not to me."

She began to flip through the pages with Gabriel's handwriting, stopping to read a specific paragraph:

There are two types of human species: primigens (homo sapiens) and valensmen (homo vis). In ancient times, valensmen were considered demigods or, in some tales, vampyres. However, the truth remains that valensmen are not immortal. Speaking as a valensmen, I can tell you that we do age, but at a significantly less drastic rate than our human counterparts, the primigens... You see, a valensman is a human with specific mutations in their epigenome. These mutations, along with our body's advanced autophagy, slow down our natural aging process by the time we reach age 17 ... Take my Father as an example: Gold King Lucien, is now more than 2,000 years old chronologically and yet he has the appearance and vitality of a man in his late twenties.

"Is he writing an item for a scientific journal?" inquired Lana.

"Maybe," said Michael. "Not sure."

"Hmmm, well I know he's already asked Lucien time and time again to start making valensmen physiology a mandatory subject across schools."

"Wouldn't hurt," said Michael. "Primigens take up 70% of the human race, and most of them appear to be willfully lacking in awareness. Even now, there are still misconceptions about our kind."

"Are there, really?"

"Some of them still think I'm a vampire," he said a matter-of-factly.

Lana bit her lip and brought the journal up to her face in an attempt to hide a silent chuckle. She knew he wouldn't care, but she still didn't have the heart to tell him that it had less to do with public ignorance over their physiology and more to do with Michael's general demeanor. He always came off as so cold and uncaring. On the rare occasions where he did show a slither of emotion, he looked hostile and impatient, like he wanted to rip someone's throat out and get it over with just so he could casually carry on with his day. It also didn't help that Michael genuinely lived up to this reputation. You couldn't be a skilled warrior and triumphant military general without slicing several heads off.

Skimming through Gabriel's notes, Lana pointedly tried to ignore her son's stare. Michael's eyes were an intimidation tactic all on their own. Whereas Lana's silver irises shined like stars, Michael's glinted like dead diamonds – the kind that were made from cremated human remains and intense heat.

She decided to ignore him.

She decided to ignore him until she couldn't take it any longer.

After several minutes, she flung the notebook shut. Unable to shake his stony stare, she snapped, "What?"

"You tell me," he said simply.

"I don't know what you mean, I'm sure," she said with unaffected breeziness as she brought a hand up to primp her dark long hair, which was pulled up and arranged in artfully placed curls and ringlets.

Michael cut his eyes at her. "What haven't you told us, Mother?"

"Only my personal opinions on the matter, which your brother didn't care to hear, *clearly*." Lana was sure Gabriel would sooner ask for Lexie's opinion than inquire after her thoughts.

"I'd like to hear it."

Lana shrugged. "It matters not. Gabe and your Father only believe in Heaven, Hell and the entire universe in between. They'd dismiss what I have to say as blasphemy."

"I'm not like them."

"No, you're not," Lana acknowledged. "You're more like me... in some ways."

It was a well-kept secret between the two. No one else in their family knew about it. Before Lucien had bestowed her with the Golden Gift, Lana had been born with a natural gift – one that Michael had inherited from her. There were many labels for this gift: Clairvoyance, Second Sight... *Psychic*, had to be the most popular term.

"Did you know this would happen?" he asked.

Lana had received visions and prophecies from a very young age. It was a blessing and a curse all at once for the visions were often powerfully accurate and usually given to her at the most inconvenient of times. That said, she had not been able to foresee their current circumstances.

"Not at all," she sighed. "Lucien's...absence ... came as a complete surprise." Dropping her perfect posture, she leaned back against the chair. "You didn't have any visions, either, I take it?"

Michael shook his head once. Always only once because he never cared to repeat himself.

Lana let out a sour little chuckle. This was why people didn't believe psychics. They didn't understand how psychics got themselves into sticky predicaments when they could allegedly prophesize everything beforehand. What they failed to grasp was that psychics had the same problem everyone else had – they couldn't see their own situation clearly because they were too emotionally attached to it.

"I have a theory," Lana said. "I think—I think he may be stuck in the Astral Realm."

The Astral Realm was a plane outside of the physical world, but not far from it. It was a place where souls exhibited and examined what had been, what should have been, and what could be before moving on.

"If that's true, then the solution is simple," said Michael.

"And that solution would be to…?"

"Do nothing." Michael had some experience travelling to the Astral Realm. He was trained by warrior monks back in the 12th century, and they had taught him many things, among which was how to have a controlled out-of-body experience. It wasn't, by any means, a fun or easy experience. But it was relatively harmless, provided the traveler knew what they were doing.

"Living visitors to the Astral Realm can never become permanent residents," he said. "Their physical bodies will always bring them back. Usually within a span of hours. The most within three days."

"What if someone didn't enter as a visitor? What if they were thrown into that realm as a prisoner?" Lana leaned forward, pressing her elbows to the table. "I know it doesn't make sense. There's no one strong enough or powerful enough to do this to the Gold King, as far as we know… and yet, I can't shake this feeling that someone did this to him."

Lana looked at Michael expectantly, but her son went silent, his jaw grimly set.

"Well?" she prompted. "Any thoughts?"

"Instinct transcends knowledge. You've always said." Michael got up and threw his tailcoat over one arm.

"So … you think I'm right?"

"I think we all need to direct our energy where it matters most." As he gathered Gabriel's leftover belongings, he added, "I know Gabe insists we'll remain at your beck and call, but you'll have to forgive us, if we can't provide you with all the attention you require. Especially *tonight*," he said, giving her another pointed stare. "He and I shall take counsel from our personal network of trusted advisors. And I expect we'll be far too preoccupied to keep you company." With a parting glance and a nod of deference, "I'll see you tomorrow, Mother."

Lana nodded her head in understanding. She knew exactly what she had to do.

"Oh boys, come along, your lunch is getting cold," she beckoned the Quartermaine twins with a wave of her hand. When they got to the table, she asked, "Do you know what the most exciting part about living in a castle is?"

"The tennis court?" said John-Marlowe.

"The maze?" supplied Jason-John.

"The swimming pools?"

"The libraries?"

"The music room?"

"The gift-wrapping rooms?"

"The dungeons?"

"The room service?"

"That's only in a hotel, dumb-dumb."

"Doesn't matter. They still have personal chefs and maids to serve you here, don't they?"

"Well, those are all perks, to be sure," nodded Lana. "But I personally always got a kick out of all the secrets this place has stored up over time … especially, the secret passageways."

The Quartermaine's jaws dropped at once. "Secret passageways?!" They shrieked eagerly.

Lana grinned. "Would you like to see them, my little Q-tees?"

"YESS!!!!"

Her grin widened. "Then how about we take one of those passageways for a top-secret trip outside of the castle tonight? Just the three of us."

Chapter 3: The Hidden House of Halkyon

"It's a waxing moon."

"It's a waning moon."

"It's clearly waxing," said John-Marlowe.

"It's obviously waning," refuted Jason-John.

"Waxing."

"Waning."

"Waxing!!"

"Waning!!"

"Boys, please." With a long-suffering sigh, Lana gently rubbed the side of her temple. She was still recovering from a migraine and being in the middle – literally – of her godsons' bickering didn't make it any better. "It's a full moon tonight, which means it's completed waxing and will begin the waning process in a moment."

The night was still young, and the three of them had already had quite the adventure. Garbed in dark hooded capes, they had all gone through a secret wall in Lana's private den that led to an elongated passageway, which led into the servant's quarters and out into a rocky pathway, which in turn, led them around to the large bridge that connected the island to the mainland.

There had been two Volucris Knights and a palomino horse by the bridge, waiting for the Queen. For a moment, the Quartermaine boys were sure they'd been clocked. But the Knights weren't there to stop them.

"Your Majesty," one of them had greeted. Like all Volucris Knights, the guard was wearing a mustard-coloured beret with a golden griffin pinned to one side along with a black and gold cravat beneath his beige jacket. "The gates are already open, and His Majesty's Shields are down," he said, referring to the portals at the end of the bridge.

The guards had bowed to Lana and handed her the reins to the horse. In return, Lana handed them a bag that contained gold bars made by King Lucien himself. Of course, the twins hadn't seen what was inside the bag and were wholly unaware that it was *hush money* Lana had stored away and used whenever she needed to flee the Cage without drawing attention to herself.

At first, the boys hadn't understood why they weren't taking modern transportation. The Golden Family had plenty – more than plenty – of automobiles and aircrafts at their disposal. Besides, it was the 19th century. No one rode horses as a means for transportation anymore, not even commoners. Not to mention, three people on a horse could get uncomfortable for both the riders and the horse, even when one of the riders was a dainty, waif-like Queen and the other two were scrawny eight-year-olds, both under eighty pounds.

"Trust me," Lana had whispered into their ears once they had all mounted the horse. She was perched at the back with Jason-John in the middle and John-Marlowe at the front. "Hold on tight," she had advised before clicking her tongue.

With the weight of three on her back, they had expected the mare to step into a slow and symmetrical four-beat gait. Instead, the horse had cantered past the bridge like it had been set on fire. Little did the boys know that the horse's hooves had been charged with the Gold King's energy.

You see, whenever a King *charged* a specific item with their energy, it meant they mentally provided a specific set of instructions, entailing exactly what they wanted said item to do. In this case, the hooves were charged for the purpose of enhancing the animal's speed from its standard limit of 55 miles per hour to a whopping 300 miles per hour.

It didn't take long for them to reach the double doors of the 20-foot gate, which blocked out the inland. The gate served two functions. The first was to look grand and elegant to the public. The second, more important purpose, was to hide the microscopic generators it had inside the doors. Said generators were also charged by the Gold King's energy and they controlled the 100-foot forcefield wall – another one of Lucien's Shields – that outlined the entire perimeter of the lake.

Like most of King Lucien's Shields, the wall was translucent and tinted in a shade of gold so pale and light that most people could never see it. Though if anyone ever tried to pass through one of those Shields while it was still up and running, they would certainly *feel* it. The Quartermaine boys still remembered the time their brother Nick-Ray had accidentally slammed into a near-invisible bell-jar-shaped Shield that Lucien had created around the twins' sandcastle. With a hanky placed tightly over Nick-Ray's bloody and broken nose, two guards had promptly rushed the eldest Quartermaine to the Cage's hospital wing for immediate repair.

Even though the Knights had assured Lana the Shields were now down, John-Marlowe and Jason-John feared they would end up hitting a steel wall like Nick-Ray. So, they kept their eyes tightly closed as the horse swept out of the gateway.

"You can open your eyes now," Lana had told them when they were several feet into the mainland.

Slowly, they blinked and released a simultaneous sigh of relief. The mare was going far too fast for any of them to crane their necks back. If they had looked back, they might've caught sight of the gates closing before them and a large beam of moonlight shining across the King's coat of arms and the inscription around it, which read: *We shine brighter than Heaven.*

Now here they were, under a yellow buck moon and out in the heart of a forest a few miles away from the Gold Kingdom's capital city, Halkyon.

After dismounting their horse, Lana tied its reins to a nearby tree. Grabbing her godson's hands, one of each, she led them down a massive copse. For a while, all they could see were silver birch trees with dark eye-shaped scars across their white barks.

The twins had immediately assumed they were lost, but their Godmother-Queen didn't look worried. Lana appeared confident and at ease, gliding through the woods like she owned it. And technically, she did own it through marriage. The woods did, after all, belong to Lucien, just like everything else in this realm. *What's his is mine, and what's mine is ours*, she had always said.

After trekking about some more, they came to a stop once they reached an unusually large gaping empty circle of dark grass. In broad daylight, it would've been the perfect spot to set up a large picnic or a seasonal festival. Under a full moon, it would've been an ideal setting for a demonic-summoning ritual. But no one ever used this location for either of those reasons. In fact, most people who hiked these trails never lingered for very long on this strangely barren spot. The few that managed to see it, ignored it, like there was nothing unusual about the sight.

"I think the trees are watching us," said John-Marlowe in a hushed voice as he tightened his grip on Lana's hand. He knew the *eyes* on a silver birch tree were nothing more than natural bark-markings. But he also knew, for certain, that the ones around them were blinking in a very unnatural way.

"Of course they are. That's their job," said Lana lightly as if it wasn't the slightest bit odd that the trees kept winking at them.

"Errr, Godmother, I thought you said we were here to visit a friend of yours," said Jason-John, shooting a nervous glance over his shoulder.

"That, we are."

"But there's no one here," he said, "Unless your friend is a talking tree."

"They talk too?!" hissed John-Marlowe, who was still weirded out by all the blinking.

"Don't insult the trees, dear. They take offence." Releasing a deep breath, she said, "Now, you boys remember the little poem I taught you on the way here?"

They nodded.

"Chant it with me now," commanded Lana. "Say it with confidence. And no matter what happens, you needn't be alarmed. I shall be right here with you."

The boys shrugged at one another. They hadn't the faintest idea what their Godmother was talking about. What harm could a little poem do? What was so alarming about it?

Slowly, softly, and seriously, the trio began to recite together:

"Heart light and mind bright,
I mean no harm nor fright.
Let my eyes shine bright across the night,
Show me all that's hidden in plain sight."

They kept the chorus going for a long while – at least it felt that way to the twins. In actuality, only three minutes had transpired. By the time they reached the five-minute mark, the boys grew weary.

The Quartermaines exchanged silent glances as they attempted to read one another's minds. Mind you, they couldn't pry into other people's minds, only their own. It was their own thing. Their *twin thing.* And right now, they needed to use their twin thing to find a way to delicately tell their Godmother-Queen: *We're bored now. Even the trees look like they're about to fall asleep. This isn't fun anymore. Let's go home.* Naturally, they couldn't use those exact words. It had to be phrased to perfection so that their Queen wouldn't feel insulted by them, and their Godmother wouldn't be disappointed with them.

The boys' chants began to dwindle and fall into noncommitted mumbles. But just as they were about to give up, things got interesting.

Heavy slashes of wind shot past the trio like invisible bullets. It swept their hoods off their heads and their bangs away from their temples. And, if Lana hadn't been holding onto them so tightly, it would've undoubtedly sent both boys flying backwards.

Even as the wind settled down, there remained an intense chill in the air that made their bodies tremor and their teeth chatter.

High above them, gloomy clouds suddenly appeared out of nowhere, taking up residence across a dark sky, which, one mere moment ago, had been adorned solely by a full moon.

All around them, the silver birch trees were going berserk. A second ago, their eyes had looked almost droopy, like they were about to nod off. Now, they were wide awake once more, rattling their branches about and working themselves into a tizzy. If the trees had been placidly observing them before, they were raucously scrutinizing them now. The eye-scars on their barks began to blink in rapid succession, emitting a beeping noise that sounded like a sensor examining a subject's biometrics before granting access.

Just when the boys thought it was all over, another wind-induced vibration coursed through them. Instinctively, they closed their eyes and clutched onto Lana's sides, wrapping their little arms tightly around her waist.

Shortly afterwards, they felt Lana's hands stroking their hair back into place. "It's alright, my little Q-ties," they heard her say softly, "It's all over now. You can open your eyes … and you can stop screaming as well."

They opened their eyes together, at the same time, just as they had done when they were first born. Jason-John was older by three minutes, but as the story was told, he had waited for his brother to be by his side before gazing out into the world.

Blinking slowly, the first thing they saw was a large house standing proudly in the middle of the previously bare gap in the soil.

"Where did that house come from?" gaped Jason-John.

Entirely black in colour, the multistoried house was a stunning semidetached with three towers. Each tower had pitched roofs with dormers sticking out. And, judging by the columns of windows on every tower, there had to be up to five floors as well. The unexpected fog that crept its way around the estate gave the overall impression of something straight out of a gothic fairy tale.

The house wasn't by any means comparable to the grandness of the Gilded Cage. It didn't even seem to be as large as the Quartermaine's family estate. Nevertheless, the children were fascinated for they had surely discovered a haunted house in the middle of a dark forest.

"Did you do that, Godmother? With the Golden Gift?" John-Marlowe asked, craning his neck to look up at Lana.

"No, dear. I didn't create or conjure this house. It's always been here, covered by an enchantment," she said.

It was all rather simple. The enchantment hid the house from passersby, and the trees protected the property from trespassers.

The twins shared a perplexed look at her explanation, which led Lana to elaborate, "It was all done with old-world magic."

"Old-world magic…" repeated Jason-John.

"But that means…" registered John-Marlowe.

"Witchcraft!" They shouted, jaws dropping.

Lana nodded, not at all surprised by their reaction.

"Does that mean you're a witch?" inquired John-Marlowe.

Lana looked down at them blankly.

"But Godmother, you could get into trouble for that!" Jason-John tugged at the side of her robe with urgency. "Witches get executed here!"

"*Prosecuted*, you mean," corrected John-Marlowe.

Jason-John narrowed his eyes at his brother. "I know what I mean, and I mean *executed*."

"Prosecuted."

"Executed."

"Prosecuted, you prat!"

"Executed, you d—"

"Neither is true," interrupted Lana. "Witches do not face prosecution or execution in this realm. There aren't any witch-hunts here … This isn't the Red Kingdom, boys."

It wasn't entirely true. In the Gold Kingdom, witches were neither prosecuted nor executed, but that didn't mean they weren't persecuted by their fellow Goldizens (Golden citizens). Hence, the hidden homes and secret sorcery.

Witchcraft was an ancient practice, available to everyone, and long preceding the emergence of Chosen Kings. But then, men with Divine Totems had come into power; the majority of them had outlawed the practice of sorcery, claiming that the only true source of magic came from a King's energy.

Lucien was a little different. Unlike many of his fellow Kings, he allowed for freedom of religion and freedom of expression across his realm. People were allowed to express their religious beliefs and partake in their spiritual practices however they pleased, provided they were loyal to the Golden Crown. That was how it appeared on paper.

Realistically, Lucien was so obstinately Catholic that there were moments where he made the Pope look like a heathen. The Gold King had never prosecuted-executed any of his subjects for their personal beliefs, but he had also never publicly endorsed any religion outside of the Christian faith. He was more open minded with monotheism, in general. But he was particularly dismissive of polytheistic faiths, highly critical of pagans who still worshiped the old gods, and widely distrustful of pagans who engaged in the practice of witchcraft. At the best of times, he seemed to bitterly tolerate the pagans the way a parent would reluctantly endure a wayward child's *unconventional lifestyle choices*.

In Lana's opinion, it was such a shame how so many of the ancient traditions had become forgotten and obscure over the centuries. Both Lana and Lucien had, in fact, been born and bred in the time of old ways and old gods. But somewhere down the line, Lucien had converted and never looked back. Lana, naturally, was expected to follow her Husband-King.

"Someone's coming," Jason-John whispered hotly, pulling at Lana's robe once again and pointing to the front entrance of the central tower.

"That would be my friend," said Lana. "The owner of this house."

A woman with a gas lantern in hand came slowly through the door and down the front steps. She appeared to be dressed entirely in black.

"She's pretty," said John-Marlowe. "Is she a witch?"

"Pretty creepy, you mean," said Jason-John as he clasped his hand tightly around Lana's. "And, obviously, she's a witch. Just look at her. The Dark Lady of the Dark House."

The Gold Queen inwardly sighed. She didn't bother explaining that the House of Halkyon Forest was somewhat sentient, and it wasn't always dressed in black – unlike its owner, Greta Anatolia, who never wore anything but black.

Lana was unaccustomed to seeing the house with such a dark exterior. It usually coloured itself a stark shade of swan-white whenever she dropped by. On occasion, she'd even seen the house change from ivory to a periwinkle blue or a sparkling silver. The Queen could only presume the house was currently hamming it up with a dark-and-dreary aesthetic, complete with heavy fog makeup and bushes of large venus flytraps, to frighten and excite the children in equal measure. Judging by their reactions, it was certainly working.

"Now boys," she said quietly as they strode forward to meet the lady of the house, "You musn't judge by appearances. Ms. Anatolia happens to be a very pleasant young valenswoman, and I want you boys to behave. No roughhousing. No bickering. We're guests in her home, so we must mind our manners, yes?"

"Yes, Godmother," they mumbled.

The twins tried their hardest not to openly gawk at the woman once they reached the foot of the steps. But it was difficult not to stare for they had never seen a woman like her before. Back when their mother was alive, the twins had subconsciously compared every woman they had ever met to her. Now that their mother was gone, they were doing the same thing with Lana.

Standing across from the Queen, Ms. Greta Anatolia looked like Lana's opposite in nearly every possible way. Greta was unconventionally pretty whereas Lana was divinely beautiful. She was short whereas Lana was tall. Her complexion was fish-belly white whereas Lana's skin tone practically radiated a golden glow. And then, of course, there were the clothes they were wearing.

Beneath her dark cape, Lana was dressed, as she often was outside of formal events, in a simple ivory silk chiffon gown. She wore no jewelry apart from her wedding ring, a 10-carat princess cut canary diamond ring with a gold band that was made by the King himself. There were people three planets away who could probably see her ring glistening in the night sky.

Greta, on the other hand, was wearing a black empire-waist dress with dark puffy sleeves. It wouldn't have been sartorially shocking… had the dress not been made entirely of leather and embellished with dark spikes and black feathers. The only accessory she appeared to be sporting was a necklace, made with a thick black string of yarn, around her throat. From a distance, it didn't look very special or peculiar. But up close, the twins noticed that the necklace had a charm and a pendant attached to it. The charm was shaped like a small golden key. The pendant was hiding behind the key, and it was much larger. From their vantage point, they couldn't make out that the pendant was a heart-shaped glass vial with the cork tightly sealed with red wax. Inside the vial were a mixture of olive oil and herbs like mugwort, wormwood, yarrow and lavender.

"Your Majesty," Greta curtsied, "You enchant us with your presence."

"Darling Greta," Lana kissed her on both cheeks and smiled, feeling relieved that Greta looked like she had been expecting a visit from her. "I take it you received my message?"

It had been Lana's first time sending a message with the Golden Gift. Lucien did it all the time, claiming it was the easiest and safest form of communication since messages sent via Divine energy couldn't be intercepted or recorded in any way, as far as he knew. It was easy for Lucien, obviously, since he was the current proprietor of said energy. It hadn't been so easy for Lana; after sending one message to Greta, she was left feeling nauseous and dizzy, and with a headache that was akin to someone stabbing a blade right between her eyes. But it had to be done. Greta lived entirely off the grid, and this was the fastest way to reach her.

"Your message was received most… clearly, ma'am," Greta nodded with a tight smile.

It had happened earlier in the day while Greta was seeing to her garden. There she was, innocently checking in on her foxgloves and nightshades when a massive golden holographic head with Queen Lana's features floated above her.

"GRETA! I HOPE THIS MESSAGE FINDS YOU WELL! I NEED YOUR HELP. PLEASE KNOW THIS MATTER REQUIRES THE UTMOST SECRECY…" Lana had gone on to explain her entire situation in great length and with considerable volume. It reminded Greta of a child using a telephone for the very first time in their life. It was a mercy there were so many protection wards around the property; otherwise, Greta was certain Lana's booming voice would've inadvertently broadcasted her dilemma to the entire realm. What Greta didn't know, however, was that telepathic messages sent through Divine energy were protected. Only the receiver of the message could see and hear it. So, it really didn't matter how loud Lana had been, no one else would've caught wind of her memo except Greta.

"What a relief, I was worried it wouldn't get through," chuckled Lana, blissfully ignorant of how unnecessarily loud her message had been. "These are my godsons, Jason-John and John-Marlowe. Their brother is Nicholas-Ray Quartermaine, the Duke of Firefinch."

The twins' faces shot up, away from the curious-looking pendant lying across Greta's chest and over to her dark eyes.

When Greta dropped her head to greet them, both boys huddled closer to Lana's sides. "Hello," they said a little shyly and nervously. Like many children, their extroverted personalities turned bashful and muted around strangers.

"Welcome to my home," she said kindly.

The twins bowed to her, even though it wasn't required of them. They were aristocracy, whereas this woman – this *witch* – was most likely a commoner. A wealthy commoner, judging by the grand house, but a commoner all the same. Witches weren't persecuted-executed in the Golden realm, but the boys were pretty sure King Lucien didn't honour them with noble titles. Nevertheless, their Godmother-Queen expected them to be polite, so they politely bowed.

"Please. Do come in," said Greta, turning to lead them up the steps. "I trust you didn't have any trouble passing the barrier."

"No, the trees gave us entrance straight away," Lana had never received such speedy access into Greta's home before. Usually, the trees would make her stand there and chant for at least an hour before revealing the house. "I suspect it was the children. They must've sensed the purity in them."

They went up a wide set of stairs, through a large, paneled doorway and into the foyer, where Greta collected their capes and placed them inside a closet. The entrance hall was dark, spotless and practically barren with hardly any furnishings save two statement pieces. The first was hanging on the wall; it was a gigantic portrait of Greta, still clad in black, and flanked by two other people, a man and a woman, who shared similar facial features. The second was a larger-than-life-sized black marble pillar of a triple goddess – same goddess depicted thrice over – with an entirely naked chest and torso. The goddess stood tall beside a spiral stairway as though she were guarding it.

The twins expected Greta to lead them up the stairs. Instead, she escorted them straight ahead, turned left and down a long, slim corridor. As they sauntered across the blackwood floor of the hall, the twins took sneak peaks into some of the rooms they came across.

The interior of the house was not at all what the boys had expected. From the outside, it all seemed delightfully doom-and-gloom. Inside, however, the rooms had more of a charming cottage aesthetic with large roaring fireplaces, red tweed sofas, gigantic armchairs and hand-painted wallpaper. Much to their relief and dismay, there wasn't anything frighteningly sinister about it.

Every now and then, the house shook, but it didn't feel ominous. It was as if the house didn't want to instill fear anymore. If anything, it rumbled as though it were releasing a giggle.

"My home was created in the seventh century. If you have any questions about it, you're more than welcome to ask," said Greta, as though reading their young minds.

"Is this house haunted?" Jason-John asked right away just as John-Marlowe inquired, "There aren't any demons here, are there?"

"Boys," Lana reprimanded in a low voice, "What did I say about minding your manners?"

"I don't mind, Your Majesty. Truly." Gazing down at Jason-John, Greta said, "Yes, it is haunted just as all houses are."

There was a saying: the older the house, the more infested it was with spirits.

"Haunted by a demon?" pressed John-Marlowe worriedly.

"By many different spirits," said Greta, "Chief among them would be my great, great grand-father. He died recently." By *recently*, she meant two centuries ago.

"Was he a demon?" asked Jason-John eagerly.

"Not really. He was usually labeled a troublemaker more than anything else," Greta grinned. "Though he was known to be a demon on the dancefloor... as you well remember, Your Majesty."

The house shook pleasantly as though emitting a belly laugh.

"I remember," Lana said with fondness. "He was a man far ahead of his time."

The late Mr. Anatolia had certainly caused a stir when he first introduced the Golden realm to the waltz back in the 13th century. It had caused quite a scandal – a couple dancing with their bodies in such proximity, and in public no less. Lucien had clutched his chest and nearly fainted at the sight of it. It took nearly half a century for both Lana and the Pope to convince him that waltzing wasn't a sacrilegious act.

Lana chuckled to herself. She wondered how her conservative Husband-King would react to the latest new dance craze that was making the rounds – the *tango*. If an innocent waltz had made him wheeze, then the tango was sure to send him into cardiac arrest.

"What's so funny, Godmother?" John-Marlowe peered up at her curiously.

"Oh, it's nothing." Lana shook her head. "I was just thinking about your Godfather-King."

"Do you miss him?"

Lana's grin fell. "He's not gone, my darling."

"I know," said John-Marlowe gently. "But… he's not here either… What if Jase's right? What happens if he doesn't wake up?"

Lana wasn't sure how to respond to that. Thankfully, she didn't have to. Jason-John's boisterous demeanor diverted their attention back to him.

"Tell us more about spirits!" Jason-John begged Greta. His head whizzed around, searching for spirits as though they'd magically appear before him at any given moment. "What are they like? How many of them are here? Are they everywhere? Are they evil?"

"Calm yourself, Jason-John," said Lana, placing a placating hand on the boy's shoulder.

"Spirits are not so different from you and I," replied Greta, not the slightest bit bothered by the series of inquiries. "They're made of energy just as we are. Most of them mean no harm. Many of them want to help. Several wander about lost and confused. Some feel angry and lash out at others. But only a select few are exceptionally malevolent."

Jason-John scrunched up his face as he mulled over her response. "You didn't answer all my questions."

"I believe you've had more than enough answers for now," said Lana firmly.

They reached the back of the house, coming to a large kitchen with a long farmhouse table in the center of the room. There was a black cast iron stove on one side of the wall and double sinks on the other side. Above the faucets were open cabinets full of glass jars containing all sorts of items, ranging from common herbs to the strangest of concoctions. There were jars of cinnamon, dried basil, orange peels and cardamom. There were also jars labelled graveyard dirt, sea urchin spines, powdered poison ivy, mistletoe berries, fox teeth, vulture feathers and cat whiskers.

At the tail end of the room were a set of glass doors, which were wide open, making way for an idyllic transition into the conservatory.

"Here we are, the most important room in the house," presented Greta.

"It's a kitchen," muttered Jason-John, unimpressed. He had never bothered stepping into the kitchens of his family's ancestral home. Why would he? It was where chefs, cooks, and servants assembled.

"Precisely," nodded Greta. "For commoners, such as myself, the kitchen is where everyone inevitably ends up gathering."

"But there's no one here," John-Marlowe pointed out, gesturing to all the empty chairs surrounding the table.

"Not true. You're here now," she said.

"And the spirits are here too," added Jason-John.

"Indeed, they are," nodded Greta.

"What's your house called, Ms. Anatolia?" asked John-Marlowe.

"We call it home," said Greta.

"No, I mean… what do people call your house?" John-Marlowe tried again, this time with examples. "Like, our family home is called Jasper House. And our Godfather's castle is called the Gilded Cage."

"We don't have such titles here. To me and my family, this place doesn't require a name. It's simply home."

"I bet it's 'cause commoners can't afford names for their houses," Jason-John whispered into his brother's ear.

"Nonsense, Jase. It doesn't cost money to name a house," said John-Marlowe. "We can come up with a name for you, if you like?" he proposed to Greta. "How about Blackrose Park? Or Blackflame Castle? … No, it's not big enough for a castle… Ooh, what about the Black House?"

"How original," muttered Jason-John, rolling his eyes.

"Brilliant suggestions, but I'm not sure any of those would work," said Greta. "You see, this house has very eclectic tastes... that is to say, it isn't always dressed in black." Motioning toward the sweet platters on the table, she offered, "Would you care for some refreshments? Some tea and cake perhaps? I've made some devil's food cake and orchard apple pie."

"Is it made from the guts and organs of unsuspecting children who come across your house?" Predictably, it was Jason-John who asked.

"I was fresh out, I'm afraid," Greta shrugged. "I had to make do with golden sugar. A subpar substitute to young flesh, I'm sure, but desperate times."

Jason-John frowned a little. She sounded serious, but he was reasonably certain she was teasing him. "We'll have a slice of devil's food cake, then."

"No, I want apple pie." disputed John-Marlowe.

"Devil's food!"

"Apple pie!"

"Dev—"

Knowing her godsons could carry on in such a manner until they starved to death, Lana quickly interrupted, "We can indulge in a sweet treat a little later, perhaps... *After* Greta and I have had a nice conversation."

Her tone was a reminder that this wasn't a social call. They were here for a purpose, not for pleasantries.

"Of course, Your Majesty." Greta nodded in understanding. "Please follow me."

Chapter 4: A Secret Society of Witches

Greta picked up her lantern once more and led them into the greenhouse, where they passed through rows of organic vegetables and fruits before stepping out into the back yard.

Her garden was a meadow with small water fountains hidden under foliage and wildflowers blooming everywhere. It was nowhere near as vast and intricate as Lucien's maze. There weren't separate rooms of gardens for the twins to find, explore, and get lost in. There didn't seem to be any rare flowers planted anywhere. There were no massive fountains with water flowing out of the mouths of stony griffin gargoyles. But the meadow did have a calm, relaxing ambience, which was further enhanced by the sounds of birds and crickets in the backdrop.

The four of them lined up and went down a narrow footpath until they reached a small, white-bricked outhouse with the doors entirely stripped out. The twins' eyes collectively lit up at the sight of all the animals. Two large black dogs, who were chasing one another in circles, stopped as they approached. They howled and barked excitedly upon seeing their owner. There was another dog, identical to them, lying down beside the entranceway. He was fast asleep with a fluffy grey cat curled contently on top of him.

The two dogs, named Selena and Gomez, ran over to the humans and began sniffing at the twins. The Quartermaine boys giggled as the dogs licked their faces. They began to pet them until they heard squeals and the patter of tiny feet. Interested in knowing what all the fuss was about, three tiny pigs shot out of the house and into their path.

"They've got pigs too!" John-Marlowe nudged his brother.

"There are more of them inside the outhouse. Along with some chickens," said Greta. "Feel free to take your pick."

"We get to keep them?" said Jason-John, who without waiting for an answer, dashed forward.

"Not quite," said Greta in a cryptic tone as she watched the boys run eagerly into the outhouse with the dogs on their trail.

Lana frowned, knowing where this was headed. "Will that really be necessary?" she asked Greta.

"I'm afraid so, Your Majesty. My brother is our family's primary spellcaster, as you may remember. And as diverse as he is with his craft, he remains highly traditional in some ways."

Traditional, she had said, meaning blood sacrifice would be involved. It was very old-school witchcraft. Most modern witches didn't bother with animal sacrifices anymore, but Lana knew there were still a fair number who remained faithful to the elder methods.

"Well, I suppose if there's no way around it…" Lana sighed and crossed her arms. "But tell him to place blindfolds over my godsons when he sacrifices the pigs. Their young eyes needn't witness every step of the procedure."

Procedure was the word Lana often used in reference to a *spell*. Truthfully, Lana wished this little procedure wasn't required at all. But her sons were right about her godsons. The Quartermaine boys knowing about Lucien's predicament was too much of a confidentiality risk.

The Valentas could have used the Golden Gift to enforce a pact of secrecy upon the boys, just as Lucien did with all his sentry and servants. But there was generally a hard rule against using Divine energy on minors, especially since there was a chance that such power would be too aggressive and intense on bodies that were still undergoing development.

It left Lana with no choice but to put them under a *Secret Screen* – that was what this particular spell was called. Lana had never tried it before, but it sounded simple enough. It involved:

- a pig's tongue,
- small bits of paper to write down the full names and dates of birth of people who needed to keep a secret, and
- small bits of paper to write down the secret itself.

Once all these materials and ingredients had been acquired, the spellcaster would have to cut slits into the pig's tongue, fold and stuff the papers into the slits and tie it down with pins, sprinkle the tongue with Four Thieves vinegar, spit rice wine onto it, and then dress it with salt, black pepper and cayenne pepper. Afterwards, the tongue would be placed in an icebox indefinitely.

If the spell proved successful, the Quartermaine twins would never tell another soul about the King's current dilemma, not even their eldest brother. For the remainder of their lives, they'd feel compelled to keep it between themselves as though it were a private joke.

The boys didn't take long and quickly returned, carrying a sleepy spotted pig. The animal was so large they each had to pick up one end of it. Jason-John held him by the front, while John-Marlowe caught hold of its rear.

"We want this one, Godmother," said Jason-John.

"We decided to call him Wilberforce!" exclaimed John-Marlowe.

Lana gave them a pitying look. She really wished they hadn't named it.

"Do you have any more animals about?" Jason-John asked Greta.

"We have a chicken coup just down the path," she replied.

"Can we see it?"

Everyone turned to Lana for her authorization.

The Queen shook her head. "Boys, need I remind you we have an exotic petting zoo, aviaries, and stables back in the Cage?"

"But it's not the same, Godmother," whined John-Marlowe. "Those animals are too rare."

Jason-John nodded in agreement. "And this is our first time in a commoner's house—"

"—with common animals!" finished his brother.

"We haven't the time for such distractions," Lana started, but at her godsons' pleading looks, she gave in, "Oh very well. A quick stopover to the chickens and then we really must be heading back. Ms. Anatolia and I have very important matters to discuss."

"What sort of matters, Godmother?" asked Jason-John.

"Private matters."

"It's about Godfather-Lucien, obviously," John-Marlowe said in a hushed voice. "It's always about him."

They went further down the trail. A small grey henhouse was only a stone's throw away. All they needed to do was take a turn right at the end of the footpath. From a distance, they couldn't hear any chickens – likely because they had all retired for the night. They did, however, hear something entirely different. There were a series of chimes, followed up with a guttural voice bashing out a tune in a mysterious language.

They took a sharp turn right and everyone's eyes bugged out. All human eyes, that is. The animals were undisturbed. The pig was still snoozing away in the twins' arms, and the dogs had already seen this scene play out too many times to even bark in surprise or enthusiasm.

Two blocks away was a perfectly ordinary henhouse.

One block away was a man who didn't look the slightest bit ordinary.

Waving his tambourine in the air and prancing about the meadow, the man seemed entirely unaware of his audience as he continued to chant up at the night sky. The twins hadn't the faintest idea what he was saying. Lana and Greta, however, knew exactly how to translate the Ancient Greek dialect he was using:

Oh, Dionysos, Ivory-crowned God of Wine, I invoke thee!

Great Liberator of the Earth, hear my prayers!

Bring mirth and cheer to all the seconds of my minutes,

And all the minutes of my hours,

And all the hours of my days and nights,

Grant me a life so heavenly and free!

Let me move and sway without impediment.

Like the best wine, let me go down smoothly for my beloved.

Aid me in selfishly indulging in all that I covet.

Show me how to be selfless and giving to all my lovers,

And guide me in making all my foes and rivals shove it…

John-Marlowe blinked several times. "What is your gamekeeper doing, Ms. Anatolia?"

"He's not the gamekeeper, dummy," said Jason-John before Greta could form a response. "Commoners don't have gamekeepers."

"Who is he then?"

"Look at his profile. It's the same guy from the portrait. I'm betting it's her brother."

"Could be her husband."

"I don't think *Ms.* Anatolia is married."

"Oh, right… but why is he dancing about like that? And what's he saying? I can't understand a word of it."

"Forget what he's saying," scoffed Jason-John. "Why is he naked?!"

On any other night, they might have seen less of Greta's younger brother, Basilius Anatolia. But under the heavy glare of a full moon shining a spotlight across his entire body, they saw far more of him than necessary.

"Alright boys. We've ventured far enough. It's time to head back," Lana said in a tone that booked no room for debate.

Beside her, Greta's face had begun to twitch. Panic spread across her eyes as she glanced nervously between the Queen and her brother. It was the first time Lana had ever seen the woman look like anything other than the perfect picture of dark serenity.

"My sincerest apologies, Your Majesty," she said in a very low whisper and gave a deep curtsy. "I must beg your forgiveness. I wasn't aware my brother would be performing his prayers outside tonight."

Lana waved her off. She wasn't the slightest bit offended by the nudity. She understood that many witches considered clothing as a barrier that blocked the flow of magic. If anything, she was mostly worried about her godsons. Being very young and impressionable, it could turn out to be a social disaster if the twins felt inspired to behave so liberally, especially among the ultra-conservative circles of Lucien's court.

"Please, feel free to roam the house while I have a private word with my Basilius. I shan't be long." After another deep curtsy, Greta turned and made a beeline toward her brother's figure while Lana dragged the twins by their collars back down the path. The last thing they heard before turning the corner was Greta raising her voice, "*We are in the presence of the Queen, the very heart and soul of the Golden realm, and she's calling on our family on a matter of nationwide, nay, empire-wide importance. So, for goddess' sake, put some damn clothes on and cover that hideous vegetable of yours!*"

"Godmother, what was that man doing?" John-Marlowe asked as they headed back toward the house.

"He was … he was simply foraging." Lana nodded. "Yes, that's exactly what he was doing. Greta's family home doesn't run on modern technology. The Anatolias prefer to live in the old ways. Therefore, they must forage and hunt for food. He was out for a nightly stroll to pick organic mossberries. Perfectly harmless."

It wasn't the most believable lie, but it was the first thing that came to mind, likely because Lucien was a gardening enthusiast and health fanatic, and a few weeks ago, he'd made a passing comment about the newfound mossberries in one of his gardens.

"*Take a look at these, Lana. Organic mossberries. Full of antioxidants,*" Lucien had gushed to his uninterested wife, "*They're ideal for warding off colds and eliminating free radicals in the body, you know.*"

"Isn't he likely to catch a cold out here without any attire?" said John-Marlowe.

"Which is exactly why he needs those mossberries," said Lana primly. "They're ideal for warding off colds and eliminating free radicals in the body, you know."

"But does one have to forage for berries *that way*?" John-Marlowe continued, still utterly perplexed. "I mean, is being naked a requirement for foraging?"

"Well…I … I suspect it's part of the process … in ensuring the berries are organic." Lana would drag out this lie to the end of the universe if she had to.

Returning to the kitchen, the boys gently laid a still slumbering Wilberforce on the table.

"I bet he wasn't foraging at all," said Jason-John. "I heard what Ms. Anatolia said. He was out there praying."

"I've never seen someone pray without any clothes on before," said his brother skeptically.

Jason-John leaned toward his brother, lowering his voice. "That's because they don't pray to God like the rest of us. They're witches. They worship the Devil."

Lana sighed and rolled her eyes. "Witchcraft is a practice, not a religion, my darlings. And there's no Devil-worship involved."

"There isn't?" Jason-John looked a little disappointed.

"No," said Lana. "Mr. Anatolia was praying to one of the pagan gods, Dionysus, not the Devil."

"Are all pagans witches?"

"Not at all. Most aren't, in fact. Only a select few choose to practice the craft."

"What alien language do you think he was speaking?" John-Marlowe wondered.

"Whatever it was, it certainly wasn't anything like the Earth Standard Sole," remarked his brother.

"He doesn't look like an alien though."

"Maybe he's a halfie like our Nick-Ray," remarked Jason-John, "Or he could be human-passing like—"

"Boys, this type of conversation is highly inappropriate for polite society," Lana reminded them. "But if you must know, the Anatolias are valensmen, just as much as we are. And Mr. Anatolia was speaking in Greek – an ancient language that existed on Earth long before the time of Chosen Kings."

Their world now lived and breathed under one global language: the Earth Standard Sole. But that hadn't always been the case. Lana, herself, was still fluent in Greek, Norse, Aramaic, Egyptian,

Sanskrit and Akkadian. Not that any of those languages existed anymore, not outside of small esoteric circles. In her opinion, it was a pity the newer generations would never know any of the dialects that had once inhabited their planet. The loss of language always equated to the loss of culture.

"That still doesn't explain why he was naked," shrugged Jason-John.

"The nudity is optional among witches, dear." Lana frowned, bringing a hand up to her temple to lightly massage it. She was still nursing a headache from the telepathic message she had sent out earlier.

"Are you unwell, Godmother?" John-Marlowe reached over to grab her free hand.

"I'm quite alright." Lana tried to smile down at him. "You needn't worry… But perhaps I ought to sit down…somewhere else," she said, eyeing the spotted pig that was now awake and helping himself to Greta's homemade apple pie.

His last meal, Lana thought sadly as the pig's snout burrowed deep into the pie. "Why don't we wait for Ms. Anatolia in the library?" she suggested. "Leave Wilberforce here," she told Jason-John before his small palms could grab hold of the animal.

"By himself?"

"I assure you he shan't be alone for much longer." Lana headed out the door, expecting her godsons to follow. "Come along now, boys."

They expected to find the library silent and vacant. It was neither.

Someone was already there, teetering on the step ladder beside a wall of books. A petite woman, she had frizzy blond curls which were tied back in a messy updo and she wore a puffy organza dress with yards of skirt in a colour that the twins could only describe as being painfully pink. She looked entirely out of place in the dark and earthy scholarly aesthetic of the room. Going by her profile, the Quartermaines recognized her as the other woman from the portrait. *Must be the sister,* they thought in unison.

She didn't turn around upon hearing someone enter the room. Instead, she began to yell in a frenzy, "G! G! Where's that grimoire I had back in the 11th century?!" She was hastily scanning through one book after another, throwing each one to the ground and letting the precious tomes fall with a careless clunk.

"It's the one that had all those potent love spells… Oh, where the deuce did you hide it, G?! And don't lie to me. I know you hid it. Just like I know it was you who locked away all the open razors in the house," she began to weep, "You knew it was going to happen, didn't you? You knew he'd leave me." With a deep dramatic inhale, she wiped her tears and bravely trudged on, "Well, you were right. But I don't care! I want him back! … I need my old love spells! And before you start, I don't want to hear you go on about how unethical they are. This is an emergency, and those incantations are far more effective than any of that modern self-love drivel all these youngblood witches today are bashing out."

She yanked a few more books out of the fifth shelf and placed them in her left arm before taking fast steps down the rungs of the ladder. "Ugh, I swear, I can't sleep, I can't eat, I can't breathe without Mr. Butterfrost!" Upon reaching the penultimate rung, she leaped onto the floor, her puffy skirts shaking around her. "Oh, I know you never liked him. You always called him a repulsive swine — I suppose he is a rake, but I love him so! And—and I'll die if he doesn't come back to me. I'll—I'll kill myself. Yes, I swear I'll do just that. I'll kill myself! And then I'll kill him."

"You'll have to kill him first, then yourself," said Lana simply. "It's him, then you. Otherwise, you're bound to come across quite the challenge, dispatching someone from beyond the grave."

"What are—" Finally turning around to face her guests, her jaw dropped along with all her books. "Oh my gods! Holy Lady-of-Cythera! Your Majesty!" She stepped forward, hastening to drop into a low curtsy. The only thing she dropped, however, was herself as she clumsily tripped over all the books she had discarded.

The Queen and the Quartermaines shot their heads downwards, following the woman's undignified descent to the floor. Though, she didn't exactly fall to the ground. If anything, she flew across the floor as though she were going belly down on a waterslide. The crown of her head stopped just short of Lana's feet.

"Your sister's not entirely wrong, Ms. Anatolia," Lana leaned forward and held out her hand as the woman scrambled to her knees. After helping the woman to her feet, the Queen added, "Spells of a romantic nature can be a touch too hostile, especially if there's an influx of ..." She paused to search for a nice synonym for *psychotic*. "... *rambunctious* energy attached to it."

Azaelea Anatolia gaped down at the dainty hand that held hers as though it were a pot of gold. She had never been touched by a royal before. No one was allowed to place a hand on them, even casually, unless they made the first move.

She lifted her eyes to meet the Queen's gaze only to drop her head once more. "Your Majesty! I salute the goddess within you! Please forgive the rancor in my speech. Such words were never meant for your untarnished ears." Dropping to the floor once more, this time on purpose, she begged in a loud voice, "Allow me to prostrate myself before you!"

"Oh, that's more than enough prostration, I rather think." Lana gently pulled the woman back up again. "Please, do get up, my darling. I assure you no respectable woman gets anywhere in life by staying on her knees for too long."

Up until now Azaelea had been blushing a pretty pink to match her dress. Now, her face was a volcano ready to detonate. *Queen Lana called me her darling!!!!* She internally squealed.

The twins gawked at her behaviour.

"The other one might look creepy, but ..." Jason-John whispered over to his twin.

"But this one's flat-out crazy," finished John-Marlowe with a nod of agreement.

Azaelea Anatolia had unknowingly accomplished something rare: she'd gotten the Quartermaine twins to wholeheartedly agree about something.

"Your Majesty," came Greta's voice from the doorway, "Allow me to apologize once more on my brother's behalf. He wasn't aware of your arrival and—Az! What are you doing here?"

"Your sister and I were conversing," said Lana, bringing her up to speed. "It appears she's been left bereft and abandoned by a Mr. Butterfrost and I was about to discourage her from taking any sort of action – magical or otherwise – in her current state of mind." Grabbing Azaelea's hand once more, she gave it a small pat. "You're far better off summoning a genuine soulmate than demanding the return of a lackluster love, my dear."

Azaelea nodded ferociously in agreement. "You're so wise, Your Majesty! I thank you for your guidance. Your heart is as vast as the sky, and your beauty is incomparable to anything on Earth. It's no wonder Helen went mad at the mere sight of you."

"You're too kind," Lana smiled politely, not bothering to correct her. In actuality, Helen of Troy was a primigen, and one who existed *long* before Lana's time. She had never even met the woman. The narrative was inadvertently started by Lucien. Back when they were first courting, Lucien would tell her, "*Lana, your beauty could make Helen of Troy seethe in jealousy!*" He must have said it often enough and loud enough for others to hear and spread.

"Please excuse us for a moment, Your Majesty." Greta came between them and dragged her sister out of the room by the elbow.

"Az!" she hissed once they were deep into the hallway. "I specifically asked you to stay away from my side of the house tonight."

"That's why you wanted privacy??" Azaelea shrieked accusingly. "You knew she'd be here tonight, and you didn't even tell me. Some sister you are! You know it's always been a lifelong dream for me to meet the Queen."

"Then consider your dream accomplished," Greta said tightly. "You can leave now and carry on with the real-life nightmare that is your relationship."

"There is no relationship anymore. It's over between me and Mr. Butterfrost."

"Tossed you aside like an unwanted salad, did he?" Greta raised a brow. "I told you he would."

"That's not how it played out!" Azaelea scowled, before softly conceding, "Not entirely."

"Well, out with it then, what happened? You may as well tell me."

"Ugh, I can't believe him! He promised me eternal loyalty, and then I catch him sneaking back to his wife!"

Greta blinked at her sister.

"It doesn't matter anymore. I'm over it now, thanks to the Queen," Azaelea shrugged happily. "I think I shall stay and offer Her Majesty a cup of tea."

Greta pinched her sister's arm to keep her in place. "Her Majesty is here for a private consultation with me."

"You, you, you." Azaelea glared as she wrangled away from Greta's grasp. "It's always about you. I don't see why you should have our Queen all to yourself! You're not the only classically-trained witch in this family," she finished with an indignant sniff.

"Of course not," agreed Greta, "We have Baz as well."

"I have plenty to offer too!" bellowed Azaelea. She resented the way Greta behaved sometimes, as though she was the only Anatolia heir with the blessing and burden of ensuring the survival of their family's occult dynasty.

Running her eyes down her sister's form with distaste, Greta sneered, "The Queen is not interested in the type of services you can provide."

"How dare—"

"Hush!" Greta growled out in a whisper. "Now is hardly the time to get into it… If you truly want to help, then you can escort her godsons over to Baz." Making an about-face, she strode back down the hall, toward the library. "He ought to be fully dressed by now," she said over her shoulder.

Azaelea's heels clucked loudly behind her sister's trail. "Why Baz?"

"He'll be performing a Silent Screen on them."

They returned to find the Queen and the Quartermaine boys picking up discarded books and restocking the shelves.

"Your Majesty," said Greta, "I must apologize once more for all these … unexpected inconveniences. If your godsons will follow my sister, you and I can retire to the reading room."

"Isn't this the reading room?" said John-Marlowe.

"It's the library, Young Mr. Quartermaine."

"Is there a diff?" snorted Jason-John.

"There is, actually," Greta insisted, but didn't bother to expand and explain. "Please, if you'll follow Azaelea, she'll escort you back into the kitchen." And to Lana, she reassured, "My brother's made himself presentable now."

The twins whipped their heads over to Lana. They didn't want to follow the pink-Ms. Anatolia. But at Lana's encouraging nod, they knew they had no choice but to do so.

Slowly, reluctantly, they made their way over to Azaelea, who grinned down at them. "Such charming twins!"

Their brows shot up at the same time.

"How'd you know we were twins?" demanded Jason-John.

"We don't look the slightest bit alike," nodded John-Marlowe. "I'm cuter."

"I'm taller."

"My eyes are bigger."

"My lashes are longer."

"My hair's more of a garnet," said John-Marlowe.

"Mine's ruby!" said Jason-John as though he had the superior shade.

"It's too ginger to be ruby!"

"Is not!"

"Oh, you're both far too adorable!" Azaelea tossed her head back and laughed. "But I could tell you were twins by your aura." Squinting down at them, she said, "You see, I have a knack for reading people's energy and you two have a very strong aura, which appears to be interconnected rather than separated. That usually only happens with people who are twins." Before the boys could refute, she held out her hands to them, wiggling her fingers about in a silly gesture, "Now, why don't we go check in on what mischief my brother Baz is up to, yes?"

They threw their heads back, looking to Lana once more for her approval.

"Go on, my darlings," said Lana encouragingly. "Oh, and Ms. Anatolia, do remind your brother to use blindfolds throughout the process."

"Yes, Your Majesty!" exclaimed Azaelea, smiling widely. "I shall return in a jiff!"

Greta cut her eyes at her sister once more. "Azaelea," she started warningly.

"Ms. Anatolia," Lana said before any passive-aggressive sisterly dispute could disrupt, "My godsons, like most boys, tend to get overexcited. If you could remain with them throughout the entire process, it would be an enormous help to me, as I'm sure they'll feel much more mollified with a feminine presence nearby."

"Oh, absolutely, Your Majesty!" Azaelea nodded hastily and gave a curtsy so low her nose might as well have been touching the floor. "Happy to be of service!"

Greta forced herself to refrain from rolling her eyes. The Gold Queen could have told her sister to head to the nearest body of water and drown herself, and Azaelea would've done it happily and with that same ridiculous smile on her face to boot.

When there were only two left in the library, Greta found herself looking away, feeling sheepish and mortified. Lana, however, was heavily amused.

"Darling Greta," she said with a bright smile, "I used to have so many questions about you. But now, after meeting more of your family… they've all been answered."

Greta's face twitched and cringed like a raisin before falling back into place. "I—um—" Unsure of how to respond, she indicated to the cerulean-coloured door next to the bookshelves. "Shall we, my Queen?"

Lana's smile never broke. "Lead the way."

Chapter 5: A Kingdom with a Million Cities

The reading room was nothing like the library. It was a little smaller and far tidier. One wall had a built-in wooden cabinet set topped with open shelves. Instead of books, the shelves were stocked with black candles, ancient scrolls, jars of moon water (which was water that had been left out under a full moon), tarot decks, oracle cards, and scrying bowls. There was a tiny woodburning stove with a kettle on top in one corner of the room. At the center was a large round table covered in a long cloth of black linen, surrounded by a series of empty chairs.

"Please, have a seat, Your Majesty," said Greta as she made her way over to the stove to fix a cup of tea.

This was Greta's unofficial office, where she carried out her work as an unofficial psychic consultant. It was all off-the-record, naturally, since she couldn't very well claim any tax deductions as a mystic. Her clients were diverse, ranging from a coven of sea witches from the Carnelian Islands to the Madhyama yogis of the Green Kingdom to the Gold Queen herself.

It certainly wasn't the easiest of professions. Having Second Sight and the ability to gaze into the Fading Future was as much a curse as it was a blessing. Nevertheless, the Anatolia family had an occult legacy to carry forward. Greta was merely doing her bit for the family's sake. Basilius was their spellcaster, Greta was the psychic medium and channeler, and Azaelea was—well, it was best not to mention her magical specialties in the presence of polite society.

"I'm aware this is stating the obvious," Lana said from her seat as she watched the woman pour hot water into a cup. "But I must remind you, Greta, this situation requires the utmost confidentiality."

"I am the soul of discretion." Greta slowly strutted toward the table, a small silver cup and saucer in hand. Laying the cup gently before Lana, she added, "As are my siblings, even though they may not exude such an impression. Rest assured, we shan't tell anyone about the King's dilemma."

"I didn't know you were one for tasseography." Lana nodded down at the teacup.

"Oh no, I never bother reading tea leaves. Waste of time, I rather think. That's for your headache, ma'am."

"Ah, I see. Thank you."

"Before we begin, Your Majesty," said Greta, taking a seat directly across from the Queen, which placed her back to the shelves. "I know you're a talented scryer in your own right. Therefore, I must ask, have you not been able to see anything?"

Scrying was the practice of seeing the past, present, and future by looking into specific objects or elements. A bowl of water, a candle flame, a crystal ball… things of that nature.

"I'm not in the best condition to scry at the moment." Lana had already depleted a lot of energy with the Golden message she had sent out earlier. Added to that, she was far too emotionally attached to get a clear reading.

"I see." Greta turned around to extract a deck of tarot cards from the shelf and two papyrus scrolls from one of the cabinets. "Perhaps we can try the cards. See what messages and guidance the Spirits have for us."

Lana frowned as Greta pulled out a traditional deck of tarot cards and began shuffling. She was acquainted with Greta long enough to know that reading tarot cards was an alternative for the witch – a back-up plan when things went wrong with her channeling. She also knew Greta had a propensity for overpreparing. The witch would've composed a strategy long before Lana arrived. Knowing Greta, she would've gone into a meditative trance to enter a deeper state of consciousness, and thereafter engage with whomever she was trying to contact from another realm of existence.

"Why do I have the feeling you're about to deliver some bad news?" Lana arched a brow as half of Greta's deck flew out of her hand and flopped onto the table.

"It's not completely terrible," said Greta slowly as she picked up the scattered cards.

"Start with the parts that aren't *completely terrible* and work your way down from there."

Greta unrolled one of the scrolls and laid it out on the table. "Would you happen to have anything that belongs to the King on your person?"

Without hesitation, Lana slipped her wedding band out of her finger and handed it over. "This gold was made by the King, with his Divine energy."

"May I?" At the Queen's nod, Greta took the ring and turned around again to remove a long string of yarn that was previously tied around a deck of oracle cards.

Meanwhile, Lana leaned forward to read the contents of the papyrus. It was a large circle divided into three quadrants with a small circle, a nucleus, in the middle. The quadrants were labelled *Physical Realm*, *Mental Realm*, *Spiritual Realm* respectively. The nucleus was categorized as the *Astral Realm*.

They were considered the Key Realms of Existence, and this was one way of explaining all the secret dimensions of the universe in a neat little package. But depending on who you asked – and what their religious, spiritual, and mystical inclinations may be – there could be anywhere between three to an infinite number of planes of existence.

Still, there seemed to be some sort of consensus around how these realms worked:

- The Physical Realm referred to anything in the three-dimensional mortal world. They were living in it, obviously.
- The Mental Realm included the vast landscapes of the subconscious mind. It was a place where thoughts, ideas, memories and dreams collided and reigned supreme.

- The Spiritual Realm was the place of Divinity, where the *higher ones* lived. Depending on one's personal beliefs, this referred to God(s), demigods, angels, and the most enlightened of prophets. It was the place where paradise existed.

The Astral Realm was like the crossroads where three roads would meet. It supposedly worked as an intersection between all three realms. Though Lana had read accounts from more than one spiritualist who claimed the Mental Realm was just as much of a gateway as the Astral. It explained why people sometimes had dreams concerning places and circumstances in their everyday lives, and other times, they had dreams where they felt like they had entered another world – because they had.

Outside the large circle, far off to the corner, Lana spotted a much smaller circle, unlabeled and coloured in like a black hole. Not that she needed a label to know what it was referring to. It marked the dwelling of the lower entities, the ones who were cast out of the Spiritual Realm. In monotheism, it was Hell, the place of fallen angels and demons. In classical pagan circles, it was Tartarus, where all the souls of damned went, along with the Titans that once wreaked havoc on Earth.

Turning to face Lana once again, Greta slid the ring through the string, clasping and fisting it at the ends. The ring dangled down in front of them like a pendant.

Keeping her hand fisted tightly and without tremor, she hovered the ring just above the scroll, to the point where it was barely grazing the paper. Greta then said a quick prayer and asked the spirit within the room to indicate the King's location.

For several seconds, the ring remained still, with no visible movement. Then, gradually, and without any physical movement on Greta's part, the ring began to shift like a pendulum. It caroused around the circle, one lap after another. This went on for a while longer until the ring landed onto the paper in a loud thud.

Both women peered down at where it landed. The Spiritual Realm.

"This confirms it." Greta didn't look the least bit surprised by the pendulum's answer. "When I channeled my spirit guides earlier, they said the same. His Majesty's soul has travelled outside of his body and into the Spiritual Realm. But thankfully, he's not trapped in the Astral."

"And that's a good thing?"

Greta nodded. "The Astral Realm is volatile to say the least. Souls and entities usually pass through it as they please, but the ones that linger there are not always... agreeable in nature. If His Majesty is in fact in one of the higher realms of existence, he's less likely to be harmed or in any danger."

Lana supposed that tracked. The Spiritual Realm was meant to be paradise, so it had the poshest neighborhoods in the cosmos. The Astral – while nowhere near as sinister and diabolical as the realm of lower entities – was akin to the chaotic hustle and bustle of a big city, with all sorts of sketchy and odd characters roaming about.

Still, if that was the good news, then Lana felt like she needed to brace herself for what she was about to hear next.

"However, the other side of it is," Greta began, "that even though we know he's in the Spiritual Realm, my spirits were not able to pinpoint his exact location. People often think of the place as one large, perfect patch of land. *Elysium*, *Heaven*, *Valhalla*, *Svargaloka*, whatever they prefer to call it. But both my magical and spiritual educators have said otherwise, calling it a Kingdom with a Million Cities."

"You wouldn't happen to have a scroll with a detailed map of each of those cities, would you?"

"Sadly, I do not."

"Hypothetically, let's say we manage to determine his whereabouts in the Spiritual Realm. What then?" said Lana.

"Then we would have to send someone over there to guide His Majesty to the Astral Realm. It's the bridge where everything intersects. Once he's there, he can travel straight back into his body. Or he can go into the Mental Realm and enter the dream state. The soul reattaches to the body in the mental plane—"

"Which means, he'd return to the physical land of the living once he awakens from whatever dream he's having," Lana finished with an understanding nod.

"In fact, the King needn't take any action once he reaches the Astral. As long as he remains alive and well, his soul will naturally be drawn back to his physical body."

"Living visitors to the Astral realm can never become permanent residents," Michael's voice shot through Lana's head as a reminder. *"Their physical bodies will always bring them back. Usually within the span of hours. The most within three days."*

"No matter what happens, you musn't let anyone else near my body!" Lucien's voice chimed in a moment later.

Lana's eyes momentarily screwed closed against her pounding headache. "Surely, there must be something we can do," she sighed. "Why not send out a traveler?"

Travelling across dimensions was a difficult spiritual medium to be proficient in. But there were still a fair few within highly esoteric circles. Lana's mind quickly sped to Michael, only to drop the thought like a sack of bricks. She didn't want to risk endangering her son in any way. Even if she did take it into consideration, it was unlikely to prove successful. Michael was trained in traveling to the streets of the Astral Realm, but he hadn't reached the ability where he could go beyond those city limits.

At Greta's sudden silence, Lana persisted, "You must have a roster of resources at your disposal."

"I do, but…"

"But what? What about Anu St. John? She could surge through the cosmos like a dream, if I recall correctly."

"You certainly do recall correctly, ma'am," said Greta hesitantly. "She was indeed a highly skilled traveler, but… she's also very much dead."

"Dead?? Are you sure?"

"Unless it was someone else I saw inside her coffin at her funeral, then yes, I'm quite sure, ma'am."

Leaning back in her chair, Lana crossed her arms. "Well, I wouldn't rule out that possibility – it has been known to happen amongst our crowd." After giving it another thought, she came up with, "Rose de Padua María Severino Garcia! Travelling was like taking a vacation for the likes of her."

"Also dead," said Greta plainly, and at Lana's reaction, went on to explain, "Hunting accident. Her life-partner forgot his specs and confused her for a boar."

"Ulysses Bartleby? Mind you, he's a bit of a last resort." From what Lana could remember, the man wasn't the most adept traveler and relied far too much on exotic vegetables from the Green Kingdom to get him into other-worldly dimensions and altered states of consciousness.

"Dead. Jumped out of a tenth-floor window after consuming one too many fungi from the Green realm."

Lana rolled her eyes. The use of psychedelics was an effortless means of spiritual travel. Unfortunately, it also meant the complete loss of control over one's physical and mental properties. Hence, all the drugged-up gurus leaping out of windows.

"Come now," huffed Lana. "There must be someone! Preferably someone who doesn't fuel up on psychedelic plants to get where we need them to be."

The Queen provided a few more names, including the likes of Tiberius Goodfellow, Gopal Gopalaswami, and Harsha Reddy.

Greta's response to each traveler was always the same: *dead, dead* and *dead*.

Lana couldn't believe what she was hearing. "How is that possible? How can they all be dead?"

"Old age," was Greta's reply.

"Nonsense, I saw them just a few centuries ago."

"They were *primigens*, Your Majesty," Greta reminded her. "They died between their eighth and ninth decade of life."

"Ugh, how inconvenient." Lana blinked wearily down at her untouched teacup. "Though my heart goes out to their kind. It's quite tragic, really. The lives of our primigenius counterparts. They die young even when they're old."

Greta nodded in agreement. She was back at her cards, shuffling them, waiting for one to slip out an appropriate answer and solution to their predicament. A general rule of thumb with tarot was that the first card that came out maintained the strongest energy in regard to one's personal situation. The trouble was, however, that Greta's deck kept unleashing multiple cards all at once.

"There must be some valensmen travelers with whom you're acquainted," said Lana, eyeing the tarots cards dubiously.

"The best ones are the monks and yogis in the Green Kingdom," said Greta, and before Lana could encourage her to reach out to one of them, she explained, "Way over in the mountains. Secluded in an ashram. Without any means of physical communication. It would take me up to a month to get a letter over there by messenger."

"By means of a mortal messenger, perhaps. But why can't you send one of your spirit guides to communicate with them? Better yet, why not use one of your guides to find Lucien and bring him back?"

"To answer your first question, their ashram is heavily warded with the Green King's energy to prevent entry of any unauthorized spirits. And to answer your second, I've already asked, and they said no."

"They said *no*?" repeated Lana in an offended tone.
"They mean no offence, Your Majesty. I believe they only declined because they are unable to fulfill such a request. As you know, not all spirits are created equal. Many wouldn't have access to the higher realms of existence." Greta pondered as she shuffled. "We could, however, find and bind a more powerful spirit to complete the task."

Lana didn't like the process of finding and binding. It meant summoning a powerful entity and entrapping them until they did your bidding. After which point, the spirit would be released. (Contrary to popular belief, you couldn't bind a spirit to you forever.) As with all situations like these, there was a best- and worst-case scenario. Best case: the spirit politely did as it was told, it was released, and everyone carried on with their day. Worst case: the spirit bitterly did as it was told, it was released, and it made sure you rued the day you ever thought to enslave it.

"Hmm… Let's consider that a fallback plan, shall we?"

"Then perhaps, ma'am, you could use your Gift to send out another message? The Golden energy is thought to be the most powerful among all Divine energies. It could be strong enough to surpass the Green King's wards."

If Lana had mastered the art of utilizing the Golden energy to her will, it would've been an ideal solution. Unfortunately, sending out one simple telepathic message from her home and across the forest had left her nursing the worst migraine of her life. She was quite sure she'd end up with an aneurysm if she even attempted to emit another message, especially one that had to be delivered to another Kingdom far from their realm.

"I'm afraid that's not an option," she said sadly. "Any other ideas?"

"If I may ask, ma'am…" still shuffling, Greta gazed up at the Queen and fixed her with a sharp stare, "When was the last time you prayed to your Divine Mother?"

Lana gave her a long look. After a while, she picked up her teacup and said in a quiet, steady voice, "I confess it's been some time. My faith has been…dormant in the last few centuries for obvious reasons."

Seven cards slipped out of Greta's palm all at once. Lana pursed her lips at the recurrence. "What's happening with your cards?"

As far as Lana knew, Greta didn't have a clumsy bone in her body. Her hands were always steady and unlikely to drop anything in its grasp … unless of course, there were outside forces making her drop them.

"I'm not sure," said Greta. "I can't seem to shuffle them properly."

As Greta gathered the cards back into the deck, Lana couldn't help but notice the synchronicity in them. *Ace of Blades. Two of Blades. Three of Blades. King of Blades*, etc. … All seven cards belonged to the Suit of Blades.

There were 56 cards in the minor arcana of every tarot deck, and they were divided into four suits: Wands, Goblets, Diamonds, and Blades. Each suit represented different things. Wands represented creativity and fire. Goblets embodied emotions and relationships. Diamonds stood for wealth and prosperity. The Blades, however, were the most aggressive of the lot. Cards with blades symbolized mind and intelligence, but also misfortune.

The Blades weren't the most pleasant of cards to receive in a tarot reading. But Lana supposed the one good thing about them was that they were fast-acting. Unlike the other cards, which implied one would have to wait anywhere from weeks to years for any visible results, the Blades were as fast and sharp as a guillotine. This meant that whatever needed to happen, good or bad, would play out rapidly in the span of a few days.

Lana moved to take a sip of her tea, but stopped short at the sound of shrieks and bustling from another room. There was a great outcry echoing about the house. It got louder, reaching the library, and blasted on full volume as the Quartermaine twins shot into the room.

"Godmother!! Godmother!!!!!" they both bellowed in fright as they ran to Lana.

Tears came out of their eyes as screams shot out of their mouths. "What's that?!" John-Marlowe's eyes gawked at the cup in Lana's hand as though it were filled to the brim with hellfire. Then, flinging an accusing look toward Greta, he said, "Did *she* give that to you?"

"Don't drink that, Godmother," In a flash, Jason-John flung his hand to the side and sent the cup diving to the ground. "It's poison!"

"It's peppermint, actually," said Greta primly as she eyed the broken cup with displeasure.

"Peppermint-flavoured poison, more like!" growled Jason-John.

"Boys, calm yourselves at once!" Lana was completely baffled by their behaviour. "We are guests in Ms. Anatolia's home, and you are to maintain an atmosphere of elegance and decorum. This is not an appropriate way for a gentleman, let alone two gentlemen, to behave. Now take a deep breath and tell me what's brought all this on?"

John-Marlowe started, "Godmother, you don't understand. These people aren't just witches—"

"They're murderers!" finished Jason-John.

Azaelea and Basilius Anatolia burst through the door, frantically searching for the twins. Basilius – Baz as he was known – was now fully attired in a suede vest, clean white shirt with the sleeves rolled up to the elbows, and form-fitting trousers, most of which was covered up by a bloody apron.

Spotting Lana, Baz stepped forward into a deep kneel, "Your Majesty! Please forgive the dramatics of the night. It tends to happen whenever a full moon and mercury retrograde collide."

"There he is!" Jason-John pointed an accusing finger his way. "There's the murderer!"

"He killed Wilberforce!" John-Marlowe wept into Lana's chest. "Then he cut out his tongue, and now he's going to make us eat it."

"He'll probably cut out our tongues and make us eat them too!" Shooting Baz a scathing look, Jason-John shouted, "Stay back you, you…swine-slayer!! That's why you have that barn house, isn't it? Just to kill innocent piglets!"

Baz sighed as he righted himself. "That is the purpose of a barn. And are you lot honestly about to tell me you've never had bacon in your young lives?"

"Never from a pig we knew personally!" cried John-Marlowe.

"I gave you specific instructions to use blindfolds," Greta growled out.

"Oh, but we did," said Azaelea, placing a hand on her brother's arm, "Both Baz and the pig were blindfolded the whole time."

Baz nodded in confirmation.

Greta shut her eyes for a second. *Oh, dearest Hekate, great champion of darkness, give me strength*, she inwardly prayed. Nervously, she glanced over at Lana, who had her arms around her godsons and was currently consoling them with hugs and soothing noises.

"There, there, my little Q-tips," Lana shushed the crying boys, "It's all over now." Her silver eyes shot toward Baz. "I'm assuming the procedure was completed?"

"Indeed, Your Majesty," Baz nodded at her.

"How long will it take to be properly administered?" asked Lana.

The spell was done, but it would be a while before any visible results were manifested. That was the difference between old-world magic and the Divine energy that came from the King's Gift.

Divine energy originated from a source of higher power far beyond their physical world, whereas witchcraft harnessed the power of natural elements all around them. A person who was highly skilled at using Divine energy could manifest whatever they desired in the span of seconds. A witch who was highly skilled in the art of spellcasting could manifest their desires anywhere from three days to six months.

"It'll be three days if they eat the tongue right now, ma'am," he said.

"Nooo!! We don't want to eat Wilberforce's tongue," cried John-Marlowe.

"Oh, you don't have to eat it, sweetlings," cooed Azaelea. "Preserving it in an icebox should do the trick. Won't it, Baz?"

"The consumption is optional." Baz shrugged indifferently. "But it'll take longer – seven days, I expect – before the Silent Screen activates."

"Seven days should be enough time." Lana patted the boys on their backs as they cried on her shoulders, literally. Not that she minded. It reminded her of when her son Gabriel had been little.

"You love it whenever he swans over to you, sobbing and slobbering," Lucien had told her once with a scoff. He knew how much Lana loved playing hero and over-mothering their sons at the same time.

"Your Majesty," said Greta, "Might I recommend we venture into the forest and partake in a little moonlight promenade?" Indicating to the boys, she continued, "From my experience, it does wonders to calm the nerves… we can take the dogs, as well."

Chapter 6: The Gold Queen's Choice

Wilberforce the Pig received a far more dignified funeral than most of his contemporaries. They had placed the animal in a large chest – which was crafted by hand out of elaborately carved cherry wood and forged from wrought iron – and buried it in the heart of Halkyon Forest.

To the Anatolias, the box was an antique, long in their family's possession. It was beautifully footed, meticulously designed, and had acquired a stunning patina from age. To the Quartermaines, it made for a prestigious coffin for a most precious pig.

"Once the Queen and those brats are gone, we're going to come back and dig that chest back up," Baz muttered into his sister's ear as the Quartermaine boys carried on with their impromptu funeral. He couldn't believe the night he was having. First, he'd been interrupted during his nocturnal prayers and subsequently body-shamed by his eldest sister. Then, he'd been accused of murder by a pair of spoiled young aristocrats. Now, he was out in the woods with a shovel in hand and sweat on his brow after digging a six-foot hole for a pig.

"Shh! Keep your voice down." Azaelea elbowed her brother in response. "And we're not touching that chest, Bazzie. Don't you dare come back here in the morn'."

"That's our dear, dead grandmama's chest!" Baz whisper-hissed indignantly.

"It's not like we hauled her out of it to make way for the pig," murmured Azaelea. "Besides, it's for a good cause."

"What good cause?" scoffed Baz.

"It's for our Queen," she said adamantly, then amended, "Well, it's for her godsons. But still, it's upon Her Majesty's wishes… Speaking of, doesn't the Queen look ever-so ethereal and enchanting by moonlight!"

Baz rolled his eyes. His sister, like many people in the Golden realm, was insanely infatuated with the Queen. He was pretty sure

Azaelea would cut herself into pieces to fit into a box provided it was upon Lana's wishes.

"Her wishes come at a great loss for us," said Baz, still peeved, "That chest was an antique… and it's a waste of perfectly good ham and bacon."

A few feet away, the Queen and the Quartermaines were hovering over the burial site.

"I like to think he's happier now," said John-Marlowe, holding Lana's left land, "That he's somewhere sunny, with lots of space to muck about, and an endless supply of apple pies."

"That sounds like a rather delightful afterlife to me," Lana smiled down at him before turning to her right to stare down at Jason-John, who had gone strangely quiet ever since they had cloaked up and stepped out of the Anatolia house.

The group had ventured well beyond the lines of the Anatolia estate. Gone were the watchful eyes of silver birch trees. Instead, they were deep into the woods, surrounded by towering oaks.

"What about you, Jason-John?" Lana asked, squeezing his little hand. She expected a response that reflected the very opposite of his brother's opinion. "Where do you think he is right now?"

"Oh, you musn't ask him, Godmother," John-Marlowe shook his head. "Jase doesn't believe in the afterlife."

"Yes, I do," Jason-John refuted quickly, keeping his eyes fixed on the chest several feet below them. "I'm just not sure where he is in the afterlife, is all."

If anyone had asked him a year ago, Jason-John would've responded exactly as his twin brother had predicted. He would've said he didn't believe in the afterlife. That wasn't the case anymore. He believed in it now, if only for one reason: he wanted to see his mother again, someday.

Sensing what was passing through the child's mind, Lana was ready to respond, until the sound of dogs barking two yards east pulled her attention away. "I'll be right back, boys."

In the absence of the energy from her soft soothing palms, the boys held one another and continued to stare down at the grave in dismay.

Lana went eastward, toward the crossroads where Greta was perched in front of an altar. At the center of the altar was a small golden statue of Hekate, goddess of magic and witchcraft. It looked like a doll-sized version of the massive pillar statue that dwelled inside Greta's family home. Behind the statuette, was a teepee campfire. There were two tiny burners a few inches away, bordering the fire, and emitting lavender resin into the air.

Greta's two dogs stopped circling the crossroads and howled enthusiastically as they saw Lana approach. The witch, however, didn't acknowledge Lana's presence right away. Her eyes were closed, and she was muttering softly into the night air. Every now and then, Lana heard her say in Greek, phrases like, *"Mother, Maiden, Crone, hear and grant my prayer… O' great mistress of darkness, hear and grant my prayer."*

Greta didn't open her eyes, not until Lana was three steps away from her.

"My apologies," said Lana, "I didn't mean to interrupt your prayers."

"Not at all, Your Majesty," Greta nodded, and shooting a brief glance toward the funeral at work, she said, "If anything, I'm the one who must apologize for everything that's transpired tonight—"

"Ugh, please stop apologizing!" Lana flopped onto the earth and sat down crossed-legged – unladylike, but no one could tell with her cloak and gown flowing all around her. "As a whole, I feel as though our gender apologizes far too much as it is."

Greta nodded in assent.

Gesturing toward the two other members of the Anatolia family, Lana said, "I must say you and your siblings have a rather… fascinating dynamic. I can't relate personally, but I've witnessed something similar with my children. They're all so very different and yet very much united at the same time… If only the rest of the world could follow such an example."

"So, we can all be one big happy family?" offered Greta.

"More or less," Lana shrugged.

They went silent for a few seconds, watching the fire and listening to the dogs.

"I almost forgot that you moonlight as a priestess of Hekate," said Lana. "How is your coven faring these days?"

"Not so well," said Greta stoically, her eyes still trained on the fire. "Our numbers are dwindling."

"I'm sorry to hear that." After a moment's pause, she asked, "What were you praying for just now, if you don't mind me asking?"

Greta turned her head to face the Gold Queen. "For the King, of course. His Majesty requires a guide to return to you. There's no one better than our gracious goddess."

"Is that so?"

"Have you forgotten, ma'am? After Persephone was kidnapped by Hades and bound to the Underworld for half a year, every year, it was Hekate who consoled and guided her back to her mother. And it was she who guided Persephone back to Hades whenever her six-month term on Earth expired."

"It wasn't a kidnapping," Lana said softly. "It was her choice."

"I beg your pardon?"

Lana stared into the fire. "They changed the story over the centuries. They stripped away her power and made her out to be a victim. A kidnapping had more dramatic appeal to listeners, I suspect. But Persephone chose to be his Queen. She chose to be with him, alongside him, in his world of infinite wealth and perpetual death. That's how it originally went." She nodded, and then repeated, "It was her choice."

Greta blinked at her, unsure of how to respond.

"As for Hekate, I suppose she is a powerful anomaly among gods – being the only Titan goddess to avoid jailtime in Tartarus, and one of the few deities with the freedom to travel between the celestial, terrestrial, and chthonic realms," Lana went on to fill the silence, "In that sense, you're right. There is no better guide than my Divine Mother."

Have you forgotten, ma'am? Lana let out a bitter little chuckle. That was the trouble. She hadn't forgotten a damn thing. She was, to be sure, the daughter of Hekate. At least, that's what Lana had always been told.

Long ago, long before the time of Chosen Kings, there was a small coven situated in the Ancient Greek colony of Apollonia. One night, under a supermoon, its members had prayed for a sign of the dark goddess's favour. The next night, they had found Lana – then, a mere infant – swaddled inside a silver cradle, in front of their doorstep. With no parents to claim the baby, the coven wholeheartedly acknowledged Lana as their sign. As she grew up, Lana proved to be a timeless beauty, further solidifying her place as a demi-goddess.

Lana wondered what those coven members – all primigens, now long gone – would think of her now. Heavily demoted from demi-goddess to Queen.

"Does she always answer your prayers?" asked Lana.

"Sometimes, but not always," said Greta. "As you know, she's highly selective when it comes to those she exalts with her favour. She provides blessings only to those she deems worthy… such as yourself."

"That was a long time ago," said Lana somberly. "As I said, my faith has been dormant."

Lucien had converted ages ago. He'd turned his back on the old gods to look up to the *One True God* ages ago. As his wife, Lana was expected to follow in his footsteps.

It would've been all too easy to throw all the blame on her husband. Tell everyone, *Lucien made me do it.* But she couldn't make him out to be the villain of her story. Had he expected her to convert? Naturally. But had he forced her? Never. She was the one who chose to turn her back on her faith to make her Husband-

King happy. Had it been the right choice? She didn't know. But it was still her choice. It had always been her choice.

Greta watched her quietly for several heartbeats. She considered her next few words carefully. "Whether you believe in one God or several, there's a saying that higher powers never abandon us. We abandon them. But they're always here —"

"Is this the part where you tell me, if we ever need them, then we need only ask?"

"Actually, I was about to say they're always here, waiting for us to come crawling back like a regretful lover with a large bouquet of dark roses in our hands and lashings of apologies on our lips."

Lana snorted out a laugh. She was about to suggest they head back before the night got even stranger. But apparently, she hadn't spoken up soon enough.

The campfire behind the statue of Hekate roared ferociously like a roused dragon. The flames shot up seven feet in the air. But Lana barely took notice of it. She was too taken back at the sight of Greta falling back onto the earth in a starfish-like pose. The witch's eyes rolled back, and her body began to shake violently as though it were experiencing a seizure.

"Greta!" Lana screamed, causing the Quartermaine- and Anatolia-siblings to take notice and dash towards them. The dogs let out a piercing howl as their mistress trembled on the ground floor.

It was a while before everything mellowed down again. Greta's body had continued to convulse for three minutes before lapsing back into calmness.

"You needn't worry." Azaelea told their guests. "She gets like this sometimes, whenever she attracts a message from a powerful spirit."

"What was the message?" said John-Marlowe just as Jason-John asked, "Who was the spirit?"

"Boys, Ms. Anatolia is still recovering. Let's not inundate her with any more questions," said Lana sternly.

As Greta's heartbeat returned to normal, Azaelea pulled her sister back into a seating position and brought a vintage flask to her lips. "Here, drink this, G."

"Oh Az, you're not giving her old mumsy's crazy juice, are you?" said Baz, appalled.

"This little cocktail can cure everything and anything." refuted Azaelea insistently, "Why, I'd wager, it could grow back a limb faster than a lizard. It's practically a miracle tonic!"

"Yeah," grunted Baz, "A miracle no one's died from it yet."

"I think," Greta started slowly, softly, "It's been a very eventful night and it's time for all of us to retire."

"I agree," said Lana, coming to a stand.

Slowly getting to her feet, Greta told her brother, "Why don't you go patch up that grave, Baz?" Turning to the Queen, "Your Majesty. If I may have a private word before we all take our leave?"

Lana nodded. "Boys, go and give Mr. Anatolia a helping hand," she ordered the twins. "I shan't be long."

Greta waited until Azaelea and the twins were out of earshot to speak. Her dogs, however, remained by her side. "Your Majesty, I received a message from your Divine Mother. I was told to relay it to you.

Lana's brow wrinkled in confusion. "Why wouldn't she tell me herself?"

"In your own words, your faith has been dormant. Once your faith returns, so shall she."

"I see," sighed Lana. "Well, what was the message then?"

"She said to trust your instincts. You believe someone has done this to your King and they have."

Lana's brows immediately narrowed, her hands fisted in anger. "Who?" she hissed with righteous fury.

"Our dark goddess didn't say. She showed me two perfect circles. One within another. The outer circle was perfectly intact. The inner circle was broken. Then, she mentioned there's been a significant change of some sort. A severe shift in our world. And what's happening to the King now is a direct consequence of this change."

The Queen waited, as though she were expecting more.

"That's it," added Greta. "That's all she said."

"She's as mysterious as ever," said Lana dryly. "What *change* could she be referring to?"

"I'm not sure," said Greta thoughtfully. "Sometimes serious changes that ultimately impact our fates are due to minor changes we make to our everyday lives... Has the King been behaving oddly as of late?"

"What do you mean, *as of late*? My Lucien has always been the oddest being in existence."

"I mean, has he been doing anything different? Something outside of his usual routine?"

"He hasn't done anything different in the last two hundred years." Lana would know. She shared a bed with the man.

"Are you sure?"

"Of course, I'm sure!" huffed Lana. "I'm his wife. I would know."

"With respect, Your Majesty," Greta said cautiously. "You probably wouldn't know *because* you're his wife."

Chapter 7: Shine Like Gold in a Rocky World

"I can't believe you're being so cavalier about all this, Mother! Need I waste breath reminding you what a scandal this could've been had anyone other than myself chanced upon this obscene… *scene*! Am I the only one in this family, save Father, who worries of scandal?"

"My darling, calm yourself," said Lana in a relaxed tone, "You needn't get so huffy-puffy over this."

"Hufffffy… puffy?!!!" Gabriel huffed out heatedly between puffs of air. "I am not being huffy-puffy! I am appalled! Utterly appalled!"

Such was the conversation booming out of Lucien's private study.

The double doors were left wide open, flanked by two Volucris Knights who were standing by, pretending not to listen. It was rare for Michael to see any members of the sentry guarding one of Lucien's private rooms. Royal guards existed solely to protect the King's family. Chosen Kings – powerful ones like Lucien, at least – never had any need for them because they were vessels of infinite power.

"Bodyguard?" Lucien had said with a dismissive laugh, many centuries ago. He supposed his Knights meant well at the recommendation. Bless their little souls, they didn't know any better. They weren't Divinely chosen to lead the way he was. "God is my bodyguard."

Michael side-eyed the guards, unimpressed as they flinched before his presence. He strode into his Father-King's study and held up a hand, which blazed brightly in gold. At his gesture, the doors instantly slammed shut behind him.

"What's happening?" Michael said stiffly as his eyes swept across the room.

Lucien's study took up three floors. The interior resembled more of a church than a private office. There were so many arches and massive windows, and it was all crowned with a painted ceiling.

92

On the first floor, there was a large fireplace, and a gigantic double partners' desk made from oak timbers. The King's throne chair was right behind it.

To the left of the desk was a floor-to-ceiling bookshelf that took up the entire wall. The shelf held numerous editions of the Bible – mostly King Lucien Versions – as the Gold King had spent the better part of a century translating biblical scrolls from Hebrew, Aramaic and Greek into the Earth Standard Sole.

Everything in the study looked perfectly well-kept, organized and intact. The same couldn't be said of the room's current occupants.

Gabriel was standing beside the desk. His pale face was now red and fuming. He reminded Michael of a snowy volcano – nearly everything from the neck up was ready to detonate.

Meanwhile, Lana looked perfectly calm, if not bored. Lying across the desk as though it were a comfortable bedspread, Lana wore a long white silk sleeping gown that rested above her ankles. She looked very much like a painting of a beautiful woman on a chaise, one hand to her forehead as though she'd perish of ennui at any given moment.

"Everything alright?" said Michael.

"Alright? Alright?!" repeated Gabriel furiously as though the smartest man in the world had just asked him the stupidest question in the universe.

With his shoulders deflating and his face crumbling, Gabriel ran over to place his head despairingly on Michael's shoulder. "Brother, everything is not alright! Everything is horrible!"

Lana peered over at them and tried not to crack a smile. She loved watching her sons hold one another. Gabriel was probably the only person in existence – save for herself – who could embrace Michael and get away unscathed.

Michael firmly, awkwardly patted his brother's back. He was usually uncomfortable with such open displays of intimacy, but he was always unwilling to deny his little brother anything. "Tell me what has happened."

"It's been dreadful, Brother," Gabriel cried into his shoulder. "I entered this room not ten minutes ago and what should I find? But our Mother *interacting* with Sir Oliver."

Sir Oliver Pinkard was their Father's Chief Private Secretary. He was a valensman. Average-looking in appearance, and meticulously organized in personality and every other aspect of his life.

Michael lifted a brow. "By interacting, you mean…?"

Gabriel's head shot back to Lana. "Isn't it obvious? Look at the state of her. Lounging about in broad daylight in her undergarments with her hair down and her ankles exposed for all to see. That's how I found her, chatting up that puckered old persimmon!"

"That's rather harsh, Gabe, don't you think?" said Lana casually. "Pinky is only in his Fourth Millennia of life. As for our interactions, it was all perfectly innocent. We were merely conversing… perhaps, a little harmless flirtation was exchanged—"

"I'd be more inclined to believe that if I hadn't caught you batting your lashes and flashing your ankles about!" said Gabriel hotly.

"Where's the persimmon now?" asked Michael.

"I gave him a proper reprimand and ejected him from this room," said Gabriel. "He's lucky I didn't toss him right out the balcony."

"Because you have so much experience tossing people out of balconies, do you?" Lana knew it was an empty threat. Her second son didn't have a violent bone in his body.

"Mother, I know this is a troubling time for you, with Father being *out-of-Kingdom*, but acting out the way you have as of late—"

"Acting out?" Lana shot up to a seated position on the desk, her legs dangling off the edge.

The sternness in her voice made Gabriel pause.

He drew his shoulders back, determined to get this off his chest. "That's right, Mother. I feel I should warn you—"

"Warn me?" Lana bit out tightly.

"This Cage has eyes and ears – too many of them, in fact – and word of your late-night escapades have been spreading rampant throughout our halls," said Gabriel evenly.

The household staff and guards were contractually bound by the King's energy to keep all royal affairs private. That meant their servants couldn't leak anything out of the Gilded Cage. That said, it didn't stop them from rumour-mongering within the confines of the castle itself.

"Tell me, Mother," Gabriel continued, "Where exactly did you swan off to the other night – without your security detail? And before you try to deny you went unchaperoned, I'll remind you those Quartermaines' are not a proper substitute for our Knights."

"You should watch yourself, Gabriel," Lana said coldly. She was absolutely done being amused by her son's dramatics. "The Queen's private affairs are exactly that – private. It's nothing with which a Prince needs to concern himself."

"No, but a mother's safety shall always be a son's primary concern," Gabriel refuted with a level of frostiness that matched Lana's tone.

They glared at one another for a second, until Gabriel said, "You went to see that witch, didn't you? The one in the forest."

"So, what if I had?"

Gabriel sighed, walking back over to the desk. "It's natural to seek guidance in times of confusion and despair, but Mother, I implore you, turn to God, turn to us," he indicated to Michael and himself, "But please, do not damn yourself by listening to a mad witch and her croakings of doom."

"You don't even know her."

"I don't need to know her. It's bad enough that I've seen her!"

"You have?" Lana was surprised to hear that. Greta and Gabriel didn't exactly run in the same circles. A shame, really, because they both had more in common than they realized. Both sticklers for formality. Both unshakably devout to their chosen deities. Gabriel to his God, Greta to her goddess.

"I laid eyes on her once, from afar, out in the capital." Gabriel remembered the first time he'd seen the witch out in Halkyon City. Her hair was madness, and her frock could only be described as a large pink-eyesore.

A member of his camarilla had pointed her out. *"Look, Your Royal Highness, there she is. The mad witch of Halkyon Forest! They say she lives alone in the woods with only phantoms to keep her company."*

"She was making a scene," said Gabriel, "Sulking loudly about like a spurned strumpet on the street."

"Oh, that wasn't her," said Lana. "That was her sister."

"That hardly matters," said Gabriel primly. "A person's family is a direct reflection upon them. Everyone knows that." Straightening the edges of his vest, he said, "Anyhow, let's not digress. Instead of putting all this time and energy into other families, we ought to be focused on our own."

"I am thinking of our family."

"Are you truly? If that were so, you would be attending to Lexie in her nursery right now, instead of engaging in *harmless flirtations* with the help."

"Lexie?"

Gabriel nodded. "I went to take her for our morning stroll not five hours ago and what should I find? My baby sister completely alone in her crib!"

"What?" Lana leapt off the desk, ready to run to the nursery. "She was all by herself? Completely unattended?"

"That's right. She was all alone with those wet nurses and nannies of hers."

Lana rolled her eyes and sat back on the edge of Lucien's desk.

Putting a hand to his chest, Gabriel said, "It breaks my heart when I think of her, ill and distressed with nothing but the subpar solace of nurserymaids to see her through these fearful, fatherless days. My poor sister!"

Lana nearly laughed. It was ironic calling Lexie *poor*. Golden Princess Alexandra Raphael Leonor Fátima Valenta, first of her name, was anything but. At the ripe age of nine months, Lexie had already topped *The Gold and Mail* newspaper's annual list of "10 Richest Kids Under 10." How? To start, she was the only daughter of a King who was literally a gold-making machine. Apart from that, said King, had also set up a trust for her – one so enormous, it could feed five planets for five millennia.

There was a belief among spiritualists that our souls chose our parents before incarnation. *If that's true*, Lana thought, *then Lexie came to a great fortune simply by selecting Lucien from a catalogue of potential fathers.*

"Lexie has a minor cold," sighed Lana. "Babies have them all the time, Gabe. It's nothing to make a fuss about."

"It was those egregious Quartermaine boys! They did this to her!" Gabriel said accusingly. "They're always there, hovering around her, breathing up all her clean air and releasing their vile germs upon her perfection."

Lana thought her son was being ridiculous. He knew kids were adorable little germ vectors, and that Lexie would be healthy again in a matter of days. Besides, she was pretty sure Gabriel had collected far more germs in his youth. Not to mention what he might've picked up all those centuries ago, when he left the Golden realm to serve as a missionary at a leper colony.

"I saw them go into her room just now," said Michael, finally contributing to the conversation, but only because he had a strong desire to end it.

Gabriel whipped his head back to him. "You did?"

"Yes, perhaps you ought to intervene, Brother," suggested Michael. "Keep them away from our beloved sister. Who knows what they might've brought back from that witch's house?"

His little brother's eyes widened in fear. "I must go to Lexie at once, ward those dreadful boys away." Little did Gabriel know, he'd be warding boys away from his sister for a great deal of her life.

Gabriel embraced Michael and planted a kiss on his left cheek. "Brother, please, I beg of you," he said seriously, "Make sure our Mother doesn't traipse out of here with bare ankles."

The Second Golden Prince made to leave, but paused just short of the doorway. With a sigh, he marched back to Lana. Angry as he was with her, she was still his Mother and his Queen. Despite his emotions, he knew it was his Princely duty to perpetually maintain an air of decorum and courtesy. So, he kissed her on both cheeks and dropped his head in deference. "May God bless and forgive you, Mother."

"It's the other way around," said Lana sarcastically to Gabriel's fast retreating back. "It's *forgive*, then *bless*. He's going to have to forgive me before he can bless me. Forgiveness comes first."

When the doors slammed shut, Lana's eyes shifted over to her eldest son. "What the dickens has gotten into him? Such histrionics are usually not his style." But with a mutter, she added, "Then again, he does have Lucien's melodramatic blood coursing through him."

"Don't hold it against him," said Michael. "His outbursts come from a place of fear."

"Fear?"

"The novelty of Father exploring the celestial realms has fast faded. Gabe expected him to be awake by now."

Physically, Lucien's body was perfectly healthy. There was no logical reason for the King to remain comatose. In fact, there wasn't a logical explanation as to why and how he had slipped into a coma to begin with.

"Gabe won't admit it, but he's worried," continued Michael. "Not only for the King, but for all of us."

In their world of Chosen Kings, bloodline held no influence over succession. Totems picked the King and thus far, in their history, it had never selected any royal progeny as a successor. Without King Lucien, the Valenta family were at risk of losing their titles, their power, their home… everything.

"There's nothing to fear." The lie was meant more for herself than her son. "As long as the Golden energy remains in your Father's body—"

"You and I both know what happens to Divine energy when it's left idle for too long," said Michael.

They'd seen it happen time after time. It was a classic *use-it-or-lose-it* situation. If a King didn't use the Divine energy bestowed upon them, then the Totem would shift over to another chosen leader.

"We still have time," Lana said quietly, "Your Father always keeps his word, and he said seven days… We're only on—"

"We're *already* on day three," clipped Michael calmly.

"A lot can happen in four days," insisted Lana.

They'd seen that happen time after time as well. A few days was all it took for turbulent hurricanes to strip a rival Kingdom bare. Mere hours were all that was required for 30,000 of their troops to miraculously defeat 100,000 foes. A few seconds had been enough to create unforeseen circumstances, which led to the greatest of misfortunes for their enemies. In the end, the Valentas had always thrived whereas others barely survived. Lana didn't see why this situation should be any different.

The Gold Queen and the First Golden Prince stared blankly at one another for a while, both likely thinking the same thing at that very moment.

It was Michael who broke the silence. "What did the witch say?"

"The witch has a name, dear."

"I'm aware."

Lana sighed. Her eldest was tolerant of witchcraft, but that didn't mean he cared for it. "Greta confirmed he's in the Spiritual Realm, but we don't have an exact compass bearing at hand. Apparently, we need to find a guide – one who can surpass the Astral bridge and into the celestial to bring him back… She also said my suspicions were correct. Someone has done this to him, but there's no way of knowing who. Not yet, anyhow."

"And?" Michael speculated there was more.

"And… she said there's been a shift of some sort," Lana admitted reluctantly. "Something rather serious… She asked if Lucien had been doing anything different as of late."

"I doubt he's done anything different in the last century."

"Two centuries, more like," said Lana. "I told her as much. But she seems convinced it has something to do with a change in his routine."

"It's possible," said Michael with a nod.

There was something to be said about *the butterfly effect*, where the minor impacted the major. An insect flapping its wings in their gardens right now could very well unleash an early monsoon many miles away in the Green Kingdom.

Michael briefly wondered if Lana had communicated this theory back to Lucien. He doubted it. Lucien was just as disapproving and patronizing as Gabriel was about Lana's witchy inclinations. Nevertheless, he had to make sure. "Have you conveyed any of this back to the King?"

Lana scoffed and crossed her arms over her chest. "I have far better things to do then wait by the phone for hours on end for a celestial call from the likes of him," she said sourly, refusing to admit that she had done exactly that.

Upon returning from her visit to the Anatolia house, the Queen had probed her ladies-in-waiting with questions concerning her husband's phone. She had kept the bedroom doors locked and sealed with Golden energy before leaving her ladies with strict instructions to remain in the den until she returned.

"Did it ring? At any time?" She had pressed. They weren't allowed to answer it, of course. But surely, they would know if it rang.

"No, not once, Your Majesty," answered one of the women, confused as to why the Queen was suddenly obsessed with the telephone.

Instead of going to bed, Lana had spent the better part of the early morning hours hovering around the telephone with a glass of wine in her hand, steaming and fuming at the thought of Lucien keeping something from her. *"You probably wouldn't know because you're his wife,"* Greta's words had circled her mind like a shiver of sharks.

Her mood had only worsened with every passing hour that went by without a ringtone. *That swine*, she had thought angrily, cursing her Husband-King's name, *he promised he'd ring*. Balling her fists up, she strode toward Lucien's washroom. She returned to her marriage bed with his razor in hand. In a fit of drunken wifely fury, she leaned over Lucien's body and shaved off his perfectly structured sideburns.

Michael quietly inspected the acrid expression on his Mother's face and drew his own conclusions. "He hasn't called you then." he said blandly. "I'm assuming that's why you were *interacting* with that persimmon?"

"Sir Oliver knows every single item in your Father's itinerary – both on- and off-the-record."

"He wouldn't give anything away. Not even for a set of appealing ankles," Michael said flatly. He knew Lucien's private secretary was devoutly loyal. True, Sir Oliver Pinkard was smitten with Lana, most people were, and he treated her with respect and deference like the Queen she was. But he revered and feared Lucien as though he were more of a God than a King.

"No, he didn't tell me anything," Lana admitted, slightly miffed on behalf of her ankles, "But sometimes body language speaks louder than words." Her silver eyes moved pointedly toward the wall of books. "He kept shooting glances at it."

Michael's silver eyes followed hers. "Tell me we aren't expected to pour extensively through all these biblical tomes."

"Please," snorted Lana. She pulled out a long golden necklace hidden behind her clothes. "I couldn't even get past Exodus, and that was only Chapter Two."

"Book Two," corrected Michael, eyeing the bottled pendant at the end of his Mother's necklace with curiosity.

"Oh, same diff," said Lana as she reached behind her neck to undo the clasp.

"Before you take your leave," Greta had held her hand out to the Queen, offering her the pendant. The one she never took off. Until now, apparently. "This bottle contains herbs and oils, powered by our goddess herself during a blood wolf moon. She told me to give it to you."

"Why?" asked Lana.

"She said you'll need it, ma'am."

"We can use this as a pendulum. It's already powered-up," said Lana.

"Powered with what?"

"Never you mind," she said dismissively. She held the necklace up tightly by the ends, letting the pendant dangle freely. "Listen, my darling, in order for this to work, I'm going to need to mix the energy in this bottle with Golden energy. I'll require your help to complete such a task. After everything that transpired yesterday, I'm feeling a touch drained."

Michael immediately held out his right palm, so that it faced the front of the pendant. Lana's left palm covered the back. Together, they closed their eyes and visualized, calling forth the Golden energy that Lucien had given them access to. Within seconds, their hands lit up, going from their natural olive skin tone to a sparkly golden gleam.

"Show us the way, Great One," Lana opened her eyes and chanted out loud, "Show us the way. Guide us on the right path and lead us not astray."

Lana and Michael moved their hands away and observed the pendant. At first, it slowly shifted from side to side. Every now and then, Michael would observe the steadiness in Lana's hand to ensure the pendulum was moving of its own volition. After a few seconds, the pendulum moved around in a large circle, and then another, and another, stopping only after five laps in the air.

"Five circles," said Lana, "Fifth shelf."

They went toward the bookcase. Lana held the necklace up to the fifth shelf. The pendant moved eastward and kept on the path, before stopping to tap thrice at a spine.

Michael removed the book from its perch. It didn't look any different than the other tomes on the shelf. Leather-bound in black, heavily gilded on the front and back covers, with gold-tipped pages in between. Michael tried to open it, only to find he couldn't. There was no visible lock or clasp on the book, but—

"It's Shielded," gathered Lana, who then pulled out a few more books to test a theory. "None of the others are locked. Lucien must have fortified that one for good reason."

Michael laid his palm on the book. He closed his eyes and visualized the book opening before him. Just as Lucien taught him.

"You can have anything, my sons. Anything at all, doesn't matter what it is, for I have given you the King's Gift. All you need to do is see it in your mind's eye and it'll come to pass," Lucien had once told them with a flourish, sparkles of gold flowing out of his arm as though it were a magic wand instead of a human limb. "That's how your Father-King accomplished all of this. That's how I built a Kingdom of Gold in a rocky world," he added brightly before manifesting a magnificent pair of golden wings and leaping out of a large open window.

"Did he actually have somewhere to go or did he just fly off for dramatic effect?" Gabriel had asked his brother as they watched their Father-King soar over the horizon.

His Father-King had always made it sound so simple, as if mastering supernatural energy was mere child's play. That's how everyday people, the ones who didn't have the King's Gift – the *ungifted*, as they were called – saw it as well. Those who were Gifted knew better. They knew how much concentration and discipline it took just to use Divine energy for the simplest of tasks.

Michael could feel the book heating up beneath him. He thought it was working, until his hand sprang back as if burned – because it was. The Shield had rejected and spurned him.

"Are you hurt?" asked Lana, her tone laced with worry. Lucien's Shields were the ultimate defense, but they could also release the most malicious offense.

Anyone else would've bowled over in pain. Golden Prince Michael – Prince of Princes, General of Generals, Warrior-Prince, Dark Warrior of Gold – however, was not like anyone else. Hardwired to endure pain from a young age, he had been trained and tortured by the very best. So, his response was a small grunt of irritation. "I can't open it."

Lana bent to inspect the book her son had dropped. Giving the cover a quick tap to ensure it was no longer scorching, she picked it up carefully. "Let's go put your hand in some ice water."

Two hours later, Lana was back in her private den, lounging on the settee with the phone behind her and the book directly in front of her. If Michael couldn't open it, then she certainly didn't stand a chance. Only the Gold King himself – or perhaps a Golden Master, at the very least – would be able to break through this Shield. And for all their natural skills and abilities, Lana and Michael weren't supernaturally inclined in such a manner. They were neither King nor Master of any Divine energy.

Lana sighed. If only they were talented enough with the Golden Gift. Or, if only this book required a traditional lock and key, then they could look—

The Queen froze. Hastily fishing out the pendant, she nearly laughed. She had almost forgotten about the charm attached to the pendant: a small golden key.

"It can't possibly be that easy," she said to herself, fully knowing that the simplest solutions were often the best ones.

She gently laid the pendant over the tome. Placing her hand above it, she envisioned a circle of golden light encompassing the items beneath her hand. Three minutes later, a mysterious humming sound shot through her ears. Taking that as a cue, her eyes flew open. She moved her hand towards the edge of the front cover.

Slowly, easily, she opened the book.

Little did Lana know, she was about to enter a secret society of Kings.

Chapter 8: A Secret Society of Kings

Date: 18 August 1828
Location: Neutral Desert
Subject: The Blessed Tree

His Majesty King Lucien, 1st King of the Golden Empire:
My fellow Kings and dear friends—

His Majesty King Caleb, 125th King of the Red Kingdom:
We're not friends.

HM Gold King Lucien:
We may have had our share of quarrels and clashes in the past,
but we stand here today, on neutral soil, as equals—

HM Red King Caleb:
We're not equals either. And we're only standing because
there's nowhere for me to park my as—

HM Gold King Lucien:
Surrounded by the most magnificent natural wonder—

HM Red King Caleb:
We're in the bloody desert! It's like being trapped in a sand
bottle.

HM Gold King Lucien:
All the great prophets ventured lonesome into the desert and
returned with the most powerful messages from the Almighty.
What better place to embrace the Fatherhood of God? What
better time to acknowledge the Brotherhood of Man, and who *we*

are as men? For we are the Extraordinary, destined from birth to live a life less ordinary. Not existing as God, but beings who are one with God. The breadth of the cosmos lies within our flesh. The macrocosm contained in the microcosm. Selected by Divine right to build and lead great nations. We are the Chosen! We are the Kings blessed by—

HM Red King Caleb:
Enough with the monologuing already! Must you do this every time? At every meeting?

His Majesty King Idris, 88th King of the Blue Kingdom:
In the interest of saving time, Lucien, perhaps we can hasten things along? Why have you requested our presence here?

HM Red King Caleb:
And where are the others? Why's it only the three of us? And what's with that over-glowing book you've got?

HM Gold King Lucien:
Let's start with your last question and work our way back…
This book is merely for record-keeping. I've charged it with my energy to transcribe our entire conversation.

HM Red King Caleb:
What do you need notes for?

HM Gold King Lucien:
Why does anyone have a need for them? It's for reviewing, connecting and synthesizing ideas, of course. You're free to make your own.

HM Red King Caleb:
How? By writing on the sand with my fingers?

HM Gold King Lucien:
Good Heavens, Caleb. Are you a King, or not? You have a Totem's Divine energy inside you. Use it! Conjure up some materials if you need to.

HM Red King Caleb:
Not all of us can use our Divine energy so frivolously, you know?!

HM Gold King Lucien:
Well, I'm happy to provide hard copies of my notes for your convenience.

HM Red King Caleb:
How generous of you.

HM Blue King Idris:
Let us get on with this, *please*.

HM Gold King Lucien:
Right… As you both know, we are in a unique position, being the only planet with multiple monarchs and separate realms. If the last galactic war taught us anything, it's that we must maintain a certain degree of unity—

HM Red King Caleb:
We already have the Alliance. What more do we need?

At the reference to the Alliance, Lana paused in her reading. The Alliance was a military coalition wherein all the tellurian Kingdoms came together to either ward off or fight off a potential alien invasion. Was that what all this was about? Was there some sort of forthcoming global threat that led Lucien to gather three heavyweight Kings in one formal setting? She shook her head. She couldn't jump to such conclusions, not without reading the entire transcript from start to finish.

HM Blue King Idris:
It wouldn't hurt to formally present ourselves as united leaders. Off-planet, we're seen as a perniciously polarized society.

HM Red King Caleb:
Which we are.

HM Blue King Idris:
It doesn't mean *they* have to see that. The fact that they do see it is partly why non-tellurian rulers regard us as easy targets.

HM Red King Caleb:
But we've already proven we're not easy targets. *Twice.* More than, even… And what's all this sudden talk about *formally* presenting ourselves as a united front? I thought this was supposed to be a private Kings-only club that Goldie cooked up? You know, to keep any potential neophyte-Kings at bay?

Lana blinked, wondering if she had read that right. *Neophyte?*

HM Blue King Idris:
Lucien?

HM Gold King Lucien:
I hadn't intended to go public with our quaint little society of Kings… Not yet, that is.

HM Blue King Idris:
What are your intentions then? And where are the other three Kings?

HM Red King Caleb:
Two, you mean. The Grey King would never associate with us.
He prefers to live isolated in his dinky lot of land by the sea.
Bastard didn't even lend us a helping hand in the last galactic war.

HM Blue King Idris:
Grey King Harald, excluded. The other two attended all your
previous meetings. Why aren't they here now, Lucien?

HM Red King Caleb:
You certainly weren't taking any notes during those meetings.

HM Gold King Lucien:
As members of The Divinely Chosen—

HM Red King Caleb:
Geez, you make us sound like a religious boyband.

HM Gold King Lucien:
As members of *the Divinely Chosen*, the Indigo King and the
Green King have my respect. But as idolators, I could not
include them in the preliminary stages of my passion project.
They hold no reverence for the Fatherhood of God. They refuse
to acknowledge the Lord as their one true source of strength.
They have gravely erred on their Divine path—

HM Red King Caleb:
Get to the point! Not all of us have centuries and millennia to
spare.

HM Gold King Lucien:
Of course we do! Are we not all valensmen?

HM Red King Caleb:
I'm also the *Red* King… Big Blue here is on the same boat.

Lana couldn't help but think Caleb made a fair point. There was a reason Red and Blue were always referred to as the *Cursed Kings*. The Red energy had a long-standing record of searing through its Kings like a clan of starving dragons. Every Red King in history, thus far, had been a human grenade that detonated without warning. It was highly unlikely that Caleb would ever be a special exception to that rule. As for all the Blue Kings throughout history, Idris included … their situation was different, but no less cursed.

HM Gold King Lucien:
Come now, you musn't let all that Cursed Kings
nonsense discourage you. Everyone knows that a curse is
nothing but a blessing in disguise.

So, that's where John-Marlowe picked up that line, thought Lana.

HM Red King Caleb:
How have you lived this long without someone punching you
in the face? Saying such things with that smug-assed smile, you're
practically begging to be struck. Can I be the first, Idris? Please?
Can I punch him in the face? Just once!

HM Blue King Idris:
I strongly advise against taking such action, Caleb… Now,
Lucien, you mentioned a passion project.

HM Gold King Lucien:
That I did. As men of God, we're all familiar with the Tree of
Life, I'm sure.

HM Red King Caleb:
Never heard of it.

HM Gold King Lucien:
How could you not?! You were sired from a bloodline of the most prestigious Kabbalah and Cabala mystics the world has ever known.

HM Red King Caleb:
You said Kabbalah twice.

HM Blue King Idris:
He didn't. It's Kabbalah with a K and Cabala with a C.

HM Red King Caleb:
What's the difference?

Lana could imagine both Lucien and Idris rolling their eyes at Caleb's ignorance. *Kabbalah* referred to Jewish mysticism and inner teachings based on the study of the Torah and other scriptures. *Cabala,* however, was a form of Christian mysticism that was heavily influenced by Jewish esotericism.

HM Gold King Lucien:
Your father would have explained all this to you. He must have at least mentioned the Tree of Life used in Rabbinical Judaism.

HM Red King Caleb:
Doesn't mean I bothered to listen. I'm not really one for religion.

HM Gold King Lucien:
How can you possibly say that when Divine energy courses through your veins?!

HM Red King Caleb:

It's easy for you to be all holier-than-thou, isn't it, you priggish prick? With your nose high in the air and your hair so pretentiously tall. But not all of us were blessed with the ability to discharge gold out of every damn orifice! Some of us were tossed right into a pit of never-ending boiling sulfur and left to drown. If you had to endure a fraction of what the Red Totem serves out to me on the daily, then you might think twice about your faultless, flawless God. And before you shoot your mouth off with self-righteous indignation, I just want to say – on the record – that in spite of everything, my faith hasn't wavered. I do still believe in God. But I refuse to support any harrowing institution that calls itself a religion and and claims every damning decision they make was done in His name ... That's all I have to say about the matter.

...

...

...

There were several sets of ellipses after Caleb's words, which Lana figured must have indicated a prolonged silence.

HM Blue King Idris:
Let us backpedal for a moment. The Tree of Life. It's mentioned in the Torah, the Bible, and the Quran.

HM Gold King Lucien:
Yes, and in the Bible, it exists in Eden. The Tree itself represents God's life, and His regenerative and creative power. The first humans were allowed to eat from it, thereby absorbing God's own Divine energy and gaining eternal life. Unfortunately, on the way to the Tree of Life, they had to pass by another sapling – the Tree of the Knowledge of Good and Evil.

HM Red King Caleb:

That's the one where Eve eats from, gets Adam to do the same, and they're eternally exiled from paradise. This part of the story, I remember.

HM Blue King Idris:
That's the trouble. Everyone remembers *that* Tree, and in doing so, they forget the one that truly matters. Mind you, this is the direct physical interpretation of the Tree of Life. There also exists the spiritual interpretation, which – among Kabbalists – is represented through a diagram of ten interconnected spheres called sefirots. Each sefirot contained attributes that God used to create the universe. All these attributes – wisdom, severity, mercy, victory, to name a few – they exist in the cosmos just as they exist within mankind. The macrocosm in the microcosm, as Lucien would say… Granted, there's far more to it. But that's the abridged version.

HM Red King Caleb:
I'll admit it's somewhat fascinating. But what's the point of it all? Are you trying to find out whether this Tree is real or not? And where do we fit into it, Goldie?

HM Gold King Lucien:
Idris brings up a great debate around the Tree of Life. Is it physical or metaphysical? … Or, going by my theory, is it both? What happens if you take a tree – not just any tree, mind – and charge it with Divine energy for all to consume?

HM Blue King Idris:
Are you saying you want to create your own Tree of Life?

HM Gold King Lucien:
Why not? If man was cast out of paradise as punishment, then perhaps he can redeem himself by creating Heaven on Earth.

HM Red King Caleb:
Then go ahead and do that. Why do you need us?

HM Gold King Lucien:
Have you not been listening to anything we've said? There are different sefirots, which equate to different facets of the universe, which equate to different personas in man. Different personalities, different energies, different Kings – all combined to generate one eternal source of life, power, and creation.

Lana could picture Lucien ending that sentence with a wave of golden sparkles emanating from his hand. It was a gesture which Idris would have considered mildly endearing, and Caleb would have found severely annoying.

HM Gold King Lucien:
Besides, I tried doing it on my own. Didn't quite take. I only ended up with a tree that unfurls gold instead of leaves and fruit from its branches.

HM Red King Caleb:
You were able to make money grow on trees? Our hearts bleed for you, Goldie.

HM Gold King Lucien:
Well, it's not as though I can run about in a frenzy, making gold trees for everyone, can I?

HM Blue King Idris:
Are you worried it would deplete your energy?

HM Gold King Lucien:

Not at all, energy can always be restored. I'm worried it would devalue the price of my gold. Rest assured, I had that tree eviscerated at once lest someone else came across it.

HM Red King Caleb:
Wait a minute. Idris said there were ten spheres. Doesn't that mean there needs to be ten Kings? We only have six, and discounting Old Grey, that makes five.

HM Blue King Idris:
That could change … The Indigo King – the previous one that is – released a very intriguing prophecy before he died. He had a vision that three, possibly four, new Totems would emerge in the coming years.

HM Red King Caleb:
I know. We all know.

The Gold Queen frowned. *No*, everyone did not know that. She certainly wasn't aware that such a prophecy existed until this very moment. It appeared to be a well-kept secret, among Kings only.

HM Red King Caleb:
But even if it comes to pass, how would it work? Where would these new-Kings reign? All the land's been claimed and divvied up for centuries now.

HM Blue King Idris:
Perhaps they'll acquire it through other means? Land could always be provided to them.

HM Red King Caleb:
A King giving away their own land?! Who the hell would do that?

HM Gold King Lucien:
For once, the Red King speaks with sense. Only the most ridiculous of Kings would willingly forfeit their own territory… Anyhow, the theory of ten sefirots is exactly that. A theory. It doesn't necessarily mean we require ten Divine energies to see this experiment through. We can begin testing it out with three energies, or even five – if the Indigo- and Green- Kings are amenable.

HM Red King Caleb:
They aren't amenable to you, though, are they? If they were, you'd have invited them to this little clandestine meeting.

HM Gold King Lucien:
Idris, I know you're on friendly terms with the current Indigo King… and Caleb, rumour has it, you've had a previous… *association*… with the Green King.

HM Red King Caleb:
That was a long time ago.

HM Gold King Lucien:
It couldn't have been more than a year ago… That's nothing for a valensmen. It's not even enough to make up a spec of sand in an hourglass.

HM Red King Caleb:
You want us to convince them on your behalf, then? Ask them to make a contribution of their Divine essence? Like donors in a sperm bank?

HM Gold King Lucien:
A *what* bank??!!!

Lana snorted. Sperm banks had yet to be established in the Golden realm. It was still a relatively new concept, currently catering to married couples who had difficulty conceiving. She was certain her overly orthodox Husband-King would be absolutely scandalized that such facilities existed in the world.

HM Blue King Idris:
Do not answer that, Caleb … Lucien, say we all agree to contribute to the creation of this …New Tree of Life, then we must consider the physical side of it as well. What tree did you have in mind? As you said, it can't be any old sapling.

HM Gold King Lucien:
Quite right, Idris. It would have to be a tree that we know, with enough conviction, that Divine inspiration took place.

…
…
…

HM Blue King Idris:
Absolutely not.

HM Gold King Lucien:
Idris—

HM Blue King Idris:
No!

HM Red King Caleb:
What? What is it? What am I missing here?

HM Blue King Idris:
He wants to use the Tree of Al-Buqayawiyya.

HM Gold King Lucien:
It lies within your borders, Idris.

HM Blue King Idris:
Yes, it is in my domain. And no, you can not use it.

HM Red King Caleb:
I'm sorry - the tree of Al-what?

HM Blue King Idris:
Al-Buqayawiyya. It's said that the prophet Muhammad sat under this tree as a child. And, it's also where a monk named Bahira foretold his prophethood. It's now a sacred site in my realm. No one's allowed near it. Even touching it would incite the wrath of 90 million Muslims across the world.

HM Gold King Lucien:
Those Muslims might be willing to cool their fiery engines, if it had your backing, my dear Idris.

HM Blue King Idris:
It does *not* have my backing. And it never will.

HM Gold King Lucien:
Well! I never thought I'd see the day where you would behave in a manner so difficult and belligerent, Blue King… I expected better of you… but I'm not one to dwell on disappointment … Very well, then. At least, give us access to the Burning Bush. That falls on your turf, as well.

HM Blue King Idris:
Lucien! That's just as bad! Possibly worse!

HM Red King Caleb:

FARHANA UDDIN

What's the Burning Bush?

HM Gold King Lucien:
You truly know nothing, do you?

HM Blue King Idris:
In the Old Testament, Moses encountered God on a desert
tree on top of a mountain. The tree was actually a bush that was
on fire, but it was incapable of being destroyed by the flames.
The bush was thought to be radiating with God's life and
power… Today, many theologians believe that bush exists in the
northwest corner of my Kingdom.

HM Red King Caleb:
And we can't use it because… ?

HM Blue King Idris:
Because it's also sacred ground, and we risk evoking the anger
of everyone in the monotheistic world if we were to utilize it in
any way.

HM Gold King Lucien:
That's not necessarily true. If we were to use it for malevolent
purposes, it would certainly provoke. But we're not. You wanted
a formal display of unity, this is it, Idris… Have you never
wondered why there are multiple Totems, multiple Kings, instead
of one? Why are we the only planet in the universe with mystical
power? What we have here is so very precious and rare. But why?
Why do we have it? It could be for this very reason. Our Divine
energies merged into one and charged into the natural elements
of our world. For what is a tree if not a symbol of
interconnectedness, life and regeneration? If we're successful,
such a plant would not only bear fruit. It would create an endless
flow of energy that could feed and heal everyone in the world…
including Cursed Kings.

119

Lana flipped the page, only to find several more ellipses before the conversation continued.

HM Blue King Idris:
If I do manage to live a day longer than expected, it'll only be to regret this very moment – You'll have my support.

HM Gold King Lucien:
Idris, you shan't reg—

HM Blue King Idris:
Provided it's a *last* resort. That goes for both the Burning Bush and the Tree of Al-Buqayawiyya.

HM Gold King Lucien:
I suppose we can always start with other trees and see what results flare up. Mind, it may be difficult to scavenge for one that's already blessed by another prophet or saint. Everything got rather mucked around after the Golden Bang.

Understatement, thought Lana. The Golden Bang referred to a world-changing event that took place in the year 1027 AD. The event was Lucien's body merging with the Golden Totem for the very first time. The vibration of the Totem's energy synergizing with Lucien had caused a blast so powerful that it literally broke and blended all the landmasses of the world. Gone were ancient domains like the Roman Empire, Japan, Kashmir, and Liao Dynasty. In its place came new domains run by Kings with Divine energy, which appeared to the mortal eye in colours like gold, red, blue, green, and grey.

HM Red King Caleb:

Uh-huh. And whose fault was that?

HM Gold King Lucien:
It's not as though I did it intentionally.

HM Red King Caleb:
You realize not all of us have as much time and money on our hands to go scouting for lost trees where holy men once perched in constipation?

HM Blue King Idris:
Contemplation.

HM Red King Caleb
Same thing. My point is, while you're discharging gold bars on the regular, some of us are busy keeping our Kingdoms from going down in flames – literally.

HM Gold King Lucien:
Well, I'm more than happy to fully fund and facilitate this grand undertaking, provided I have your vote in two months' time.

HM Red King Caleb:
That's it! I knew it! I knew it! That's what you were after from the very beginning. You want us to elect you Dominus of our circle of Kings. You don't care about healing the world. You certainly don't give a damn about healing us. You only care about controlling the world by controlling us. Power-hungry prick!

HM Gold King Lucien:
The faint-hearted Red King is pre-inclined to assume the worst in everyone—

HM Red King Caleb:
Not true. That assumption is reserved especially for you,
Goldie.

HM Gold King Lucien:
But you know me better, Idris. You and I have our differences,
but we share an unfaltering belief in God. And you know, as I
do, that a King always works in service for his subjects just as
God is always working for his people.

. . .

. . .

HM Blue King Idris:
I'll need a moment to discuss this with Caleb. If you don't
mind?

HM Gold King Lucien:
Not at all. Please, have a seat and a refreshing glass of iced tea.

HM Red King Caleb:
Seriously?!! You conjure up chairs, a table and full set of
brassware now?? Why didn't you have this out from the start
instead of making us stand around like a bunch of boiling dandies
under the sun?!!

HM Blue King Idris:
Our conversation will need to be off-the-record as well.

HM Gold King Lucien:
Of course. Let me close this good book and give you a touch
of privacy. But before I go, allow me a moment to recap the
importance of this Divine undertaking and all the infinite
possibilities that may emerge from it should we move forward
together in grace and harmony. After all, it was Jesus – or *Yeshua*
or *Isa*, if you prefer – who said that he was the vine, and we are

the branches. For Jesus was a seed of God's life that would die in the ground, but then grow and flourish into—

HM Red King Caleb:
Oh, for the love of Jesus! Would you piss off already?

HM Gold King Lucien:
Yes, well… I trust you'll make the right decision. At least, I know you will, Idris… I'll take a few laps around the skies, shall I? Cheerio!
…
…
HM Red King Caleb:
Flash Bastard. Always showing off by flying off somewhere. Mr. "*Look-at-me-I-can-manifest-a-pair-of-golden-wings-and-dash-off-into-the-susnset*." As if that's worthy of impression. I could fly too, you know?

Lana doubted it. Thus far, Lucien was the only King – and only person, for that matter – on the planet with flight capabilities.

HM Blue King Idris:
Can you really?

HM Red King Caleb:
Well… no…but it's only because I have no interest in taking flight. I bet I could do it though, if I really wanted to.

HM Blue King Idris:
I'm sure … Please have a seat, Caleb, and let us discuss this calmly. Bear in mind, our conversation may still be earwigged. Rumour has it, Lucien can use his energy for advanced hearing. They say he can hear a nail being hammered into a coffin a million miles away, should he so please.

Lana knew that much to be true. Lucien's hearing was better than that of a lion's – when he bothered to listen, that was. It was highly likely that he had eavesdropped on their entire conversation after flying off. And, as for why the book was continuing to transcribe even after being shut – Lana knew the only reason Lucien's energy was keeping an official record of this private confab between Red and Blue was because her beloved Husband-King really was that much of a bastard.

Chapter 9: Among Cursed Kings Only

Caleb:
What's there to discuss? We can't trust a man like him, with all
that hair and teeth and uppity posturing.

Idris:
Lots of hair, teeth and class… Isn't that the type you usually go
for? The exact opposite of you.

Caleb:
Shut it, Idris!

Idris:
It was Lucien's idea to have this covenant of Kings. Perhaps
it's only fair we elect him as Dominus.

Caleb:
Covenant? Please… And the only reason he even cooked all this
up is to control us. Hell, the man wants to control everyone and
everything around him. If an unwanted gust of wind came in his
direction, he'd probably reprimand it and force it to turn around
in shame. That's what he wants to do to us, only worse: he'll
lecture us half to death and then order us around until we drop.
He wants to control us because he can't conquer us. And the
only thing that's ever stopped him from fully conquering our
world is—

Idris:
Is the exact same thing that stops all Chosen Kings from taking
over the world. Don't pretend as though the thought of world

domination has never crossed your mind. I'll admit, it's crossed mine in the past.

Lana furrowed her brows in confusion. She had always wondered why Lucien hadn't bothered taking the world for himself. He was certainly powerful enough. What was stopping him? Apparently, it was the same thing stopping every other King.

Caleb:
Fine! … But my point is…actually, I can't remember what my point was… Anyhow, don't call it a *covenant*.

Idris:
If it were up to you, we'd be calling it a men's club.

Caleb:
Don't be silly. Not all Kings are men … unfortunately.

Idris:
A society. A circle. An alliance. Whatever you wish to call it. Who would you rather have to lead it?

Caleb:
Anyone but him… You remember Goldie's initial meeting last month, don't you? I thought that was the unspoken agreement among the four of us. Red, Blue, Indigo, and Green – we were all thinking it, weren't we? *Anyone but him. Anything but Gold.* … He already has enough power as it is. More than enough. If we make him Dominus of this … *society* of Kings, he'll have even more power. He'll mark himself down in history as a King of Kings… What am I saying? He's already done that. That's how he promotes himself off-planet, you know, to the aliens—

Idris:

Non-tellurians, Caleb.

Caleb:
Don't get all politically correct on me. You've seen how they look, how they dress, how they speak. You can't honestly tell me you look at them and see anything but an alien?

Idris:
They don't all have such… unconventional features. Some of them look just like us.

Caleb:
That's even more terrifying.

Idris:
You realize you sound exactly like Lucien when you make such remarks.

Caleb:
I thought you wanted a calm, civilized conversation? No need to hurl insults like that.

Idris:
Let's not digress… regardless of your personal feelings, you can't deny, that he is a natural leader. We wouldn't have won any galactic battles without the Gold King. Out of all of us, he has the most wealth, the most experience as a King, and the most control over his Divine energy. If any new Kings do arise and cause trouble in the coming years, Lucien would be the only one strong enough to rein them in and prevent a world war… We may have silently agreed on *anyone but him*, but we now must come to terms with the fact there isn't anyone else except him… What are our alternatives? The Indigo King is—

Caleb:
Is a woman! Out of the question!

Idris:
I was about to say, is a young King.

Caleb:
Young? She's an 80-year-old *primigen*. Their lot can't even
surpass their First Century of life.

Idris:
Based on her chronological age and primigenious biology, she
is an old woman. But she's only reigned for five years, thus far,
making her a young King… then there's the Green King – barely
into his Second Century of life and second year as a ruler, he's a
young valensman and a young King… As for Grey King Harald,
he has as much experience as Lucien, but he's —

Caleb:
An even bigger bastard than Goldie.

Idris:
Harald is a very mercurial man and immensely isolated from his
fellow Kings… Do the math, Caleb, we have no other choice but
to go for Gold.

Caleb:
Oiy… I should just let my Totem kill me now.

Idris:
This could work for our benefit. For all his warmth and
outlandishness, Lucien can be a very calculated and cold-hearted
man. This society of ours may be a way to keep an eye on him.

Caleb:
What? A checks-and-balances system? Doesn't exist among absolute monarchs and you know it… And, how come you haven't mentioned me as a contender?

Idris:
You're also a very young King, Caleb.

Caleb:
Doesn't mean I don't have the experience. I contributed to the last galactic war, remember? My Red energy's plenty powerful—

Idris:
So powerful that you nearly killed half our allied troops with it.

Caleb:
That was an accident!

It had been an accident, Lana remembered. But it was also an extremely embarrassing situation. Had Lucien not been present to Shield everyone from the Red King's unexpected cosmic blast of fire, the Alliance would most definitely have lost that war.

Idris:
I'm aware. But it still stands to reason, you don't have enough control over the Red Totem.

…

…

Caleb:
What about you, Idris? Out of all of us, you've got the most integrity, diplomacy and compassion.

Idris:
You believe I'm the best of the lot, do you?

Caleb:
Don't let it get to your head. I think you're the *least worst* in a society of demons posing as angels.

Idris:
I suppose there's a compliment in there somewhere... Alas, like you, I'm far too busy—

Caleb:
Trying not to die.

Idris:
Quite... if I'm lucky, I may have another half-century in me. But it's a mere possibility, not a promise.

Caleb:
You're not going to make it unless you do away with that pesky savior-complex of yours. That last plague you cured nearly did you in.

Lana nodded. Such was the curse of the Blue Kings. They could heal everyone but themselves. And the more they helped others, the more harm came their way.

Idris:
But that's precisely why the Blue Totem chose me, and all those before me. We're people whose souls chose to enter this world for the sole purpose of wanting to heal it.

Caleb:
Ugh. I take it back. You're far too much of a sap to be a Dominus.

...

...
...

Caleb:
You truly believe he can pull this off? Replicate this all-healing
Tree of Life for everyone to experience and enjoy?

Idris:
It would be a group effort. He, himself, admitted he couldn't
do it on his own. If he could, he wouldn't have included us.

Caleb:
That's true. He'd have run off and told the world – taken all
the glory for himself. The way he always does. Goddamn prick.

Idris:
Yes. He can be horribly smug and self-regarding. But out of all
of us, he is the only one with the time, resources and energy to
see this plan through to the very end.

Caleb:
You know what pains me the most? More than the Red Totem
dwelling inside me? ... It's the fact that centuries from now, even
millennia from now, he'll still be here. Still the first and only
Gold King in history. Whereas I—I—well, the chances of me
still walking the Earth even half a century from now is a
moonshot.

Idris:
There's always a chance. This little project could be our chance
to rebrand ourselves and finally put an end to the lineage of
Cursed Kings.

Caleb:

Who are you kidding? It's nothing but a dog's chance of succeeding.

Idris:
You said you still believed in God, Caleb.

Caleb:
So? What of it?

Idris:
We're all here to play out a story... A story that the highest of powers wrote for us. In our mortal-minded haze we can't remember, but our souls once agreed to act out all these parts.

Caleb:
I still don't know where you're going with this.

Idris:
There's no story that God loves writing more than one about an underdog. It's been told a million times in a million different ways, hasn't it? Someone who enters this world with nothing for the sole purpose of proving they can gain everything.

Caleb:
If that's true, then how do you explain someone like Goldie? They called him a demigod in ancient times and today they call him the First Chosen King. He entered this world with everything and every day, in every way, he keeps getting more than he deserves. He's out there thriving while the rest of us are barely surviving. Hardly seems fair.

Idris:
You make it sound as though everything comes easily for him.

Caleb:
Because it does. Obviously.

Idris:
Lucien has a flair for showmanship. He likes to keep up appearances and make all aspects of his life appear effortless and elegant. But at the end of the day, he's still a King… A supernova exists inside his body, and he's containing it relentlessly. Granted, his situation isn't as severe as ours—

Caleb:
Damn right. His Golden Totem isn't out to kill him, is it?

Idris:
Nevertheless, he's had his share of pain and losses.

Caleb:
Losses?? I bet he's never suffered a day in his life.

Idris:
You're only reading the middle of his story. You have no idea how it shall end for him. And, you're neglecting his origins… I know you weren't born at the time of the Royal Purge in the Golden realm. But surely, you've heard of it?

Lana shifted uncomfortably in her seat. She didn't like thinking about the Royal Purge. It was a dark moment in Golden history. It had taken place during the early years of Lucien's Kinghood. His six half-brothers had plotted against him and collectively attempted regicide. In an act of self-defense, Lucien had instinctively unleashed a highly concentrated wave of Golden energy. Unfortunately, being a young King at the time, he was unable control the intensity of its eruption.

Caleb:
Yes…well…

Idris:
Caleb, you lost control of your Divine energy and came very close to killing your own Knights. Lucien lost control once, and inadvertently killed all his brothers. Does that not give you an explanation for his incessant need to control everything around him?

…

…

…

Caleb:
This is why I hate talking to you, Idris. Everything that exits your mouth is so … sensible and sympathetic. It's pathetic. And I hate it! … And I hate you as well!

Idris:
Then why are you always calling on me to converse?

Caleb:
… Because we Cursed Kings need to stick together.

Idris:
Well, for what it's worth, I'm rather fond of our little chats. I hope we'll continue to have them in five centuries' time.

Caleb:
I might not even have five years left in me… unless this works… Fine, let's put it the test. See if God truly does love a flaming underdog just as much as he adores a golden boy… But if I vote for him, I want it somewhere in writing that he doesn't start and end every damn meeting with a speech. If I'm cursed to

combust, I refuse to go down listening to the likes of Lucien *"The-party-doesn't-start-until-I-fly-in-with-my-prissy-golden-wings"* Valenta.

Idris:
I wish you luck with that. I can tell you from experience, he starts monologuing even if there's only one person in the room.

Lana snorted. She knew Lucien was prone to monologuing even when he was alone in a room.

Idris:
I'll send out a signal and beckon him back.

Caleb:
Not yet. Let's take a gander at this book of his first, shall we? See what his Divine energy was really taking down.

….

Idris:
What's the matter?

Caleb:
I can't open it!

Idris:
Er—Caleb, I think you should set that book down. Immediately.

Caleb:
It's as if the pages are stuck together… as though it's locked and— AHHHHHH!!!!! MY HAND!!!!!!

The Gold Queen quickly searched through the remainder of the book to see if there were any more transcripts, any more secret meetings between Kings ... There weren't. Every other page appeared to be Lucien's private notes.

Skimming through the pages, Lana could see that Lucien's handwritten observations were as agonizingly lengthy as his monologues, possibly worse. She could tell right away it wasn't going to be a fraction as entertaining as the confab between Kings.

Lana sighed as the pages fanned before her. This had to be worse than all those biblical poetry readings Lucien had made her sit through – the ones where he recited his own verses and kept his eyes trained solely on her to ensure she didn't fall asleep. She knew from experience that one needed to be equipped with two things to get through her husband's written ramblings: patience and a sense of readerly broad-mindedness. Two gifts that she did not possess. Not without a drink, or two, or three...

Chapter 10: The Phantom Husband

She did it.

She had finally read through all of Lucien's notes.

It had only taken her four hours and one, two... three bottles of gooseberry wine to get through the book without perishing of ennui.

There were over 200 pages of notes on various items, including:

- customized prayers invoking God Almighty and the Princes of Heaven,
- speeches Lucien had planned for future meetings once he was named Dominus,
- agenda items Lucien had planned for future meetings once he was named Dominus,
- a labyrinthine legal code on how the Kings can maintain international peace and security,
- a meticulously detailed strategy on supporting sustainable development and climate action,
- design sketches on robes, wigs, crowns and shoes all Kings were required to wear during their meetings,
- preliminary sketches of a combined coat of arms, featuring the Totems of all the Kings (excluding the Grey King) and
- theories on how this New Tree of Life could be created.

The last part was the only bit that Lana had found slightly interesting. There was some scientific language similar to what Gabriel had told her a few days prior. Lucien's theory was that the Kings had to charge a blessed tree with their Divine energies to recreate the Tree of Life. But it wasn't as simple as it sounded:

As Kings, we can only control the power of our Totems through the power of our own minds – that is, through absolute focus and unbending composure, Lucien wrote. *In order for this project to work, I speculate we need to find a way to synchronize our brainwave patterns before we collectively charge a tree with our powers. The trouble is all our Divine energies vibrate at different frequencies. Added difficulty: we not only have to align our brainwaves, but we may also have to align them in frequency patterns of brain activity associated with relaxed and meditative states of mind – Theta and Delta are ideal, but Alpha is likely the most feasible. It's easy for a King of my caliber and possibly even Idris to enter such mental states, but how we could ever get a meatball-head like Caleb to calm himself down long enough to complete such a task is beyond me…*

Lana thumbed through the pages once more, stopping when she came to an illustration. There weren't many illustrations in the book, but Lana was grateful for the few that existed – it gave her eyes a much-needed respite from Lucien's handwriting.

The one she was seeing now was an initial illustration of the Kings' combined coat of arms. Lucien's Golden Griffin was at the center and three tiny Green Butterflies were dotted near it; coiled all around them was a Blue Snake and an eel-like Red Dragon. The symbol of the Indigo King's Totem appeared to be missing, but Lucien had left a footnote stating, *Not sure how to incorporate her Mustang without damaging the symmetry of the visual. Will find a way to squeeze Indigo in at a more convenient time.*

Lana slammed the book shut and peered over to the man sitting on the chair across from her. "So, this is what you've been doing behind my back, is it? A mystical science experiment with your little cult of Kings?"

Lucien gave her one of his smiles. It was the kind of smile that was so polite, it was downright rude. "I wouldn't call it a cult. It's more of a… society, really. Or perhaps I'll call it something else. A concordat? A convocation? I'll figure it out soon enough," he said with a casual shrug. "And really, that ever-so accusing tone of yours, Lana. You make it sound like I've been keeping this from you."

"You have."

"It's not as though you bothered to ask what I was up to in my spare."

"How do you even have spare time to do anything? You're an absolute monarch with control issues and a hovering husband to boot."

"I have a massive talent for multitasking, as you well know."

"I know you have a massive talent for being an ass—"

"You shouldn't be imbibing by your lonesome, Lana," he reprimanded.

Respectable women drank in small proportions and only during social settings – and always in the presence of their husbands. Lana merely snorted and poured herself another glass. She scowled when she missed the goblet, and the dark maroon liquid dripped onto the mulberry silk fabric of the settee.

"Who's going to stop me? You?" She snorted again, uncaring of how unladylike she was being. "You're not even here."

Somewhere in the back of her mind, the part of her that wasn't completely hammered knew that she wasn't really talking to her husband. Lucien's body was still comatose in their bedroom, several feet behind her. Lucien's soul was dancing through celestial planes, several dimensions away. This entity in front of her was merely a phantom. A hallucination taking the shape of her husband and dressed entirely in black. Black satin knee breeches, black waistcoat and a black tailcoat. It was Lana's favourite outfit on him. The dark colours and exquisite tailoring perfectly accentuated his physique. More importantly, there weren't any outlandish frills and laces, nothing to take the focus away from Lucien's beautiful face and pleasing form.

"You—you—you don't love me anymore!" Lana hurled the glass across the room. It flew right over Lucien's head. The sound of it shattering felt congruent with the sound of her heart breaking.

"Lana, please, calm yourself," Phantom-Lucien said evenly.

He didn't make any movement to get up and physically soothe her. Instead, he gave a small offering of verbal solace. "My love for you is greater than gold, I've always said."

It might have sounded comforting had he not said it so emotionlessly.

"Then you don't trust me anymore!" Lana tried standing up, only to find her legs failing her, "You used to tell me avery-avery...avery-thing... *Everything*, even things I didn't want to know. Espeshhh—espeshhh—espeshhiallly things I didn't want nor care to know. Like whenever your morning urine isn't green enough to your liking... Or, or the time you were worroorririeed you had back acne and made me check. Or, or-or-or—the time you thought the spirit of your dreadful dead Aunt Agnes came back to possess your fourth-favourite horse and asked me to exercise, exercise," she hiccuped, "*exorcise* it."

"It was never my intention to upset you, Lana," said Lucien, his tone still unemotional. "But there are certain matters that can only be discussed among Kings."

"But I'm your life!!! *Wife*, I mean, wife! And your Queen!"

"But you aren't a King," he said quietly. "And there are facets of my life you can never be privy to until you're a King."

Lana blinked. "You mean *unless* I'm a King."

"Is that not what I said?"

"I—I—I don't know," she hiccuped again, "I don't think so."

"Well, I'm sure it's what I meant." Lucien's smile returned, this time showing far too many teeth.

"I dun't-dun't-doo not care if you had to break some sort of King's code," she said huffily, "You shouldn't be keeping any sucretssss—secrets from me."

"I thought you liked secrets," he said. "Weren't you the one who once told me that secrets tied people together."

"I lick—lick—like secrets when they're being shared with me, not when they're being kept from me."

"And how many secrets have you kept from me over the past millennia?"

Lana shook her head and yelled, "That's not the same thing!"

"Is it not?"

"When wolves—wives keep secrets, it's an act of self-perverssh...self-preservassshion. When husbendersss do it, it's suspishhhhhh...susfishessss"

140

"It's late. You should get some rest, Lana."

Ignoring his suggestion, Lana groaned out, "Why did you have to do this? Why did you have to get mixxeddd up with those…Cun…Cuss…Cursed Kings? They're called *cursed* for a good ransom—reason." She threw a thumb back behind her, indicating toward their bedroom where his body dwelled. "And now their curse has rubbed off on you, Sleeping Beauty."

Lucien smiled again. "Curses are merely blessings in disguise. Everyone knows that, don't they?"

"Ugggghhh." Lana dropped her head, face down, onto a throw pillow and let out a shrill scream.

"You could always try waking me with true love's kiss," he said sardonically.

Lifting herself back up, she admitted, "That was John-Marshmallow's advice… And I already tried… Didn't work."

After emitting a long guttural growl, she said, "Just once, I wish you could be like every other husband in the world and, and, and—"

"And what?"

"And be lazy! Sit around. Do nuthin'. Scratch yourself inapprorrriateeely. Or-or-or-I dunno, go off and have an affair!"

Lucien raised a brow. "You'd rather I have an affair?" Then added with a cringe, "And scratch myself in an obscene manner?"

Lana sobered up a little at the thought of Lucien having an affair. He never would, she knew. But she also knew exactly what she would do if that ever happened. She would kill the other woman and then she'd kill Lucien. Or maybe, she'd kill Lucien first. Either way, problem solved.

"I'd rather you bee-hive normally," she muttered, sinking back into the couch. "Can't you ever be normal?"

Lucien gave her a long, empty stare. Then, he leaned forward and said, "I am a Divinely chosen being with limitless power wedged into this mortal meat-vessel of a body, whose soul was assigned to enter the terrestrial realm for the sole purpose of creating and leading the greatest empire ever known to man. I can turn absolutely nothing and everything into the most precious of gold. I can create electric storms across the realm with one mere thought. I can send bolts of lightning two Kingdoms over and get them to report back to me. If I so please, I can hear a butterfly flapping its wings on the other side of the planet. If I so wish, I can fly straight to the Sun without ever once having to stop on the Moon. … With all that in mind, the answer to your question is a profound, *No… No, I can never be normal.*"

Lana blinked at him, perplexed. She had trouble understanding Lucien when she was sober. Now that she was thoroughly sloshed, it was as though he were speaking in an alien language. "Uggghhh… just tell me who did this to you … Red or Blue. Which one did this? Tell me. And I'll-I'll—"

"You'll what, my dear?"

"I'll squash them like a bunch of grapes! I'll kill them!" she shouted severely, before hissing out in a low voice, "And then I'll kill you."

"Oh, I shall yield to my grave someday, calling out your name with my very last breath. Of that, I have no doubt," Lucien grinned. "But what makes you think it was one of them? What possible reason do they have to harm me?"

It didn't make sense to her. Both the Red- and Blue- Kings were invested in Lucien's experiment; both benefited from its potential success. True, the Red King despised him, and the Blue King distrusted him. But neither of them had any genuine cause to put the Gold King out of commission in such a manner.

"I dunno… but who else could it have been?" Lana began to flop around the divan, looking less like a graceful swan and more like a fish out of water. "It has to be Red or Blue … Only a King is strong enough to go up against another King… but you're the one with the most power. How could any of them ever challenge you and win?"

For the first time since their conversation started, Lucien got out of his seat. Once near enough, he knelt beside her. "Look at the state of you, Lana," he whispered, gently stroking tendrils of dark hair away from her face. His hand felt like a frozen lake. "If only our subjects could see you now. Their perfect, elegant Gold Queen appearing so unkempt and disorderly and… pathetic. Strangely enough, I rather fancy this side of you."

"Go away," she mumbled, tossing her face to the side to avoid the iciness issuing from the hallucination, the phantom, the ghost. Whatever this entity was, he wasn't Lucien. Her Lucien always ran hot. Too hot, in fact. She was sure there was enough thermal energy in him to create a second sun.

"Before I go, I'll let you in on a little secret… No, I tell a lie. I'll give away the *biggest* secret that exists about Chosen Kings."

"I already know about your little secret society of Kings."

"Oh, that's not much of a secret. Not really." Lucien tossed his head back and chuckled darkly. "This is something that I've kept to myself ever since I was chosen. Oh, and it's a doozy. No other King in the world has realized it yet."

Lana peered over at him. "What is it?"

Lucien smiled *that smile* again, an act of polite rudeness. "I'm not the most powerful King."

"What???" If Lana had the energy, she would have sprung right up. As it was, her legs felt like boulders. So, she laid there limply like a cadaver with eyes wide open. "But then… who is?"

"No one."

"But… but," said Lana. "You can do things that the other Kings can never do."

"Because I tell myself I can." The real-Lucien had always responded with the same line whenever anyone asked him how he was capable of using his Divine energy for diverse purposes. The real-Lucien would laugh through his answer, as though it were merely a jest. This phantom-Lucien, however, didn't chuckle or smile obligingly as he delivered his go-to line. This phantom was stoic and dead serious.

"You can fly… and make gold—"

"Because I tell myself I can," he repeated with indifference.

143

"—make thunder, lightning and electricity…and have conversations with thunder, lightning and electricity, and —"

"Because I tell myself I can," he repeated thrice-over.

"—and start earthquakes … and seismic shifts—"

"Because I tell myself I can."

"I don't understand," she whispered.

"That's the secret, Lana. There's no such thing as one Totem being stronger than another, one King being more powerful than his counterparts. It's a lie I've fed them for centuries, and they swallow it like starving swines, every time. But the truth is, all our Divine energies are sourced from the same eternal power, the same infinite intelligence… I prefer to call this source *God*, but everyone has their own labels these days … Anyhow, as Kings we all have unlimited access to this power, and we have the ability – for the most part, at least – to do as we please with it."

"So, you're saying … the Kings and all their Divine energies are equal by spiritual law?"

"That's correct."

"Then why can't the other Kings tap into this infinite power as easily as you?"

"It's all mind over matter, really."

"How do you mean?" she said softly, before snapping, "And don't say '*Because I tell myself I can*'!!!"

"But that's the only genuine answer." Lucien stared down at her. "Think of it this way: it boils down to what we say about ourselves and *to* ourselves every night before falling asleep… The Red King goes to bed, telling himself he's cursed to combust and that God's out to punish him. So, that's exactly what he experiences with his energy. The Blue King dozes off thinking he's pre-destined for a life of self-sacrifice. And that's precisely what he manifests with his powers… As for me… well, I'm not one to limit myself. I've always believed that all things were possible to me. I told myself that if six billion people have to simultaneously drop and kneel in order for me to get everything I want, then by God, *they will kneel*," he finished darkly.

Then, a beat later: "Mind you, I've held these thoughts and beliefs since I was a child. So, I suppose I hold an unfair advantage. It's always easier to believe in all the possibilities of the impossible when you're a bright young thing, isn't it?" Lucien uttered with a light-hearted laugh, as if he hadn't spoken like a maniacal overlord not three seconds ago. "Do you understand me now, Lana?"

"Uh huh." Lana eyed him skeptically. "Why have you never told me any of this before?"

"But I did, many centuries ago."

"No... no, you didn't. I would've remembered."

"*You?* You would have remembered?" Lucien's cold smile suddenly broke into cruel, condescending laughter. "You can't even remember a simple anniversary date." His frosty palm covered her forehead. "My poor little swan, you're the unreliable narrator of your own life and you don't even know it... Tell me, what do you say about yourself, to yourself, before you retire for the night? That you're the Gold Queen, always perfect, always alone in a world of people staring into her every move and judging her? Is that it? Did I get that right?"

If Lana had enough strength right then, she would have punched him in the face. Instead, she settled for shouting, "I tell myself I'm an idiot for marrying such an insufferable buttard... bastard!! Ugh! Just go away, will you?"

"In case you haven't noticed, I'm already gone," said Lucien.

Lana blinked. She was alone in her den once again. The phantom of her husband had disappeared.

It took her awhile to eject herself from the chaise. When she finally managed to stand again, it was only to fall unceremoniously to the ground. A normal person might have tried to get back on their feet. A normal person might have admitted defeat and fallen into a drunken stupor. Lana, however, had bellycrawled across the floor and over to her bedroom.

She couldn't remember how she did it, but somehow, she was able to get back onto the bed without causing any more damage. Once there, she scrambled close to her husband's body. She grabbed his arm, threw one of her legs over his, placed her head atop his chest and huddled close. The body did not make any reaction as though refusing to acknowledge her.

For a few short moments, she laid there listening to his heartbeat alongside the beeps and dings of all the monitors Gabriel had set up around the room to keep tabs on the Gold King's pulse rate and brain activity.

Lucien's body was now literally glowing, fully encapsulated by his Golden aura. His everlasting warmth was still there, even though his mind and soul had been spirited away. He was within her grasp and far beyond her reach at the same time. Right there beside her and yet it was impossible for her not to be conscious of his absence.

It was so typical of him. Even his absence had become a presence.

Bastard, was her last thought before succumbing to sleep.

Chapter 11:
Fairy Tales and Tragedies are One and the Same

"It's a fairy tale," insisted John-Marlowe.

"It's a tragedy," refuted Jason-John.

"A fairy tale."

"A tragedy."

"A fairy tale!"

"A tragedy!!"

"Godfather-Lucien is like a beautiful princess who's fallen under a witch's curse—"

"Except he's a King."

"—and our Godmother's the handsome prince who rides up on a noble steed to free him from the hex—"

"Except she's a Queen and a witch. For all we know, she's the one who hexed him."

"—and once she's saved him, it'll become obvious that the curse was a blessing all along. And they'll fall madly in love with each other—"

"They're already married! It's too late for them to fall in love now!"

"—and then they'll get married—"

"They're already married, dummy!!"

"We're watching destiny unfold as we speak! Two people, meant to be, written in the stars. They lose each other only to find one another all over again. This is a love story! This is a tearjerker! This is a fairy tale, Jase!!!"

"All fairy tales are destined to become tragedies in the end. Everyone knows that, Marshmallow."

"Boys, please stop jumping on my bed," Lana said politely but loud enough so they could hear her command from the den.

"Yes, Godmother," said the twins before resuming their verbal dispute beside Lucien's body.

Lana was laid out on her chaise, just as she had been last night. Only this time, she was in a state of sobriety. The crapulence she felt from yesterday's libations had left her bedridden for the better part of the day. When she finally wakened, the world outside of her windows had turned dark. The sun had gone down and Lucien still wasn't up.

They were closing off on Day 4, and with no solution in sight.

She had consumed the entirety of Lucien's book, mentally noting everything of interest and trying not to drop off into oblivion at all the tedious details. But ultimately, it felt like an exercise in futility. She wasn't any closer to discovering who had *cursed* – as the twins called it – her Husband-King. Nor did she have any ideas on how to bring him back.

She gazed listlessly at the high ceiling. The twins' latest ongoing quarrel wafted from the bedroom, into her private quarters and through her ears. *Was this a fairy tale or a tragedy?* She thought to herself.

Fairy tales had simple solutions. One good kiss and you were set for life.

Tragedies were complicated. There were a million roads to take, a million decisions to make. By the time everything was finished, someone either ended up dead or they stayed alive only to wish they were dead… like the man who killed his father, romanced his mother and scratched his own eyes out when he realized what he'd done. What was his name? Lana couldn't remember. Not that it mattered.

Maybe this is the intermission, she thought in dismay, *The fairy tale in the process of becoming a tragedy.*

A part of her wanted to give up. Leave all the heavy lifting to her sons – that was what sons existed for, after all. Or, she could leave it to chance – let everything resolve itself on its own. Yes, perhaps she would do exactly that. She was a Queen, which meant she had the luxury of sitting back and doing nothing. Giving up sounded like the perfect solution right then…

But this was the funny thing about giving up: just as you're about to do it, you're reminded of why you should never do it. For Lana, that reminder came in the form of a voice. One she hadn't heard in centuries.

"*You mortals. You all want simple solutions to get out of your self-inflicted situations. Yet every single one of you refuses to believe a simple solution can even exist. It's like watching a witch who doesn't believe in magic.*"

Lana sat up, her eyes zipping around the room. The twins were still inside her bedroom. She was alone in the den. But instinctively, she knew another energy – another entity – had entered the room.

"Mother?" she said in a muted voice so the twins couldn't hear her. "Is that you?"

No response came, but Lana didn't feel discouraged. She went on, "Great Mother of Darkness, if you're listening, and I know you are… I need your help… I need your help finding my husband."

"*Find yourself another one.*"

Lana rolled her eyes. That confirmed it. It was definitely her Divine Mother speaking to her. "I'm rather fond of the one I have now."

"*Why?*"

"Because I love him."

"*But does he love you?*"

"Absolutely. His love for me is greater than his love for gold."

"*But not greater than the love he holds for his God.*"

Lana's lips tightened into a thin line. She didn't know how to disprove that. She couldn't disprove that. It was true, wasn't it? She had chosen Lucien over her own faith, but he had never once returned the favour.

"Just tell me what I need to do, Mother."

"*You already know what to do.*"

"No, I don't. If I did, I wouldn't be asking."

"*You're not asking now.*"

"Allow me to rearticulate. Will you tell me what to do? Please?" begged Lana.

"*You already know what to do.*"

Lana opened her mouth to release a mute groan of frustration. "Mother," she hissed, keeping one eye toward the bedroom to ensure the twins weren't eavesdropping. "I'm begging you."

"*A spoiled brat like you knows nothing of begging.*"

Shoulders deflating, Lana dropped back onto the divan.

Several silent moments passed before the voice returned, "*When you were but sixteen, you casted a circle by a river and summoned a water spirit. It was your very first attempt at beckoning and binding a spirit. Do you remember?*"

"No."

"*You spent hours, looking out into the river and chanting invocations to conjure the spirit. Three hours of chanting on your part. And two hours and fifty-five minutes of the water spirit screaming, 'Hello! I am here, maiden! … You've already summoned me. You can stop calling my name now… For the love of Poseidon's Favourite Trident, I am right here, you foolish girl!!!! Stop saying my name!!!'*"

Lana flushed a little. She still couldn't remember that particular incident. But it certainly sounded like something that could've happened to her. It was a common mistake among beginner witches: successfully calling forth a spirit but failing to sense its presence. Seeing spirits didn't come naturally to mortals. Only a select few were gifted at it. Over the centuries, Lana had learned to rely on other means to sense a spirit – such as a drop in air temperature, an unexpected ringing or buzzing sound, or the flickering of candles or lights.

"*The spirit appeared before you within three minutes, and yet you droned on for three hours.*"

"So… you're saying what I need to know is right in front of me?"

"*In front of you. Behind you. Inside you. All around you… It's everywhere, but you're not looking.*"

"What? What is it? What am I failing to see?"

"*Figure it out yourself. You know what to do.*"

"But I—"

"Your First Sight is far from right. You can only see the light with your Second Sight."

There were no windows in the den, no entryway for a draft, and yet she felt a wave of cold air brush her hair to the side and fly past her, signaling the entity was no longer present.

With newfound energy and determination, Lana stood up. She knew what she had to do. It was something she should have done from the start.

When it came to witchcraft, Lana wasn't the greatest spellcaster around nor did she excel at channeling spirits. Nevertheless, she did have natural psychic and clairvoyant abilities – *Second Sight*, as some would call it.

Usually, divinatory visions came to her whenever they pleased. But when they didn't, she could always draw them out through the process of scrying.

She crossed the room and silently shut the doors to her bedroom. The Quartermaine twins took no notice. Gabriel had already attached various monitors onto Lucien's chest and cranium. They were wirelessly connected to a series of screens, which were hung up on the wall beside Lucien. Each screen measured a different pattern – heart rate, breathing, blood pressure, intracranial pressure and cerebral perfusion pressure. The twins were now far too immersed in all the equipment to acknowledge Lana's presence.

On the way back to her lounge area, Lana shut off the lights and stopped to grab a few items from a carved walnut armoire: a packet of matches and a candle that Greta had gifted her – a large black pillar made entirely from beeswax.

She gracefully fell into a seated position on the floor and laid the candle on the table in front of her. Before drawing a match, she closed her eyes and focused on her breathing. She inhaled for four beats and exhaled for six. She continued this breathing process consistently for ten minutes. Breathwork wasn't necessarily required for scrying, but it helped calm and emotionally detach the mind, which in turn, made divination a lot easier.

At the ten-minute mark, she returned her breathing to its normal state. Her silver eyes flew open, shimmering like diamonds against the darkness of the room. When she felt ready, she lit the candle and watched the flame.

Scrying wasn't the easiest divination method to master. Most people thought it was nothing more than a witch's joke – looking into a crystal ball and making up predictions. But in actuality, it required a lot of energy and focus. You had to stare directly into an object or entity – be it a crystal ball, a flame, a bowl of water, etc. – and keep your concentration on it while simultaneously allowing yourself to be submerged into a trancelike state, much like a child gazing up at the sky and seeing images in ordinary clouds. Once fully immersed in the trance, the visions came naturally to your mind's eye.

Lana kept her eyes trained on the flickering flame, which resembled three teardrops of decreasing size placed one inside of another. At the center, the flame gleamed gold. Surrounding the golden core, the flame appeared in a luminous red orange. And outlining the blazing teardrop was a vibrant line of blue.

Upon first glance, it didn't look like anything more than an ordinary well-kept flame on a mundane pillar candle. But Lana kept her gaze and mind trained on it, allowing herself to become dazed with the sight of the fire blinking and blazing. Every time a stray thought entered her head, she ignored it and returned her attention to the flame.

She didn't know how long she sat there, staring into the turbulent void. But somewhere along the line, the ring of blue surrounding the flame had dissipated completely. The gold and orange hues soon followed, becoming fully engulfed by a bright red.

For a while, the fire remained stubbornly red as though it were testing Lana to see if she would be the one to blink first. When she didn't, the red flame grew larger and danced wildly before shifting into its complimentary colour – green.

Then it happened.

Lana was no longer in her private chambers. Instead, she was falling endlessly through a large olive-green wormhole and into another pocket of time.

When she finally landed on her feet, it was to see earth and grass beneath her bare toes. Above her was a fortress of daylight, but the sun felt soft instead of scorching. The atmosphere carried an aroma of roses, sandalwood and cinnamon mixed with a slight metallic tinge that reminded Lana of bronze statues and prayer bowls.

There was a man several feet in front of her, looking out at a row of mountains covered in green trees. It was a view so idyllic, it belonged in a painting.

With his back turned, she couldn't see his face. His hair was dark and long, and he was dressed in loose-fitting beryl-coloured robes. He only appeared to have one accessory on him. Lana squinted at it. *No*, scratch that. It wasn't *on* him. It was directly above him, hovering a few feet over his head. A kaleidoscope of green butterflies flapped around in a circle, forming a sentient crown above him.

It reminded her of the first time she had ever seen Lucien. Even back then, before he had been Chosen, Lana had foreseen a shiny golden crown floating over him like a halo. The Golden crown she'd witnessed back then had felt unyielding, like it was shouting at her, demanding everything from her. This crown she was encountering now was different. It wasn't loud and aiming to conquer her soul. It felt forgiving and apologetic, like it was trying to soothe her soul.

"Godmother? … Hello! Godmother? … Jason-John! Come quick! Something's wrong with Godmother!"

Lana wanted to reach out to the man. But every time she tried to step forward, she felt herself being wrenched back.

"Godmother? … Godmother!!"

The Gold Queen gasped loudly and scrambled away. It took her a moment to absorb her surroundings and realize she was – both physically and mentally – back in her private rooms. Her two godsons were regarding her warily. Fraternal twins with an identical look of concern on their faces.

"Boys," Lana exhaled deeply. She tried to lighten the heaviness in her chest, which seemed to materialize every time she came out of a scrying session. "What—what are you doing?"

"What are *you* doing?" Jason-John tossed back with genuine curiosity. "Sitting on the floor." He knew his Godmother was unconventional, but she was still a Queen. Women of her standard didn't lie about on the ground like a scullery maid. "And alone in the dark, no less."

John-Marlowe leaned forward and whispered to her, "Is this a ...*witchy* thing?"

"Not really," muttered Lana, all the while searching for an excuse. "I was...er..." Gesturing to the candle, she said, "Blowing out a candle...for my birthday."

"Is today your birthday?" asked Jason-John.

"Um... no," said Lana lamely before snuffing out the candle with one large breath. "But I was practicing...for my next birthday."

"Oh," nodded John-Marlowe. "That makes sense."

"No, it doesn't," Jason-John scowled at him. "That makes no sense whatsoever!"

"Yes, it does."

"No, it doesn't."

"Yes, it does!" insisted John-Marlowe. "I do it! I strategize for our birthday every year. I practice my surprise-face for our surprise party. And then, I think about the cake we'll have – golden sponge cake with apricot marmalade and cream, this year. And then, I think about our presents, what Nick-Ray's going to get us, what Mama's going to get us—"

John-Marlowe stopped, practically choking on his words as realization hit him.

Jason-John nearly staggered back at the agonizing reminder that sliced through his mind.

Lana let out a small gasp and drew a hand to her chest. This year would be the first birthday the Quartermaine twins would spend without their mother.

"I'm sorry…I—I forgot." John-Marlowe's lips began to tremble, his shoulders started to shake and his eyes were blinking rapidly.

Lana could tell he was trying his hardest not to cry. A new wave of resolve coursed through her. She knew she could never detach the boys from the pain of losing their parents; unfortunately, they had no choice but to experience it. Nevertheless, Lana was determined to distract them from this pain for as long as she could.

"Boys, how about I give you an early birthday present, hmm?"

"What is it?" Jason-John asked as he walked over to place a comforting arm around his brother's shoulder.

"Why don't we go on another adventure? Just the three of us… and my security detail."

John-Marlowe sniffed a little, still trying to keep the tears at bay. "Are we going back to the witchy house?"

"No, my little love. It's a place much further away. And it's not in a witch's house, but I assure you, it's no less magical."

The twins nodded at her.

With a deep exhale, Lana's eyes drifted toward her bedroom. The doors were wide open, and she had a clear vision of Lucien, still in a state of strange soporose. She knew there was only one person who could get him out of his current predicament. Incidentally, it was the same person who placed him there to begin with. And now, Lana knew exactly who they were.

Chapter 12: The Ashram Beneath the Rosebud

Getting out of the Golden realm was never easy, not for Lana at least. Lucien was able to fly freely, *literally*, out-of-Kingdom whenever he pleased. Lana, however, had to endure a chain of unnecessarily lengthy inquiries from her security detail, especially if she was travelling without the company of her Husband-King.

It was the dullest dance in the world – a series of byzantine queries followed by Lana's clipped responses. *Where's your final destination, Your Majesty?* (Svarga City, Green Kingdom.) *What's the purpose of your visit?* (Confidential.) *Who shall you be meeting?* (Also confidential.) *How many people will be present at your intended location?* (Unknown.) *What's the current political landscape of the Green Kingdom?* (How the devil should I know??)

Lana had maintained her poise throughout most of it. She didn't snap – not until they asked her: "Shouldn't His Royal Highnesses Prince Michael and Prince Gabriel be accompanying you, ma'am?"

"Why would they need to escort me?" Lana had asked kindly, coldly.

"Because, ma'am…" the Knight had hesitated a little under Lana's scrutinizing gaze, "A woman of your rank requires a chaperone."

"A woman of my rank," Lana had bit out, "requires no chaperone. A woman of my rank outranks you and this entire moronic lot of minions devoted to my husband. And if I recall correctly – as I always do – a Queen outranks her Princes just as a mother always outranks her sons. This conversation is finished. Get the Leviathan up and running. We shall depart immediately … Why are you still standing here gawking? Get to it!

"Yes, Your Majesty!"

Lana shook off the memory. It was a minor irritation, nothing to get riled up over, especially now that they were so close to their intended destination. She unbuckled her seat and arose to glide across the empty span of Gabriel's private airship, the Leviathan. Inside, the ship was minimal, steel-like and expansive with massive windows. From the outside, however, observers would have thought they were witnessing a giant golden whale with windows serving as large teeth. It was an odd-looking dirigible, one that appeared better suited under the sea than up in the sky. Despite its strange appearance, Lana had chosen the Leviathan of all the other family air-vehicles for its spaciousness and speed. It was sure to get them to the Green Kingdom by lunch and have them back on Golden soil by supper… a very late supper.

She met up with her godsons by the tinted windows. The Quartermaine twins had their noses pressed against the glass as they surveyed a forest on the outskirts of Svarga City with keen interest. They were 10,000 feet up in the air with nothing but green beneath him until John-Marlowe spotted something that piked his interest.

"Over there, Jase!" he said excitedly, pointing to a gigantic grass sculpture of a rosebud situated right in the middle of the forest. "That must be the place Godmother was telling us about."

Jason-John craned his neck up at Lana. "Is there really a house underneath that rosebud?"

"I wouldn't refer to it as a house, per se," said Lana.

"Is it a castle?" asked John-Marlowe.

"Hmm… you could call it that," nodded Lana. "The person who owns it certainly sees it as his castle."

"Is it invisible like Ms. Anatolia's house?"

"Ms. Anatolia's house wasn't invisible, silly." John-Marlowe shook his head. "It was merely hidden."

"Same diff!" huffed Jason-John.

"Hardly," refuted his brother.

Lana crouched down to whisper at them, ensuring her sentry couldn't overhear their conversation. "Just between the three of us, I can tell you, it isn't invisible nor is it hidden in plain sight. However, there's something you boys ought to know," leaning forward a little more, she said in a low voice, "Getting into this castle is half the adventure. You see, not everyone can pass through. Acquiring entry to such a place requires considerable energy and a great deal of mental strength."

"You needn't fret, Godmother," said John-Marlowe, putting a thumb to his chest, "I have energy to spare and I'm plenty mentally strong. People tell me so all the time."

Jason-John scoffed. "They tell you that you're mentally—"

"To gain admission," Lana interrupted purposefully, "We must remain calm at all times. Think of the trees near Ms. Anatolia's home. They looked fearsome in the darkness, but they meant no harm. They were only there to protect you. That's what you need to remember when we step out of this ship. Whatever you see, whatever you encounter, no matter how petrifying it may seem, it will not harm you. Keep your composure, refrain from making any noises, do not be alarmed, and most of all – *do not* make a run for it. Understood?"

"Yes, Godmother," they said.

"And I know I needn't remind you both to mind your manners. We're guests in this Kingdom, and as Golden citizens attending alongside the Queen, you're expected to maintain a level of professional decorum. Consider yourselves diplomats today. That means your behaviour here will be a reflection on our realm. I'm relying on you both to carry yourselves with dignity and show everyone that men of Gold always uphold the highest of standards.

"Just like our Godfather-King," smiled John-Marlowe. "He always says the Golden realm is where the higher standards prevail."

"Precisely. Conduct yourselves the way your Godfather would," Lana nodded in agreement, until she remembered something. "Well, perhaps not entirely like him. You don't want to be a..." She paused and attempted to drum up a polite way of saying *'Refrain from behaving like a vain, insufferable, pompous, holier-than-thou snob with too much product in his hair.'* She couldn't figure out the best way to phrase it for her godsons, but eventually settled for saying, "You needn't be as *puffed up* as your Godfather. But you get the gist, I'm sure."

"We'll be ever-so good, Godmother," promised John-Marlowe.

Lana smiled at him. "I'm sure you will."

"We shan't embarrass you," added Jason-John.

Lana's smile faded a little. "I hope you won't." She lifted herself back upright and held out her hands for them to take. "Remember, nothing you see here will harm you unless you allow it. Chin up. Back straight. And always keep your composure intact."

Upon landing on a high alpine meadow, they changed into clothing less restrictive and more reflective of the region they were visiting. The twins wore identical golden sherwanis – which, to them, felt like a hybrid of a frock coat and an achkan – with loose-fitted linen trousers underneath. Lana wore a simple white sari. It was a long stretch of soft fabric arranged elegantly over her body as a robe. One end of it was attached to her waist while the other rested over her shoulder like a stole. Their guards, however, remained in their standard Volucris uniforms.

With two Knights in front of them and two behind, Lana and the twins were boxed in as they exited the Leviathan, trekked through the meadow, and disappeared into a forest of evergreen trees.

After a half-hour hike, the twins were underwhelmed. They had seen nothing but trees, so far. Sure, the trees were nice enough, but they weren't that impressive. Not compared to the birch trees they had recently encountered back home.

The twins were growing bored and weary. They wondered how much longer they would need to walk before reaching this secret castle in the woods.

Jason-John tugged at Lana's sari, ready to whine. But she came to a stop and placed a finger to her lips, signaling for silence. The Knights stopped as well. They could hear a rustle, a movement behind the bushes.

The twins didn't know how it happened. Out of nowhere an ambush of white tigers appeared, surrounding them from all sides.

They were growling and snarling, their silver eyes squinted in scrutiny.

"Keep quiet boys and stay close to me," Lana whispered to them before reminding her sentry, "Drop your rifles. They're a protected species in this realm."

"But Your Majesty—" one of the Knights started, but didn't get a chance to finish.

The tigers were on the Knights in a flash, tossing away their rifles as though they were rattles on a baby's palm. Lana supposed it was for the best. The Volucris Knights all carried weapons charged with the Gold King's energy, which meant a single blast could put a gaping hole right through its target.

At the loss of their weapons, two of the Knights backed away and pushed their palms together as a trigger to manifest Shields. Angry at the sudden appearance of translucent Golden walls keeping them from their prey, the tigers began roaring and pounding at the Shields.

As the Gold King, Lucien could keep a Shield up and running for years on end without recharging. His Knights, however, weren't as talented. Their Shields barely managed to stay up for more than ten minutes. So, it wasn't long before the tigers broke right through.

"RUN!!!" One of the Knights screamed as they fled.

Lana tightened her grip on her godsons. "Stay where you are."

The three of them watched as half the white tiger clan ran westward, chasing after the absconding Knights.

Certainly not the best and bravest of Lucien's lot, Lana thought to herself as she heard the echo of their undignified shrieks.

"Godmother," whispered John-Marlowe anxiously as the remaining five tigers began circling them.

"Remember what I told you," she said calmly. "You needn't be alarmed. They won't hurt you."

One of the tigers slowly approached them, coming close to John-Marlowe, who huddled closer to Lana's side in response. The tiger sniffed at the boy for a second, nodded its head once and proceeded to nuzzle the side of his furry face against John-Marlowe's cheek.

"Hey, that tickles!" chuckled John-Marlowe.

It didn't take long for another tiger to trot over to Jason-John, giving him the same treatment.

"They're actually very friendly!" John-Marlowe gently caressed the tiger's fur.

"I told you they wouldn't harm you." Three tigers came up to Lana. For a moment, it was three sets of silver eyes staring into Lana's own. Then, as if intuitively sensing they were in the presence of royalty, they crouched before her, exuding the semblance of a bow.

Lana knew they had to keep moving forward, but she couldn't deny her godsons this rare treat. So, they stayed put for another half-hour, giving the twins time to enjoy playing with the tigers. Not that any of the tigers were rolling around and running about. Rather, they were lying on the grass boredly yet patiently as the twins jumped on their backs and petted them. A few of them curled up at Lana's footsteps and dozed off into a nap.

"Godmother," John-Marlowe piped up whilst straddling one of the tigers, "Why didn't your Knights remain calm as you said? Didn't they know these tigers were nice?"

"Oh, I must have forgotten to let them in on the secret…silly me," said Lana, feigning innocence. In actuality, she had purposely omitted these little details to her guards. She didn't want them anywhere near where she was headed.

"What will happen to them?" asked Jason-John as he tickled a tiger's ear. The feline on the receiving end of his attention merely yawned in tedium.

"They'll be fine," Lana reassured the twins. "Look at these beautiful creatures, they're as sweet as kittens. They wouldn't harm a soul."

The white tigers in this region were well-trained. Lana knew they would merely chase her guards around the forest and bare their teeth at them, but nothing more.

Lana slowly stepped over the three sleeping tigers in front of her. "Listen, my darlings, it's time to forge ahead. We still have a bit of a walk ahead of us."

The twins groaned.

"Come along now," ordered Lana, holding out her palms. "We can get reacquainted with them on our way back."

Jason-John sighed and gave his chosen tiger one last pat on the head. "Bye Taylor."

John-Marlowe hopped off his tiger and placed a soft kiss between their eyes. "Bye Swift."

The twins returned to Lana, each grabbing hold of one of her hands.

The trio continued down the path through the forest. They hiked on for another half mile until coming to a stop. There was a blockage in their path in the form of a tall wall of thorny plants. It was a strange mix of firehorns with bright red berries and honey locusts covered with foot-long dagger-like brown thorns.

"Now what, Godmother?" asked John-Marlowe.

"Go on through," said Lana.

"But there's no door."

"It doesn't need one."

"But it's full of thorns!" objected Jason-John.

"What did I tell you?" Lana reminded them.

"Nothing here will harm us unless we allow it," said John-Marlowe, eyeing the plants with uncertainty, "But …"

"I need you to trust me. You do trust me, don't you, boys?" When no response came, Lana added, "Your mother always trusted me. She trusted with her—" The Queen halted in her verbal tracks. *With her life*, was what she came close to uttering. But look how that situation turned out? With the Quartermaine matriarch six feet under.

Clearing her throat, she went on to say, "She trusted me wholeheartedly. I need you boys to do the same."

"We do trust you, Godmother." John-Marlowe squeezed her hand to reassure her. "We trust you with the world."

"But we don't trust the world at all," countered Jason-John. "Look at the size of those thorns. They're sure to pierce like swords and you know how easily John-Marlowe bruises."

"Like a peach," nodded John-Marlowe in agreement.

"We'll go together." Lana gave them a relaxed smile. "You needn't fear. I shall be with you."

Lana pulled them along, heading confidently toward the thorny wall. The twins screwed their eyes shut as they walked into it. Had they opened their eyes, they would've seen all the thorns and berries light up in a translucent emerald shade. Every thorn that touched their faces and bodies felt like a soft kiss from a flower petal, lulling and pacifying their nerves.

"You can open your eyes now," Lana told them.

The twins blinked in unison, their eyes staring into what felt like a brand-new world.

"Welcome to the Green Ashram," said Lana.

Chapter 13: A Secret Society of Spirits

Behind them was the wall of thorns, covering a vast wilderness. In front of them, however, was a green paradise. There were sentient plants everywhere. There was a row of bushes with roses that were life-size and towered over them. There were children running around, playing. There was a woman near a massive lemon tree, which was beaming with the same translucent green glow from the vines. One of the branches of the tree wrapped around her waist and hauled her up, allowing her to pick lemons with convenience. Every time she snapped one out, another lemon magically appeared in its place.

To the east, a group of bald men were sitting on the grass beside a small firepit; they were gathered in a circle, chanting in a language unfamiliar to the twins. The fire shot up and changed form, creating various auspicious geometric shapes and symbols in line with whatever they were chanting. Sensing their presence, some of them men looked their way and gaped at the sight of Lana. Everyone – men, women, and children – was dressed in the same beryl-coloured robes.

When the shade suddenly disappeared, the twins squinted up to find a ceiling made of grass opening and blossoming as the sunlight poured in. Realization struck them: they were inside the grass rosebud.

Not only were they inside a rosebud, but there was a similar structure directly in front of them. It was a large seafoam-coloured building shaped like a rosebud. There were ten petal-shaped panels making up the roof and directly beneath it was a circular row of large sage-tinted windows.

"Now, my darlings, there's something I've neglected to mention about our host. He's—where's Jason-John?" Absorbed as she had been with her surroundings, she hadn't noticed one of her godsons stray away from her.

Lana and John-Marlowe swiveled around, looking for Jason-John. Their eyes came to a halt at the sight of two small feet with a pair of walking boots sticking out of a gigantic rose.

"Jason-John!" Lana ran over to him. "Oh, the nerve! Release my godson at once!"

The plant instantly obeyed the Queen and gently placed the boy's feet on the ground and stretched out its petals to release him. Lana scolded it some more and the rose shrank back like a child shamed by a parent.

Jason-John swayed and fumbled around for a few moments, a glassy look in his eyes.

"Darling, are you alright?"

"That was… so much fun!!!!" he screamed in delight. "It felt like riding a magical cloud!"

John-Marlowe held up his hand and jumped in the air. "I want to have a go at it!"

"*No*," Lana said sternly.

"I can hear my eyes moving," said Jason-John euphorically.

Lana gave him a light shake. "Jason-John, please, pull yourself together, child."

A woman, the same one from the lemon tree, suddenly appeared beside them and handed Jason-John a goblet of tonic water with passionflower and chamomile. "This will help," she said in a broken Earth Standard dialect.

"Oh, thank you," Lana gave the woman a grateful smile before returning to her godson. "Drink up, my darling." She gently poured half the water down Jason-John's throat and waited for it to take effect. Once she was certain the boy's mind was firmly grounded back to reality, Lana picked up where she left off. "As I was saying, there's something you need to know about our host—"

"Is that him?" John-Marlowe pointed in the direction of the temple.

Lana turned around to find a handsome man approaching them. He was dressed in the current fashions of the Gold- and the Red-realms, with a plush emerald coattail, a velvet green vest, and a white cravat paired with beige trousers and brown boots. His skin was heavily tanned, and his hair was drawn back in a ponytail, resembling a long dark waterfall. To top it off, there was a swarm of green butterflies circling above him like a sentient crown.

He was a young valensmen, to be sure. Barely into his Second Century of life, he looked no older than 18 years old by primigenious standards.

With a broad smile, the man went straight toward Lana, holding out his arms for an embrace. "Gold Queen Lana," he kissed her on both cheeks. "Always unforgettable. Eternally enthralling. You enchant us with your presence."

"My dear sweet Ivaan," Lana returned warmly, "Nice crown."

Ivaan blushed a little, as though he'd forgotten the butterflies were even there. "I took inspiration from King Lucien. Obviously."

Throughout his Kinghood, Lucien had never owned a physical crown. Instead, he had always manifested one to hover above him like a halo whenever the occasion called for it.

Feeling bashful, the man silently ordered the butterflies to scatter. They did so, but not before tickling their wings past the twins' cheeks.

"You don't look too surprised to see me," observed Lana. "Did you happen to foretell my arrival?"

Ivaan chuckled, shaking his head. "The Indigo King is the one who holds the gift of prophecy. Not me."

"Then did the trees warn you of my presence?"

"They *told* me," corrected Ivaan. "They would've warned me had it been your husband… or any other King for that matter."

Lana supposed that tracked. The only thing a King ever had to fear was another King.

"And even if they hadn't told me," said Ivaan. "I always get alerts from border patrol whenever Royal entities enter my realm."

"Of course," nodded Lana.

"I noticed you were getting acquainted with my plants. I hope they weren't causing any mischief."

"They're very beautiful… if only they weren't so clingy."

Ivaan brought a hand to cover his mouth as he broke into a bout of laughter. "Apologies," he coughed, clearing his throat. "I couldn't help myself. You see … that's precisely what King Lucien once said about you."

"A jest! A mere jest. He is ever-so amusing that way, isn't he?" Lana smiled and laughed outwardly, all the while fuming inwardly. *I'll kill him once I have him back*, she swore to herself.

"How is Lucien? Keeping well as usual, I suspect?"

"Of course. He'd never allow himself to be otherwise." It was a polite lie, but Lana felt it was far too early to drop any truth-grenades into the conversation. "You know him, he could frighten off a flu simply by lecturing it half to death …"

While Ivaan and Lana exchanged pleasantries, the twins marveled at their host. Ivaan reminded them so much of Lucien. He even looked like he could pass for Lucien's little brother, or perhaps his son.

"Jase! Jase!" John-Marlowe elbowed his brother. "Look! It's the Green King!"

"Yes, I can see that. Stop poking me!"

"He's quite dashing."

"I suppose some might regard him as such." Jason-John looked away, determined to appear unimpressed and trying to exude an air of indifference.

Jason-John knew that all Kings had their own personal branding. The Gold King was famous for being beautiful and powerful. The Blue King was known to be charitable and intelligent. The Indigo King was proving to be wise and compassionate. The Red King was notorious for being grumpy, hot-headed and stoutish like an over-boiling kettle. And as for the Grey King – well, he had a reputation for being stark raving mad.

Up until recently, Lucien had been the only handsome and charismatic King in their world. It didn't sit right with Jason-John that some new Green upstart should come along and try to steal the spotlight away from his Godfather-King and the Golden empire.

"Should we bow to him, do you think?" suggested John-Marlowe.

"I should think not," huffed Jason-John. "He's not our King."

"But he is *a* King—"

"Foreigners aren't required to display any deference to me," said Ivaan, gazing down at the twins.

John-Marlowe's eyes widened. "How did you know what we were talking about?"

"Did you use your powers to eavesdrop?" inquired Jason-John.

"I used the power of my human ears to overhear a conversation taking place directly in front of me," he said with a smile. "You weren't exactly whispering."

"Oh… right," said John-Marlowe sheepishly.

"These little red Q-tips are my godsons, King Ivaan." Lana introduced them, placing a palm above their heads as she did so. "Jason-John Quartermaine and John-Marlowe Quartermaine. They decided to accompany me. I hope you don't mind."

"Not at all." Ivaan kneeled until he was eye-level with the twins. "Welcome Mr. Quartermaine and Mr. Quartermaine. Twins, are you?"

"Yes, Your Majesty," said John-Marlowe. "But we're not identical. We're fraternal."

"I never would have guessed," said Ivaan with an amused look. "Is this your first time in the Green Kingdom?"

"It is!" gushed John-Marlowe, always happy to be on the receiving end of anyone's attention. "It's our first time meeting a King too… well, a King beside our Gold-Godfather-King, that is."

"Hmm… well, I'm not sure I'm capable of making as memorable of a first impression as your Godfather," said Ivaan.

"Oh, but you are!" said John-Marlowe. "You even look like our Godfather-King… except your hair is darker and longer. *A lot* longer."

"And you're not as tall as he is," quipped Jason-John.

"And your teeth aren't as big as his."

"And you're not as handsome as he is."

"Boys!" Lana cringed in embarrassment.

Ivaan tossed his head back and laughed. "Your godsons are unfiltered. They speak without mercy."

"Allow me to apologize on their behalf."

"No apology necessary." Ivaan shot back up, brushing off bits of grass from his trousers along the way. "I'm well aware I can't compete with the Gold King's beauty. Most men can't."

Lana bit her lip. She couldn't deny that sentiment. Internally, Lucien was highly pretentious, vain and intolerable. Externally, Lucien's face and body formed the nuclear fantasy of the perfect man. Why else would Lana have put up with him for so long? She certainly wouldn't have been able to endure him if his aesthetic wasn't so pleasing to the eyes.

"Oh, I meant to ask, Queen Lana, how are your sons?" said Ivaan.

"They're well, thank you." It was another polite lie. Gabriel was still going berserk back home. And Michael lived in such a state of perpetual apathy that it was impossible to decipher how the man was truly feeling – assuming he felt anything at all these days.

"And your daughters? Are they in good health?"

Lana furrowed her brows. "You mean my *daughter*? I think I would have remembered having more than one."

Ivaan blinked. "Of course, my mistake. Your godsons have me seeing and thinking in doubles." He chuckled awkwardly and rubbed the back of his neck. "How is she?"

"Alexandra has a bit of a cold at the moment, but children are always catching bugs and ailments. I'm sure she'll recover soon enough."

"I shall send blessings of good health her way."

"Thank you, that's most kin—" Lana paused as something caught her attention from the corner of her eye. There were a swarm of monks gawking at her, many of whom had ran out of the Ashram with cameras on hand. "I wasn't aware your clerics were so technologically inclined... I always assumed all monks were luddites."

"Now it's my turn to apologize." Ivaan shook his head, half in disapproval, half in amusement. "Even the most enlightened of men can become starstruck, especially in the presence of someone like you."

"They do this with every Queen that comes their way, I'm sure."

"Not at all. You're the special exception," insisted Ivaan. "There are several Queens in this world, but only the Gold Queen can garner a level of universal attention that surpasses all expectations."

Lana waved her hand in the air casually. "A testament to Lucien's popularity…and notoriety."

"Don't underestimate yourself." That was the last remark he made on the matter before returning his attention to the twins. "Would you gents like a tour?"

The twins nodded eagerly.

"Follow me."

They went down the footed path, straight toward the Ashram. Lana nodded politely at all the monks and smiled for their cameras as they passed.

"Is this really your castle?" Jason-John asked the Green King as they made it up to the steps and onto the circular pavement surrounding the temple.

"This is my primary residence pro tempore, and I am a King, so … yes, I suppose this is technically my castle."

"Is your castle haunted?" inquired John-Marlowe.

"It's *spirited*." Ivaan winked down at him.

"Where are your Knights?"

"You're looking at them."

"These monks??" scoffed Jason-John. "They're your Knights? They're not even armed."

"Knights don't need to carry weapons," John-Marlowe nudged at his brother. "Not if they have the King's Gift." Back home, they'd seen a few members of the Volucris rely solely on the power of the Golden energy for combative and protective purposes.

"Quite right," Ivaan nodded. "They don't require a weapon, because they are the weapon."

The Green King guided them around, occasionally pausing beside one of the large windows to point out a specific room.

At one point, they stopped to peer into a room where everyone had their arms on the floor, their backs in a deep bend, and their legs flung over their heads. Their bodies mirrored a scorpion's raised tail.

John-Marlowe lightly tapped at the window and pointed at them. "What kind of dance is that?"

"That's not a dance, dear." Lana gently grabbed his hand to stop the boy from persisting with his needless pointing. "That's yoga." At the twins' perplexed looks, she explained, "It's a physical, mental, and spiritual discipline. It's meant to help control and calm the mind."

"I don't think I'd feel very calm if I did that," said John-Marlowe.

"I wouldn't recommend trying it," warned Ivaan. "It's not for beginners. This pose is for more advanced practitioners."

"Can you do it, Green King?" wondered Jason-John.

Ivaan snorted. "Not without breaking my body in half."

They carried on, passing by a large room full of dancing purple passion flowers. In the center was an indoor firepit where a monk was conducting a puja. Another room showed people sitting on the floor while eating food laid out on tiny desks.

"Why is everyone so quiet?" asked John-Marlowe.

"Everyone eats in silence here as a way to appreciate the food," said Ivaan.

As they moved on, the twins noticed a pair of monks walking by, carrying brass containers with cavities. Smoke was emerging from its holes, leaving behind a powerful aroma in its wake.

John-Marlowe sniffed cinnamon and roses. "That smells nice."

"That's our custom-made incense," said Ivaan. "It's meant to help with the spirits."

"Ms. Anatolia says spirits are all around us."

"Ms. Anatolia?"

"She's a wit—"

"A dear friend of mine," interjected Lana.

"Well, your friend is correct," remarked Ivaan. "There's a secret society of spirits surrounding us. One thing you need to know about spirits is that most of them have terribly poor eyesight. To make up for it, they're gifted with a stellar sense of smell. Certain fragrances and herbs attract well-meaning spirits, while repelling the ones who lack the best of intentions. Granted, now that the Ashram is protected with my Green energy, it no longer requires so much incense."

"Why do you have it then?" asked Jason-John.

Ivaan shrugged. "Because it smells nice."

"If spirits are all around us," said John-Marlowe. "Why can't we see them?"

"Some people can see them. It's a gift, given to a select few," said Ivaan. "Mind you, animals are much better at detecting them than we are. Have you ever seen a dog bark at a blank wall or at an empty corner or at nothing in particular?"

The twins nodded.

"I assure you: they aren't barking at *nothing*. There's always something, someone there, concealed from our delicate mortal eyes."

"Can you see them, Your Majesty?" asked John-Marlowe.

"Oh, I can do a little more than that these days," replied Ivaan in a cryptic tone. "Ah, speaking of sight, *this* you must see," he said, halting at a window.

The twins stepped closer to get a better glimpse. Inside were half a dozen child monks with their legs crossed in a sitting pose, levitating five feet in the air.

"Jase, look! Those children are flying!"

"But how??" Jason-John gaped. "Do they have the King's Gift?"

"I do not grant the Green Gift to minors," Ivaan shook his head. "No, this isn't Divine energy at work. These are natural and

172

manmade elements at play. You can't hear it because the windows are insulated, but these kids are using a combination of chanting and acoustic sound waves to counteract gravity and levitate."

"Can we learn how to do that? Please!" begged John-Marlowe.

"Certainly. But before you do, you must take a gander at our fountain," he led them around to the back of the Ashram. "I had it installed recently."

The back garden was a field cluttered with even more sentient plants, but the twins barely took notice. They were too enthralled by the massive swimming fountain. The water was naturally blue, of course, but the algae had clearly conquered and devoured the pool, giving it a vibrant lime colour. The edge of the fountain was lined with beryl crystals, which were glistening with Green energy. There was a large statue smack in the middle, of a man playing a flute while standing on a serpent with a hundred heads. A couple of children were swimming around, their heads poking out of the green water. A few others were climbing up the necks of the snakes.

Ivaan's hand glowed up and emitted a line of Green energy straight onto the statue of the man, causing the stone to come to life and play its flute.

"That statue's dancing with the serpents," said John-Marlowe.

"He's actually dancing on top of them in order to defeat them," Ivaan clarified. "At least, that's how the story originally went."

Before the twins could inquire any further, they heard a loud rumble that sounded much like a trumpet. A swirly grey trunk shot out of the water. For a moment, they assumed it was the snake statue coming to life. But upon further inspection, they realized—

"It's a baby elephant!" John-Marlowe cried enthusiastically. "Can we go swimming and play with it?"

"Of course." Turning to Lana, he reassured her, "The water was blessed by the Blue King's healing grace, and all the algae is charged with my Green energy. It's perfectly safe."

John-Marlowe tugged at the Green King's sleeve. "You're not going to cut out the elephant's tongue later and make everyone eat it, are you?"

Ivaan rose a brow. "I beg your pardon?"

"Don't mind them," Lana chuckled uncomfortably, pulling John-Marlowe back to her. "They jest! Such wicked boys! Much like their Godfather, they wield a most unusual sense of humour."

"Right." Ivaan's brow still hadn't come down. "Pleased as I am to have such intriguing visitors, I'm curious as to what brings you all here today?"

"It's an early birthday present for me and Jase."

"Oh?"

"Yes, Godmother feels bad for us because our Mama is d—"

Sensing his brother was about to over-share once again, Jason-John elbowed him. "Marshmallow! Shh!"

"I see." Ivaan's eyes softened. "Well, if it's a birthday, then I should bestow a gift upon you as well...if your Godmother-Queen will allow it, that is."

They whipped their heads around to face her.

Lana rolled her eyes at her godsons' reaction. "Drop the pleading puppy eyes and artificial stares of innocence. I shan't stop you from collecting your present."

Ivaan kneeled before them and held out his hands. John-Marlowe grasped his right, Jason-John gripped his left.

"It may be too much to ask you to trust a man you met not twenty minutes ago," said Ivaan.

"It is," said Jason-John curtly.

"Nevertheless, for this to work, I'll require your trust."

John-Marlowe nodded without hesitation. Jason-John did the same, reluctantly, and only because he wanted his birthday present.

"You needn't be afraid, nothing here will—"

"Will harm us," Jason-John finished off. "We know. Our Godmother already told us."

"Let's crack on then. Keep your hold on me at all times," instructed Ivaan.

The Green King closed his eyes and took a deep breath. When he exhaled, a small puff of green light emitted from his breath.

It grew.

It continued to grow.

It didn't stop growing until all three of them were properly engulfed in a semitransparent circle of green. It wrapped around them like an impenetrable protective blanket.

For a moment, nothing happened. There was nothing but the world around them, seen through lime-coloured lenses.

Then, suddenly, it was as though an invisible veil had been lifted. The twins could now see the unseen. The secret world of spirits clashing against the mortal domain of men. They were everywhere. Some of the spirits looked frightening with multiple heads or disfigured features. Some looked like ordinary people. Some appeared as creatures. Some were orbs and wisps, merely puffs of coloured energy.

The twins held their breath as they witnessed a gigantic centipede-like spirit with a million legs, a serpentine body as long as a train, and three human-looking faces attached to the head. The spirit climbed out of the rosebud-roof and headed over to fountain.

John-Marlowe used his free hand to grab hold of his brother's arm. "Jase! There are ghosts everywhere!" he hissed in equal parts exhilaration and fear.

The centipede-looking spirit halted in its tracks. One of its faces shot over to the twins.

"I think it heard you, Marshmallow," whispered Jason-John.

The spirit's third face squinted at them and without even moving its mouth, it said, "To us, *you* are the ghosts."

With that shattering remark, the spirit dashed away to dive into the fountain.

John-Marlowe might have called after the spirit, had another one not grabbed his attention.

This one appeared as a soft red orb, not much bigger than an apple. While the other spirits had remained outside the Green

King's circle of protection, this one materialized right in front of them, covering part of Ivaan's face.

Instinctively, the twins knew exactly what it was… *who* it was.

"My dear, sweet boys," said the spirit of their mother, "I never meant to hurt you… I never meant to hurt you … You must know that I never left you. Through golden roads and burning bridges, I am with you, now, always and forever … My greatest blessing in this life was having you and your brother as my family… I promise to stay with you… I won't pass on to the next place…the next life… not until I'm sure we can be together again… In the meantime, Jason-John, try to see the best in people. They're not all out to destroy you. And John-Marlowe, try to see the truth in them. They're not all living out a fairy tale for your amusement … Be kind to yourselves. And be kind to Nick-Ray. The future will not be kind to him, so you must make up for it … And take care with your Godmother… she will someday endure the most brutal of fates, one from which no one can save her… So, be good to her, she loves you both so … but don't let our chef give her chef my secret souffle recipe… Goodbye for now, my loves. I'll see you soon. The centuries, the millennia will fly by, I promise… Goodbye… I love you…I love you both so much … and remember, my souffle must remain in the family."

The red orb vanished just as the bubble of green broke in a loud pop.

The spirits were gone. The invisible veil had returned, putting everything back in place and neatly dividing the world of spirits and men once more.

"Boys! Boys!" Lana sped over to them the second the circle had snapped. "What happened?" she demanded, concerned by the sudden flood of tears on the twins' cheeks.

Instead of answering her, the twins threw themselves at Ivaan, embracing him tightly.

Lana watched in confusion and curiosity as her godsons wept on the Green King's shoulders.

176

They pulled away a short while later, wiping their tear-stained faces with their sleeves.

"Thank you, King Ivaan," sniffed Jason-John.

"You're welcome."

Once they had regained their composure, they turned to Lana. "Can we go play with the elephant now, Godmother?" said John-Marlowe.

With a baffled expression, Lana nodded. "Er…yes, I suppose so."

They Quartermaine boys made a run for it, only to stop mid-way through. They looked at one another and nodded sharply, as though they had collectively remembered something significant. Dashing back, they returned to Lana and clung to her waist.

"What's brought all this on?" Lana was still nonplussed.

"We couldn't save mama," started John-Marlowe.

"But we promise we'll try to save you someday, Godmother," finished Jason-John.

That remark certainly didn't help dissipate Lana's confusion. "Oh … er… thank you, dears." She patted them on their backs. "You boys run along and play… Go on now… Have fun."

Lana watched them sprint toward the fountain, removing their sherwanis as they drew near the water. "What did you give them, Ivaan?"

As an observer, all Lana had seen were the three of them inside a flashy green orb. There had been an unexpected chill, but apart from feeling a gust of cold air, she hadn't heard or seen any of the spirits they had encountered.

Ivaan came up beside her. "I couldn't give them what they wanted most in the world. So, I settled for giving them what they needed right now."

Lana gave him a sidelong glance. She knew what they wanted most: their mother back. Given the impossibility of such a resurrection, the second-best option had to be—

"Gold Queen Lana," Ivaan held out his arm for her to take, "Why don't we have a spot of tea?"

Chapter 14: Nebulas Drenched in Blood

Ivaan led her past the fountain and into a copse of evergreen trees. It was a short ten-minute walk until they surpassed all the foliage to find themselves on a large empty patch of grass near the edge of a cliff. There was a small, elegant table for two with desserts and a silver tea set laid out before them. A few feet away perched a stone fire pit. Much like the fire she had seen earlier, this one also appeared to be sentient. The flames kept changing form and shape, going back and forth from a griffin to a butterfly.

Beyond the precipice, was the view Lana had seen in her visions: a sea of massive tree-covered mountains.

Lana took a deep breath, soaking up the fresh air. "It's beautiful out here."

"In a month's time, all these mountains will be masked in powder."

The Green Kingdom usually ran hot, but the Ashram was located so far north, the area experienced all the seasons.

"That'll make it even more stunning." Lana kept her gaze on the view as Ivaan escorted her to a seat.

"There's another ashram further northwest, deep in the mountains." He seated himself across from her and pointed toward a specific patch of trees. "But I prefer this one."

"Why is that?"

"The other one is far too soundless and secluded for my liking. You've got monks as old as dinosaurs –   and I mean that somewhat literally – roaming about, taking lengthy vows of silence."

Lana was suddenly reminded of what Greta had told her. "*The best ones are the monks and yogis in the Green Kingdom,*" she had said. "*Way over in the mountains. Secluded in the Ashram. Without any means of physical communication. It would take me up to a month to get a letter over there by messenger.*"

That *other* ashram was the one Greta had spoken of. Most of the monks in that hermitage were considered the original mystics, valensmen who were born several millennia ago, long before the emergence of Chosen Kings. They weren't people who waited around to be *Divinely selected* at a *Divinely specific time* in their lives. They were people who had learned how to master the powers of manifestation and divination without the use of any energy beyond what they were provided at birth.

"Please, allow me." Ivaan moved to grab the teapot and fill her cup. The cups were already half-filled with tea leaves that were green and brown in colour and resembled knotted ropes. "I don't believe you were served this the last time you came by, but I hope it's to your taste. It's a rock tea grown from these mountains. The leaves look like death, I know, but out of all the teas in the world, this one has the longest-lasting taste. It lingers longer and stronger than a flask of whiskey."

"I'm sure it'll be delightful." Lana watched as the tea began to brew, the clear hot liquid transforming into a bright orange-yellow colour.

"Do help yourself to some sweets as well," he nodded over to the tray of rectangle-shaped desserts. Half the bars were dyed with green food colouring while the others remained in their natural golden hue. There was also a small plate of pistachio kulfis that were charged with Ivaan's energy to keep them from melting too quickly under the sun.

"Oh, I do love all the cuisine and desserts you have in your Kingdom. Every dish looks exquisite, and tastes so flavourful and healthy. I swear, back home, everything is drenched with butter. It's a mercy the rate of heart-attacks among Goldizens hasn't skyrocketed… What are these bars made of?"

Ivaan shot her an amused look as he poured himself a cup of tea. "Mostly butter and ghee."

"Ghee?"

"More butter. Well, it's clarified butter, but still…butter."

They took their time, enjoying the tea, the refreshments, and the view. Eventually, Lana found her eyes straying from the scenery and toward Ivaan's profile. The twins weren't wrong. He did look a bit like Lucien with his perfectly high cheekbones, strong jawline, broad shoulders and lean physique. Being out here with him evoked memories of the early days of her and Lucien's courtship – back when her husband had taken her to his favourite nature spots. She had assumed he was taking her to those spots for one significant purpose: sex. Instead, he had taken her there only to romance and regale her with his pathetic poetry. When Lana had suggested they get to *know* one another, Lucien had shot her down immediately, claiming that he knew Lana was destined to be his wife someday and wouldn't dare disrespect her with something as uncouth and unsanitary as intercourse. Lana had sighed in dismay. She'd been a maiden back then and had so desperately wanted to be disrespected.

Lana blinked and looked away before Ivaan could catch her staring. The reality of it was that he wasn't Lucien, and this wasn't a date nor was it a social call. She'd have to ruin the moment with official business, soon enough.

"I must say, King Ivaan, I hadn't expected you to be attired in such familiar fashions."

Ivaan's well-tailored jacket-and-cravat ensemble was more common in the Gold, Grey, and Red Kingdoms, but not often seen among the Green, Blue, and Indigo realms, where the attire was a little more shapeless and relaxed.

"Out of habit, I'm afraid. I had grown so accustomed to the wardrobe in the Red Kingdom that by the time I returned here, I found myself having difficulty re-acclimating – sartorially speaking at least."

Lana nodded. "You served as the Green Ambassador to the Red Kingdom for quite some time."

"Only a half a century, give or take," shrugged Ivaan. "A mere spec in time for a valensman."

"Even so, for a young valensman such as yourself, it must have been a life-changing experience… so much so that you've brought a bit of it back with you." Lana gestured to the firepit behind him. She had noticed it before as well: the flames didn't have the orange and yellow hues that came with natural fire. Rather, the flames' shade was a cross between ruby and garnet, which was the foundation and trademark of the Red King's energy.

Having perfectly understood what she was indicating, Ivaan didn't bother looking back. "When I was Chosen two years ago, all the other Kings – well, most of them, anyhow – welcomed me into the Divine fold with gifts. The Blue King provided me with a supply of water charged with his energy for healing and self-purification. As you've seen, I've used it for the fountain."

"That was most generous of him."

"Yes, it was," he agreed solemnly. "I protested at first. Told him it wasn't necessary. But he insisted." Like everyone else, Ivaan knew that the Blue King reduced his own lifespan every time he used his Divine energy. And yet, the calling of an imminent death never stopped King Idris from exercising his powers as he saw fit.

"And what did my husband give you?"

"A hundred bars of his handmade gold."

"Such a rare peace offering from Lucien," lied Lana. She knew it was Lucien's standard gift for nearly every special occasion with foreign dignitaries, both in- and off-planet.

"Is it?" Ivaan smiled wryly. "I hear he hands them out like dinner invitations."

"Nonsense! He'd never do that. It would devalue the price of gold," smirked Lana. "And… the fire was a gift from the Red King, I take it?"

"Yes," he replied after a beat of silence, "I suppose it's meant to be a memento of my time in his realm."

"Do you miss it very much?" *Do you miss him very much*, was what she had really wanted to ask.

"No." And then, after another heartbeat of silence, added, "No, I don't miss it at all."

Lana gave him a soft sympathetic smile. "Would have been more believable if you hadn't repeated the *no* in such a tone."

"I didn't have a tone," he denied.

"Oh, there was definitely a tone."

Ivaan chuckled, a little bitterly. "I suppose there's some irony to it," he sighed. "When I was there, I was constantly homesick, and now that I'm back home, I'm… I'm…"

"Lovesick?"

"You speak without mercy as well," he said with a small laugh. "It must be a Golden trait."

Lana leaned forward in her seat a little. "If you'll allow me, I'm going to say something because I feel an impulsive, dire urge to say it."

"I hear it's dangerous to resist an impulse. So, if you must…"

"I'm not one to pry into other people's personal relationships—"

"But you're going to do it anyway."

"—well… yes, but only briefly. I shan't go on at length."

Ivaan reluctantly nodded.

"As I was saying, I'm *usually* not one to pry, but I know how close you and Caleb were and speaking as someone who has a few more centuries of life experience than you—"

"But I thought you were well past your First Millennia of life?"

Lana frowned. "Are you going to keep interrupting with inconsequential quips? And in *that tone*, no less?"

"Apologies." Ivaan held up a hand for mercy. "You don't look a day past your Third Century, truly … Please, do go on."

"All this to say," she waited a second to ensure he wouldn't interrupt, "To be so very young and in love with another soul who reciprocates that feeling in equal measure is the most exquisite sensation in the universe… and not something to be taken for granted."

Ivaan shook his head. "I'm afraid the situation is far more complex when both parties are—"

"Are men?"

"—when both parties are Kings," he finished with finality.

Neither Caleb nor Ivaan were worried about any archaic laws against sodomy. They were Chosen Kings and absolute monarchs. They could easily break and make the laws in their respective nations whenever they pleased. But because they were Kings, there were other blockages in their path.

"Two Kings can never be together," he went on, "There's always destined to be a clash of crowns and egos." Letting out a deep exhale, he said, "Anyhow, I'm sure you didn't come all this way to discuss my love life, or lack thereof… nor do I believe you're here solely to entertain your godsons."

Lana straightened up in her seat. It was time to get on to business. "But it's true, I did want them to see this place. They've never strayed a step out of Golden soil until today. And it's a little treat for myself as well. Much time has passed since I've visited the Green Kingdom." Turning to the scenery, she said, "Such a beautiful nation, full of colour and life… and with such a *unique* history. Until you came along, it was run by a democratic government, wasn't it? As I recall your predecessor, the last Green King, departed over five centuries ago… It's highly unusual for a Kingless realm to remain unoccupied for so long." Her silver eyes darted sharply back to him. "Why do you think that was?"

"I wouldn't know." Ivaan's posture was stiff, and his tone was now all businesslike. "No one knows for sure. It's one of those great unsolved mysteries of our world."

"Indeed. It's as though there was a seal of divine protection around this Kingdom, preventing any foreign monarchs from conquering it. Quite the phenomenon."

"Quite," he agreed severely.

"And how are you coping with your newfound powers, Ivaan?" When Ivaan didn't respond, she surged on, "The first few years into Kinghood are always the most difficult. I remember how Lucien struggled with the Golden energy in his early days."

"Well, that was to be expected. The Golden energy, from what I've heard and seen, is far more demanding and unforgiving. By contrast, my Green energy is on the opposite side of the spectrum."

Lana narrowed her eyes. "That may be true, but there's still a King's Conversion process to consider."

The Conversion occurred whenever the Divine energy of a Totem established a symbiosis with a Chosen King's body. The entire process took nearly a decade to reach completion. Whenever a Totem penetrated the vessel of its appointed King, it placed a massive star of unlimited power within that body. Power that could ultimately be too much for the mortal form to control. It was why the first few years of Kinghood were particularly painful for a monarch. The Conversion was a time where a King had to learn how to properly control their newfound powers all the while coping with chronic pain day-in and day-out. If a King couldn't complete their Conversion, they would have to endure the same inevitable fate of all stars: a complete supernova in which they'd explode in a brilliant burst of light.

"Regardless of whatever *personality* your Totem carries, it stands to reason, there's a destructive star inside you now, Ivaan. Maintaining it requires a great deal of time and focus… along with an unbearable amount of pain."

"We're all stars beneath flesh and bone," said Ivaan, rather dismissively. "Even our brains resemble nebulas drenched in blood."

Lana frowned. She could tell he was trying to divert her attention away from the subject at hand. "It's different for Kings, as you well know, and your Conversion—"

"I'm sorry, Queen Lana, but it's highly inappropriate for me to discuss the details of my Conversion with you."

"Why? Because I'm a woman?"

"Because you're not a King," he clarified. "With all due respect, these are subject matters that are meant for deliberation among Kings, and *only* among Kings."

"Ugh, so typical of you Kings, with all the cloak-and-dagger around your powers." Lana rolled her eyes. "It's most unnecessary, just like that ridiculous little society you're all setting up."

Ivaan's mouth opened and closed a few times, fishlike, before settling into a thin-lipped frown of suspicion. "How do you know about that?"

"Lucien told me."

The Gold Queen had said it with enough conviction in her voice, but the Green King didn't believe her. Now that Ivaan was among the Chosen, he knew how Kings operated. They always kept the true extent of their powers to themselves. They didn't go about publishing papers on the exact mechanisms behind their abilities, and for good reason.

"Your husband strikes me as a man whose secrets have secrets. I doubt he'd share them with anyone so freely."

"I'm not anyone," said Lana tersely. "I'm his wife."

"As if that matters." Ivaan huffed out a small snort. "Kings tend to love their Queens the most and trust them the least."

Lana stared at him with well-contained fury. It was funny how quickly his charismatic allure could convert into casual cruelty. Just like Lucien. "It appears you're capable of speaking without mercy as well. Perhaps it's not an attribute exclusive to the Golden realm."

"I'm sorry." Ivaan appeared ashamed after having made such a remark. "Forgive me, Lana. That was insensitive."

"Yes, it was," Lana said with a steely edge to her voice. "As a Queen, I may be more ornamental than functional in the eyes of the world. I may not be privy to all the great secrets of the universe the way Kings are, but I've lived and endured beside one long enough to know how things work… You hide it beautifully, King Ivaan, but all that power stored in your body must be eating away at you. Lucien had me to help him through such a challenging time. Who do you have?"

Ivaan didn't answer her. He remained seated and silent, jaw grimly set.

It was a harsh question that didn't need to be asked because she already knew the answer. Ivaan didn't have anyone. No remaining family. No emotional attachments except to a man who was too busy ruling his own Kingdom on the other side of the world.

"I promise, I'm getting to a point. But before I can do that, I need you to tell me, in earnest, have there been any complications on your end?"

Ivaan kept quiet for a few seconds.

Then, slowly, softly, he confessed, "I'll admit, it is a physical adjustment. My body is still in the process of adapting to the power within. However, it's highly unlikely my powers could unleash something as lethal as another Golden Bang."

"No, I fear your powers have gone beyond that and done something significantly worse," she said portentously.

When Lucien released the Golden Bang, he had done so inadvertently, and created a seismic shift that visibly altered their atlas forever. Ivaan, however, appeared to have generated a much more fatal shift – one so subtle and formidable that no one had even noticed it had happened.

Ivaan waited for her to expand and explain. When she didn't, he sighed, "I don't understand where you're going with any of this, Lana, or why you've come to see me."

Lana wasn't sure whether to believe him. She couldn't tell whether he was lying or not. The trouble was, he really did remind her of Lucien, with his effortless confidence and sharp features. She wondered if Ivaan was also as morally ambiguous as her husband was. Lucien always preferred to be an honest man, but he was more than capable of playing the beautiful liar when the situation called for it. Her intuition was telling her that Ivaan was cut from the same pretentious cloth.

When Lana continued to remain silent, Ivaan pressed, "Does King Lucien know you're here?"

A rush of wind came between them, sending their hair flying and leaving the silverware chattering.

"He's travelling," she said simply.

"Where?"

"You tell me."

Ivaan no longer bothered to hide his confusion. "How should I know?"

Lana cut her eyes at him. "This nation has remained Kingless for so long that I nearly forgot your predecessor, Ivaan… but I remember him quite clearly now. Did you know he had a natural gift for entering altered states of consciousness and travelling across different realms of existence? Those powers magnified exponentially after he was Chosen. As a King, he behaved much like a phantom without borders, crossing through terrestrial, astral and spiritual lines as he pleased. However, unlike his successor, he was never powerful enough to trap anyone within those celestial borders."

Ivaan frowned. Lana could see something, a notion, sliding into place inside his head.

"Are you implying King Lucien is confined… in a non-physical realm?" Tilting his head to one side, he added, "And that I'm the one who placed him there?"

"Let's not be completely ingenuous. You know exactly what has happened." Lana stared him down. "What I don't understand is *why*? Why would you do this?"

"Lana, I assure you, until this moment, I was not aware of the Gold King's … *whereabouts*. And I most certainly did not entrap him. I now carry my predecessor's Divine energy, but I don't possess the exact same skill set he once had – I'm not even a spiritual traveler for goodness sake!"

"Perhaps you didn't do any of this intentionally, but it was still you, King Ivaan. I know it! I've *seen* it!" Lana snapped, slamming a dainty hand against the table. "So, I repeat: why would you do this?"

"I hadn't even realized I was doing anything!" Ivaan shot back with equal parts irritation and confusion.

"Hadn't you? Surely, Lucien's current predicament isn't the only abnormality that's occurred recently. There have been changes on your end too, I suspect."

Ivaan leaned back in his chair and rubbed a hand along his face. "I don't know what happened, truly," he confessed, his tone and posture now laced with disquietude. "It started a couple days ago, I think. I simply went to sleep one night, and when I woke up, the world was slightly… different."

"How so?"

"There've been minor changes," he said, before correcting himself, "*Comparatively* minor, depending on your perspective. Certain plants and animals that were previously extinct have miraculously returned. Certain people now have different titles, different professions, while certain others … are no longer present."

"You mean they're now dead?"

"No, not dead, per se," Ivaan scratched the back of his neck. He suddenly looked very uncomfortable. "Rather … they never existed to begin with. And no one seems to have any recollection of them. No one, but me."

Lana sank back into her seat, shocked. "And you call that a minor impact?"

"Well… as I said, it's all a matter of perspective, really."

"My gods, Ivaan! Exactly how many people have you erased from the face of the earth?"

"I have no way of knowing," he responded tersely. "I'm not acquainted with every single being wandering the planet and roaming the universe."

Lana was ready to clobber him, verbally and physically. But a thought struck her like a silver dagger between the eyes, freezing her in place. It was a seed of a concept. One that a phantom had planted inside her head the other night. "*Think of it this way: it boils down to what we say about ourselves and to ourselves every night before falling asleep… Tell me, what do you say about yourself, to yourself, before you retire for the night?*"

"You said you fell asleep and woke up to a different world." Lana locked eyes with him. "What did you do before you went to bed that night?"

"Nothing out of the ordinary." Ivaan found the question rather odd. "I was supposed to attend a fire puja with the monks and then head off to a festival at the capitol, but the Green Totem had taken a lot out of me that day. I felt like my body was being sheared apart by pressure from two opposite directions. Everything hurt—" He stopped for a second as if to remind himself to omit the details. A King's Conversion was meant to be a private process, after all. "Anyhow, I decided to forego all the formalities of the night and headed straight to bed."

"What did you *tell* yourself before you went to sleep?"

"Tell myself? Lana, I've been patient throughout this unusual line of questioning, but —"

"I know how strange this sounds, but please, indulge me with this, Ivaan. I know I'm not a King nor am I particularly masterful with the King's Gift, but I have studied and dabbled in many forms of mysticism my entire life. If you answer me with veracity, I may be able to help you undo… whatever it is you weren't aware you were doing to begin with."

Ivaan observed Lana with skepticism. He liked her well enough, but he didn't fully trust her. He suspected the feeling was mutual. Nonetheless, he didn't know who else he could turn to right now.

With a long sigh, Ivaan tossed his head back over to the mountains. Gazing into the green landscape, he tried to pull up the details of everything that had transpired in his reality six nights prior.

"I'm not sure I told myself anything before going to bed," he said thoughtfully. "But I remember I thought to myself, just as I was about to drop into a slumber… I thought to myself, I never asked to be a King. I never held a desire to be Chosen. But when the opportunity presented itself, when my Totem appeared before me as an irradiated green butterfly, I knew I couldn't refuse. I readily accepted all the terms and conditions that came with

Kinghood. And yet that night… I was so tired, there was an engine of pain running across me and I yearned to be somewhere else, doing something else… and I thought, how many others share my sentiments? I meet them all the time, not here, but in other ashrams open to the public. They always show up on weekends, always grateful for the weekend break because they despise all the other days of their lives. It's depressing when you think about it, all these people, only living for two days out of every seven and detesting a great fraction of their life span. They're all out there wishing their current circumstances could magically change. So, I thought to myself, how wonderful would it be if everyone could be exactly where they wanted to be, doing exactly what they wanted to be doing with their lives… the last thing I remember was carrying that thought with me right into my dreams."

Ivaan's eyes steered back to Lana, who was watching him with a somber, pensive look.

Considering her next words carefully, she said, "It sounds like you were using your powers while you were falling asleep… perhaps, you were even using them in your sleep."

"But that's not possible… is it?" Ivaan straightened in his chair, suddenly spellbound by Lana's theory. "I mean, using Divine energy requires intense focus and concentration. Two things that do not come easily or naturally to us in the dream state."

Lana blinked at him. The phantom inside her head returned with a cruel laugh. "*I've always believed that all things were possible to me. I told myself that if six billion people have to simultaneously drop and kneel in order for me to get everything and anything I want, then by God, they will kneel… Mind you, I've held these thoughts and beliefs since I was a child. So, I suppose I hold an unfair advantage. It's always easier to believe in all the possibilities of the impossible when you're a bright young thing, isn't it?*"

Sometimes, it was easier to make dreams come true when you're young… because it was easier to believe in the impossible when you're young. That's precisely what Ivaan was: a young valensman and a young King.

"Have you tried to undo it?" Lana had no current interest in diving into the limitless capabilities of a King's power. All she wanted was everything back to status quo: namely, having Lucien up and alive. She wasn't particularly bothered by any of the other changes. She didn't concern herself with any previously existing entity that might've been hastily erased.

"In order to undo it, I have to know exactly what I did to begin with," said Ivaan reflectively. "Like I said, all I remember was being in a state of drowsiness and having a few thoughts here and there. I don't ever recall using my Green energy in my sleep."

Lana looked askance at that remark. Did the man not realize the sheer power knotted within a *few thoughts*? In the old days, and even now in modern times, both the most amateur and the most competent of witches could take a few thoughts and transform them into the direst of spells and hexes. Looking back, it suddenly occurred to her: this had been Lucien's predominant method of manifestation, long before he turned King. Granted, he had never run about naked under the moonlight, chanting spells, but Lucien always got his way, every damn time, simply because *he told himself he could.*

"I'm not sure there's a way for me to reverse everything that's transpired."

"You must find a way!" she shouted, dropping her ladylike manners and slamming both palms down on the table. "You have to undo this, immediately!"

"Lana—"

"I'm not asking." Lana gritted out. "This isn't a polite request from an old friend that you can freely decline. This is an irrefutable demand from the Gold Queen. We've been allies since you came into your Kinghood, Ivaan, and I'd like us to remain on such amenable terms. But that isn't likely to happen if my Husband-King's soul is out there, liaising with angels."

"I can sense the Golden energy within you, and all around you," Ivaan drifted his eyes across her frame, which was now irradiating with Golden fury. "Which means Lucien's body must still be alive and unimpaired."

191

"Of course it is," Lana admitted. "It's heavily protected at the moment," she added, in case the Green King tried anything untoward.

"And he hasn't woken up?"

"Not in the last five days."

"Fascinating," Ivaan mused with a studious look. Staring out at the scenery, he took a deep breath, granting himself a moment of hesitation. Returning to Lana, he said, "I have a postulation, a theory of sorts."

"What is it?"

"Have you considered the possibility that he doesn't want to return?"

"What?" Lana bit out, gnashing her teeth.

Ivaan felt the need to bring his palms up a peaceful gesture – one that requested grace and mercy, especially since Lana now very much resembled a swan ready to attack. "Please, let me explain," he said, "I know Lucien's not where he needs to be at the moment. But perhaps, I sent him exactly where he wants to be."

"No one knows Lucien better than me, and I know the only thing he wants is to come home to me."

"I'm certainly not as familiar with King Lucien as you are—"

"I should hope not."

"— but from my encounters with him, he always struck me as a man seeking enlightenment. He wishes to experience enlightenment because he's already experienced achievement everywhere else. He probably does want to go back home, but that home doesn't necessarily equate to his Kingdom. He wants to return to his real home and become one with his true source – *God* as he would call it."

"True, he is a devout man," acknowledged Lana, "But he wants to be *here*, I know it. His life's purpose is to create Heaven on Earth, he's always said."

"He's already done that. He's already experienced Heaven on Earth. He's created a great nation, a formidable empire, a momentous castle. And he's enjoyed an all-consuming romance and a long-lasting love worth emulating," Ivaan gestured a hand over to her, "He's lived and thrived for millennia in all matters of life: family, career, artistry, love… What else is left for him here?"

Lana's gaze bore into him. For a brief moment, Ivaan was grateful Lana wasn't dexterous with the Golden Gift. Otherwise, he was sure she would've used her eyes to blast a Golden laser beam right through him like an enraged cyclops.

The Gold Queen tried to calm herself by absorbing the beauty of the mountains. When her heartrate dropped back to normal, she faced Ivaan. Calmly, quietly, she said, "Anyone meeting you for the first time, Ivaan, would think you were wise beyond your centuries. I had thought so too. But now, I can clearly see your youth – it's so painfully obvious and it looks profoundly tacky on such a pretty face. That's right, it's *tacky* for a Chosen King to dwell in such an ignorant state of mind. How little you know about life, and about your own Divine purpose. Out of all the Kings, the Green energy under your proprietorship is meant to have the strongest connection to the Earth, and yet you know nothing about it."

Ivaan opened his mouth to contest, but Lana immediately shot a hand up for silence. "I'm still speaking," she said tersely. "Let me share my postulations with you, Ivaan. You're so gifted when it comes to seeing spirits and interacting with them, that you neglect the mortal experience taking place right in front of you… You can feel the endless love that spirits carry for those they left behind, how much they miss them, and yet you were so quick to walk away from the only great love you've ever known, thus far."

The Green King kept quiet, his face had turned cold, and his dark eyes were now somber.

Lana sighed. "I confess, I can not see spirits or speak to them as easily as you do, but I can sense their presence, and I know far more about them than you ever will. Out of all the realms of existence, why do you think so many spirits – billions of them in fact – choose to linger here in the physical world? Why do you think so many of them refuse to pass on? It's because they can't properly experience things beyond the veil. It's only here that we can feel and enjoy everything – food, art, power, wealth, beauty, friendship, hatred and love… Lucien might have his head in the clouds half the time, but I assure you he's very much grounded for the other half. He treasures every moment of his life because he knows every heartbeat is more valuable than all the bars of gold in the universe. He understands that what we have here is so rare and precious even our spiritual superiors covet it. And he recognizes what it means to be a valensman. It means you need to find reasons to get up every morning for centuries and millennia on end. You don't drop all sense of perseverance and call it quits because you've *been there and done that*. Your soul chose to become a valensman because it wanted to keep going, longer and stronger than most. It wanted to experience everything in this world, watch it all change drastically, and experience it all over again in a million different ways."

By the end of it, Lana was tired. She plunged back into her chair with a long exhale. It was out-of-character for her to run her mouth off into a monologue. It appeared that after all this time, her husband's bad habits had finally rubbed off on her. *Bastard*, she thought fondly.

The Green King didn't say anything for a long while. For the first time since Lana had met Ivaan, his face was entirely unreadable. It was impossible to tell what he was thinking.

When he finally spoke, it was with a tone that was practically robotic. "You speak with undeniable wisdom, Queen Lana. I must say, I don't think I've ever had someone berate my soul as thoroughly as you just have… I can only imagine how harrowing these past few days have been for you. Being in a husbandless, Kingless state is undoubtedly a great cross to bear for a woman and a Queen. I appreciate the agony you've endured, and I extend my deepest apologies for being the cause of it. I promise you it was unconsciously done."

Lana was anticipating a bit more than an official, backhanded apology like that.

When it became apparent he wasn't going to offer anything else, she leaned forward with an appalled expression. She had expected more from him. She had expected better from him. "Is that all?" she demanded. "Is that all you have to say to me?"

"What else would you like me to say to you?" he said firmly.

"I would like you to tell me you're determined to bring my husband back! That you'll find a way to do so and persevere until the day he returns to vex the world with his priggish personality and atrocious poetry."

"Lana, I told you—"

"Don't tell me you can't do it. Don't tell *yourself* you can't do it," Lana exploded on him. "Start telling yourself you can find a solution until the solution magically appears. Get to work!" She pointed her index finger at him as though it were a wand that could force him to do her bidding. "I recommend you do this for your own benefit. You don't want to make an enemy out of me, King Ivaan. Husbandless and Kingless I may be at present, but I assure you, I'm not a woman to be trifled with. I'm not sworn to any spoken or unspoken oath of secrecy, and I hold no qualms with publicizing the full extent of your newfound abilities and what you've done to a most-beloved Golden monarch. It's sure be discussed and debated at great length, both among Kings and the public."

Ivaan's stony expression shattered into a glare. They both knew other Kings – or anyone else for that matter – wouldn't take kindly to the possibility that he could alter their entire reality on a whim. "I suggest you become more cautious with your words, Queen Lana," he said icily. "We've always been on pleasant terms, and I wish to preserve our alliance, but you're in no position to threaten me."

Technically, that was true. Like a chessboard, a Queen carried much power, but that power only existed as long as the King remained standing. Nevertheless, Lana was confident she still had the upper hand.

"Oh, I don't need to toss any threats your way, King Ivaan," she said darkly. "You will be the maker of your own undoing, I'm sure of it. For history has shown us, time and time again, *exactly* what happens to Chosen Kings who fail to control their own powers."

With that ominous observation, the Gold Queen stood up, signaling the end of their conversation.

Chapter 15: The Heart Works on Muscle Memory

"Truly, I don't know what I ever saw in you… Except for maybe the towering length of your body, those annoyingly attractive features, shoulders that could take up the wingspan of an eagle, more money than Hades, all the power of Zeus and then some … but apart from a few redeeming qualities, you were never marriage material, Lucien," she mumbled, running a long nail across her husband's smooth, sideburn-less face.

Lana waited politely for a response, taking a long sip of gooseberry wine – straight from the bottle – throughout the entire length of the pause.

Nothing.

The Gold Queen stared down at her husband's stationary body. She was in bed with him, hovering over his body with an entire bottle of liquid-dynamite on hand. It was where she had remained for the better part of Day 6. Nightfall was slowly creeping in. They were fast approaching Day 7, and there still wasn't a trace of movement from Lucien except for the steady rise and fall of his heartbeat.

"I should never have married you," Lana carried on whilst taking random pauses to consume more wine. "You're obnoxiously vain, stupidly oblivious at the best of times, horribly honest at the worst of them… You're stuffy. Your opinion of yourself is much too high. I could've done far better. … I could have!" She swore loudly as though Lucien had sprung to life and scoffed at her instead of remaining idle. "You think you were the only offer I had on the table? There were kings fighting over me, starting wars and uprisings for my hand! … Well, I mean, not *Kings*, but kings … you know the ones from before—oh, you know precisely what I mean! Don't even try to deny it!"

There was a huge difference between Chosen Kings with a capital K, the ones who were granted limitless supernatural power, and the powerless kings of ancient times, before 1027 AD, back when monarchs merely inherited their titles by birth and blood.

"Ugh, Luccieeeennnnn," she whined after taking another swig of wine, "This is no way for us to spend our anniversary! … Or the eve of our anniversary… Or is it the eve of the eve of our anniversary? Blast, I can't remember!"

Lana ran her free hand down his body. She suddenly wondered if *every* part of him would remain idle. Lucien was a marvelous sight of a man, to be sure, but he was still just a man. Aside from his brainwaves and his heartbeat, there had to be other significant parts of him that still ran on autopilot.

As her hand crept lower across his torso, she convinced herself she wasn't doing anything wrong. Lucien did give her permission to use his body to satisfy any carnal urges that arose in his absence. Even if he was unconscious, this was still consensual… moderately consensual.

"You don't have to worry about us," she whispered to him, "The children are fine. I'm fine," she lied, "I'm perfectly fine. I haven't been missing you at all."

"Clearly," came a deep voice from behind.

"MICHAELLL!!!!" The bottle went airborne, and Lana released the most undignified of squawks as she flew back like a clumsy swan.

Luckily for her, Michael's instincts were first class. Her eldest son managed to grab the bottle in the air with one hand. He wrapped his other hand around his Mother before she could reach the edge of the bed and hit the floor.

"Mother," he said in his usual cold, formal tone.

"I—I was just—"

"I can see what you were just," he said flatly.

"It's not how it seems!" She insisted even though it was entirely how it seemed.

"I'm sure."

"It's not! I was… I wasn't …. This is simply a matter of habit. Your Father and I have grown into a set routine over the centuries, you see —"

"I've seen enough. You needn't explain any further."

"—and really, this was nothing more than muscle memory at work," Lana blustered on, "The heart is a muscle after all and so are our gen—"

"Mother," Michael said gravely, "I don't need to hear this."

"Right." Lana sobered up a little as mortification smacked her across the face. Nevertheless, she was relieved it was only her eldest child. It could have been worse. Imagine the embarrassment had it been the twins bursting in on such a scene. Fortunately, the twins had already left her side an hour ago to go play in Lucien's labyrinth of gardens. That would certainly keep them occupied for a while.

"Don't worry, Godmother. We know you'll find a way to break Godfather's curse!" John-Marlowe had assured her after they had returned from the Green Kingdom.

"Hah!" Jason-John had shouted triumphantly. "So, you admit it, it's a cur—"

"A curse, which everyone knows is a blessing in disguise," John-Marlowe had said adamantly, quickly cutting off his brother before returning to Lana, "Maybe if you kissed him?"

Lana had smiled sadly and cupped the boy's sweet face. "I already tried, my little Q-tip. It didn't work."

"Try it again until it does work!" John-Marlowe stomped his foot with staunch determination. "Are you his One True Love or aren't you?" As he and his brother dashed off, she could hear him mutter in vexation, "Adults. They give up too easy."

She couldn't deny, her godson had a point. In some ways, a child's heart was so much stronger, so much more resilient. They kept crawling and falling until they could walk. They kept climbing the tallest tree, no matter how many scrapes they acquired along the way, until they reached the top. Adults, however, were more inclined to crack open a new case of gooseberry wine and drop into a dramatic drought of despair at the first sight of failure.

199

Lana rubbed her temple as the memory of her godsons faded off into a dark corner of her mind. She could already feel a headache forming. "I didn't hear you enter," she told Michael. "How can a boy your size move with such inaudibility? It's unnatural."

Michael gently brought her up onto a seated position in bed. "Even elephants can move in absolute silence."

"Can they, really? Huh, how fascinating." Blinking up at him, she asked, "What brought you here, my darling?" A wonderful thought suddenly occurred to her, and she laid her hands on his arms. "Oh, I bet I know. Did my first baby want his Mother to tuck him in? Hmm?"

"This baby of yours is in his Ninth Century of life," he said monotonously.

"Oh yes, I suppose you are." Lana visibly drooped. She had almost forgotten. Her boys still looked like teenagers. It made it difficult to remember their true valensmen ages, especially when she was smashed and under the influence. "It feels like only yesterday I was in my Ninth Century... and now look at me," she laid her head upon her son's chest and began to weep, "Well past my First Millennia and..." Her cries grew louder as she drunkenly reflected on her lost youth, "And I've been told I look like... like a 24-year-old! ... By primigenious standards, obviously."

She could feel Michael's large hand stiffly caress the crown of her head in comfort. If he was rolling his eyes heavenward, she couldn't see it, busy as she was soaking his jacket with her tears.

Sniffing, she blinked up at him. "You know, one can never grow too old to be coddled by one's Mother. Are you certain you wouldn't like me to tuck you in? It'll do us a world of good. It'll make me feel much better, I'm sure."

"Later, perhaps," he said, "I have a few more items on my agenda before I retire for the night."

"Well, at least have a drink with me before you dash," she said, unnecessarily straightening his cravat. "Now that you're over 21, you and I can finally share a drink together."

"I think you've had enough for tonight," he said, holding up the near-empty bottle.

"Ugh. Don't be a such a stickler," Lana rolled her eyes. "Go on and pour your dear Mother a stiffener!"

Michael focused on the bottle until it blazed up in a sheen of golden light. It took several minutes, during which time Michael's face looked rather constipated. Finally, with a mighty pop, the bottle disappeared.

Lana pouted when she realized he had used his Golden Gift to banish her bottle.

"I came here to fetch you," said Michael. "Gabe wants to have a family meeting to discuss—" He jutted his chin toward Lucien in lieu of finishing the sentence.

"Why now?"

"Because we're approaching Day 7."

"Yes, so we are," she said, her voice turning soft. If Lucien didn't wake up by tomorrow, they would need to come up with a strategy. Something to appease their subjects who would undoubtedly be inquiring after their King. She supposed Michael could serve as Regent for the time being, if needed.

"Given your current disposition, however, I think we should postpone until tomorrow."

"Yes, of course. Let us gather tomorrow morning. First thing."

"*Later* in the morning, I rather think." Michael swept his eyes over the room, scanning for more bottles. "Much later."

Lana rolled her eyes again. Did Michael truly think she was such a lightweight? Granted, as a woman of considerable rank, she didn't get much practice with the art of drinking outside of heavily chaperoned social occasions. But for someone with so little practice, she thought herself to be remarkably great at holding her liquor. And she wasn't nearly as drunk as Michael thought her to be – not tonight anyhow. She was only one bottle in at this point. She wouldn't start slurring and seeing ghosts until she was on her third bottle, at the very least.

When Michael remained in place, making no motion to leave, she inquired, "Was there something else?"

Michael stared at her. "Why did you visit King Ivaan?"

"I took the boys to the Green realm," she responded with a small laugh, "What makes you think I went to visit their King?"

Michael continued to stare down at her in silence, refusing to answer such a pointless question.

With a sigh, Lana confessed, "I thought he could be of some use to us."

Instead of diving for specific details, Michael merely asked, "Was he?"

"He carries a pleasant, sunny disposition that gives you the feeling he can be completely trusted." Lana shook her head bitterly. "But it's all frontage and facade."

"Much like Father."

"Indeed." Lana leaned forward to grab his arms once more. "Let that be a lesson to you, my darling boy. Should you ever fall in love with someone of a seemingly sunny disposition, I want you to remember this: the sun's sole purpose of existence is to burn everything to death."

"I'll bear that in mind," he said with disinterest. "Anything else I need to know?"

Lana bit her lip. She thought back to the moment she had stormed away from Ivaan, only to have him materialize in front of her in a whisp of Green energy.

"Lana, please wait," Ivaan held out a hand. "I don't wish for us to part with such hatred in our hearts. You're right, there may be a way for me to bring Lucien back," he'd said charily. "My powers make it easy for me to summon spirits. There's a chance I could summon his soul back into his body. But," he added quickly, sharply, before Lana could get her hopes up, "There's something I shall require in return."

Ivaan's conditions were that she make a pact – sealed with Divine energy – promising two things: (1) no harm would come to his realm after Lucien awoke and (2) neither Lucien nor anyone else would ever learn about the full extent of his abilities.

From Ivaan's perspective, the accord made sense. Lucien could be a very capricious, egotistical man. He wouldn't take kindly to finding out there was another King who could potentially get the better of him. But Lana remained uncertain and uneasy over the idea of signing a Divinely-sealed contract. She had left promptly after that, but not before telling Ivaaan that she would need time to think it over before reaching a decision.

Lana gazed up at Michael, misery and uncertainty in her eyes. He was still waiting for an answer. "Let's discuss it tomorrow," she told him. "I'm a touch too sloshed at the moment. I think I shall retire early to bed."

Michael could sense she was hiding something, but he did not press. "Very well, then," he said with a vacant look. "I bid you good night, Mother."

"Goodnight, my love."

He dropped a kiss on her forehead and left her bedroom and private chambers as silently as he had entered it.

Lana returned to her place in bed, beside Lucien. She placed her head above his heart and draped a lithe arm around him.

It was odd. She didn't have that much to drink – or so she thought – and yet she couldn't seem to keep her eyes open. She dropped off, an idyllic vision of the mountains appearing in her mind's eye. It lasted for a brief spell. And then the earth and the skies opened together, making way for an empty, black abyss that swallowed her whole and carried her away as though she were as light as a feather.

Chapter 16: The Anniversary Gift

Lana didn't know what she was doing here or how she came to be here. She was wearing a long white nightdress that came just short of her ankles. Still in her sleepwear, even though she was out in public… not that there seemed to be anyone from the public roaming the long, cold hallways.

It had been quite some time since she had visited this place. It was called the Goldsmith Museum. As one of the most popular exhibitions in the capital city of Halkyon, it was a massive tourist attraction.

Maybe it's closed, she thought to herself, *It must be late*. The corridor she was passing through was lined on one side with a row of large windows and bars of moonlight pouring in. The other side had open doors that led to rooms where temporary exhibits were being held. She glided by them, occasionally stopping to look at some of the plaque cards identifying each exhibit.

There was *Shakespeare: Celebrating His Fourth Century*. Lana nearly rolled her eyes. The Fourth Century was hardly a milestone birthday for a valensman. And was that bard still around? His poetry was nearly as bad as Lucien's, in her opinion. Not to mention he was a hack. He pretty much recycled everything from ancient Greek mythology and called it an *homage*.

Then there was *Centuries of the King's Gold*. An exhibit that tracked and showcased the evolution of Lucien's Divinely handmade golden bars since the beginning of his Kinghood. It came with interactive historical data on the price of gold over time, including inflation-adjusted numbers. Lana nearly yawned in boredom after reading the place card.

And there was the *Coronation of the First Gold King*. It was an oil painting Lucien had commissioned during his official coronation ceremony in 1030 AD. It depicted the very moment Lucien had placed a golden crown – one which he'd made himself – atop

Lana's head amidst a lavish ceremony. The painting was more than 30 feet wide. Its usual residence was in the Gilded Cage, but Lucien occasionally leant it out to museums across the realm. She remembered how the painter had originally called it the "Coronation of King Lucien" before quickly changing it to honour the place of the First Gold King in their nation's history.

Lana cracked a little smile. If only that painter knew then what they knew now. Here they were, centuries later, still under the reign of the same monarch. No Second King necessary… Her smile soured in a flash. It dawned on her that it might come to that should Lucien never return.

Turning sharply, she hurried down the corridor until she reached a pair of doors leading into a gigantic outdoor space complete with pristine marble flooring and lined with towering columns. It was a famous spot. Millions of visitors came and went through this area every year, but there was only one permanent entity that lived here and that was the 50-foot-tall golden statue of Lucien sitting on a throne and gazing out into the view of a lake, which was the size and shape of a football field. Not far behind the body of water, was the Senate House – the Glaring Chamber, as they called it.

Lana strode over to the statue. It was a very good likeness of the current state of her husband: beautiful, golden and unmoving. The only difference was this one had his eyes open. Hanging above the statue's head was a plaque bearing one of Lucien's (many) mottos: *In God and Gold we trust.*

Most people didn't know, but Lucien had built this statue for her as an anniversary gift a few centuries back. She hadn't understood how a statue of *him* could be considered a gift for her. With a toothy grin, his response had been, if she recalled correctly, "*It's for when you're missing me, you devastating creature! I know how much you love your nightly strolls. You try to hide it, but I always know. Now, whenever I'm away on business—*" Said 'business' meant he'd be off invading other planets. "*—you can swing by during nightfall and stagger back in admiration of your Husband-King. Feel free to gaze upon it at length. I already have and I can tell you from experience, just looking at it makes for countless hours of inner grace and tranquility… Well, what do you think?*"

"I—" Lana hadn't really known how to respond in a favorable light to such a gift, "I—I think it's…"

"So magnificent that I should have a replica inserted in our home for your convenience?" Lucien had finished for her. Putting an arm around her, he pulled her toward his chest and flashed another wide smile. "Already done."

"Some anniversary gift you were," Lana scowled up at the statue. "And let the record show, I'm not missing you at all. Why would I? You're always too demanding, too overbearing, too much of… everything. And me? I'm the fool who gave you everything in return. But it was never enough for you. I gave you my heart and you reciprocated by demanding my soul."

"Obviously," came the deep, familiar voice of her husband. "Hearts are ephemeral, but the soul… the soul is eternal. That's what we are, Lana. An entity for eternity."

Lana swung around. Lucien was there, bright, golden and fully conscious.

She ran to embrace him. She was dreaming, she had to be. He was another phantom, another ghost in her head. Another alcohol-induced hallucination. But she couldn't bring herself to care, especially when he felt so real and warm. She could feel his chest shaking in laughter.

"This is how you greet someone who you haven't missed in the slightest, is it?" He grinned, returning her embrace. "By hurling and thrusting yourself wantonly at them?"

"I'm still mad at you." Lana shifted away from his arms and gave him a light, harmless punch in the chest. "You swine! You promised you'd ring me back!"

"I tried!" Lucien said defensively. "It's not as if that telephone booth had a redial button or a call log containing our household digits. I was right back where I started, going through every Lana in every blessed and cursed reality in existence. Do you have any idea how many heartless women with your namesake are out there across time and space? The number of them that were uncaring of my woes. Not to mention all the ones who suggested I place the telephone receiver up my underdrawers. Mind you, I found them preferable to the ones who recommended I remove my drawers entirely and send them video evidence!" He gasped out in an appalled tone. "The way they carried on, puffing and panting on the line, you would think they'd never heard the voice of a desirable man in the whole of their lives! And don't get me started on my Golden Totem. The number of times I called out to it and still, it's been as silent as a sundial in the shade. Not that this is entirely unprecedented behaviour from my Totem, but in all these centuries of Divine symbiosis, it's never …."

Lana smiled as Lucien prattled on. She couldn't help it. This illusion of her husband didn't feel like a phantom ready to taunt her. This one was so similar to *her Lucien* with his prudish manners and his long-winded chatter. Her life had been so unpleasantly quiet these past few nights and now she remembered why. He hadn't been there to keep her up at night with all his frivolous musings.

"… You wouldn't believe the things I've seen and endured these past few—" He didn't know how to finish that sentence. Time was a man-made concept, one that didn't exist beyond the Physical Realm. "How long has it been? I can't tell if minutes or millennia have passed."

"We're approaching Day 7," Lana told him, "You need to come back to us, Lucien, and you—wait, what are you wearing?"

"Fancy it on me, do you?" Lucien preened, adjusting the cravat – if it could even be called that. It looked far too slim, like a piece of silky rope. "An entity I passed by along the way gave it to me. Called it a black suit-and-tie. Said it would be all the rage among men of my standing when it pushes out into the Physical Realm in a few centuries time. Naturally, I asked for the cravat—the *tie*, that is—to be in gold."

"Naturally." Lana nodded. She couldn't deny its appeal, especially on Lucien's body. "This was another… *Angel*, I take it?" She said, her voice laced with more than a little skepticism.

"Not sure. It had three goat-heads, which was rather disconcerting. But it couldn't have been—" He broke off, his eyes running down Lana's form. "Speaking of clothes, where are yours? Have you taken leave of your senses? Out here in broad…nightlight… in a state of undress?!" He hurried to remove his dark jacket. "My God, woman, you could drive a man to the brink of madness exposing yourself in such a manner!"

"I'm fully covered, Lucien," Lana rolled her eyes as he threw his jacket around her shoulders, drowning her in black silk and wool. It smelled so much like him, a blend of sandalwood and citrus.

"Not with those bare ankles, you aren't!" scowled Lucien, his eyes widening as they drifted lower. "And bare feet for that matter! Where are your shoes?"

"I—I'm not sure… I can't even tell you how I got here," she muttered, "I really must be dreaming."

"You and me both, I suspect." Placing one arm under her legs and the other on her back, he picked her up like a groom carrying his bride through the threshold for the first time. "Let us go then, you and I."

"You want to leave?"

Turning to her with a raised brow, he smiled, "Would you rather stay and ogle my likeness some more?"

This time, Lana didn't hesitate to place her arms around his neck. "Let's get out of here."

With all the naturalness of a bird of prey, Lucien flew off into the night with Lana in his arms.

As Lucien flew them over the capital, Lana began to question whether she was dreaming or not. Halkyon City looked exactly like it did in real life with its blend of gothic and classic architecture. Lana admired the view below as they swept past grand boulevards lined by large, elegant buildings with wrought iron details and griffin gargoyles perched atop rooftops.

She looked away for a moment to give her husband a sidelong glance. It was strange for Lana to see Lucien flying without his golden wings. Not that he needed them to fly. But he usually manifested them whenever he was airborne, namely for two reasons:

- It was a defensive maneuver as he could easily turn the wings from shining and beautiful to steely and bullet-proof (and laser-proof, nuclear-bomb-proof, etc.) whenever he pleased.
- He truly was a *flash bastard* – as the Red King liked to put it – and loved to show off whenever he pleased.

She could only assume he kept his wings to himself because they were all alone. Looking down at the empty capital, Lana couldn't spot another soul wandering around. It looked completely unoccupied. That would never have happened in real life. Not for a famous city like Halkyon.

Probably why he's not grandstanding like a peacock for once, Lana thought to herself. *There's no one around to see it.*

Raking a long fingernail down his left sideburn, she concluded she had to be dreaming. She had already shaved off his sideburns in the land of the living. It confirmed her suspicions that this Lucien was another delusion of hers. Yet, she still couldn't bring herself to care.

Meanwhile, Lucien continued to natter about everything he had witnessed in the Spiritual Realm. In doing so, he was completely oblivious of the way his wife was looking at him. Had he bothered to turn his head, he might've noticed Lana was staring at him the same way she did the first time they met – like he was the shiniest star in the universe, something completely unattainable, something she could only admire from afar. It made sense in a way. She was a witch and witches loved the darkness, because they were always looking for the brightest stars.

With a sigh, she tightened her arms around his neck and embraced him with more vigor.

"After I abandoned that blasted telephone, I forged ahead, and I tell you, Lana," said Lucien, "Beyond those invisible veils is an utterly chaotic system of everlasting peace, light and unity. I came across this one region – well, I call it a region for lack of a better word – where they had operating tables lined up like a war hospital and all these spirits were popping in to receive energy. Sounds pleasant, doesn't it? But it was all such a mess! There were spirits stacking up on top of one another like a dogpile. Absolutely no sense of organization. What's the point of having such harmony if it's all in shambles? And—Lana? Lana! Are you listening?"

"Mm-hmm."

"Don't fall asleep on me now."

"I'm already asleep," she mumbled. "This is a dream."

"Even so, it's discourteous to drift off during a dialogue. Now…where was I?" Lucien kept on. "Anyhow, for celestial beings that operate on a higher frequency, I must say they came across as clueless as newborn babes. I couldn't find a single entity to tell me where I was or conjure up a decent map for me. I told them they ought to visit my Golden realm and witness the interactive maps I ordered to have conveniently placed across all major cities. Rest assured, no one ever loses their way with me as their leader."

"Mm-hmm," yawned Lana. "And how did they respond?"

"I couldn't say … most of them flew off while I was mid-sentence."

"Mid-monologue, more likely," she muttered under her breath.

"One of them did provide me with a guide dog."

"Dog?" She hummed.

"Oh yes, a dark, massive thing with a face that looked like it was melting. I tried explaining that I held more of an affinity for cats and birds, but it didn't seem to care… It led me straight here, you know. So, I suppose it proved useful in the end. Mind, it disappeared on me the moment I spotted you and —Lana! Wake up!"

"Hmm?" Lana babbled, struggling to keep her eyelids up.

Lucien sighed. "Let's go a touch higher, shall we? Perhaps a gust of wind will perk your senses up."

The air grew colder as Lucien flew higher. It felt like a bucket of ice had dropped right over Lana's head. She was wide awake now. Wide awake inside her dream.

Lucien continued to go on at length at everything he had seen as he traveled through all the circles of Heaven.

"I came across a grand hall that contained the Akashic records," said Lucien, "Also dreadfully unorganized. Can you believe it? A complete compendium of every universal thought, event and emotion all throughout existence – all of which was arranged nonalphabetically…"

Lana tried to listen, but she found herself far too distracted with how high Lucien was flying. The clouds had parted for them. The city below now looked like a gigantic circuit board.

"Um, Lucien?"

"Then there was the Great Library of Alexandria. You know the one that burned down ages ago. Apparently, it was resurrected in the afterlife. I thought the Akashic records were muddled, but then I saw the state of this library…"

"Lucien," Lana latched onto him tightly. She no longer felt comfortable looking down. And she was pretty sure she was inhaling stardust.

"Oh, and I musn't forget this Kingdom I came across, residing and functioning under a purple ocean. I couldn't verify, but I'm fairly confident I saw Atlantis and—"

"Lucien!"

"What?"

"How high up are you taking us?!"

"We're only a touch over 10,000 feet," he replied calmly.

Lana stared at him. "Get us down," she said sharply. "Now!"

"Alright!" huffed Lucien. "No need to make a fuss."

On the way back down, Lana decided to commandeer the conversation. She had to. Otherwise, Lucien was likely to go off on another tangent.

As Lucien dived slowly toward the city, Lana told him everything that had occurred in the physical world while he'd been off on his spiritual sabbatical. *Nearly* everything, that was. She omitted a few key details, particularly her collaboration with the Anatolia siblings. Lucien heavily frowned upon the use of witchcraft in their lives, and she didn't want to hear another lengthy lecture about it. Instead, Lana told him she'd discovered his hidden book through his private secretary and subsequently learned more about the secret society he was forming with all the Kings.

By the time they approached their world's most famous cathedral, the Luce Domina, Lana had finished telling him about her meeting with King Ivaan – the only factor she'd left out was the pact the Green King had proposed. At first, she was reluctant to mention Ivaan's part in their predicament. But she quickly changed her mind, convincing herself it didn't matter. This wasn't the *real* Lucien, so what was the harm?

Reaching the balcony of the cathedral, Lucien gently set her down on the stone pavement – close to the balustrade, beside a row of grumpy griffin gargoyles – but not before manifesting a pair of pointy golden slides on her feet.

"I knew that young man couldn't be trusted," said Lucien as he zipped around to stand beside her. "Especially given his … *association*… with the Red King."

Lucien grimaced in disapproval. He hated even bringing up such a relationship on consecrated grounds.

"You know, he re…" Whatever it was Lana was trying to say, Lucien couldn't hear it.

Behind them, seven blessed 13-ton bells within the Luce's soaring tower began ringing in F sharp.

"What was that?" Lucien asked once the melody came to an end.

"I said, Ivaan reminds me of you in some ways."

"I'm nothing like him, Lana!" Lucien practically shouted, forever appalled. "How dare you compare!"

Lana laid her elbows on the railing and faced the beautiful view of the city. She tried to hide her smirk. Of course, the Gold King got a little green with jealousy whenever Ivaan was mentioned. Lucien wasn't accustomed to another tellurian King garnering so much attention. He was a man who was highly inexperienced with having such competition.

Even though their world had multiple monarchs, whenever people across the galaxy thought of the King of Earth, the vibrant and beautiful Gold King immediately came front and center in their minds. But no one had predicted that another Green King would emerge, not after so many centuries. And, much to Lucien's irritation, no one could've predicted that the new Green King would be so aesthetically well-made in form and features.

"I hope you haven't taken a liking to that boy, Lana," Lucien said snidely. "Not that such affection from the likes of you would have any impact on the likes of him. You don't have any of *the parts* he desires in a mate."

"Don't be unkind, Lucien."

"Me unkind?" Lucien brought a hand to his chest. "Need I remind you that he's the cause of all this!"

"It was an accident... I think," shrugged Lana. "Despite everything, I don't believe Ivaan meant any harm."

Lucien threw her a look of incredulity. "I may very well lose my Kingdom and for what? An accident of fate? Intwined destinies clashing?"

"Kingdoms have fallen for far less." They had both been alive long enough to see many realms collapse into ruin over the most ridiculous of reasons: a mistranslated memo between diplomats, a dispute over a slaughtered boar, a want of a good fucking...the list dragged on, really.

"Well, I refuse to have our Empire disintegrate simply because some young-upstart-fetus-of-a-King used one tiny braincell in his head to form a cataclysmic world-altering event," scoffed Lucien. "Fancy, having to explain this to our subjects. Or worse, having it displayed in history books for everyone and anyone to see. The shame of it all!"

Lana had to bite down on her lower lip to keep from laughing. She knew it wasn't really a laughing matter, but it always amused her how far Lucien would go to keep up appearances. The thought of losing their Kingdom didn't seem to hurt him as much as the thought of everyone knowing about it.

A silence came between them. They used the moment to stare out into the warm glow of monuments, buildings and streetlights. They had created all this together. They had taken it all from a pile of rocks and earth and transformed it to look like a golden palace of fairy tales. This was *theirs*. But for how much longer? Lana took a few deep breaths, willing herself to believe she could release all her anxiety and anguish with every exhale.

Sensing the change in his wife's mood, Lucien placed his hand over hers. "You needn't despair, my dear. I still have a plan."

"You do?" Lana turned to him, a hopeful glint in her silver eyes.

"Certainly!" Lucien nodded. "I'll be back in a jiffy. There isn't a doubt in my mind."

"How? What are you going to do?"

"Same thing I always do," he smiled at her. "I'm going to tell myself I can head back home with speed and ease."

Lana rolled her eyes until they rotated back over to the skyline. "Is that your solution to everything?" she said irritably. "You tell yourself you can?"

"Well… yes… that, and prayer," he said encouragingly. "Prayer is always the answer."

"Have you been praying to God for a solution out of this?"

"Of course I have! I've already said a millennia's worth of prayers since I've been here."

Lana lifted a brow, unimpressed. "And they've all gone unanswered, I take it? Just like all your calls and summons to your Totem?"

Displeased with his wife's pessimism, Lucien said in a stern voice, "I'm not one to waste energy on unrequited romances, Lana."

"What does that mean?"

214

"It means my prayers are a form of my affections, and my affections – whether they're from you, our subjects, my Totem, or God Himself – have never gone unrequited. It's only a matter of time – minutes really, a few days at the most – until destiny turns the wheels of fortune in my favour once again."

"Uh huh," said Lana, utterly unconvinced.

"Oh, buck up, my dear!" Lucien threw an arm around her shoulder. "You can't tell me you're not having a spot of fun with this."

"Fun?!" Lana shoved his arm off. "How is this fun for me?"

"We're the same, Lana. You deny it, but it's true," he winked at her, a flock of golden sparkles flew out of his eye and splashed her across the face before vanishing. "You love to sweep in and save the day as much as I do."

"I don't know how to save you from this, Lucien." That was a lie. She knew exactly what she needed to do – seal a Divine pact with the Green King – but she wasn't sure she wanted to do it. There had to be an easier way, a better way to bring Lucien back.

"I'm sure you'll think of something."

"Leaving it all to me, are you?"

Lucien gave her one of his camera-ready smiles. "A real-life King perched on a throne isn't so different to one standing tall on a chessboard. Both require a strong, powerful queen to come to their rescue whenever the situation turns dire."

"What is this? Are you trying to *charm* me? Please!" derided Lana. "Your charms have never work on me, and you know it."

Lucien's face nearly fell into a pout. "It worked in the beginning."

"Oh, not even!"

"We wouldn't be here if it hadn't worked," reasoned Lucien.

Lana slammed a hand against the rail. Her face became more ferocious-looking than the gargoyle behind her. "We are *here* because of you!" She shrieked, stabbing a bony finger to his chest. "You, and the ridiculous mess you always manage to get yourself into!"

"This is hardly my doing!"

"Nevertheless, this is something that could only have happened to someone like you because you're *you*." Lana walked away from him and began pacing across the long terrace. "Ever since we met, you've attracted such madness and brought it into our lives on the regular!" Looking heavenwards, she groaned out, "Ugggghhhh, why did I ever marry you?"

Lucien shrugged. He was still smiling, much to Lana's displeasure.

"It was the two big Is."

Lana pulled a face. "Two big eyes?"

"Inevitability and Ineffability. Powerful combination," said Lucien. "That's what we were from the very beginning."

Lana lifted her nose to the air. "Quit pouring on the charm. I'm immune to it, especially when it comes from you."

"Indeed, you are a difficult woman to please… but I do so love a challenge." Lucien lifted a finger to the air as a thought struck him. "Ah, before I forget, I left something inside my jacket." He gestured toward the black lounge coat Lana was still wearing. "Do you mind? It's within the jetted pocket."

Keeping her eyes on him, she fished into the inner pocket and pulled out a tiny glass bottle with white confetti inside. "What's this?"

Lucien's right palm shone gold and with a snap of his fingers, the tiny bottle converted into a large jar that Lana needed to hold with both hands. "*That* is for you, my dear. Happy Anniversary."

With confusion, Lana removed the lid and looked inside. There were over 1,000 tiny strings of paper inside jumbled together.

"I hope you like it. I did exert a fair amount of thought and time into it." Lucien reverted his gaze toward the city, turning his back to her. "Though, I had nothing but time on my hands, really. Not that time exists here, or over there, which is where I was before I was here. It's funny when we think about our concept of time and the illusion of it in the realms of higher frequencies. I always knew time isn't linear, but I've found that, perhaps, it's circular and overlapping in our system of reality – or realities, I should say – and what's fascinating is that it's being held together by a sphere that's connected to the infinite intelligence that is God…"

While Lucien prated on, Lana busied herself with the contents of the jar. Every slip of paper appeared to have writing on it. It wasn't written by hand, but it was printed in a familiar dark antique golden font, which Lana recognized as the same print from Lucien's transcripts. This meant Lucien had used his Divine energy to jot down everything on these slips.

"You see, Lana, we're all drifting in a continuous motion of experience in order to witness our own self-transformation and evolution throughout life…"

Lana ignored her husband's ramblings and began reading every slip, one by one:

- Under the sunlight, your eyes look like the colour of starlight.
- You can easily make up rhymes and songs about anything and everything.
- Whenever you can't tamper down your temper, a piece of hair at the very top of your head will slowly start to shift upwards like the moon moving across the sky.
- You always roll over and embrace me in your sleep, and always with your hands slipping beneath my nightshirt, even on nights when you retire to bed in anger.
- Polished as a swan in public, and uncontrollable as a phoenix in the bedroom.
- The laugh you make around me. It's different from the way you laugh around everyone else.
- The smiles you offer me. They're different from the way you smile at everyone else.
- Your pupils still widen every time you see me naked.
- You try to stay awake during my poetry readings.
- You could drive anyone mad looking so attractive all the time.

- The colours of your aura. You can't see it, but I can. There's an entire galaxy of black, white and silver orbiting you.
- You're light and darkness in equal measure. A combination of compassion and cruelty. Such a fusion makes for the perfect Queen.
- No one in the universe knows me better…

It went on for ages. Lana didn't understand straight away. She should have, but she didn't. It wasn't until she was more than three-quarters through the entire jar that she realized: this was a list of everything Lucien loved about her.

"… It's rather amusing really. Physically, we reside in a universe that holds a specific form, which in return holds a central basis in time. As I said previously, time is what we use to measure our evolution throughout life," said Lucien, "But now that I've encountered these non-physical realms, I can claim with certainty that time doesn't exist – well, not out here, where we're in a state of constant eternal stillness. All this to say, time is indeed an illusion, but in the physical realm, we must respect the illusion because our senses and bodies perceive it as real. Isn't that the kicker? And if—oof!"

Lucien came to an abrupt stop as a pair of arms embraced him, suddenly and fiercely, from behind.

"Still as clingy as an octopus in heat, I see," Lucien said with an amused grin as Lana clasped her hands securely around his slim waist.

Pressing her cheek into his back, she mumbled, "Male octopuses die after mating, you know."

"Do they really? How unfortunate… and uncouth… Then again, sexual cannibalism is all the rage in the animal kingdom. I suspect the female consumes its mate after copulation?"

She tightened her hold on him. "I don't think it works that way…not for octopuses, at least."

"Putting all mollusks aside, might I ask, what's brought on this precipitous display of affection?"

"I liked your anniversary gift," she admitted. "A considerable improvement from last year."

The previous year, he'd presented her with one of his epic poems. With more than 300,000 individual verse lines and long prose passages, Lana hadn't made it past the first ten stanzas without flaking out. When Lucien had asked for her critique, she'd smiled, nodded and recounted a line or two that she had miraculously managed to remember. "*That part about how 'once a bond is established, it echoes throughout eternity' – that was my favourite bit, dear*," she had told him.

She planted a small kiss on his back. "I must say, I like this version of you much more than the other one." Smudging her cheek against his back once more, she said, "You're so much warmer. Sweeter."

"What *other one*??" said Lucien, suspicion creeping into his voice.

"You know."

"No. I don't," he said tightly.

"Yes, you do. Remember? The night I got sloshed and you got into my head and revealed all those little details about a King's energy and how it all works."

"I haven't the faintest idea what you're talking about." Lucien removed her hands from his frame and turned around with a deep frown on his face. "What do you mean by *sloshed*? Lana, I hope you weren't imbibing wine unchaperoned. *Again*."

"Well…"

"Lana! Tell me you didn't have more than three sips."

"I can honestly say I didn't have three sips." The truth: she had consumed three bottles.

Lucien narrowed his eyes. "And who the devil were you talking to in regard to the King's energy?"

Lana stared at him, assessing the look of confusion and chariness on her husband's handsome face. It dawned on her that the phantom she'd seen a few nights prior had been a mere projection of her own subconscious taunting her with big little truths. Details sowed deep into her mind. Things she already knew but had left forgotten inside of her for far too long. The phantom-Lucien had drudged it all back up to the surface of her consciousness.

This Lucien before her, however, wasn't a phantom nor a fantasy. He was—

"Lucien! Is that really you?" She fisted her hands around his shirt and began tugging at it, almost wildly.

"Of course it's me! I should hope you don't make a habit of hurling and latching yourself onto other men with such ferocity, Lana."

"You said a dog brought you here," she remembered. An image of a large black canine flew into her mind's eye.

"Yes. It's gone now. Vanished like a ghost the second you showed up."

A burst of unseen energy shot through her, heavy and acute, much like it did that night she spoke to Hekate, and Lana knew without a doubt that a higher power had intervened. Her Divine Mother had done as she had requested and brought Lucien back to her.

"Lucien! It's you! It's been you this whole time. But… is this your dream or mine?"

"I'm not sure." Lucien continued to give her a dubious stare. He didn't know what to make of his wife's odd little outburst. "Does it matter?"

"No… No, it does not," she realized as her conversation with Greta came rushing back to her:

"Hypothetically, let's say we manage to determine his whereabouts in the Spiritual Realm. What then?" Lana had asked Greta.

"Then we would have to send someone over there to guide His Majesty to the Astral Realm. It's the bridge where everything intersects. Once he's there, he can travel straight back into his body. Or, he can go into the Mental Realm and enter the dream state. The soul reattaches to the body in the mental plane—"

"Which means, he'd return to the physical land of the living once he awakens from whatever dream he's having."

Dreams were rarely ever isolated. If anything, people's dreams, much like their lives, usually intersected with one another. They were both in a dream, which was part of the Mental Realm. Lucien's soul must have already recoupled with its body by now, which meant there was only one thing left to do.

"Oh my goodness, Lucien," Lana shook her head at their own stupidity. "We've been such fools!" Like a pair of fishes swimming around in search of water, clueless as to what water even looked like.

"How do you mean?"

"We're in the dream state. The Mental Realm! Don't you see?" She brought both palms up to cup his face. "Lucien, I know what to do! I know how to save you. I know how to break the curse."

"Curse? What curse?!" said Lucien hotly. "You said it was an accident. You didn't mention anything about sorcery!"

"My darling, listen to me, you are in a dream," she said to him calmly, slowly as though he were a fledgling or a newborn kitten. "We. Are. In. A. Dream."

Slips of white paper began flying around them like wisps of snow. The city was starting to disintegrate, block by block. But neither of them noticed. They were focused solely on each other.

Lucien blinked down at her.

Lana couldn't understand how someone as intelligent as her husband often failed to see the obvious solution. "Wake up, you fool!"

"How?"

"Do what you always do: *tell yourself you can*," said Lana. "Tell yourself to wake up!"

"Well—I—I—I can't do it if you keep watching me with those eyes of yours!"

Lana rolled those eyes of hers. "Oh, for goddess' sake!" Without a moment's hesitation, she pulled his face down to hers and pressed her lips against his.

It hadn't been their steamiest kiss nor was it their most romantic one. It wouldn't have even made their list of top 10 kisses throughout their centuries-spanning marriage. But when they both woke up in each other's arms on Day 7, they realized, it might've been their most miraculous kiss.

Chapter 17: Engraved in Her Mind

Lana expected everything to return to normal once Lucien returned.

It was a ridiculous expectation, given that nothing was ever normal where Lucien Valenta was concerned.

Lucien had resumed his usual royal schedule. He took part in senatorial sessions where he decided which laws to pass and which ones to deny. He attended mass at the Luce every Sunday. He met with dignitaries and diplomats from across the globe and galaxy. He delivered speeches at various public and formal events. He smiled and waved to the masses whenever the occasion called for it. Looking at him, no one – apart from his immediate family and members of their household staff – would've sensed that something was amiss with the Gold King.

But behind closed doors and away from the cameras, Lucien's calm, charming disposition disappeared all at once like the final spark on a burnt sheet of paper. He was unusually rattled and discomposed, with his mood changing from troubled to terrifying in less than a heartbeat.

He was regularly snapping at his sons and at the staff. His sons weren't too perturbed by it. Michael and Gabriel had endured far worse than a few verbal lashings from Lucien in the past. His staff, however, were taken back. They were accustomed to haughty reprimands and verbose lectures from their King, but they'd never been on the receiving end of Lucien's ire before. They had never witnessed Lucien being crass and brusque with his words – not until now.

To ensure his outer world reflected his inner turmoil, Lucien had also taken to manifesting thunderstorms nearly every day. His family knew the storms weren't natural because the colour, sound and force of the lightning bolts were distinctive to Lucien's Divine energy.

Added to all that, he was ignoring Lana at every turn. She barely saw him during the day, and instead of retiring to bed every night, he had taken to either staying up late in his study or pacing and towering around Lexie's crib like a guard dog.

Lana didn't know what was more disturbing:

- the nights where she lingered by the doors to his study and overheard him screaming – seemingly at no one, but Lana knew he was arguing with the Golden Totem inside him. ("*Let me bring her back!*" Lucien had shouted, and whatever response the Totem had provided in the privacy of his mind obviously did nothing to appease him because his next words were, "*Because she's my daughter, you bastard!*"), or

- the nights when she caught him in Lexie's nursery, watching over their daughter as though she'd vanish if he so much as blinked.

The nursery was where she found him once again on yet another thunderous night. Still dressed in formal attire, Lucien was cradling a sleeping-Lexie in his arms all the while floating around the room like a ghoul.

"Lucien?" she started softly as she entered the dark room. All the lights were off. The only source of illumination came from the occasional golden bolts of lightning that appeared from the large semi-circle window that took up the better part of the east wall.

Lucien didn't acknowledge her, but she persisted. "You missed dinner."

"I wasn't hungry," he said tersely.

"You missed lunch as well."

"I wasn't hungry," he repeated.

"Gabe's been asking about you. He still wants to pick your brain about everything you witnessed in the celestial realms. I figured you wouldn't want to discuss it. So, I told him you couldn't remember. That it all felt like a dream where everything seemed unreal and distorted. I suppose it wasn't entirely a lie, was it?"

Lucien didn't respond. He wouldn't even look her way. His focus remained solely on their daughter.

"The boys—the twins, that is, have been inquiring after you as well," Lana carried on. "They haven't seen you in awhile and were worried you'd gone off into another… spiritual sabbatical."

At Lucien's continued silence, Lana began walking slowly around the room, carefully avoiding his personal space. There was an army of stuffed animals surrounding them, observing their exchange.

"You needn't worry about those boys running their mouths off. I took precautions to ensure they kept everything hush-hush." By that, she meant the *Silent Screen* Baz had casted was now in effect. She had been monitoring the twins, and thus far, they hadn't spoken of Lucien's previous predicament to anyone. Even on occasions where their eldest brother called, the twins hadn't said a word about anything concerning secret witches, curses and spiritual encounters.

"Nick-Ray phoned today. He said his business in the Red Kingdom is taking longer than expected. I told him we'd be happy to care for the boys in his absence."

Lucien grunted in response. Lana could only assume it was a sound of agreement.

"The boys were also wondering when they could see the baby again. You haven't allowed anyone near her—"

"No!" Lucien shouted and subsequently winced as Lexie began to stir and cry. "Her immune system has been compromised. She's not well enough to receive visitors," he told his wife before making soothing, shushing noises at his daughter.

"It's a mere cold, Lucien. Babies get them all the time."

"Colds don't linger on for more than three weeks," said Lucien quietly. "Something's changed. She wasn't like this before… I called Idris, requested he provide some of his healing energy. Lord knows he owes me a favour. Several favours, for that matter."

"You truly believe it's that serious?"

"I wouldn't have called for him otherwise, now would I?" he said crossly.

Lana knew he wouldn't. Lucien wasn't one to go around asking for help. He was the Gold King. People came to him on their knees, pleading for favours. Not the other way around. Admitting he needed support in any capacity would've torched his ego. The fact that he'd done so anyway made Lana anxious about the state of Lexie's health.

"But isn't it harmful to use Divine energy on a baby?"

"The Blue King's energy holds vast healing properties that have proven beneficial and innocuous for all ages," Lucien explained. "Applied in small dosages at a time, it should be safe for her."

Lana slowly crept closer to him. The nearer she got, the more she could see the lassitude on his features, the dark half-moons under his eyes. His clothes were a little wrinkled and there was a slight tremble to his hands – something she didn't see very often in a man as confident as her husband. Lucien's persona was fairly consistent: he was over-the-top yet controlled, calculated and carefully curated. She hadn't seen him so discombobulated and edgy since the early years of his Kinghood.

"Lucien, you've barely slept since you awakened… Why don't you give her to me and get some rest?"

Ignoring her suggestion, Lucien held Lexie to his chest and began stroking her back rhythmically in an attempt to soothe her cries.

"Lucien, please, give her to me. I think your energy is distressing her."

Not his Golden energy, but the restlessness pouring out of him like a broken dam.

"Suddenly you care?" Lucien lashed at her. "You speak as though you haven't been shirking your maternal obligations to her as of late. Maybe our daughter would still be healthy had you been paying more attention to her instead of swanning off to other realms in my absence and getting drunk all the time!"

Lexie released a high-pitch shriek just as a bolt of lightning blasted across the sky. The brief moment of illumination that splashed across the room gave Lana enough time to see the regret on Lucien's face.

"Lana, I didn't—"

"Unless the next words out of your mouth are an apology, I don't want to hear it," she said coldly. "Hand me my daughter."

"Darling, you musn't get—"

"Give her to me…NOW!"

Lucien did as he was told, silently surrendering Lexie.

With her daughter tucked safely in her arms, Lana promptly left the room without so much as a backward glance. Maybe he would come around and apologize later. It was probably for the best if the apology came later. She wasn't in a forgiving mood.

On the long walk back to her room, Lana tried to calm Lexie. And once the baby had quietened, she tried to calm herself. Arguments were inevitable and ineffable in a marriage, she reminded herself. And sometimes, no matter how many wonderful centuries you've spent with someone, all it takes is an incident, a few sentences, a small string of messy words, to make you regret the relationship.

Five days later, Lana broke their marital silence and confronted him. "What did you do?" she said in an accusing voice.

Deskbound in his study, Lucien raised his tired eyes up to see his wife with her arms crossed, her eyes narrowed and her svelte frame looming over him like a small storm cloud. "Lana, I haven't the faintest—"

"The Green King has been officially declared missing," she said, suspending him mid-sentence. "What did you do?"

Lucien rubbed his eyes and reclined on his high-back chair. Judging by the gauntness in his features, Lana could tell he was running on fumes.

"Why do you immediately assume I had a part to play?"

"Because no one else knew about what Ivaan did. So… What. Did. You. Do?"

Lucien lightly tossed the paper he had previously been scouring aside. "The whereabouts of the Green King have little to no impact on our Kingdom. And even if it did, such political affairs should be discussed among Kings, and only among Kings. You know that. You needn't concern yourself with any of this."

"Oh, you Kings and your precious code," scowled Lana. "You can take your book of secrets and clandestine meetings and tree-hugging plans and shove it all up your breeches!"

"Thank you for the suggestion, but I see little practical merit in performing such a task at the moment," said Lucien snootily. "Now if you'll excuse me, I must return to the work at hand and reject these ludicrous proposals from Senator Wartface—"

"Wexford," corrected Lana.

"— because *no,* I won't allow any of my Golden citizens to vote on whether my realm should ever enter any given war and *no,* I shan't legalize interspecies marriage," he said tiredly.

"Why are my Senators always carping on at length?" Lucien had once complained to her after returning from a lengthy senatorial session. "They've got it easy. All they have to do is come up with ideas to make my realm better. I'm the one who has to accept or decline their proposals. I'm the one who has to decide what to do. And whether my choices are right or wrong, it all comes back down on my shoulders, doesn't it?" With a drawn-out sigh, he said, "I swear, there's nothing more tiresome than having to make a choice."

Lucien resumed his work, expecting to hear Lana stomp away.

"Was there something else?" He asked as she lingered by his desk, purposefully grating her talon-like nails against his woodblock.

"He was right."

Lucien's dark eyes flickered back over to her. "Who?"

"The Green King. He told me Kings love their Queens the most and trust them the least," she nodded. "Clearly, he was right."

Lucien watched her leave with an indecipherable expression on his face.

Lana wanted a brief escape from her husband. But it was hard to do even in a castle with over 1,000 rooms. It was nearly impossible to find a spot of space that didn't have Lucien's smug face painted on a wall or carved on a statue.

The Gold Queen wasn't sure if it was fate or fury that led her to the Traitor Room, but it was one of the few spots on the royal premises where she was guaranteed to remain unbothered.

Almost guaranteed, she mentally revised as the doors swung open followed by the sound of footsteps.

"There you are." With his usual confident gait, Lucien strode inside the large, circular stone room. "Where have you been? … Well, clearly you've been here, but you know what I meant…"

Lana knew he was purposefully noisy, both with his steps and his voice. The man could fly, run and glide as fast as the speed of sound. Lucien knew perfectly well how to silence his presence. The problem was, he never wanted to silence himself in any way. He enjoyed being heard and seen in every capacity. He felt it was his royal obligation to earn all forms of recognition.

"It's my duty to be well-perceived by anyone at any given time, Lana," Lucien had told her once, *"My people would wish it! Any attention directed towards me, is attention for our Kingdom, for the Empire!"*

It was during such moments, Lana remembered how obtuse and oblivious her husband could be. "Your 6 ft. 4" and you look like …. like you… people will notice you simply for existing, you dumb oaf!" She'd shouted at him.

"Ah, yes," With an unbothered, patronizing smile, he had tossed back, "But there's no point in existing if there's no one around to notice, is there?"

"That doesn't even make any sense!"

"Lana! Lana! Where are you going?"

"Lana! Lana! Did you hear me?" Lucien came up to her, his voice snapping her out of the memory. "You're not listening, are you? I can always tell. If there's one thing that infuriates me more than another is people not listening."

"Lucien—"

"I've been searching ages for you only to find you standing here not listening to me." It was a lie. He hadn't really searched for her. She carried his Divine energy, which meant he could easily trace her from virtually anywhere in the world – the *physical* world, that is. Nevertheless, she didn't need to know that.

Lana didn't look his way. She kept her focus straight ahead and with a flat voice, said, "An hour hasn't so much as passed since we last spoke."

"I've been searching ages for the better part of an hour then, haven't I?" Lucien shook his head at her as though she was the one being ridiculous.

"Obviously, you've found me," she sighed out.

"Of course, I did." Lucien wrapped a strong hand around her waist. "I'll always find you."

Lana frowned. *I'll always find you.* He used to say it as a romantic sentiment, complete with a cute smile. But now it sounded more like a threat, and the smile that accompanied such a line had shifted from cute to creepy over the centuries.

"Why are you *here*, anyway?" Lucien shot her a curious look.

She turned to him, crossing her arms. "Why does anyone come here?"

"No one comes here."

"You do," she refuted.

"Well, on occasion …yes…"

"Why?" She mirrored his curiosity, threw it back at him.

Lucien paused for a beat before responding in a quiet voice, "Because they were my brothers."

They exchanged empty stares for a moment before turning towards the other occupants in the room: the six marble statues displayed and lined up in a semi-circle. Each sculpture depicted a man who bared a passing resemblance to Lucien.

Like most statues, they were built in remembrance, and these men would always be retained in history as the late half-brothers of the Gold King and traitors to the realm.

The sculptures were the only items that preserved their likeness. Their bodies had disintegrated once Lucien had unleashed his energy on them. Not a single trace of blood and bone had been left behind.

There weren't any remaining photographs, portraits, or documentations of his brothers either. Lucien had destroyed them during the Royal Purge, along with revoking their royal titles and the ones belonging to their children, and in doing so, he had erased them from the Golden narrative.

This was all that was left of them: pieces of rock in a cold empty room.

"They look as dour as ever," noted Lucien.

"A most accurate depiction," Lana nodded. "They looked like that even when they were alive."

"Did they? I suppose I never took any notice of it … Not until it was too late," said Lucien regretfully. Rocking on his feet, he turned to her and confessed, "Perhaps I've been a touch dour myself as of late."

"Really? I hadn't noticed," she said sarcastically.

"I know. I've always upheld such a merry temperament," he nodded, lacking in self-awareness as usual. "My unexpected grimness must have come as a shock to your delicate senses."

"Lucien—"

"Hear me, Lana… just hear me," he said, almost pleadingly.

"Alright." She waited for him to speak, but there was nothing but silence on his end.

"Well?" she pressed. "Go on, then."

Lucien groaned and teared away from her. "I can't talk to you when you're looking at me with those eyes of yours," he muttered.

"What would you rather have me use to look at you? A telescope?"

Staring at the sculptures, he began, "Love and trust are much like brothers—No. Scratch that. Love and trust are like twins. They look similar, sometimes congruent. They go hand in hand. You could separate them, but it hurts to do so. Like all twins, people are so quick to label them. This one's the good child, the easy one, and that one's the difficult one, the problem child... Love is easy. You've always made it easy for me, Lana. Trust, however, is the problem ..." He trailed off, gesturing toward his brothers. "Anyhow, the point I'm trying to make is, like most twins, love and trust are misunderstood... They're misunderstood because we think they're emotions. But the truth is, love and trust are *decisions*. The most important decisions we'll ever make in our lifetime... I can't speak from experience, but I've heard that making the wrong choice in love doesn't necessarily equate to making a bad decision because the memories of happiness often remain... But if you choose to trust the wrong person, the wrong people, it undoubtedly leads to regret. Every time.... And that I do know from experience."

Lana watched him carefully, taking note of all the small cracks in his voice and slight twitches of his jaw. When she was sure he was done, she took hold of his hand. "I know, my darling," she said tenderly. "I know all your greatest regrets. I don't need statues to remind me of them. I have a list of all their names permanently engraved on my mind. And I have the names of all their children as well, in case betrayal passes into bloodline." With a deep breath, her tone turned terse. "But Lucien, I'm not on that list. I'm not standing here before you as a chunk of stone symbolic of sorrow. I don't belong amongst those who stabbed you in the back. And I refuse to take the heat for it."

Lucien looked into her eyes. Lana wasn't sure what he was searching for in them. Reassurance? Solace? Confirmation of some kind? Whatever it was, he seemed to have found it. Not a moment later, he nodded.

"Of course not. Backstabbing isn't your style. Don't witches prefer castration?" he smiled slightly in an attempt to lighten the mood. "And you should know by now… I do trust you, more than anyone."

"Then tell me what's happening with you."

Lucien entwined their fingers. "It might be easier if I showed you."

"Then show me."

"It might also be worse if I show you."

"Show me anyway."

Chapter 18: To Kill a King

Lucien had manifested a pair of translucent golden wings before flying them to the island on the other side of the Silver Sea.

The isle had no name and very few occupants. Surrounded by shrubbery, there was only one man-made structure in sight. It was a tower built like a steely silo. It ran so far up it nearly touched the clouds. Striking through the grey clouds were stripes of golden lightning that looked as though they were ready to touch down on the building at any moment.

All the residents of the island lived in that tower.

All the residents were prisoners and the tower – The Volt, as it was called – was their dungeon.

"Stay close to me," Lucien had told her, seven centuries ago, back when he had first given her a tour of the premises. "I'm their maker," he'd said, pointing towards the lightning, "My Bolts shan't harm you… provided you cling to me, that is."

"Are they really necessary?" Lana had asked, raising her voice to be heard over the claps of thunder.

"Of course. My Bolts are the ones guarding the Volt." He gestured to the end of the footed path where said building was perched.

"Don't we have actual guards for … guarding?"

Lucien had laughed as though she'd told a daft joke. "Please, Lana. Guards are the equivalent of toy soldiers. They exist mostly for display purposes, you ought to know that by now. No. You see, I've given these Bolts specific instructions not to harm the island or the building, only those who dare to step so much as a toe out of it."

"How will you get the prisoners inside in one piece? Are you planning on escorting them in personally?"

"Don't be silly. Of course not. They'll be transported into the building through carriages protected by my Shields, thereby evading my Bolts."

Lana winced and latched on tightly to his arm as another terrifying thunderclap roared above her. "What happens if anyone manages to escape this electric inferno?"

"My Bolts shall notify me straight away," Lucien had said grimly. "Rest assured, any fugitives shan't get far… not without being deep-fried."

As Lucien gently placed her feet back on solid earth, Lana realized she hadn't returned to this place since his initial grand tour. And for good reason. It wasn't exactly what anyone would call an island getaway.

Lucien gripped her hand. "Stay close to me," he reminded her.

Lana knew it wasn't a warning about the prisoners inside – they were harmless. The only genuine threats were outside, several feet up in the air, menacingly slicing up the sky. Lightning would strike her down the second she released him.

Huddled closely together, they walked down the path, toward the Volt.

As they approached the front of the building, the iron portcullis was immediately raised, granting them access.

"Your Majesties!" The wardens stood to attention and saluted as the Gold King entered the Volt with his Queen in hand.

Lana didn't release her grasp on her husband until they were several feet inside and hidden from his lightning bolts.

Lucien called for one of the wardens and gave the man instructions to escort them up to the 22nd floor. Lana noticed how this guard had additional tassels and badges to uniform, suggesting he was of a higher rank than his colleagues.

Lana felt bad for all the wardens here. In a sense, they were also prisoners. Like the inmates, the Knights assigned to the Volt couldn't leave the building without facing death by electrocution. They were only given a respite once a year when Lucien dropped by to re-charge his Bolts.

"A minor flaw in my coding," Lucien had previously explained. "I'm working to rectify it. Soon enough, I'll be able to set customized exceptions to all my energetically-charged weapons and defenses."

"Uh huh," Lana had said disbelievingly. "What exactly does that mean?"

"For starters, it means you and our children will have the ability to breeze right through all my Shields and Bolts, unharmed and unfazed… much like ghosts." Then with a light-hearted chuckle, he added, "And I'll never have to worry about turning any of you into gold by accident."

The first floor was a round, near-empty lobby room with a few fully armed guards scattered about in strategic spots, in case they had any intruders or escapees. Neither of which would ever happen, for obvious reasons. But as Lucien had said, they existed for decorative purposes.

As the head warden ushered them across the lobby and into a slim stoney spiral stairway at the back, Lana could see how little had changed. The Volt was as medieval as ever with its narrow passageways, walls of limestone and granite, and floors of flint and slate. There was no central heating, so the atmosphere was practically teeth-shattering during the cooler seasons.

Upon reaching the second floor, they went through a slender aisle in the middle. Lana purposefully didn't look to her left or right as they swept down the hall. There were rows of cells on either side of them. The second floor was where low-level criminals were sent, back in the day when the Volt was one of the few penitentiaries in the realm. She was pretty sure these cells were now entirely empty seeing as they didn't send regular civilians to the Volt anymore. Still, she kept her eyes ahead, hoping not to draw the attention of any spirits haunting around, spying through rectangular peepholes.

They got to the end of the hall and stopped short of a large manual elevator covered with a translucent Golden Shield. Using the Golden Gift, the warden raised his arm downwards, summoning the Shield to temporarily vanish. He then lifted the diamond-patterned cast iron gates by hand and moved aside for the Royals to enter.

Once everyone was inside and the gates were back in place, the Shield immediately resurfaced. The warden then grabbed the hand-operated lever and shifted it to the right. With a jolt, the lift shot upwards.

Lana tried to remember the purpose of each level as they zipped by them, one by one. The majority of them were cells that had once held various degrees of criminals. More ghosts of men in iron masks wandering around, no doubt. The only floor she recalled with a little more clarity was the 13th floor. Lucien had spared her the specifics, but she knew exactly what transpired on that level. That had been Lucien's interrogation floor, stacked with some of the cruelest instruments of torture known to man, and created by man. Though she couldn't imagine any man-made device being worse than having someone strapped down onto a table to receive Lucien's Divinely customized version of electroshock therapy.

There was another jerk in the lift, indicating they had reached their intended floor. The guard lifted the gates, then the Shield.

Ahead of them were more rows of cells. But unlike the other floors, this one had at least three guards on patrol, suggesting the cells weren't empty.

Lana walked out first, Lucien behind her. The Gold King placed one hand on the back of his wife's waist, gently guiding her ahead. He lifted his spare hand in the air, a silent command for the warden to stay behind.

They went further down the hall. Lana practically trembled with every step forward. She had a sinking feeling in her chest and knots in her stomach, all of which instinctively told her she knew exactly what she was about to see. And when they stopped at a Shielded door, she knew wasn't going to like what was behind it.

Lucien waved a hand in the air, stripping away the translucent golden Shield.

Sucking in a breath, Lana brought her eyes to the iron lattice covering the boxy peephole. There was a tall man inside facing a small, caged window. His back was half-covered with his long dark hair. As if sensing another presence, he slowly turned around to face her.

Ivaan stared back at her, his eyes and expression entirely impassive. Lana forced herself not to scream the second she noticed how his face was now scarred with two dark circles on his forehead, right above his brows.

She leapt away from the door as though it had burned her. The Shield immediately came back up.

"Lana? Lana?" Lucien followed her as she marched back down the hall. "Where are you going?"

"Away from you," she shouted over her shoulder. "I'm leaving. I've had enough of this place… Stop following me!"

It was a command that she had bellowed many times in the course of their marriage. Not that Lucien had ever obeyed such an order. She was pretty sure he'd follow her to the end of the universe, partly because he wanted to and partly because she would tell him not to.

"You must remain by my side, Lana! My Bolts could harm you if you step out there without me."

"Let them! The soul is eternal, is it not? I'll reincarnate eventually. Maybe next time, I'll be smarter when it comes down to spousal selection. Maybe next time, I won't marry such an idiot!"

"Come now, my dear, you needn't get so emotional over this. That's your trouble, you know. You're always getting emotional," he said, trailing behind her like a puppy desperate for its owner's attention. "Lana! Give me a moment to explain… or at least wait for me to evanesce my Bolts before you dash out all feral-like into the wilderness."

If Lana were less angry, she might've turned around to tell him exactly what he could do with his Bolts. But seeing as she was in a state far beyond mild irritation, she didn't look back and wait for him to catch up. She kicked off her shoes, picked up the long skirts of her dress and made a run for it.

Lana made it into the elevator swiftly enough, but before she could so much as order the befuddled-looking warden to shut the gates, Lucien had already zoomed inside in a whirl of Golden energy.

"Get out!" He shouted at the guard. Grabbing the man's collar, Lucien tossed him effortlessly out of the lift as though he were made of paper.

With a snap of the Gold King's fingers, the gates came down vertically to lock them in. The Shield followed suit, putting up a defensive layer of protection.

"How do you move this thing?" Lana grumbled heatedly as she pulled at the lever.

"You're going up! You need to move it left if you want to go down… No, not the middle, to the left! … Left! … Your left!"

"We're facing the same way. My left is the same as yours."

"And yet, you keep pulling right," snarked Lucien. "Here, stand aside, I'll maneuver it."

"You keep away! I know what I'm doing!"

"Clearly," huffed Lucien.

"Don't touch me! Idiots aren't allowed to touch me!"

"I'm not trying to touch you! I'm trying to properly operate this lift! You keep pulling us heavenward!" He screamed back at her. "Honestly, you're the one who can't tell left from right and somehow, I'm the idiot?"

They both wrestled for control of the lever, with Lucien occasionally squirming away to save his precious face from her pointy elbows. "Watch the face, Lana! Watch the face! It's the face of our Kingdom!"

"It's a stupid face!"

It would've been easy to use his powers or even his natural strength to push her aside, but Lucien didn't want to risk hurting her. Releasing the lever in aggravation, he bristled, "Lana, will you please desist!"

After a deep, long-suffering exhale, Lana let go of the handle. With a heavy jolt, they came to an abrupt stop on the 30th floor.

"Listen—"

Lana whirled back to him, her face furious. "That's exactly the problem! I have been listening to you for centuries on end. I know all the prolonged speeches you've delivered, the poetic lines which are nothing but a tissue of lies with a small snot of truth!" She inched closer to him. "What? What? What is it going to be today? You'll tell me that you needed to do this. That there's a method to your madness. That this was a small step in the Great Golden Dynastic Plan of yours. That there was an overwhelmingly justifiable reason for you to *lobotomize* a King. To lobotomize yet another King!"

Lucien paused for a moment. "Well, as a matter of fact—"

"Oh, shut up!" Lana growled at him. "Just… shut your cakehole, Lucien!"

Lucien went silent as Lana circled around him like a bird of prey. He had endured countless celestial phone calls with so many antagonistic- and verbally combative-Lanas from other universes. Now, he was starting to think he was married to the one with the most anger management issues.

After a few more laps around the lift and several deep breaths, Lana acquiesced, "Alright… I'll hear you out." She crossed her arms and leaned against the west wall of the lift. Before Lucien could start speaking, she held a finger up for silence, "Under the condition that I ask the questions and you – *you* – will, for the moment, break this horrendous lifetime habit of monologuing and respond with clear, crisp answers, no longer than one sentence." Knowing he could stretch out a sentence like a bungee cord, she included, "And preferably no more than ten words per sentence."

"Very well." Lucien mirrored her pose, pressing his back against the east wall. "I shall endeavor to be compendious with my words."

"That was eleven words. Already off to an unpromising start," she grumbled under her breath. Heaving another sigh, she began, "The Greens only recently announced Ivaan's disappearance. They wouldn't have done so at all unless they believed the situation was severe. So, I'm to assume *this* happened quite some time ago?"

"Four weeks ago, to be exact."

"And you did *that* to him, where? Hopefully not on Green turf."

Lucien's Golden energy was strong, but it was also loud, hot and easily detectable with the use of modern-day thermal tracers.

"Certainly not," scoffed Lucien. "Do you take me for a fool? … Don't answer that… I met with him in the desert, dealt with him there."

"The desert? Which desert? The Neutral Desert?"

"Yes."

"Isn't that area considered sacred grounds? I thought no one was allowed to commit any violence there."

"Kings can do as they please," he said proudly.

Lana unleashed a cruel little laugh. "You call yourselves Kings, and yet you act like little boys who make up new rules in a game the moment they realize they're losing." She shook her head. "But yes, you're right. You and all the other high and mighty, toffee-nosed tyrants are free to do whatever you please without facing any Divine repercussions … except kill another King."

"I didn't kill him… I neutralized him. He's still alive."

"If you can call that living," Lana said, grinding her teeth. "Am I to assume you'll give Ivaan the same treatment as all his predecessors?"

It wasn't impossible to kill a Chosen King, but it was a grave sin, one that came with Divine consequences. No one ever got away unscathed for it. No one except Lucien. He had managed to find a loophole to discard his rivals and contemporaries whenever necessary. That loophole came in the form of a lobotomy. All he had to do was shoot a pair of heated golden rays out of his eyes and straight through the frontal lobes of his enemies. It did a spectacular job of *neutralizing* them. After such an attack – a *procedure*, as Lucien would call it – his victims no longer had any desire to use their Divine energy. They no longer had any desire to do anything at all.

"You and I both know what happens to Divine energy when it's left idle for too long," Michael's voice rang through her.

Yes, and it didn't end there. Once Lucien had turned his counterparts into artichokes, vegetables with hearts, he ensured they remained alive until all their Divine energy departed their bodies. By that point, they were no longer Kings, and Lucien was no longer obligated to keep them around.

"I had no choice, Lana. I—"

"No!" Lana raised her hand. "Stop. We'll get to that part in a bit… First, tell me who else knows he's here?"

"The wardens, who are all bound to secrecy by Divinely-sealed contracts … and now you."

"What about Mike and Gabe?"

"I haven't mentioned anything to them about the Green King, not even his involvement in my absence. Did you?"

"No. We were supposed to have a family meeting on Day 7, but then you woke up and we never got a chance to discuss it. Mind you, Michael is aware I visited Ivaan in the Green Kingdom, and I'm sure he suspects—Wait. Let's take a few steps back. Ivaan never trusted you. He certainly wouldn't have met with you in private. How did you get him alone?"

Lucien looked away from her. "He may have been under the impression that he was about to attend a meeting for my covenant."

"Ah right, your little private boys club for Kings."

Lucien frowned at her. He hated it when she trivialized and belittled his work. "It's not all men. The Indigo King is involved as well."

"So, you deceived him into making an appearance, but how do you know he didn't mention his whereabouts to anyone else?"

"These meetings are highly confidential, exclusive to Kings," said Lucien, hoisting his nose up to the air. "We're not supposed to talk about it all willy-nilly with anyone."

"You did. Your private secretary knew where you were."

"He most certainly did not. Pinkard was instructed to keep half my schedule clear every Thursday. The most he knew was that I disappeared once a week with a Bible in hand."

At Lana's dubious expression, Lucien added, "Even if Ivaan did tell anyone beforehand, what does it matter? All my communications to him were sent through private Divinely telepathic messages, so there's no trail – paper, digital or otherwise. Besides… they can't prove anything without a body."

"That's it." Lana snapped her fingers. "We have to make sure the Greens find a body."

"Why?"

"Kings generally don't disappear into thin air, Lucien."

"No, but Ivaan was barely into his second year of monarchy. They'll simply assume he didn't survive the Conversion period."

"His personal advisors may draw such conclusions. But not everyone knows about the Conversion process."

"People aren't aware of the specifics – that's true – but it's not uncommon for Kings to die from spontaneous combustion. Red Kings aren't the only ones with a propensity for self-detonation," he said. "History will mark Ivaan down as yet another King who failed to contain the power within. End of story."

Lana bit down on her lower lip. He had somewhat of a point. While commonly associated with Red monarchs, they all knew self-combustion was possible with any King. Once again, Lucien seemed to be the only special exception to this rule. In the past, whenever he had lost control of his powers, Lucien had disintegrated everything and everyone around him – hence, the dead brothers; his own body, however, remained perfectly intact.

"Yes, but there can't be an ending to this story without a body," she said, expecting Lucien to understand where she was headed. Judging by the confusion in his eyes, she knew he was failing to see the obvious.

"Don't you see? If we want everyone to assume he combusted, there needs to be a trail of evidence," she explained. "Bits of the body here and there. An ear or a nose scattered around. A few teeth planted somewhere subtle yet noticeable, carelessly yet conveniently."

"Well, that can be arranged. Once the Green energy has left him, I'll assign a special C.R.O.W. agent to oversee the situation."

The Covert Royal Operations Wing (C.R.O.W.) was a sector of the Gold King's secret security. Most agents had the Golden Gift and were licensed to use it for both defensive and combative purposes. However, there were a few select spies and assassins who did not have any access to Lucien's energy and relied solely on their natural skills to accomplish their missions. This was done intentionally, of course. If no one could detect any traces of Divine energy on a kill, they would have a much harder time issuing accusations and counterattacks against any specific Kingdom.

"You're forgetting one thing," Lana brought up. "His body has been dwelling here for weeks, meaning any decent coroner will know that his corporation has been in contact with Golden energy."

Lucien hadn't taken that into consideration, but it didn't faze him. "Then we let the body wither and die here, along with those before him," he shrugged, "What does it matter if it looks a touch suspicious? Everyone will forget about it soon enough."

Lana highly doubted the citizens of the Green realm would forget. They hadn't had any type of glory in centuries. The arrival of their latest King must have been like feeling sunlight on your face for the very first time. Having someone as handsome and debonair as Ivaan as their monarch brought so much wonderful publicity and attention to their realm, and it placed them back on the global and universal stage. With Ivaan gone, it wouldn't be long until the Greens were shoved back into obscurity.

"It won't just look *a touch* suspicious. It'll make *you* look very suspicious," said Lana. "Think about it: the Indigo King doesn't have the energy to disable or kill a King. Idris is far too much of a holy man; he would never do something like this. Caleb might act like a scorned lover, but he adored Ivaan far too much, everyone knew it. The Red King's love for the Green King was the worst kept secret in the world... As for the Grey King, I don't think he's ever spoken to Ivaan or even acknowledged his presence... that leaves only one person, one King – you... And you did the Big Giant Face Thing."

"Big Giant Face Thing?"

"You know, when you use your energy to send a holographic message, and your face appears all big and loud to the receiver."

"Well, yes, but it's rather redundant to call it *big* and *giant*. I would simply call it—"

"Never mind that. When you sent Ivaan that message to lure him into the desert, it didn't leave a paper or digital trail, but it probably left some traces of Golden energy behind. And if anyone picked up on it, then it makes you look highly suspicious."

"It won't come to that. It was still a private communication – the contents of which could never be intercepted by anyone." Lucien still appeared unaffected. "Why are we even making such a fuss about this? The Greens can wag their fingers at me to their heart's content, it won't make a lick of difference. I'm untouchable."

Lana fixed him with a cold look. "The little spiritual sabbatical you were forced to take has proved otherwise."

"Fine. *Predominantly* untouchable," amended Lucien irritably. "But this is nothing I haven't done before—"

"Why is the Shield on the door flickering like this?" she asked abruptly, perplexed as to why the golden layer of protection was behaving like a blinking neon sign.

"It's not only the door. The entire elevator shaft is covered with a Shield. It has to dissipate on occasion to allow for the flow of oxygen. Otherwise, we'd suffer the same fate as bees sealed up in a jar."

"I suppose that explains why it's so stuffy in here," sighed Lana. "I thought it was just because of you."

"It is because of me," he said plainly. "I made the Shield. It's my Golden energy."

Running a hand through her hair, Lana took a breath and allowed for a brief standstill in the conversation. When she felt ready, she picked up where they left off. "Look, if these were the Old Days and the Old Ways, it wouldn't matter. Everyone and their great-great-grandfathers ran about pillaging and conquering back then. But in modern times, this type of behaviour would be considered unjust and grounds for war."

"War?" mocked Lucien. "The Green realm doesn't have the means to get into a war with our Empire."

"No, not on their own. But what if they allied with all the other Kingdoms against us?"

"I can take them."

Lana snorted at his arrogance. "If that's the case, then why don't you save us the trouble and take this whole world for yourself? Or better yet, why didn't you do that from the beginning? Wasn't world domination your original plan?"

"It was," he said quietly. "Once."

"But you couldn't do it," sneered Lana. "Even with all this Divine power, and all the financial and technological resources at your disposal, you still couldn't do it. Why? What stopped you then? What's stopping you now?"

It was a query she had expressed plenty of times in the past. Lucien had avoided answering it, every time. This time, he seemed conflicted. His gaze was sharp, his facial muscles were stiff. He looked as though he wanted to tell her, but literally couldn't get his mouth to discharge the words.

With an exhausted sigh, he said, "The same thing that stops every other King from conquering this world for themselves."

It took Lana a few seconds to figure out why that sounded so familiar. Then, she remembered how Idris had said the exact same thing. Neither King had provided a direct answer, but Lana had a hunch it had something to do with their Totems.

Totems were entities of Divine energy. They were the Kingmakers, the ones who got to choose the leaders of their world. Beyond that, there was still so much mystery around Totems, at least to the public. The Chosen Kings kept a great deal of information to themselves, but Lana now wondered if they even had a choice in the matter. Did Kings keep to themselves because they wanted to or was it because they were forced to do so by their

Totems? Did Kings really have free will to use their powers as they pleased or was it their Totems pulling at the strings of destiny?

"What's it like, your Totem?" Lana had asked her husband one night as they were nestled together in bed. This was way back in the early years of Lucien's Kinghood. "I know, you said it came to you in the form of pure golden light shaped like a griffin. But what's it like as a person?"

"The Golden Totem is not a person," had been Lucien's response.

"I know, but it must have a personality of some sort."

Lucien had kept his eyes on the ceiling. "I suppose he— he's not really a he, but it's easier for me to refer to it as such – he's got this voice … It's not even a voice. It almost feels like music wafting in from another room …a melody in my ear that only I can understand and decipher into words. It sounds like a gentle hymn and an angry anthem all at once… and as for personality… I don't know how to provide a precise description. I'm not sure I can … except to say, if he were a real person, he'd be the best and the worst man I had ever met."

The Gold Queen had stared at her King through the darkness. She wondered if Lucien had even realized he was describing himself.

"Lana? Lana? Did you hear me?"

She blinked and straightened her posture. Lost in thoughts of the past, she was neglecting the present. "Hmm? Sorry, what were you saying?"

"I said, my reasons for neutralizing him are not groundless. If the other Kings knew, if everyone knew what Ivaan had done, what he was capable of doing without even realizing—"

"Yes, I know, then the other Kings – most of them, anyhow – might be more accepting of your actions. But do you really want to plant that seed in their minds? Give them the idea that they could emulate Ivaan and attempt to create an alternate reality, an alternate timeline, or do something similar with their powers?"

Lucien didn't respond. He didn't have to. The answer was obvious.

"And as for the public," said Lana. "They haven't noticed so much as a spot of change in their lives. Ivaan mentioned there were people that went missing – no, not missing, people that became nonexistent and were completely erased from everyone's memories. If that's the case, how can we go about proving that to anyone? It's not as though you can miss someone who never existed to begin with, is it? Not to mention we have to take— Lucien? Lucien? What's wrong?!"

She didn't understand what was happening. One second, her husband had been standing there, posture perfect and picture perfect, with the usual air of pretentiousness and superiority set firmly in place on his face. The next, he was sliding down the wall, lifting a hand to hide his shattered expression.

Lana dashed over to kneel beside him on the floor. "Lucien?" She gently pulled his hand away from his face. She couldn't remember the last time she'd seen her Husband-King shed a tear. It seemed surreal to witness it now. "What is it? Tell me!"

Lucien swiped at his face, forcing it to regain some level of restraint. He knew being so emotional wasn't a good look on him. "Michael and Gabriel have no memory of her," he said despairingly. "No one does. Not even you."

"Who?"

Locking eyes with her, he said in a tight voice, "Our daughter."

"Lexie?"

"No," he sighed. "Much like our little godsons, Lexie didn't enter our lives alone."

"Wait, are you suggesting—" Lana processed his words, trying to make sense of them. "You're saying… no, no… I would know."

Lucien tore his dark eyes away from her.

"I would know!" She repeated in a loud voice. "I was there. I'm her Mother! I gave birth to Lexie. There was never another—"

"And your daughters? Are they in good health?" Ivaan had asked her during their previous encounter. The memory of it poured down upon her like a trembling flood.

Lana lifted a shaky hand to her mouth. "Oh gods…but… but how…"

"I believe the only reason I remember is because I wasn't here." It was as he'd told her in their dream. Timelines didn't exist in the

Spiritual Realm. It was a state of constant eternal stillness where everything – every possibility, every reality – happened all at once.

Lana was still at a loss, unsure of how to register this newfound information. There was only one thing she could think to say and that was, "Can you bring her back?

"I've been trying," said Lucien in a broken whisper.

Shutting her eyes, Lana began to piece everything together. This explained the arguments he'd been having with his Totem as of late.

"Then you shouldn't have disabled Ivaan," she said, frantically tugging at his arm, "Lucien, why would you do this? He was the only one who could've changed everything back."

Lucien grabbed her hands. "No Lana." With certainty and gentleness in his voice, he said, "I wouldn't have done that to him if I thought for one moment, he could change everything back."

"How do you know he couldn't?"

"Because that's not how it works." Bringing her hands to his chest, he said, "You slice a person across the heart, they may survive, and the body may heal and mend. But that body will never look the same, and the person who has to look at that scar in the mirror everyday will never be the same again… Even if he changed everything again, it wouldn't be the same. It would never look and feel as it once did."

After a long sigh, he carried on, "You remember Ivaan's predecessor, don't you? That's what he tried to do. He was a spiritual traveler who could enter altered states of consciousness, and he was training his brain to create ripples in time and space to influence reality… He never got far enough with it. Failed at every attempt. Ivaan, however, managed to succeed without even trying."

Cupping her cheeks, he lifted her face to meet his gaze. "Do you understand now, Lana? Why I needed to do this?" He asked as he brushed away her tears. "The power to bend an entire reality to one's will makes for great theatre, but it's a horror story when it's implemented in real life. It's why I had to neutralize him. It's why

I'll have to take the same course of action for any other King who attempts to imitate his actions. Believe me when I tell you I didn't make this decision lightly or recklessly."

After a brief pause, Lana brushed his hands away from her. Her mind was still reeling from this latest discovery, and yet, she felt compelled to continue down a line of inquiries. "Are there any other changes I should know about?"

Lucien blinked, surprised at the coldness creeping back into his wife's voice. "Everything else in our lives appears to be unaffected. Though Lexie's illness is concerning. She wasn't sick before, but—"

"Are you sure you can't bring her back?" Lana demanded. "Our—Lexie's sister, that is."

"Lana—"

"You always said you could make anything happen because you told yourself you could. Can't you do that now?"

"I've been trying."

"And?" pressed Lana.

Lucien didn't answer. He didn't want to. He refused to admit defeat. As a King, Lucien had already broken through so many boundaries. He had accomplished things that people told him were impossible. But even now, several centuries into his Kinghood, there were still impossibilities that he hadn't been able to perforate. *Not yet*, anyhow.

When his silence persisted, Lana nodded in comprehension. "I see."

"I've been consulting with my Totem," said Lucien.

"I've heard. Your side of the conversation, that is. What did it have to say?"

"It told me any attempt to rectify this matter would be futile. Lexie will be our only daughter in this timeline. Even if we tried for another girl, it would never work… There's no golden lining to this, but there may be a silver one."

"How so?"

"According to my Totem, the soul of our child, the one we los—the one that's no longer here—went back to the Astral realm. Someday, it may return to our lives, in some capacity."

"In some capacity?" Lana echoed distantly. "But not as our daughter. Then how?"

"I don't know. It refused to tell me."

Lana sprang up to a stand and began circling the boxy lift once more. She remained quiet for a long while and Lucien used that time to sort through the complex politics of expressions on his wife's face.

"Lana? My dear, perhaps this happened for the best. A few centuries down the line, we may look back on this as a blessing in disguise—"

"Get up," she ordered him.

"Pardon?"

"Stand up, Lucien. This isn't the place to have *a moment*." Lana was ready to get back to the business at hand. She'd curl up and cry later in a more appropriate place, like her private chambers or in Lexie's nursery or in the shower. She wasn't about to shed any tears out here in the presence of phantoms of dead men who were most likely thrilled to see the Valentas at a disadvantage.

After Lucien stood and righted himself, Lana began to drill him with more questions. "What about your meeting with the other Kings? Weren't you expecting to be made Dominus of your little secret society or whatever you want to call it?"

"It's been delayed due to Ivaan's disappearance," said Lucien. "It's not really a secret society. If anything, it's more of a *convocation* and—"

"Then we're back full circle to our original problem," said Lana, keeping him from diving into a tangent. "The Green realm isn't the only one investigating. The other Kings are going to make inquiries as well. We need to present them with a body. Or parts of a body, and fast."

Lucien's eyes oscillated as Lana swept back and forth past him.

"We can't let it be traced back to you, Lucien," she said. "Just because you can afford to survive and win another war, doesn't mean we should put our children and our subjects through one."

"What other choice is there? It's as you said, they'll be able to sense traces of my Golden energy if we send his body back."

An idea popped into her head. "Unless we use another body as a decoy," she suggested.

"Well, I suppose I could utilize my powers to alter a cadaver to look like Ivaan—minus the fingers and toes, that is." Footprints and fingerprints were far too unique to be perfectly replicated. "But it still generates the same problem: my Golden energetic-footprints will be all over it. There's no hiding that."

"I know. That's why I need you to stay out of it completely," she said, placing her hands on his chest. "Leave everything to me."

If Lucien were a younger, less seasoned man and King, he would've visibly pouted. He hated it whenever she said those four little words. *Leave everything to me.* He knew from experience it never ended well.

"Lana, I hope you're not thinking of resorting to ancient sorcery," he said, lifting his nose to the air in his usual manner. "You know how much I frown upon it."

"Keep frowning, then," she said darkly. "Just don't get in my way."

Chapter 19:
Kings Own the Day, Queens Rule the Night

"Are you really going to do this?" Baz asked his eldest sister. "Are you really going to say *no* to the Queen?"

Greta snapped her eyes over to the left, where her brother sat. By her right was Azaelea, biting at a fingernail with her snaggletooth. As the eldest, Greta was sitting at her usual place at the head of the table.

The Anatolia siblings huddled around their kitchen as they always did for one of two occasions: dinner or discussion. The dinners were often pleasant with light, harmless chatter. The *discussions*, however, usually involved coming up with a convenient way to escape an inconvenient mess they'd inadvertently dug themselves into. At the moment, they were dealing with the latter.

"You've never said *no* to her before," Baz went on. "Do you really have the stones to go through with it?"

"What do mean am *I* going to do this? Do *I* have the stones?" said Greta. "You're the primary spellcaster of our lot. You're involved too."

Baz leaned back on his chair, throwing an arm over the top rail. "It's easier for me to stomach this conversation if I pretend I'm not entangled."

"Then, I recommend you snap yourself out of the delusion, because as a member of this family, you are well and properly entangled," she bit out sharply.

A pensive look shot through Baz's face. "Is it too late to be disowned?

"Be serious, Baz!" scolded Azaelea.

"I am being serious! Who are we kidding? We can't say *no* the likes of her. You know how things work in this realm. The Gold King owns the day, but his Queen rules the night. She'll have our throats sliced in our sleep. Or worse, she'll have us thrown into the Volt. You know what they do to their inmates, don't you?"

"What?" gasped Azaelea.

Baz sprang forward and folded his hands in front of him on the table. "It's where the King performs lobotomies on the prisoners," he leaned in a bit more and added in a whisper, "And I hear the Queen castrates the men herself – without anesthetics. Has an entire floor devoted to performing such a procedure." Letting out a puff of air, he shuddered, "I reckon there's no harm in dropping the soap over there."

"Really?" said Azaelea, her mouth dropping in shock.

"Our Queen doesn't sterilize people, Baz. Don't be ridiculous." Greta rolled her eyes at her brother's dramatic embellishments. "Nor is she going to imprison us in the Volt. They don't put civilians there anymore."

"You're the delusional one if you truly believe that," snorted Baz.

"This spell she wants us to perform, is it truly so impossible?" asked Azaelea.

Baz scratched his cheek. "It's not impossible, per se… But it's never been done before, as far as I know, and regardless of whether it's successful or not, there's a string of danger to it… karmically speaking that is."

"Is that why you're fretting, Bazzie?" Azaelea's features smoothed over as she gave him a calming smile. "Well, that's nothing, then… isn't it? I mean, Great-Aunt Marta would've done it. She'd have done it with a cackle. She would've laughed at us sitting here, fretting over karmic reactions and regulations."

There were many different concepts of karma. To name a few, there was the ancient one, the original one from the *Rig Veda* – the oldest sacred text of Hinduism – which believed that every thought, action and intention led to reactions and consequences. Then, there was the more modern-day concept of karma, popular among new-age sectors, which basically claimed that any energy put out – be it positive or negative – would get thrown back at you like a boomerang to the face.

The Witches of the Old Ways from the Old Days would've scoffed and sneered at the contemporary notion of karma. To them, there was no sense of payback, consequences be damned. To them, witchcraft was much like wielding a blade. You could use it to slice a loaf of bread and feed others, or you can use it to slice a throat and destroy your enemies. Your choice. Do as you will.

"Great-Aunt Marta ended up being burned at the stake over in the Red Kingdom," Baz reminded her, "Not a golden example to follow, is she?"

"She wasn't burned… she was hung," said Azaelea, as if the method of execution made their aunt's story slightly less tragic. "And it wasn't her fault. That witch-hating committee had it out for. Packed with utterly unforgiving, unfeminist women, it was!"

"All of whom were the wives of Marta's lovers, if I recall correctly," said Baz dryly. "There's nothing in feminism that says you're obliged to forgive your husband's mistress."

"Maybe we can suggest another spellcaster?" suggested Azaelea. "Why does it have to be our family?"

"Baz is the best one in the realm, and the Queen knows it," answered Greta.

"Then perhaps we can perform a spell on her, one that protects us by preventing her from desiring such a task?" Azaelea barely got the recommendation out of her mouth when an invisible force of energy ruptured through the doors behind them, the ones leading to the conservatory.

The three Anatolia siblings grimaced and clung to the edges of the table as a blast of wind, equivalent to a hurricane, shot through their kitchen, sending all manner of items – pans, dishes, plates, brooms – flying about and crashing. They stayed put, while occasionally ducking their heads to avoid being pummeled by bits of kitchenware.

When it was finally over, they collectively released their breaths and inspected one another for injuries. With their hair blown up, they looked as though a stick of dynamite had exploded in front of them. But otherwise, the siblings seemed to be reasonably intact.

"You musn't say such things, Az," sighed Greta, knowing full well they were in the presence of Hekate. It appeared their goddess didn't take kindly to hearing a potential conspiracy against Queen Lana.

"I'm sorry," said Azaelea, feeling abashed. "I don't know what I was thinking. It's treason to perform spells on royalty."

"It's not that, Azzie." Baz smoothed down his hair. "In the physical world, the Queen is protected by the Crown. But beyond this realm of existence, she's Divinely protected by the Dark Mother. Any hex placed on her would merely bounce back onto the caster, ten-fold... I take it our goddess is here with us now?" He asked, looking over to Greta for confirmation.

"She is," nodded Greta.

"Oh, oh my." Azaelea's eyes shot around the room frantically, worried Hekate would reveal all her true forms right then and there. "Forgive me, goddess!" she shouted, bowing her head to the table.

"It's fine, Az." Greta placed a reassuring hand over his sister's. "It was a warning."

Baz fished out a small chain of keys from the pocket of his vest. He threw them on the table, then threw his hands up in the air in surrender. "Warning fully heeded!" he said to the unseen deity in the room. "Apologies all around. We shan't cast any spells your daughter's way. Please leave us be, your greatness ... preferably with our blood unshed and our bones unbroken."

The keys immediately vanished. *Apology accepted.*

Another ripple of invisible energy scoured past them; this time it felt gentle like a parent soothing a child immediately after scolding them. They waited until it left the room and didn't speak until the doors magically slammed shut behind them.

"Alright, listen," said Baz. "I know what to do. We'll make a run for it. I'll have the house moved to Proximar B."

"Why Proximar B?" asked Azaelea in confusion.

"Because it's a long way from here," replied Baz in a tone that suggested he was stating the obvious.

"It's only four light years off. That's a mere stone's throw away from Earth. The Queen could easily find us there."

"Fine then, we'll go one galaxy over, to the very end of the spiral Andromeda zone."

"Did you forget who she's married to? She has the means to find us there too," said Azaelea. "Besides, I don't fancy immigrating. Sure, the men beyond our galaxy are plenty exotic and bodacious, but those languages they speak are impossible to learn. They all sound so… so… alien."

"Because they *are* aliens, Az."

"That's enough. We're not going anywhere. This is our home, and that's never going to change," asserted Greta. "I am the eldest and my decision stands. We'll tell her *no*… with the utmost deference and cordiality, of course."

Baz still seemed hesitant. "Maybe we don't have to make our refusal so transparent," he said, "Let's just tell her we'll do it without having to do it."

"How do you mean?"

"This spell she wants won't work without a very specific taglock, and I highly doubt she can acquire such an item," said Baz. "So why bother denying her? We'll say, '*Yes, Your Great Goldness. Of course, we'll be happy to cast this spell for you… once we have this item.*' That's sure to leave her scouring for a taglock she'll never find, and we'll be in the clear."

"Did you not experience what transpired here a few moments ago? The gods are on her side. She'll find a way, I'm sure of it," said Greta. "Best not to get her hopes up only to disappoint her later." With a final shake of her head, she decided, "I shall tell her tomorrow and I'd like your support. Both of you."

Azaelea and Baz stared down at the table, their faces wrecked with concern and apprehension.

After a lengthy pause, Azaelea said, "I suppose, it can't be all that bad. The Queen is a kind, understanding woman and our family has always served her most devotedly. Surely, she won't penalize us for one minor refusal?"

Baz and Greta said nothing. Azaelea didn't know their Queen well enough. Sure, Lana was gentle and compassionate when it pleased her. She was the sort of woman who could easily slip into anyone's heart – unless, of course, she was in the mood to stomp all over it.

When neither of her siblings answered, Azaelea went on, "And it's not a complete refusal, is it? We're still acquiescing to part of her request. We're just politely, respectfully, tactfully refusing the other part. Right?"

When her siblings remained silent, she nodded, "Right then. Regardless of what happens, we'll stand firm and unwavering behind you, G. Won't we, Baz? … Baz!"

"Huh?" Baz shot up, clearly distracted and agitated. "Oh, yes… we're in it together, forever, sisters."

"We've acquired a cadaver with the similar height and build as King Ivaan, and placed extensive enchantments upon it," said Greta. "My brother will transport it himself into Svarga City. They'll be placed strategically in the locations listed here – areas frequented by the Green King – unless you have any objections, Your Majesty." She slid the papyrus sheet slowly across the table toward the Gold Queen.

They were back in Greta's private reading room. Only this time, the Queen hadn't come by for a consultation. Lana was here for a progress report on the latest mission she'd assigned to the Anatolia family.

As Lana examined the written contents of the paper, Greta explained, "The enchantments shall remain intact for at least seven months, during which time, King Ivaan's body – or parts of his body—that is, what they believe to be parts of his body, will most likely be gathered, medically examined and cremated."

"Most likely?" Lana lifted her face, the sharp movement of her silver eyes felt like a sword being unsheathed.

"Yes, Your Majesty," Greta forced her face to stay neutral, "The enchantments won't dictate how Green authorities will jettison the bod— parts of the body. But based on the primary religion and customs of their realm, we can only assume cremation is inevitable."

"I suppose that's convenient for us," hummed Lana. "What about fingerprints? Footprints? Blood?"

"As you know, ma'am, it's near impossible to alter such unique identifiers. However, the enchantments we've used are tenacious. Anyone who inspects the cadaver will witness something that isn't even there to begin with. They'll see what we want them to see. Regardless of what they come across – teeth, blood, bone, prints – they'll believe it's an exact match to King Ivaan."

"Anyone who comes across *these parts* shouldn't be able to draw a blood sample," determined Lana. She knew dead bodies didn't bleed. The blood in a corpse pooled and clotted very quickly after circulation ceased, making it impossible to perform any tests. "Nevertheless, whoever stumbles upon the sight, needs to see some traces of blood nearest to the ground where the limbs are found. Otherwise, they'll assume the parts were moved."

"Baz has accounted for that, ma'am. Rest assured, his enchantments shall cover all exigencies."

"And there's no way of tracing any of these enchantments back to us, correct?" Lana already knew it was true but wanted to hear the confirmation all the same.

"That's correct, Your Majesty."

Lana nodded at her. Lucien could *frown upon* her use of witchcraft all he wanted, but even he couldn't deny there was one massive perk to ancient sorcery. If done correctly, it left no energetic-footprints behind. Magic from Divine energy – when employed masterfully, that is – worked fast, like a dragon soaring through the sky, breathing fire and leaving a trail of smoke in its wake. But magic from witchcraft was like a phantom in the night, too hidden to discover and impossible to chase down.

"Might I ask, ma'am, is there a reason why the body needs to be so...fragmented?"

"You may ask and yes, there is a reason." Lana returned her focus to the document at hand. "It's a matter of feasibility, really. Kings who can't control their powers are destined for detonation. Everyone knows that."

That was pretty much all they knew. The general public weren't aware of the Conversion process new Kings had to undergo. It was purposely kept hidden from them to protect a King's safety.

"The Conversion is where the physical body of a King battles with the Divinity inside. It can put the best of us in a precarious state," Lucien had once informed her, *"We don't want our subjects knowing about it. And we certainly don't need rulers in other planets made aware of it. They'll see it as a weakness, one that could easily be used against us."*

"It's only..." Greta trailed off.

Lana kept her eyes on the papyrus. "What is it?" she asked offhandedly.

"King Ivaan didn't appear to be lacking in control and discipline with his abilities. Wouldn't anyone be suspicious?"

Lana's silver eyes shot up like a sword ready to strike. "That's what these *tenacious* enchantments are for, are they not? To ward off any accusations of foul play?"

"Yes, of course, ma'am, once they're presented with the evidence we've crafted, they'll have no choice but to diminish the likelihood of slaughter." Greta nodded in deference, all the while trying her best not to flinch.

The Queen was all business today. She had entered the Anatolia house with a smile on her face and her little godsons in tow. But Greta had seen the change after they had left the twins to enjoy a few treats in the kitchen. The moment the Queen had faced away from the young boys and looked over at the Anatolia siblings, there had been a sizeable shift in her countenance. Lana's silver eyes had gone from soft to steely, her upturned brows had narrowed, and her entire expression had morphed from calm to calculated. It was a reminder to the Anatolias: this wasn't a social call from their Queen.

"I approve of these areas you've scouted." Lana placed the papyrus back onto the table. "Upon completion of your mission, please ensure all documentation you've assembled is destroyed and eviscerated. Leave no trail behind – paper, digital, magical or otherwise."

"Yes, Your Majesty. You can rely on us to be meticulous and diligent in such matters." Greta attempted to keep her voice as even as possible as she said, "And, in regard to your other request," she lifted a hand and gestured leftward where her siblings stood. "We have decided—"

"We?"

Greta shot her head to the side to see an empty wall beside an open door. There was no one there. Her eyes went wide when she realized her siblings were no longer present in the room with her.

"Do you mean your brother and sister?" asked Lana. "They crept away while you were speaking."

Those little brats, Greta hissed in the privacy of her mind. Immersed as she'd been in her conversation with the Queen, she hadn't even sensed their departure.

"Well?" said Lana, her tone changing from sounding like a cutting sword to a loaded gun. "What is it you wanted to say about my *other* request?"

Greta smiled nervously as she fumbled over a small stack of papyrus sheets to her right. "It involves an extensive ritual," she said, thumbing through the pages, "To start, prayers to specific deities will need to be done at exact hours, beginning on a dark moon. These prayers should be recited every day for at least three months. We've created distinct sigils that can be used during the rites and in the course of enacting the spell itself."

She handed over a few sheets with the markings of sigils properly illustrated on them. To those who weren't accustomed to the occult, a sigil looked like a weird design of geometric shapes and patterns colliding together. Witches, however, knew that exactly what they were. In ancient times, sigils were like a spirit's graphic signature – something that proved useful when one was trying to summon a particular entity. Among modern-day magical practitioners, sigils were symbols that expressed ideas, intentions and outcomes. Both forms of sigils had their uses.

"The spell Baz crafted is rather unique," said Greta slowly. "So unique that it's entirely original… Such originality makes it difficult for us to determine its success rate."

"Are you suggesting it's impossible because it's never been done before? That's hardly an excuse." Lana lightly tossed the papers onto the table and crossed her arms. "Look at this table. The concept of a flat surface on fixed legs was once nonexistent, until someone thought it up. Everything in existence began as a prototype. This spell should be no different. So, what is it then that concerns you?" she asked coldly.

Greta tried to keep her features neutral, but one look from Lana told her she wasn't pulling off nonchalance as well as she'd hoped. She was hesitant and apprehensive, not at all like her usual self. Her ancestors would've disapproved, no doubt. They had taught her that a witch should always live without fear, knowing in their hearts that they were the terror that howled in the night. A great philosophy to live by, but not always easy to put into practice – especially when she was sitting six feet across from a woman who owned the night.

"True enough. There's always a chance this prototype will prove triumphant, just as much as there's a possibility it may fail," said Greta. "Regardless of the aftermath in enacting such an inexperient spell, my family and I firmly believe we must take into consideration the contentious nature of such magic."

"Contentious?" Lana tilted her head. "Are you worried about Divine retribution? You needn't be. It's not as though I'm asking you to kill a King."

Greta smoothed out her face, painting it with a coating of courage. "Your Majesty, from your perspective, I can understand why you would want this layer of protection. The Green King inadvertently caused the erasure of your child's existence," she said in a delicate tone, "And the ability to alter the whole of reality is such a dangerous power – one that places your empire at risk. So, it's obvious why you want to impose sanctions on it. But if we were to do this, ma'am, it wouldn't be a spell of protection. It would be prevention. And, from my experience, one can take great lengths to prevent an event from happening, but…"

"But what?"

The witch paused for a breath. "Let's say a traveler stumbles across a fork in the road. One track is laced with large paw prints with long sharp claws, the other is untouched. The traveler walks the clean path to avoid the wolves. But somewhere, in their journey, they'll inevitably come across a predator. They made the right choice at the time, but destiny intervened in the end," Greta leaned forward and looked straight ahead at Lana. "You may be making the best decision right now, but certain events in life are pre-destined and bound to happen … Ignoring any possibility and threat of Divine consequences, even if we prove successful with this spell, destiny will find a way to make it happen. Destiny always finds a way."

The Gold Queen stared silently at her, through her, and Greta could see storms in her eyes.

"So…it's not that you *can't* do this, it's that you *won't* do it." Lana lifted a brow. It was such a simple motion, but to Greta, it felt as though the Queen had just fired a subtle warning shot at the ceiling. "That is what you're saying, is it not? That your family won't perform this spell at my behest?"

Greta shifted in her seat and avoided her eyes. *Are you really going to say no to the Queen?* Baz's words coursed through her. *You've never said no to her before.* She highly doubted anyone had ever denied the Gold Queen of anything, in any capacity, throughout the course of her life. Like her husband, Lana had too much wealth, beauty, power and influence going for her. Greta couldn't help but worry the Queen would mistake this act of repudiation for insubordination.

A long, stilted silence descended over the room. One that Lana eventually disabled by breaking out into a chuckle.

"My goodness, Greta, I've never seen you in such a fright!" Lana laughed. "The way you look right now. As though I'm going to have you and your entire family torn into so many pieces even the vultures wouldn't be able to sniff out a single molecule of cadaverine."

Greta smiled crookedly, anxiously.

When her laughter faded into a soft sigh, Lana looked over at Greta calmly, sadly, and said, "You know, my husband once told me that Kings don't have any friends. Only followers and foes… It appears Queens are no different."

"I beg your pardon, Your Majesty?"

"Never mind," said Lana with a casual wave of hand. "If your family is uneasy with this assignment, then you needn't bother with it. Give me a list of everything that's required in this ritual, I shall find another practitioner."

"It's on the final page – just there, ma'am."

Lana pulled up the sheet and scanned all the ingredients:

- Herbs and plants: mullen, hyssop, tumbleweed, nettles, dragon's blood, cloves, guava leaves, wisteria, bay and hyacinth
- A batch of graveyard dirt
- Taglock: blood, saliva, lock of hair and nail clippings (one of each)
- Taglock: one item (anything) charged with Green energy…

The last item wouldn't be easy to acquire, especially now, given Ivaan's vegetative state of mind.

As if reading Lana's thoughts, Greta said, "I should add, my brother strongly advises against making any substitutions and exclusions."

"We can't say that with rigid certainty," countered Lana. "As mentioned, this spell is a prototype. Never been done before. For all we know, a viable substitution could work just as effectively, if not better."

"Yes, but—"

"GODMOTHER! GODMOTHER!!!" Jason-John's voice boomed into the room before he did. Baz and Azaelea followed suit with looks of distress struck across their faces.

"Jason-John Quartermaine, you know better than to cause such a chaotic interruption," scolded Lana. "*Again*."

"But Godmother!" cried the boy, jerking at her arm, "This is an emergency! John-Marlowe's missing!"

Chapter 20: To Live Forever

"John-Marlowe! John-Marlowe!"

"Marshmallow! Marshmallow!"

Lana and Jason-John's voices shot through tall oak trees with golden autumn leaves and echoed across Halkyon Forest as they searched for the young boy. Azaelea and Baz were a few feet away, by the crossroads, also on the lookout for the youngest of the Quartermaine clan. Greta had decided to stay behind at the house, in case the child returned.

"Godmother, are you sure he's here?" Jason-John tugged at her dress skirts.

"Positive," Lana said with a firm nod.

Before they had unleashed the search party, Greta had pulled out a lengthy map of the Anatolia property, along with the entirety of Halkyon Forest. Hovering a necklace with a round pendant over the map, the witch had proceeded to ask the spirits of the house to pinpoint John-Marlowe's whereabouts. The pendulum didn't hesitate to respond – it had swerved the pendant away from the house and toward the forest, before landing quickly and decisively beside the crossroads.

"Oh, this never would've happened if Nick-Ray had let me plant microchips on you boys," groused Lana.

Jason-John tilted his head up, regarding her curiously. "What?"

"Never you mind," she said, "Start calling for your brother again. He's sure to be here."

"John-Marlowe! … John-Marlowe! … MARSHMALLOW!!!!" Jason-John stopped for breath. "Maybe he can't hear me."

Lana winced at the boy's loud pitch. "People outside of our galactic postal code can hear you, dearest."

A noticeable thud came between them. They both followed the direction of the sound and gazed down to find a small book resting over the soil. It certainly hadn't been there a second ago.

"Oh no," muttered a familiar voice from above.

Lana and Jason-John's heads shot heavenward.

Jason-Join pointed at the third tree branch on the left side of the nearest oak. "Look! There he is!"

Perched on the very branch was John-Marlowe, peering down at them with a grimace. He tried covering himself with some leaves in a very poor attempt at stealth. He might've done a better job at it if they were surrounded by the pitch-black darkness of night. But in the harsh light of day, the boy's red hair stood out like wildfire.

"John-Marlowe Quartermaine! What are you doing up there?!" Lana demanded furiously. "What in the world possessed you? Running off without so much as a word! Get down from there at once and explain yourself!"

"No!" John-Marlowe hollered down at her.

"No? *No?*" echoed Lana in an offended tone. For the second time in one day, she was on the receiving end of a *no*. She wasn't accustomed to such an uncomely response. She could only hope people around her wouldn't start making a habit of it.

"I'm sorry, Godmother," amended John-Marlowe. "That's not what I meant to say to you."

"I'm glad to hear it. Now—"

"I meant to say *no, thank you*. So… no, thank you!" said the youngest Quartermaine. "Jase, can you come up and give me back my book?"

"You stay where you are, child," Lana pulled at Jason-John's collar, hauling him back as though he were a wayward kitten. "John-Marlowe, if you want repossession of this volume, you shall have to place your feet back on solid earth. Immediately."

"Where'd you get this?" Jason-John picked up the book for further inspection. "It looks like something from the Anatolia library."

"It is. Stop fussing with it. It's mine!" John-Marlowe shouted at his brother. "Mr. Anatolia gave it to me as a gift."

"Mr. *Pigkiller*? Why did he give you a gift? … And why didn't give me anything?"

"Same reason why I always get more birthday gifts than you. It's because I'm the nice one. And because I don't keep calling him Mr. Pigkiller. Now give it back!"

"John-Marlowe," Lana bellowed, "You won't get this book back until you get yourself back on solid earth. I shan't repeat myself."

"But you already have, Godmother," the boy smiled cheekily.

"*John-Marlowe*," Lana said grimly in a warning tone.

The boy's smile switched into a sulk. He narrowed his brows and bit his bottom lip, looking like he was trying to resolve a conflict inside the depths of his mind. After a moment's pause, he said, "Fine," he said softly, then loudly, "Fine! Forget it then. Forget you ever saw me!"

"Is that truly what you want?" asked Lana.

"Er… yes."

"Why?"

"Because I'm running away."

"Please, it's not like you could've gotten very far," Jason-John scoffed with amusement. "With that hair, you stick out like a clown nose."

"Look who's talking!" said John-Marlowe.

"Your Majesty! Your Majesty!" said Azaelea as she and her brother came dashing toward them. "Please, allow us to fetch your godson." By *us*, she clearly meant Baz. "Go on, Bazzie, get up there."

Baz crossed his arms. "Why me?"

"Because I have my nails to consider." Azaelea lifted her hands to display her long fingernails.

"So what if you break a few? You could do with trimming those talons."

"Stay where you are," ordered Lana. "None of you are going up there. My godson will be coming down."

"No, I shan't!" John-Marlowe continued to assert.

"Then I shall come up and fetch you," declared Lana.

"You wouldn't!" cried the boy.

"I would."

"You couldn't!"

"I could."

"But you musn't!"

"*John-Marlowe*," Lana said testily, her second and final warning.

"You can't fly up here like Godfather, and you can't climb up because you're a girl."

"Oh, you think girls can't mount trees, do you?"

"I know girls are more than capable of climbing trees." John-Marlowe lifted his little nose to the air – a pretentious mannerism he'd picked up from Lucien, no doubt. "But I also know they can't do it wearing…um… everything that girls need to wear on the daily. I regret to inform you, Godmother, but you're at a disadvantage."

"And I regret to inform you, my dear godson, a Queen is never at a disadvantage." With that remark, Lana wasted no more time.

Everyone gaped as the Gold Queen began shedding her clothes.

"Godmother!!!" flushed Jason-John. "You musn't undress yourself here for the whole world to see!"

"The entire world's not here at present. It's just the five of us in this tiny spec of the universe." Lana yanked off her coat before pulling her long white dress over her head. She bundled her clothes into a ball and threw them at Azaelea, who caught them clumsily. Thankfully, the Queen had foregone the crinoline today. Azaelea didn't fancy having a steel-hooped petticoat cage thrown at her.

"But Godmother!" Jason-John glanced sheepishly elsewhere, anywhere, to avoid Lana's form. "What if someone came by and… And saw your ankles!"

"For goodness sake, does every male specimen in this Kingdom carry an ankle-fetish?" Lana yanked and tore at the edge of her petticoat, creating a slit up to the middle of her left thigh.

Everyone's eyes bulged as they noted a leather holster, complete with a hip flask, strapped around her thigh.

"*You*! Avert your gaze!" Jason-John shouted at Baz. "How dare you openly gawk at the Queen! You're not worthy of laying eyes on her. You sorcerer. You devil-worshipper … you pigkiller!"

Baz smirked down at the tiny pot of hellfire. "But it's alright for a pervy prince like you to sneak a peek, is it?"

"I'm not a perv!"

"You're not a prince either."

"I'm her godson!"

"Uh huh. Not the same as being her real son though, is it?" Baz knew he was being petty, but he couldn't help it. Spoiled little brats like this one had a talent for bringing out all his pent-up pettiness.

Jason-John balled up his hands. His face was now as red as his hair. "Being a godson is better than that."

"Is it?" egged Baz. "How so, kid?"

"Bazzie, stop," hissed Azaelea, who now had her arms full of the Queen's clothes, shoes and jewelry.

"He started it."

"He's not even past his First Decade of life," Azaelea pointed out, "You're in your Second Millennia!"

Ignoring his sister, Baz said, "Go on, little scarlet pimpernel, explain to me how it's better."

"Because," said Jason-John, his mind searching for a reasonable answer, "Because it's in the title. *God*-son…. God Himself is directly involved in the selection process. I don't expect a devil-worshipper like you to understand."

Before Baz could return with another cutting remark, a holster with a flask was being thrusted at him.

"Hold this," commanded Lana.

Baz's eyes dropped to the holster before shooting back over to Lana, who was now down to nothing but a silk beige corset and a light skirt with a high slit.

"Er… Your Majesty." Baz cleared his throat. "Upon reflection, I think it's best if I scattered on up there to retrieve the child." If the Queen broke her neck climbing a tree, then Baz was sure the Gold King would have his on a noose for failing to protect her.

"No." Snatching the book from Jason-John's hands, she said, "It was my dear friend, who brought that precious, devious boy into this world. Now, it's my duty to bring him back down onto it."

Moving toward the tree, Lana tossed another command over her shoulder. "Give us a bit of privacy, will you? But stay close-ish."

Lana took a moment to observe the large oak. It had thick, scaly branches that were curled outward, similar to a dragon's tail. John-Marlowe was right, to an extent. She could try to use the Golden Gift to fly up there, but she'd never been successful with flight. The closest she'd gotten was levitating two inches above the ground. Even if she attempted it now, it would require an hour – possibly longer – of intense concentration and focus.

Realizing she had no other choice but to do this the manual way, she placed the small book in between her teeth to ensure her hands were free. Stepping onto the exposed roots for elevation helped her latch onto the nearest branch. With a firm grip, she popped herself up and threw her feet onto the bark before hoisting herself onto the branch like a primate. She repeated the motions onto another branch, then another, until she reached the limb where John-Marlowe was perched.

"You're wild, Godmother! Just *wild*!" John-Marlowe was aghast and amazed by her behaviour. "First with the witchcraft and devil-worship, now this. I can't believe you came up here in such a state!"

Lana pulled the book out of her mouth. "I told you, there's no devil-worship in the craft." She got to a seated position and swung her legs around so that they dangled off the branch. "And this is nothing. Even if you climbed all the way up to the clouds, I'd still come up to fetch you."

"You shouldn't take such risks, Godmother! You could've been hurt."

"The same could be said for you."

John-Marlowe looked down and began fumbling with his hands. "May I please have my book back?"

"First things first," Lana waved the book in the air. "Tell me how you managed to leave the Anatolia estate? All the doors were locked down to ensure you and your brother's safety."

"I asked the house to open one of them," he said simply.

"You *asked* it?"

"Yes." John-Marlowe nodded. "I asked it. Very nicely, if it wasn't too much trouble, if it could open a door for me."

Right. Lana closed her eyes for a moment. She had almost forgotten the house was sentient. John-Marlowe's cute face and sweet disposition made it easy for him to get any entity – living, spiritual or otherwise – to do his bidding.

"Alright, but why did you leave?"

"I already said, I'm running away."

"To where exactly?"

"Anywhere will suffice. I can blend in anywhere." When doubt struck Lana's features, the boy insisted, "Well, I could! … As soon as I dye my hair."

"I see." Lana indulged him. "So, you'll change your hair. Then what?"

"Then…then…" He hadn't thought so far ahead, but he couldn't reveal as much to his Godmother. "Then, I'll join a traveling theatre group."

"Ah yes, because actors are exactly the sort of people who wish to blend in and ward off attention."

"I bet I'd be really good at it, though. I'm the best looking out of all my brothers. Everyone always says!"

"Hmm, that is true," nodded Lana. "You are the Q-test of the Quartermaines."

"Or I could become a sorcerer like Mr. Anatolia. He even gave me his first book of spells."

"Ah, is that what this is? A grimoire." Lana ran a hand across the cover. It featured a lacquer painting of a forest with golden and pearl dust. The leaves and trees were outlined with gold foil, and there was a gilded edging that caught bits of sunlight every time she turned a page. "There are plenty of useful spells here for a beginner. And I see you've dogeared something."

"Yes, I wanted to—" John-Marlowe bit down on his lip, preventing himself from going any further.

"You wanted to… what?"

"Nothing," he mumbled.

Lana snapped the grimoire shut. "I don't think you've thought this through, my little firestorm."

"Yes, I have!"

"Oh? Have you considered Jason-John's feelings? How it must feel to be abandoned by one's own twin brother?"

"Well…" John-Marlowe trailed off.

"And how will Nick-Ray feel? Losing his youngest brother?"

A devastated look came across John-Marlowe's face as he remembered what the spirit of his mother had to say about his eldest brother. "*The future will not be kind to him, so you must make up for it.*"

"And what of me? I promised your mother I'd look after you. Would you have me fail to meet her final request?"

John-Marlowe looked away, his hands fisting up at the mention of his mother.

"Not to mention the King will be most displeased with me," continued Lana. "We're not supposed to be here, you know? He'll blow his crown right off if he discovered we snuck out, especially without my security detail."

John-Marlowe hugged his legs to his chest and leaned back on the bark. "Why are you always sneaking out, Godmother? Wouldn't it be easier just to be honest with my Godfather-King?"

"Child, please. Honesty is the most painful way to kill a marriage… You'll understand when you're older."

The child shook his head. He didn't want to understand. He didn't want to grow up and face adulthood. Adults always seemed to go out of their way to make their lives difficult. Adults were the sort of people that would rather run barefoot through a line of piping hot coals instead of walking slowly on comfortable suede shoes.

"If you run away, your Godfather-King will have my head on a golden spike, to be sure."

"No, he wouldn't. He likes your head attached to your body – way too much. I can tell."

"How can you tell?"

"He's always looking at you whenever you're not looking at him."

"Is that so?" Lana's face turned smug. "I still got it."

John-Marlowe scrunched up his features in confusion. "Got what?"

"Never you mind," said Lana, returning to the conversation at hand. "But if you're not worried for my head, then what of the Anatolias? The King holds no personal attachment to their family, and I know he wouldn't hesitate to send them to the stocks when he finds out you ran away on their watch."

"Do people still get sent to the stocks?" inquired John-Marlowe, his eyes widening in shock. He'd be wrecked with guilt and shame if the Anatolias were harmed because of him.

"Oh yes," lied Lana. "The King even provides buckets of tomatoes for onlookers to throw."

"You're lying," said John-Marlowe disbelievingly. "Godfather always says the food we receive is a blessing from God. He would never endorse such an act of nutritional waste."

"You clever boy," Lana said with a tilt to her smile, "I can't get anything by you, can I?"

John-Marlowe responded with a smile of his own.

"You believe honesty is always best, don't you?" She waited for him to nod. "Then be frank with me. Tell me what's wrong, my darling. I can't fix it unless I know."

At his silence, she carried on, "I know how challenging this past year has been for you, but after our time in the Green realm, you boys seemed to be a little more at ease—"

"The Green King is dead, isn't he?" John-Marlowe burst out. His smile was long gone, had faded with every word she'd said.

Lana blinked. "What?"

John-Marlowe made a somewhat strangled sound as he bit out, "Everyone's talking about him. About how he's gone missing."

"Yes, he has disappeared for the time being," Lana said slowly, "But what gives you the impression that he's dead?"

"I don't know… just a feeling," he said, his voice somehow sharp and gentle all at once. "When Godfather was asleep, I knew he'd wake up. Jason-John made me doubtful for a second, but even then, in the back of my mind, I still believed he'd wake up because I knew you'd save him … but with King Ivaan… I hear his parents died when he was around my age. And he doesn't have any family or a consort. He doesn't have anyone to save him!"

Lana knew that wasn't entirely true. Ivaan had Caleb. Rumour had it, the Red King had assigned nearly all his special agents to scour the entire world in search of his lost love. But it was too late for Caleb to save Ivaan. It was too late for anyone to save him.

"I'm sure he's fine." Lana hoped her lie successfully took. "He's an adult and a King. He can take care of himself."

"Why do adults say things like that?" he said angrily. "It's a lie! Everyone needs someone to take care of them! It doesn't matter who they are or how old they get!"

It suddenly struck Lana that John-Marlowe was far more insightful than she'd realized. "You're right," she conceded, "We all need someone. Even a babe left stranded in the jungle would need the love and care of apes to raise him up properly… So, if you run away, who's going to take care of you out there in the wilderness of the world? Hmm?"

John-Marlowe frowned. She had him trapped.

"Exactly," she said at his lack of response, "That's what your brothers are here for. That's what I'm here for. Now, why don't we head back down and—"

"Do you think King Ivaan will come back?"

"My darling boy…" Lana sighed.

"You don't, do you? You think he's dead too, don't you?" snarled John-Marlowe, tears welling up in his eyes. "King Ivaan was a good person. I didn't really know him. But I think he was a good person just like my mama, so why did he have to die? Why does everyone have to die? I'm sick of everyone dying!!"

Lana hadn't seen him cry like this, not since his mother's funeral. Even then, he hadn't yelled or raised his voice in resentment – only Jason-John had done that. It was as she suspected: John-Marlowe had been bottling up his anger for a long time. The child was long overdue for a tantrum.

"King Ivaan gave you a glimpse into the secret world of spirits, didn't he?" Lana wished she didn't have to discuss such a topic with a child so young, but given the circumstances, there was no avoiding it. "We're part of that world just as much as we're part of this one. We are spiritual beings brought down here to indulge in a mortal experience, a human experience… Death is a part of that experience. It's something we can not escape. If we ran and hid from it, it would only speed up to catch us. It doesn't matter what sort of people we are – good, bad or somewhere in between. Death does not judge; it's both kind and cruel in that way."

The Gold Queen reached forward to brush away her godson's tears. "My sweet boy, I wish I had the magic to change the entire world for you. Make it so that you'd never shed another tear."

"You mean that?" John-Marlowe sniffed. "Would you really do anything for me, Godmother?"

"Of course, my little love," she responded without hesitation.

"Great!" John-Marlowe's entire mood leaped 180 degrees. With delightful eagerness, he sprang forward and grabbed the grimoire. "I was reading what Mr. Anatolia wrote about petition magic." He headed for the page he'd bookmarked. "He says it's the easiest, especially for a beginner. That's when—"

"Yes, dear. I know what petition magic is." It was a very old-school, practical form of magic where the caster would write down a specific request, with the expectation that spiritual intervention would take place and manifest it for them.

"He says you can use it for anything." John-Marlowe flipped to the end of the book where a few empty pages remained. Tearing out one of the blank sheets, he said, "Let's do one together, Godmother, shall we?"

Lana's mouth thinned. "Technically, it's true. You can use it for anything. Ancient sorcery holds little to no limitations, but that doesn't mean there aren't any setbacks to what you manifest into the physical world."

"I know, I know. Mr. Anatolia wrote it in his footnotes. He said to always avoid the Big Three."

"Big Three?"

John-Marlowe held up a small fist and revealed a finger as he went through every avoidance, "Forcing someone to love you. Bringing back the dead. And altering the timeline... He said it never ends well."

"He's right."

"But I'm not trying to do any of those things."

"What are you trying to accomplish then?"

Ignoring her question, John-Marlowe laid out the sheet of paper between them. "I'll need you to write your name down, Godmother. Write it thrice." He held up three fingers for emphasis.

"I don't have a pen on me. Sorry, my dear," she said though she didn't sound the least bit apologetic. "I'm about to teeter off any moment now, I'm sure. So, why don't we continue this discussion with our feet on the ground?"

"No! I don't want anyone else to see," said John-Marlowe adamantly. "Can't you use Golden energy to write it down? The way Godfather does?"

Lana nearly rolled her eyes. She figured the child must have seen Lucien use his powers to transcribe everything he'd said into fine gilded print. Lucien could use his energy to do almost anything. What was more aggravating was how easy he made it all look. But it wasn't easy. It was challenging enough to get access to Divine energy – you had to be a King or bestowed with the King's Gift –

but utilizing such supernatural powers in any capacity required so much focus and concentration that it was extremely taxing on one's mind.

Instead of putting the effort into using her supernatural abilities, Lana was tempted to use her royal powers and command the boy back down. But judging by the obstinate look on his face and the fresh wave of tears that would undoubtedly reemerge the second she declined him, Lana knew everything would be resolved much more easily and far less painfully if she simply played along.

"Alright, I suppose I can do something similar." Lana focused on her index finger, putting all her intentions and instructions onto it. After several minutes, the tip of her finger glowed a radiant gold. Just as she was about to put finger to paper, she stopped. "Wait, why am I writing my name down? I thought this was your request."

"It is. But it's about you, Godmother."

"Oh?" said Lana, expecting an explanation.

"If I can't bring mama back to life, then I'm going to keep you alive forever, Godmother," the young boy said with steely determination.

Lana's shoulders caved in. "Were you not listening at all during my '*you can't escape death*' speech." She sighed in irritation. For a brief second, she empathized with her husband. *No wonder Lucien gets so frustrated whenever his monologues don't land*, she thought to herself.

"This isn't the same thing," insisted John-Marlowe. "A person who lives forever never has to run or escape death, because death will never come for them... So, this is more like putting a permanent stopper on death."

Lana stared at him unblinkingly. The child's thought process was like a contradiction twisting a knife into itself. "If I do this. Will you promise to come down with me and never run away again?"

John-Marlowe flashed an innocent smile. "I promise."

After a long sigh, Lana indulged the boy. Using her glowing index finger as a pen, she wrote her name down three times as though she were making a list. Within seconds, her name appeared thrice, the dark golden print marking across the papyrus sheet.

"You have to put your date of birth beside your name too. It says so right here," he said, pointing to the notes on the grimoire. "Say, how old are you, Godmother? I know Godfather's in his Third Millennia of life, that must mean you're—"

"We can waive the age component of the spell," Lana said sternly.

"But—"

"It'll work regardless."

"Are you sure, Godmother?"

"Positive, Godson."

"Alright then… Now let's see, it says to turn the paper clockwise. You must always move clockwise to make something happen and counterclockwise to repel something. That's in the footnotes."

Lana already knew all the instructions but allowed the child to dictate everything. "Done. What's next?"

John-Marlowe poked his head back into the grimoire. "It says to write out your request over all your names. Three times. But you have to write your request like it's a command – as if it's already done."

"What shall I write then?"

"Mr. Anatolia says here that it's best to keep it simple and precise." John-Marlowe's face crinkled up in thought. He mulled it over for a little while before reaching a conclusion. "Write…write… *I, Lana Valenta, shall live forever and never die.* Thrice."

Lana shook her head but nevertheless obliged him.

"Done. Now what?"

"Move it clockwise again. Then place your signature over it. Thrice."

Lana did as she was told. With so many layers of words stacked atop one another, the message now looked completely unreadable to an observer. Nothing but a bundle of gibberish.

"Now fold it towards you," said John-Marlowe. "Turn it clockwise again…fold it towards you again… clockwise again…. And fold it towards you one last time."

When she was done, Lana held out a tiny, neatly folded square of paper. "There you go."

John-Marlowe frowned as he scoured the recipe for petition magic once more. "He doesn't say what to do with the paper afterwards."

"Anything really," shrugged Lana. "You can keep it, burn it, bury it somewhere…"

"I'll bury it then." Struck by an idea, he said, "By the crossroads."

"Fine." Lana would've agreed to anything if it got them off this tree. "Let us go then, you and I."

"It'll work, right, Godmother?"

Lana looked into her godson's eyes. John-Marlowe wanted honesty, but Lana knew what he needed the most right now was a lie.

"Yes, my sweet boy. It'll work. I shall live forever and never die."

"Great!" beamed John-Marlowe. "If it works on you. I'll use it on everyone else I love."

"Why not use it on yourself?"

"I don't need it for myself. It only makes me sad when the people I love die. It wouldn't bother me if I died because I'll be too busy being dead to care."

Lana couldn't argue with that logic. "Fair enough… Now, can we please leave? If I am to live forever, I don't fancy spending my eternity on this tree."

Once they were back, feet atop soil, John-Marlowe issued another request. "Godmother, can we go back to the Green Ashram?"

"Why?"

"I want to return this." John-Marlowe unclenched his left fist to reveal a small rock with a cluster of beryl crystals.

Beryl stones were usually diverse in colouring, but the cluster in the boy's grasp was a distinct shade, a cross between a turquoise and an emerald green. The crystal itself wasn't rare. Beryls were rather common and easily obtained from certain parts of the world. What made this one unique was the evident green glow – dim, but still present – emanating from the rock. The glow, however faint, was unmistakable to anyone who knew what they were looking at. It was Divine energy. This was a crystal charged with Divine energy, more specifically the Green King's energy.

Lana took the crystal into her own hand and brought it up to eye-level. "John-Marlowe, how did you…?"

"I found it, back in the Ashram … Well, I didn't really find it… It was lying about. There were so many of them in that fountain." Worried that Lana would think he'd stolen it, the child hastened to add, "I didn't mean to take it. Honest! I was looking at it when you came to fetch us, and then, we left in such haste that I forgot to put it back."

A memory flashed into her mind. She had been so angry after her discussion with King Ivaan that she had yanked the boys rather forcefully out of the fountain and had given them no explanation as to why they were leaving with such urgency.

"Anyway, I wanted to give it back," said John-Marlowe, bashfully kicking his feet across the ground. "It's not right for me to keep it."

"Due to King Ivaan's disappearance, the Green Ashram isn't receiving any visitors for the foreseeable future." Brushing a hand across the boy's hair, she said, "But don't you worry, I'll take care of it. I'll make sure this goes exactly where it belongs."

"Marshmallow!" Jason-John came running across the woods, flanked by the Anatolia siblings.

John-Marlowe held out his arms, expecting an embrace from his brother. What he got instead was a sharp thump to his forehead.

"Ow—what was that for?" John-Marlowe scowled, rubbing at his temple.

"That's for running off!"

"I was only gone for a little bit."

"I don't care!" Jason-John crossed his arms. "What made you think you could go without me? You're not allowed to do that. Ever! We came into this world together, didn't we? It only makes sense for us to leave together!"

Jason-John expected his twin brother to feel ashamed by his reprimand. He was most disappointed when John-Marlowe smiled brightly and flung his arms around him.

"Such coddling is highly unnecessary." Jason-John didn't hug his brother back. But he didn't push him away either.

Azaelea wrapped her arm around her brother. "Aww, isn't that sweet, Bazzie?"

Lana might have melted at the sight of brotherly love as well had she not been too busy inspecting the small mass of beryls with the Green King's energy. The glow was slowly fading because Ivaan's power was growing weak from idleness. In a matter of months, the Green Totem would abandon Ivaan's body from lack of use – which meant any item he'd charged would also lose its supernatural enhancements. Until then, this rock could still prove useful. *A taglock: one item (anything) charged with Green energy.* This was exactly what Lana needed to complete the spell.

It was a unique magical procedure, one that had never been done before. This time, Lana would have to do it herself. Now that she had all the ingredients, all she needed to do was complete a ritual of prayers and then await the arrival of the dark moon to begin.

The enchantments around the fake body were only a fraction of her plan. It would cover up Ivaan's disappearance and rule Lucien out as a suspect. It was an integral part of her scheme, but Lana felt as though this spell was far more important. If successful, it would prevent the likelihood of any more chaotic changes and unexpected erasures in their timeline. Because this spell would ensure there would never be another Green King.

Trouble can't happen if the troublemaker doesn't exist to begin with. Ivaan wasn't a troublemaker, Lana knew that. The culprit was the Green energy. She felt confident in the belief that the blockage and prevention of the Green Totem from selecting another Kingly candidate was the only logical solution. *No more Green Kings, problem solved.*

After Lana had dressed herself, the group headed down the path toward the crossroads nearby. As they trekked along, John-Marlowe picked a few flowers, asters and goldenrods mostly, from the wildwood.

Jason-John was confused. The Anatolia house was in the opposite direction, and yet they were walking forwards.

"I'll explain in a bit," John-Marlowe told him, picking a few more goldenrods until he had a reasonably-sized bouquet.

Lana was a few feet away, trailing behind the group slowly. By the time she had caught up with everyone at the crossroads, John-Marlowe had finished digging a small gap in the soil with his gloved hands. He gently placed the folded petition paper into the earth before sealing it up again with dark soil.

The flowers the boy placed atop the small mountain of soil confused Lana. It felt like a funeral of sorts. Flowers for a phantom grave. It made her think of the child she had lost, the one who had been erased from this world. For the first time ever, Lana found herself missing someone who had never existed.

John-Marlowe stood up, brushing dirt off his trousers. He proceeded to tell everyone about the petition magic he was performing, though he was careful not to mention what the spell was actually about. "Now what do I do?" he asked Baz.

"Well, you could conjure a specific spirit to manifest your request. But it's tricky business, that. And it takes work. *A lot* of work. You have to find it, summon it and bind it to you. And it's not pretty if you accidentally find and bind the wrong entity. Trust me, I've been there," Baz told the child, "I'd say it's best to leave this petition for a daemon to pick up. They'll do the heavy lifting for you."

"Demon?" squeaked John-Marlowe nervously. "You didn't say anything about demons in your book."

"Not a demon. A *daemon*," clarified Baz. "They're not evil."

"What are they then?"

"Well, I suppose you could say they're like Divine spirits… guardian spirits, even."

"Guardian spirit?" said John-Marlowe. "Is that the same thing as a guardian angel?"

"Depends on who you ask…"

While they conversed, Lana thought about the promise she had made. The one that she would undoubtedly – due to the natural laws of the universe – have to break someday.

I shall live forever and never die, was what she had sworn, immortalizing herself in writing. If by some bizarre twist of fate, such an anomaly did come to pass, she couldn't decide if it would be a blessing or a curse. Not that it mattered. In the end, a curse was nothing but a blessing in disguise.

Author's note:
This novel is a companion piece and prequel to *The King's Energy* book series. For the continuation of this saga, check out Book 1 of the series, *Golden Phantoms*, available on Amazon and Barnes & Noble.

Take a Sneak Peek at *Golden Phantoms*:

Lana tried her hardest to focus on the meeting at hand. It was a standard weekly session with her two primary royal advisors – her sons – during which they discussed matters of national importance. She had to listen to what they were saying. Or at the very least, pretend to listen. But she couldn't do that either. Her mind was obsessed with one thought. One life-changing thought that was playing repeatedly in her head like a needle stuck in a groove.

"…onto the next agenda item. This one was added at Michael's request," Gabriel gestured leftward to his brother.

The Valenta brothers were in Lana's private office, sitting directly across from her on dark wingback chairs. "There's been growing hostility from the Greys by our borderlines. Security risks are increasing, and Michael believes this presents an opportunity for us to redress our chronic underspending on defense. Now, our current annual military spending—"

"I'm pregnant," Lana announced, unable to keep the thought to herself a moment longer. It wasn't the most tactful way to drop the news to her adult children. *Oh well, no use closing the barn door after you've let the horse out to trample on everyone*, she thought to herself.

From the throne chair behind her dark burl wood desk, Lana held her breath as she awaited their reactions.

For a long while, neither man spoke. Michael blinked once before fixing her with a cold stare. Gabriel's mouth opened and closed several times, all fishlike, as though he were attempting to say something, but was unable to wring out a single word.

Finally, it was Michael who broke the silence. "Who's the father?" he asked coldly.

"What do you mean '*Who's the father?*'" said Lana sharply. "It's your Father, of course."

"You—you—" Gabriel spluttered. "You mean to tell me, you and Father have been—that is to say, the two of you have…"

"Had sex recently?" supplied Lana. "Yes, dear. That's usually how it works."

"But, but, but," Gabriel couldn't seem to stop saying that word, "But you're a King now, Mother. You're both Kings!"

"Two Kings can still have sex with one another," winked Lana. "Trust me, it's been done before."

"But I… I don't understand… I mean, I don't want to understand," wheezed Gabriel. "I thought you were waiting for a divorce?"

A divorce that would never come. Lana and Lucien had been separated for a little over a century now, ever since she had been chosen for Kinghood by the Black and White Totems. She knew for a fact that someone as strait-laced and heavily Catholic as the Gold King would never consent to a divorce. And deep down, she loved that he'd never do it. Even though they had agreed to let each other go, it was clear to everyone they were still holding on.

"Yes…well… I needed something to do while I was waiting," she said breezily.

Gabriel continued to croak in shock and disgust. Michael's glare was now an icy inferno that Lana suspected could cure global climate change.

"Look here, boys. As your Mother, I don't care for your disapproval. And as your King, I don't require your approval," she said sternly. "I simply wanted to give you both the heads up… in a few months' time, you'll be greeting your new baby brother and—oh Gabe, do stop making those appalling noises! I'm not delivering a message of impending doom. A new addition to our family should put you boys in a celebratory mood." Then, with a happy realization, she chirped, "You know, I do believe this will be the first child born of two Kings. It'll make for quite the event, I'm sure."

Lana ended the meeting shortly after dropping that little grenade of an announcement. She momentarily considered sticking around and waiting for her sons to offer their congratulations. But she quickly discarded the idea. She didn't fancy waiting until the end of eternity for them to finally come around.

"I'll see you boys at dinner," she said cheerily.

With a whisp of Black energy, King Lana disappeared from her study.

"I can't believe her. I can't believe him. I can't believe them! Fancy, pulling such a stunt at their age." Gabriel dropped his head back and groaned. "Sometimes, I wish she'd never turned King. We could've stayed in the Golden realm. Father wouldn't have removed our titles as Golden Princes. More importantly, he wouldn't have rescinded our trust funds. And we wouldn't have to deal with something as tacky as—" Looking about to ensure they were alone, he said in a scandalized whisper, "As an unintended pregnancy."

"This would've happened even if we had stayed in Father's world of Gold," said Michael.

"No, it wouldn't have." Gabriel shook his head. "Had our parents stayed together for another few centuries, they could've grown weary of one another like normal spouses in every respectable marriage. Being apart has turned them into a couple of angry horndogs. Yes, that's right, I said *horndogs*… Don't look at me like that, Mike. I'm not entirely unfamiliar with colloquial language, you know … My point being, this separation has done nothing but intensify their obsession with one another… And now look at what we have to deal with."

"We're facing a new sibling, not a nuclear war," said Michael. He wasn't too pleased with the news, but he knew it wasn't the worst thing his Mother-King could've declared. Besides, they had no choice but to accept the reality of it all. There was no way to reverse their current predicament. The toothpaste was already out of the tube, so to speak.

"I still remember what Lexie was like as a child," Gabriel said with a tired sigh, "Ran rings around me. You as well… Started electrocuting people by age seven, if I recall correctly."

After a pause, Michael said, "She was a special exception…and that only happened because Father gave her the Golden Gift far too soon."

"She was a spark in the dark, to be sure … still is." A smile crept across Gabriel's face as he remembered all the wonderful times he had with his baby sister. The longer he reflected on it, the more he realized he'd enjoyed raising her and spoiling her in equal measure. And he'd missed her terribly when they'd defected from the Golden realm, leaving Lexie behind with their Father.

"Oh, maybe you're right. Perhaps, I'm overreacting," Gabriel reconsidered. "Lexie turned out perfectly, once I managed to convince her to stop *neutralizing* people. This one should be no different … I think I'll find Mother and apologize. Offer my best wishes."

"Changed your tune awful quick."

"Why not? As you said, it's not the start of an impending war. It's just a baby, after all. A child," Gabriel chuckled, "How much trouble can one child be?"

About the Author

FARHANA is the author of the books in *The King's Energy* series. *Secret Society of Kings, Witches and Spirits* and *Golden Phantoms* are merely the start of this epic saga. She has more than ten years of work experience in copywriting, editing and content marketing.

Connect with the author:

TikTok: @farhanabooks
Instagram: @farhanabooks
Tumblr: farhanabooks.tumblr.com
Linktree: https://linktr.ee/farhanabooks